KING DORK

APPROXIMATELY

ALSO BY FRANK PORTMAN

King Dork
Andromeda Klein

KING DORK APPROXIMATELY

FRANK PORTMAN

Delacorte Press

THANKS TO:

Krista Marino, Beverly Horowitz, Barbara Marcus, Angela Carlino,
Steven Malk, Tanya Turek, Lindsey Haggar, Paige O'Donoghue,
G. K. Chesterton, Mavie Portman (hi, Mom), Bobby Jordan, Ted Angel,
Jim Pittman, Chris Appelgren, Ben Perlstein, Matt Riggle, Kepi,
Franz Barcella, Diego Clemente, Stefan Tijs, Ian Brennan,
Marilena Delli, Lavinia Rosato, Alexa Alejandria, Marisa Graham

Visit us on the Web! randomhouseteens.com

Educators and librarians, for a variety of teaching tools, visit us at
RHTeachersLibrarians.com

Library of Congress Cataloging-in-Publication Data
Portman, Frank.
King Dork Approximately / Frank Portman. – First edition.
pages cm
Sequel to: King Dork.
Summary: With stitches in his head and aftereffects from surgery, Tom Henderson
finds some of his most deeply-held beliefs shattering but, somehow, "makes out"
with at least two girls by the end of tenth grade.
ISBN 978-0-385-73618-3 (hc) – ISBN 978-0-385-90591-6 (glb) –
ISBN 978-0-375-98567-6 (el)
[1. Interpersonal relations–Fiction. 2. High schools–Fiction. 3. Schools–Fiction.]
I. Title.
PZ7.P8373Kk 2014
[Fic]–dc23
2013042885

The text of this book is set in 11-point Caslon Book.
Book design by Angela Carlino

Printed in the United States of America
10 9 8 7 6 5 4 3 2 1
First Edition

for dinataruni

O'Brien is tryin' to learn to talk Hawaiian
    to his Honolulu Lou
and he's sighin' and cryin' and all the while he's tryin'
    just to say "I love you true"
with his "arra yaaka hula," "begorrah hickey dula,"
    and his Irish "Ji-ji-boo,"
O'Brien is tryin' to learn to talk Hawaiian
    to his Honolulu Lou.

–Rennie Cormack, Al Dubin,
"O'Brien Is Tryin' to Learn to Talk Hawaiian," 1916

A4   02:46

–MNLP   8003

INTRODUCTORY REMARKS

So I'm just going to pick up where I left off, if that's all right with you.

Tenth Grade, act one, was pretty awful. I wouldn't recommend tenth grade to anyone. Yet I survived. And while there was no particular reason to believe that the looming second act would be much better, the most pressing challenge, as I saw it, would merely be figuring out a new hair strategy for the upcoming semester. My previous method of preemptive self-ostracism, where I would sit with my back against the wall hiding my face behind my glasses and my glasses behind my hair and my hair behind a book, would be severely hampered because I had quite a bit less hair to work with. They had had to shave some of it off to do my surgery, and then my mom had cut the rest of it pretty short with my dad's old electric clippers once I got home from the hospital.

"You're a nice-looking boy without all that hair," she had said, causing my sister, Amanda, to collapse in melodramatic amusement.

Well, yes. I was a "nice-looking boy," and it was going to be a great year. Maybe I could get a hat or something, was my main thought.

Of course, I was as wrong as wrong could be. The horrors of Tenth Grade, act 2, would not, and could not, be solved by a mere hat.

That said, do you want to hear something weird? If yes, just read this sentence out loud:

I've done it. With a girl.

It is basically true, as in, it's pretty much the case. Except "I" is me, not you, and I guess that's more like one and a half sentences. So yeah, I screwed that up, but never mind.

Now, perhaps it didn't sound all that weird when *you* said it aloud–I don't know you. (And if you're a girl and it didn't sound weird, all I can say is, congratulations: you're hot.) But when I say it, trust me, it sounds weird. And maybe you're thinking I'm just being cagey, and it will turn out that the "it" that was done, with the girl, by me, was something like baking cookies, or playing Monopoly, or fetching a pail of water from the old well up the hill. But I assure you, it means what people usually mean by "it." I'm talking full-on, approximately literal ramoning. (If you've somehow been fortunate enough to avoid my previous explanations, I'll make it clear: ramoning is sex.)

I know you probably don't believe me about this alleged ramoning. I wouldn't believe me either. And it's true that I've been caught in an exaggeration or three when it comes to women. For instance, being strictly honest, I had, at the beginning of the stuff I'm going to tell you about, made out with three girls in my short career as a womanizer. Well, okay, technically two, but the third one kind of counts, as she was an alternate identity of one of the first two. And what if something *extra special* happened during one of these "sessions," something that went above and beyond the call of ordinary making out? Shouldn't that really count as a bit more than one? I think so. And then if I include girls who have, say, pretended to be interested in me as a Make-out/Fake-out stunt, and girls I've accidentally brushed up against, and girls where it seemed like they might have been looking at me and maybe would have possibly been potentially willing to make out with me? Well, then sometimes

I can get the total up to as high as twelve or thirteen. Once I even made it to nineteen, but since two were comic book characters and one of those was a space robot, even I can't accept that statistic as official.

But trying to be as honest and accurate as I can, we're talking making out with anywhere from three to nineteen girls, but mostly just two, and doing it with at least one. Salvador Dalí couldn't have done much better at fifteen, I'm pretty sure of that. I'll tell you what, though: math of any kind makes me dizzy these days.

So who's the lucky lady, and who's this Salvador Dalí character, you're asking? Well, Salvador Dalí–and I'm surprised at you for not knowing this–was this Spanish artist who painted things like melting clocks and ships with butterfly sails. He was a notorious lover of women, particularly of naked women, who all went wild for his crazy eyes and his big twisty mustache. There's a photo of him using a sexy lady as a desk, doing office work on her belly. Even I can imagine being interested in homework under such circumstances. One day I may attempt to pattern myself after him, if I'm not doing it already. So that's our Salvador. As for the "lucky lady," that's the thing I'm telling you about here, so don't rush me. (But the Salvador Dollies would be a great band name, and if I ever meet three willing girls I will totally Kim Fowley them and turn them into rock and roll history. Who's this Kim Fowley? Look him up, I'm tired of explaining.)

Anyway, you'll have to bear with me because even though I was promised a full recovery, my brains are still scrambled on account of this head injury, which, if you remember from my previous explanations, I received when the normal people of the world tried to kill rock and roll by hitting me in the face with a brass instrument. Words come out a little funny some-times, when I talk at all, and I find I lose track of things more easily than I believe I used to. Thanks, tuba.

Nevertheless, I've given the matter some thought, slightly, and here's how I'm going to start the story part of this.

So travel back through the mists of time, long, long months ago, in the twilight of a Christmas vacation much like any other, to a town called Hillmont, in a bathroom called "the bathroom." Free your mind of all preconceptions, put your trust in my gentle care, and then, with any luck, I think you will find, dear reader, in the end, that it will, well, you know, sort of just pretty much be okay.

PART ONE
Christmas Vacation

LIVE WIRE

I was doing the thing where you look in the mirror and try to decide if you recognize the face staring back at you. And I did recognize it. The bruises were coming along nicely, little rings of black, purple, and yellow, as if some evil hippie scientist had figured out a way to tie-dye random areas of my entire body with dark, foreboding colors, as a grim warning, perhaps, to any who dared question the sacred doctrines of recycling, organic dishwashing liquid, and the Doors. A centipede snaked across my forehead just under the hairline, the transparent legs of which, doctors had told me, would soon dissolve, leaving a legless centipede of scar tissue that would itself eventually fade to almost face color. At the moment, though, it was like a third, off-center eyebrow of fishing line. My hair, as I've already explained, was too short to cover the centipede in front, which was unfortunate, but looking on the bright side, I supposed it would allow me to test the conventional wisdom that chicks dig scars. I couldn't resist stroking it. "We shall see, my little centipede," I whispered. "We shall see."

If I held my head at just the right angle and blurred my eyes up a bit, it didn't look all that bad. Bruised as it was, I could work with it.

So I started to do the thing where you think of all the women you've had and pretend you are the Lord and Master of the Universe, making grandeur-deluded Mussolini eyes with an Angus Young lip curl and a slight head-bang, left hand idly positioned with the fingers draped over an invisible, floating guitar neck while the right index finger makes a series of rhythmic stabs, in time to which you growl tunelessly, under your breath, something like "I'm a live wire, live wire, I'm a live wire. . . ."

Don't try to tell me you've never done this. Be honest, you were probably doing it just now. Also, don't try to tell me that when you were doing it you didn't at some point become conscious of a threatening presence behind you and slightly to your right. Everyone gets caught practicing eventually, is what I mean, especially when you live in a house full of annoying family members, like you probably do. In my case, the figure standing in the bathroom door that I should have remembered to close and lock happened to be my reliably inconvenient younger sister, Amanda.

Her thoughts were clearly visible on her face, as though written there in Magic Marker. "Ah," they ran. "And another piece of the puzzle falls into place."

But what she said, with her voice, in a withering, partially italicized tone, was:

"Hey, *Live Wire*. It's your *other half* on the phone."

She was holding the telephone like a TV remote control, pointing it at me as though deciding whether to switch the channel.

"How much did you see?" I asked.

"All of it, *Live Wire*," she said. Then, after a pause, she repeated "All of it" and walked away shaking her head in an exaggerated manner, as she did in response to pretty much everything. Fortunately, she's family, so what she thinks doesn't matter.

Now, "other half" is a euphemism for "mate" or "spouse" or any other person with whom you have what they used to call "sexual relations" on a regular basis. It's meant as sweet-natured ridicule, implying that once two people have begun, you know, ramoning, they no longer have individual identities. It's kind of sad and beautiful when you pause to think about it—one of the English language's more lyrical insults, if "lyrical" means what I think it does. And an optimist might have assumed, knowing this history, that the voice on the other end of the telephone would be a female one.

But if nearly fifteen years of walking around on this godforsaken hellhole of a planet in the midst of its godforsaken hellhole of a society has taught me anything, it's that this kind of optimism is rarely warranted. My godforsaken hellhole of a sister's mocking, italicized tone said it all, transforming a gentle romantic put-down into nothing more than yet another tedious gay joke, the kind of thing that the normal people of the world, even up to and including your own sister, never ever ever *ever* seem to tire of. In other words, I was not at all surprised that the voice coming out of the telephone was not that of a female but rather that of a dude. Well, technically, anyway.

"Satan?" it said.

FOR IT WAS HE

"Mussolini, actually," I replied, marveling at the voice's keen powers of observation and deduction. All it had needed to hear was Amanda's mocking "Live Wire" to know what she had discovered me doing in the mirror.

"Better stick to Satan," said the voice.

"But I thought you were Satan," I said.

"We can all be Satan," it said, and I could see its point, which was actually pretty beautiful. The rock and roll Satan face was just the rock and roll Mussolini face with the addition of a flicking tongue. I could do that.

"Did you get the letter?" said the voice.

Letter? What letter? And who, or what, was this mysterious voice?

Okay, you know what? I'm already tired of this "for it was he" gimmick, "the voice" and everything. You and I both know it was Sam Hellerman on the phone. Who else would have been calling me to talk about Satan and Mussolini and whether I'd received some letter? He was pretty much the only person I knew.

"What are you talking about, Hellerman?" I said. For it was he. "What letter?"

It was hard to interpret the silence that followed.

"Meet me in front of Linda's in forty-five minutes to an hour," he finally said.

"Will you be the one wearing a yellow carnation?" I said, because the conversation sounded a bit like we were being spies, and that's a joke I sometimes make when proceedings have taken a spylike turn. It's from a movie, probably, though I couldn't tell you which one. One of those old black-and-white ones where the guys' pants come up to their chests and Humphrey Bogart has to stand on a box just out of frame to kiss the tall ladies.

"And bring the stuff," said Sam Hellerman, ignoring my brilliant carnation gag. Okay, Agent X-T9. I decided to give the carnation joke one more try sometime soon and then, if it didn't get a laugh, retire it for good. Why no one thinks it's funny is beyond me. I had planned to say something along the lines of "Just tell me what fucking letter. . . ." But he had hung up.

"Christ, what an idiot," I said under my breath. I was referring to myself. Sam Hellerman, as I've often remarked, is, despite considerable flaws, a genius. I'm just the one who always falls for it, whatever scheme he's working on, in which I am occasionally the target but more often a mere pawn in some grand plan beyond my understanding. He's that kind of guy.

THE IRON FIST OF THE SANTA CARLA COUNTY SCHOOL DISTRICT

Sam Hellerman, Sam Hellerman … *Sam Hellerman.* I believe I've already said all that needs to be said about Sam Hellerman. Our association began long, long ago, in the mists of elementary school. The state, having determined that its interests would best be served by turning the lives of its citizens into a living nightmare at as early an age as possible, had entrusted the day-to-day soul-crushing process to the local Santa Carla County School District. And the District found that its iron fist could most efficiently grind the aforementioned souls into a fine, terrified, inert paste if the bodies they animated were clearly marked and organized in a rigid, alphabetically ordered grid, like books, or socket sets, or fireworks. This system placed me–Henderson, Tom–always and everywhere either to the right or directly behind Hellerman, Sam. When the District's iron fist wanted to torture one of us, it had only to flip through the letters till its murderous index finger alighted on "H." And there we were. Teachers, parents, and their minions (the psychotic normal students who occupied the rest of the alphabetical grid) would obediently spring to action to take care of whatever was left.

I don't know why we ended up remaining in our assigned positions even after school, at home, onstage, pretty much everywhere. It was the path of least resistance, perhaps. And it was only natural to band together with whoever was closest at hand once the inevitable assaults began. But eventually, over time, one way or another, we got used to standing next to each other, which is pretty much the living definition of friendship.

In a way, I should be grateful to the state's iron fist, even though I am its sworn enemy, because I doubt I'd have been able to make a friend on my own. And then I wouldn't have had anyone to be in a band with once I discovered rock and roll.

Oh, you haven't heard our band? Encyclopedia Satanica? Well, that's what it was called at the time I'm describing–that is, at the beginning of Sam Hellerman's phone call about the letter. You should have seen the logo: so squashed-together and spiky that it was completely illegible. No way anyone was going to be able to read that thing. And it was really more of a sinister cult than a band. By the end of every show all audience members, especially the ladies, were thoroughly brainwashed and eager to do our bidding like sexy robot zombies. (That's why we'd been putting more effort into rehearsing our faces lately. I mean, obviously.) Now, that, my friends, was a great band. I miss it.

One of our best band names ever, too. And looking back, I'd have to say, upon careful consideration, that it was almost definitely a mistake to change it to I Hate This Jar, based on a jar my mom was having trouble opening when I walked past the kitchen just after Sam Hellerman told me to bring the stuff and hung up on me.

"I hate this jar," said my mom, like I said, holding the jar in question in both hands and banging its lid against the counter edge.

"Good band name," I said almost involuntarily, sealing Encyclopedia Satanica's fate before I could stop myself. It's just a reflex, but once it kicks in, there's no going back. The Tomster on guitar and vox, the Samster on bass and never looking back, the Shinefieldster on the drumster. First album–

This train of thought was stopped in its tracks when another train crashed into it and derailed it, scattering the first train's cars and passengers in a bloody, tangled, screeching mess all over the thought countryside. Because my mom was really bashing the hell out of the jar in question, and it was weird. I mean, it just didn't seem plausible that a human being, even my mom, could hate a jar quite that much. Though that weirdness was part of why the event warranted being memorialized in band name form for at least a few hours, it still didn't compute, and the way I'm wired, I tend to take note of things that don't compute and worry about them helplessly in that quiet, detached, brooding way I have.

Now, I don't know how well you know my mom, but even though I technically, and even literally, love her, I'd be the first to admit she has her quirks. A lot of them are charming, and even some of the less charming ones are mostly forgivable because she's pretty. She dresses like the costume room of a community theater exploded and landed on her. She professes to believe the most preposterous new age nonsense even though it is clear that in reality she doesn't believe in anything at all. She likes the Doors, and I'm not even exaggerating all that much. Also, she is unpredictable. And I don't mean just unpredictable as in, she'll get up and make a two-foot-high stack of pancakes in the middle of the night, or start tap-dancing on an airplane, or put a skillet on her head and sing "You Are My Sunshine" in a cartoon mouse voice when you least expect it; she's done all those things, though honestly she hasn't done anything that . . . what's the word here . . . "exuberant"? She hasn't done anything that exuberant in a long, long time.

No, by unpredictable I mean that even though her usual mode is subdued, distant, and silent, she can go from catatonic to berserk in a matter of seconds, well before it's possible for people within her blast radius to know what hit them. This behavior got a lot more noticeable after my dad died, I think, though it's hard to tell for certain because I was only eight and

I'm pretty sure my "we're a happy family" memories of that time are well padded with fake content that my mind invented and placed there in order to underscore how bad things got afterward. What I'm saying is that if there's anyone you might expect to overreact to a jar, it'd be my mom. But even for her, this seemed excessive.

I rounded the corner where the hallway juts off from the kitchen's mini-hallway, mainly to replace the phone in its little saddle thing before getting the hell out of there, because things were seeming like they could get pretty tense and uncomfortable at any moment. Quick as a striking cobra, Amanda's arm shot out and took possession of the phone, hardly allowing any plastic-on-plastic contact at all. She had, as usual, been silently shadowing me, waiting for her first phone-snatching opportunity. She likes to keep control of the phone as much as she can, carrying it around as she used to carry her dolls when she was younger, so much so that I tend to think of them, the phone and Amanda, as a single unit, the Amanda-phone. For all I know, she dresses it in little outfits and rocks it and pretends to feed it when no one's looking. The purpose of this–the carrying, if not the dressing and feeding–is to discourage others from using it, to be sure, but it's also to monitor who is talking to whom. She fields all calls that come in, sighing heavily and saying "Hold, please" when it's not for her, and handing the phone off to the appropriate person like some hostile secretary.

I was just shooting Amanda a puzzled look concerning the jar when I heard the voice of Little Big Tom, husband to my mom and fake dad to Amanda and me. And all became, well, not clear, but about as clear as anything ever gets around here.

"If you don't tell me what it is," he was saying, "how am

I supposed to know how to respond?" His customary placid voice twisted into a slight whine on the word "respond."

As though in answer to my puzzled look, but really, in fact, just to be a dick, Amanda cupped her hand at her mouth and stage-whispered:

"If she doesn't tell him what it is, how is he supposed to know how to respond?" She shook her head in mock concern, but underneath it all she was practically beaming. She is not a fan of Little Big Tom, and she loves it when my mom argues with him, even a little, about anything. My hospitalization had brought us all closer together for a brief time but as far as Amanda was concerned the truce was over, and hostilities resumed almost as soon as I returned home. In a way I couldn't blame her. Little Big Tom is not a bad guy, but he can be hard to take, even at his best. I find it difficult not to feel sorry for him, even though I'm not above mocking him with sympathetic regret. We all do it, even my mom. But Amanda seems immune to sentimentality when it comes to family matters. "Sympathy is for the weak," her steely eyes seem to say. Well, I mean, with regard to her eyes: they're as steely as brown eyes ever get.

IT'S NOT EASY BEING A TWELVE-YEAR-OLD GIRL

So my mom and my diminutive stepfather were having a Special Moment, and Amanda, the phone-baby, and I had barged in on it just as my mom was spicing things up by taking her frustration out on a defenseless jar. This would have been an excellent time for me to exit stage left, sans sister-phone, but Amanda's whisper had given us away.

"Hey, sport," said Little Big Tom. "Taking care of business?"

He spoke in a much jauntier manner than you'd expect from someone who was in the middle of playing Try to Guess What I'm Mad About. (This game is played all the time around here. No one, including me, ever seems to learn that the only winning move is to turn around and leave.)

I have to say, it's quite impressive how Little Big Tom can manage to have two entirely separate conversations at the same time, especially conversations with two such wildly different moods. If you've ever met him, you'll know that the key to Little Big Tom is body language. He throws his whole self into conversation, as though he's worried that words are not enough. Which is pretty astute, because what he says, in words, can be the most contentless blather, usually something along the lines of "Everything happens for a reason" or "Hang on to your dreams." His body, on the other hand, puts so much into getting the otherwise forgettable message across that it can leave you in a state of stunned bafflement that will stick with you for years to come. He would have been great in silent films, especially a silent film about a man who was split into two halves, such that his left side could have an argument with his wife while the other side could simultaneously make a sandwich one-handed and encourage the little children to do more, strive more, and be more. It's a bit like juggling, I suppose.

So Little Big Tom's right shoulder was slumped in a defeated way, and his eyes looked to my mother with pleading frustration. At the same time, he looked at me with his head cocked, his index finger in the air, and the rest of his face in that frozen half-frown it sometimes assumes when he's waiting for an answer. If you respond the way he likes, the head descends, the frown smiles on one side, the finger comes down and points as though hitting a little target hovering in front of

him, and he winks and says something like "That's the stuff."
And he may shoot you with finger guns. He was waiting to
learn whether I was, in fact, taking care of business at that
particular moment.

The scene before me was distracting, but I did my best.

"You got it . . . chief," I said, deadpan, haltingly, unable, despite Herculean efforts, if those are the kind of efforts I mean,
to keep the irony out of my voice. And my halfhearted finger
gun wound up looking a good deal more sarcastic than I'd
intended as well. I'm not capable of sincerity when it comes
to things like finger guns and saying "chief." People should just
know that about me.

But it was good enough for Little Big Tom, or at least, it was
good enough for the half of Little Big Tom that was talking to
me. The head and index finger came down while the mouth
corner went up, and yes, there was some quite exultant finger gunning too, even as he reached to put his arms around a
stiffened, uncooperative Carol Henderson and nod sympathetically into her cheek.

"Nicely done," he said, to me, evidently pleased with the confirmation that business was being taken care of. "Good stuff."

My mom disengaged from her half of Little Big Tom and
put the jar down. She picked up the three-quarters of a cigarette that had been balanced on the edge of the counter, tipped
the ash in the sink, and took a deep drag on it.

"How are you feeling, baby?" she said, placing the back of
her non-cigarette-holding hand on my forehead with surprising tenderness and motherliness and considerately turning
her head almost all the way around so that her exhaled cloud
of cigarette smoke landed somewhere other than in my face.
Which I appreciated, even though, technically, that hand-to-
forehead procedure is meant to determine whether someone is

feverish, and there not being any chance at all of my having a fever, it of course served no practical purpose. But as an empty, vague demonstration of concern and affection I still ranked it highly. It didn't happen too often. But it hadn't been all that long since I was in the hospital, and everyone was still making an effort to be nice to me. Well, everyone except Amanda, who said, just before scampering off with the phone-baby:

"Don't worry about him. He's a *live wire* and he's going to set the world on fire."

I could almost see the gears turning in both of my parents' heads, their argument temporarily forgotten as they tried to work out whether to worry that I was going to set something on fire right there. I'm sure they wouldn't have put it past me. In their world, any person who was not that interested in sports was capable of anything, arson being the least of it. But then they seemed to realize I was just being mocked, in a sisterly sort of way.

"She heard me singing a song," I said, just to make sure they got it. I explained that "setting the town on fire" was merely a metaphor for making things happen, helping your fellow man, and making the world a better place. I gave them the look that says "It's really a very positive message." Laying it on thick, I know, but the last thing I needed was to be put on pyromaniac watch.

Then, anticipating the next thing Little Big Tom was going to say, I added: "And plus, I'd rather not 'lay it on you' right now . . . chief. Still working on it." Of course it was AC/DC, not one of my own songs, as I implied, and it had been "finished" over twenty-five years ago. And if I knew Bon Scott, he'd have set a hundred towns on fire, quite literally, and Little Big Tom as well, without blinking. But there was just no way I was going to stand there singing "Live Wire" in front of my mom and Little Big Tom and try to defend it beyond a reasonable doubt. They'd put some kind of watch on me then, no question.

To my slight amazement, they bought it.

"The integrity of the artist," Little Big Tom was saying, nodding sagely, while resuming the marital strife process by glancing at my mom with a bitter but kindly "the fuck?" look on his face. "Very cool. Very, *very* cool. Any time you're ready, maestro. I'll be all ears." He wiggled his fingers at his ears, then said, "Go easy on your sister, chief. It's not easy being a twelve-year-old girl."

Thank the good Lord he didn't try to do some kind of hand gesture to illustrate "twelve-year-old girl." But I had to suppress a laugh anyway, because the earnest, solemn way he said it made it sound as though he were speaking from experience, and also because I was on edge. A few minutes of Little Big Tom's relentless jocularity, shot through with a rich vein of marital disharmony, can fray a person's nerves to the point where he's likely to shoot off an involuntary giggle or two at the least appropriate moments. Even my mom broke character and gave him a look, but she remained pointedly silent when he added, rather unwisely, it seemed to me, in her direction: "Am I right, honey?"

So now they were both "the fuck?"–ing each other. With their faces, I mean.

Evidently, I wasn't the only one who didn't know what the argument was about, but whatever it was, it must have been pretty serious. No matter how annoyed I am with Little Big Tom, he desires acknowledgment so fervently, and is satisfied with so little, that it is nearly impossible to resist throwing him some sort of bone in the end, even if it's only a grudging

"You betcha" or a fraction of a second's worth of ambivalent eye contact. My mom wasn't giving him anything, though. A tough cookie, I think the phrase goes.

"Don't forget your medicine," she finally said, to me, and left the kitchen without another word or glance at either of us. As I said, when it comes to the T. T. G. W. I. M. A. game, the first person to leave the room wins, and she almost never loses. Nerves of steel, that's what it takes.

Little Big Tom did this lip-pursed "it is what it is" thing with his face, picked up the olive jar, placed it, with resigned precision, in the cupboard on top of a tomato sauce can, and sighed heavily.

"Rock and roll," he said, the words infused with extraordinary sadness.

Now, in order to explain the next thing that happened, I have to make sure you understand something. When Little Big Tom first started hanging out with my mom and spending time around here, I was a little kid, and he, though tiny for a grown man, was still quite a bit taller than me. I guess he wasn't all that used to being taller than someone, and got a little drunk with power over it, because he rather recklessly decided he wanted to be called Big Tom, to distinguish himself from me, whom he called Little Tom, or sometimes Little Dude or Little Guy. It was annoying, but as it was an accurate reflection of our relative sizes, perfectly legal according to the United Nations or the Marquess of Queensberry or whoever it is that administers the rules of who can call whom what and what they can hit each other with.

Soon, however, I started to grow up, as people do, and it wasn't too long before I was not all that much shorter than him. That's when I started to call him, in my head, though never to his face, of course, Little Big Tom, because it was funny and there was nothing the UN or the Marquess of Queensberry could do about it. Now I'm just slightly taller than him, and though he may be a bit wider than me in the middle, there is pretty much no other sense in which he is big compared to me. I could call him Little Dude, but I don't because, as annoying as he is, I wouldn't want to hurt his feelings that bad, except behind his back. But that's why, by unspoken agreement, we've been saying "chief" and "sport" more often lately, so the subject of our relative heights won't come up, even though everyone's probably thinking it, most especially him.

So you know the thing where the dad-type figure will rumple the hair of the kid-type figure as though to say "You're a good kid and I was your age once, so run along now"? I'm way too old for that, but Little Big Tom still likes to do it, especially when he needs cheering up, and it was plain he wanted to do it now. In fact, he was all but begging for it, making the well-known "it would mean a great deal to me to rumple your hair if you could find it in your heart to allow me that one simple pleasure" face with imploring eyes. Well, my nerves must be made of something other than steel, because I just didn't have the heart to refuse, and win, by leaving the room.

Performing this operation these days involves his drawing himself up as tall as he can without too obviously standing on his toes, while I slouch and lower my head, like he's the queen and I'm bowing in preparation for being knighted.

I'll tell you what: it's not easy being anyone.

IT NEVER ALL FALLS AWAY COMPLETELY

Little Big Tom had looked at me blankly when I asked him if I had received any letters from Sam Hellerman.

"Why would he need to send a letter?" he had said. "You guys are practically joined at the hip. He could save a stamp and just hand it to you." (Little Big Tom had actually mimed the "hand it to you" part instead of putting it into words, presenting the invisible letter with a flourish and a bow, as though to say "Your missive, my liege," and making a whistling sound. Actually, you know what? Describing Little Big Tom's gestures, funny and profound as they are, is going to get pretty cumbersome if I take the time to do each one like that. From now on, just try to remember to assume that anything Little Big Tom says is going to be mostly mime, with some whistling and tongue-clicking sound effects thrown in. I think that's a good plan.)

I bristled at that "joined at the hip" remark, but he had a point: there was no reason for Sam Hellerman to send me a letter. There was no reason for him to call to remind me to meet him at Linda's at one p.m. either, as we met up there around that time pretty much every day during Christmas vacation and we had already made a specific plan for today because we were going to go from there to band practice at Shinefield's house.

Beyond that, both Sam Hellerman and my mom knew full well that there was little chance I was going to forget my medicine, otherwise known as "the stuff." I had it in my front pocket, all ready to go in little envelopes. Of the three kinds of pills I had been given at the hospital to take home, one was just an anti-inflammatory thing that was of no use to anyone who wasn't inflamed in some way. But the other two, a muscle relaxant and a painkiller with codeine, were of keen interest to Sam Hellerman. They were only to be taken "as needed," and I didn't need them all that much. Sam Hellerman, though: that boy had needs. For him, "as needed" comprehended the universe, if I'm using that phrase correctly. So before you judge me, remember: I was just following the instructions on the bottle.

The muscle relaxant makes you feel like you're made of rubber, and I suppose I can see how that might be kind of fun if you don't need your hands and feet for anything important. The painkiller just made me want to take a nap. Neither affected my centipede much, and anyway, I didn't mind the centipede; it quivered and itched from time to time, which was a strange feeling since much of the forehead it rested upon was suffused in numbness, but I could live with that. My headaches, on the other hand, could be pretty bad. But I couldn't see the use of just sleeping through them, and Sam Hellerman's love affair with the nap, a kind of nap lust, really, mattered more in the big picture than my piddling headaches and the centipede that triggered them. So it's only just and proper, and in the best interests of humanity, really, that Sam Hellerman always gets the drugs. That way, he can curl up in one of his great escapes while I stand watch, deterring predators. I wouldn't want it to be the other way around. I'd wind up handcuffed in a freight car bound for Siberia, or wake up in my underwear on a basement floor in an unknown city with a dog licking my face. The guy you don't completely trust? He's the one you want napping with relaxed muscles, not yourself.

Thankfully, once I was outside, the household tension fell away like clumps of sand sliding from the arms of a person who has been buried at the beach, and, like, he's fallen asleep and the kids cover him with sand and he wakes up and says "What the . . . ?" and scrambles to his feet to chase the kids away, waving his arms. And maybe his girlfriend or wife says, "Oh, don't worry about it, honey, they're just kids, lighten up." And the guy says, "Like hell I will," and charges after them, sand flying everywhere. So the sand that falls from his arms? That's the household tension I was referring to. Got the picture?

Long story short, as I headed to Linda's Pancakes on Broadway, the household tension fell away, et cetera. (Actually, to be honest, there was still some of that household tension in my ears and in my shorts and in between my toes. It never all falls away completely, does it?)

But the day was crisp and clear. Brisk, I think they say, about as cold as it ever gets here in Hillmont. I mean, it was probably about sixty degrees or something, but I was still shivering without my old army coat. I felt vulnerable and unprotected without it. The tuba attack had left it covered in blood—mine—and my mom had taken it away and quietly disposed of it.

"So you needed it for the case, I suppose," I had said on discovering its absence.

"The case," repeated my mom, with evident incomprehension.

"The lawsuit, then," I said.

"Lawsuit?" said my mom. "What lawsuit?"

"The lawsuit," I said, "about how I got attacked by a pack of wild normal people and almost died." I pointed to my head. "That lawsuit."

Her quizzical look had informed me of another absence: the absence of any lawsuit, any plans for any lawsuit, any inkling of the possibility of even considering the option of exploring the notion of a lawsuit. I mean, I should have known. My dad would have been all over it in a second, suing the pants off everything that had pants, and doing "police work" on them as well, I'm sure, showing up at Matt Lynch's house with a bunch of his friends from the department and beating them all senseless, and then, after the "investigation," arresting them. That would have been good. But my family sans dad was far too disorganized and apathetic an organization to implement even the most meager campaign of righteous vengeance, let alone any sort of lawsuit.

"Oh, sweetie," my mom had said, kissing me on top of the head. "You don't need to worry about that. The insurance will cover everything. You just concentrate on getting better."

As I think I've said before, when you're in the hospital it's like it's your birthday every day. You're everybody's hero. It's not a bad life at all. But I don't think I mentioned which birthday it is. It's your *fifth* birthday. Ice cream, candy, baby talk, condescension, total lack of concern for your wishes or interests, kindness. It's the kindness I miss most of all.

Little Big Tom came closest of anyone to grasping that there was an actual reason to be mad at someone in this situation, and he grasped it thusly:

"Love your enemies, sport," he said, raising an eyebrow and rumpling what was left of my hair. "It'll drive 'em crazy."

I stroked my centipede in moody silence.

A GENERAL THEORY OF THE UNIVERSE

But what was I talking about? Oh yes, my coat.

So I was down one bloodstained army coat, and feeling considerably less than a full Tom Henderson without it. The short hair didn't help, of course, but that coat had been my signature look, for what that's worth. The jeans jacket I was wearing in its place wasn't cutting it as a jacket or as a signature. It's a shame too, because I'm sure the bloodstains would have looked cool, besides serving as a constant "never forget" reminder.

Despite Little Big Tom's sage words about the best revenge

being the confusion you cause by being a good sport, it still rankled that no one seemed to care all that much that I had been attacked so brutally and so senselessly, or about much of anything at all concerning yours truly. Well, what did you expect would happen, they seemed to be saying, when you insisted on being eccentric and uninterested in football and a bit smaller than everyone else? There was, in other words, a tuba with my name on it as soon as I picked up a guitar. Of course, as I've tried to explain in previous explanations, accidentally beating up this guy named Paul Krebs and stumbling onto Assistant Principal Tony Isadore Teone's illicit sex conspiracies and memorializing them both in song probably didn't hurt. Or should that be help? Anyway, when it comes to normal people, you fare best when they notice you least. But it was apt confirmation of my General Theory of the Universe, which some, like my erstwhile therapist Dr. Hextrom, if "erstwhile" means what I think it does, have mistakenly judged to be a bit paranoid.

It is as follows:

That the normal people who attack rock and roll misfits with tubas and put defenseless nerdy kids in garbage cans and throw gum in their hair and tease fat girls into suicidosity et cetera are merely the lowest foot soldiers in an integrated, extremely well-organized totalitarian social structure that extends through the student body, the school system, the city, the state, the country and its entire population and culture as well as those of the whole world, and, ultimately, to nature itself, all organized around a pseudo-Darwinian principle that may best be described as Survival of the Cruelest and the Dumbest, and just barely masked by an increasingly threadbare curtain of pretty lies, which–the curtain of lies, I mean–is most prominently exemplified by this godforsaken hellhole of a book called *The Catcher in the Rye.*

About which–*The Catcher in the Rye,* I mean–don't even get me started.

Plus, Mr. Teone killed my dad. It's all part of the same rotten-egg omelet. And that, my friends, if any of you truly are my friends, is not the kind of omelet you can comfortably be a good sport about.

At any rate, the Hillmont world was likely going to be flooded with a great big floody flood flood flood of lawsuits about Mr. Teone's hidden Satanic cameras in the girls' and boys' bathrooms and locker rooms and such. You could think, hey, what's one more lawsuit among all the other lawsuits? Or you could think, Tom "Chi-Mo" Henderson's feeble tuba lawsuit doesn't stand a chance when competing for ratings with sex, satanism, and bathrooms. Lawsuit lawsuit lawsuit: sometimes when you say a word a certain number of times, like I just did with "lawsuit," it starts to sound strange and meaningless. Lawsuit. Now, what was I talking about?

Oh yes, lawsuits.

But let me shift gears just a bit here and return from the mists of time where I took you on a journey et cetera to the current time now when I'm saying this.

I figure there can be only two reasons why you or anyone would be interested in knowing anything at all about Hillmont High School.

First reason: you are from the future, when the genius of my world-transforming rock and roll vision has finally been recognized, and ever since hearing my face-melting yet excruciatingly beautiful fifth solo album about love's futile power you've been plagued by questions. Whence–is it "whence"? I think it's "whence"–whence came this voice of a generation? How did it find itself, and how did it triumph over the evil forces that would have it silenced? Could the answer lie in Hillmont High School, the cradle of the rock revolution? That's the first reason.

Second reason: you've seen *Halls of Innocence*.

Well, I'm a realist. I know it's probably reason number two. But for you Reason Number One–ers from the future, if you're out there, I should probably explain that *Halls of Innocence* is a TV movie that was loosely based on all that scandal stuff with the sex tapes and the hidden cameras and the bad assistant principal that happened at Hillmont High School at the end of the year and was rushed into production for the May sweeps week. (Well, from my perspective it was the end of last year; I don't know how far in the future you are, but in our calendar system, it was just at the turn of the second millennium A.D. on planet Earth, at the edge of the Orion spiral arm in the Milky Way galaxy. I hope that helps you narrow it down.)

I strongly advise you to avoid *Halls of Innocence*. It will teach you nothing. It is a piece of garbage. I mean, Hillmont High School was a piece of garbage too, granted. So *Halls of Innocence* is a piece of garbage about a piece of garbage, and it completely mischaracterizes this piece of garbage along with all the pieces of garbage that administered it and sent their kids to it and attended it.

But no, you know what? You *should* see it, actually, because it's hilarious. Everyone should. Now that I think about it, it may well be my favorite movie of all time. I mean, when the Jake character throws his jacket down and kicks his locker and tells the Christine character "I don't even know you anymore" and runs off crying, well, that, folks, is TV cinema gold. It has been quoted and reenacted over and over again around here, including by me. Amanda does a great "I don't even know you anymore." You should see it sometime.

So see *Halls of Innocence,* but keep in mind that it gets everything wrong. And I mean everything, not just little things like how they changed Hillmont to Millmont or how Mr. Teone, the assistant principal, became Mr. Cabal. (That's how it's spelled in the credits and on his desk sign, but everyone pronounces it like "cable." Which, when you think about it, is pretty darn Hillmont-y. If we excelled at nothing else at Hillmont High School—and we didn't, trust me—we were world-class mispronouncers.)

The jacket in the iconic jacket-throwing scene is one of those with a ruglike letter on it that you probably think haven't been worn by anyone not in the cast of *Grease* for decades, if ever. I was to learn a lot about these so-called jackets in the coming months, but I can assure you that they certainly were never worn at Hillmont High School. And if the "real" Jake (who appears to be a combination of Matt Lynch and Paul Krebs and maybe one or two other sadistic normal psychotic meatheads) had thrown a jacket, it would only have been over the head of, say, a developmentally disabled kid before he mimicked his way of talking and pushed him down the stairs saying something brilliant like "Eat concrete, gimp." And then everyone would high-five him and he'd get an award in a special ceremony on Center Court. Millmont High School, unlike Hillmont High School, seems like a pretty nice place to be. Sure, the assistant principal put hidden cameras in the bathrooms, but in every other respect it is far from the pit of terror, torture, and iniquity that was the real Hillmont High, if "iniquity" means what I think it does.

I know this because I was there. And because I found a code in *The Catcher in the Rye* that revealed the true depths of Mr. Teone's depravity. And because of a little guy I like to call Sam Hellerman. He may not look like much, but he is good at figuring things out and knowing things nobody else knows and understanding things with utter confidence even when the explanations don't exactly add up. Also, as I've said, he's good at taking tranquilizers. Which may or may not be related to that previous item.

But maybe you didn't know that Mr. Cabal went around killing people's dads. Did you know that the various Jakes of the school, at Mr. Cabal's direction, got together and attacked me, in the head, with marching band instruments in order to silence me? Did you know that the incisive social commentary in our rock and roll band's songs were what exposed Mr. Cabal and spooked him enough to make him flee to wherever he fled to, bringing the whole system crashing down?

Not from *Halls of Innocence,* you didn't. My band wasn't even in it at all. That should tell you all you need to know about *Halls of Innocence.* Pure garbage, basically, except for one sublime jacket-throwing scene. Oh, and I can't believe I forgot the football game part. Remind me to tell you about that one, if you haven't seen it, where Jake, I kid you not, rides his skateboard down to the tracks to save this dog from being run over by a train during a time-out and makes it back just in time to score the winning touchdown as he'd promised to do for Christine's mother, who has cancer. Unbelievable.

So now, come with me once again, on a journey through the mists of time, back to Linda's Pancakes on Broadway, where our hero is heading to meet up with Sam Hellerman before continuing on to band practice, unaware of the future contents of *Halls of Innocence.*

He–I mean, I was feeling a little down, thinking about my dad and the sands of domestic tension and lawsuits and the predations of the normal. And I was thinking about the women in my life, or the women sort of in it, anyway, one of whom, Deanna Schumacher, was refusing to return my calls, while the other, Celeste Fletcher, the one I really liked, was maintaining a similarly disconcerting distance. It had been so different when I was hospitalized–or, I think it had. To be honest, I was so drugged up when I was there that it's all a bit of a haze. Both of them visited me, I know that, and sexiness ensued, I substantially know that. And I'm all for it, don't get me wrong. I was pretty proud of myself about the whole thing, to say the least. But just once I'd like someone to play Try to Guess What I'm Mad About with me and have it come from a place of love rather than a place of weird, uncertain manipulation. Like I said before, it's the kindness I miss most of all. I wondered if I'd ever be that happy again.

Sam Hellerman was sitting at the bus stop in front of Linda's Pancakes on Broadway with his headphones on and a yellow legal pad on his knees, his bass leaning against the bus stop's windscreen thing. He was evidently making notes on the music he was listening to on this weird old beat-up portable cassette player, but when he saw me approaching he turned the notepad over, a bit furtively, I thought, and clicked pause.

I angled my guitar case up against his bass case and slid in on the bench next to him.

"See, the problem is, Henderson," he said, taking a headphone off one ear, "that no one gets the Mussolini face. No one knows who he is. They'll just think you're constipated."

I knew he was right. I only knew about Mussolini because

I'd been watching my dad's old *World at War* documentaries recently, and he had seemed suitably evil and theatrical and pretty apt for a band called Encyclopedia Satanica. But few members of our theoretical audience, I had to concede, will have been watching the Italian episodes of *The World at War.* I assured Sam Hellerman that I'd seen the light and that Mussolini was as good as forgotten.

"Then stop doing the face," he said.

"I'm not doing the face."

"You're saying that's your regular face right now?"

I nodded.

"Well, Henderson," said Sam Hellerman. He gave me the look that says: "It appears you've got bigger problems than Mussolini."

I suppose thinking about my dad and my not-really girl-friends and the sadistic structure of the universe had been causing more of a dour, frowning expression than I'd realized. I de-Mussolini-ized the best I could, though I can't say it wasn't a struggle.

Of course, it didn't matter anyway, as Encyclopedia Satanica had passed into the annals of history, if "annals" means what I think it does. I told Sam Hellerman about I Hate This Jar. He was visibly shaken, but he knew better than to fight me on a band name. On the plus side, I noted, we could still use the Encyclopedia Satanica logo, so all those hours spent on perfecting its illegibility would not have been in vain. So Sam Hellerman agreed in the end but recommended that we not tell Shinefield about the new band name till later in the day when he was good and stoned and more likely to take it in good humor. Shinefield was an agreeable sort of guy about almost everything, but we both had a feeling he wouldn't have an easy time understanding I Hate This Jar.

REMAINING ALOOF

I expected more discussion, but Sam Hellerman, to my surprise, simply sniffed and put his headphones back on. He was no longer taking notes but rather staring off into space, bizarre expressions animating his face one after the other. And he had just been complaining about *my* face! What a hypocrite.

Sometimes I don't know what to make of Sam Hellerman.

I mean, you know the type of person I'm talking about? He may seem like he's not much of a friend sometimes. He may kid around a bit and even cross the line occasionally, not caring all that much about the consequences or who happens to get hurt. His motives may not always be noble: in fact, they rarely are. And sometimes he can just be a total bastard for no reason whatsoever. Nevertheless, you know that when the chips are down he'll be there to back you up, that deep down he's a pretty good guy with something approaching a heart of gold. And somehow, coming from him, after all you've been through together, having any heart at all seems to mean more. And you have to admit, life is certainly a lot more interesting with him around. You blink in amazement at the surprising realization that in the end he turned out to be a pretty good friend.

Well, Sam Hellerman is nothing at all like that. I mean, are you kidding? Sometimes I think he might be pure evil. I'm joking. Sam Hellerman's a great guy, really, greater than the sum of his parts, whatever the hell they may be.

Figuring he must have some reason for doing what he was doing, and that chances are it would turn out to be interesting in some way, I tried to be patient. But just sitting there next to him in silence while he listened to his tape and contorted his face was eventually too much of a strain. After what seemed

33

like two and a quarter centuries of trying to make my own face communicate something along the lines of "What the hell are you doing, Hellerman?" I finally resorted to the spoken word, much as I hated to do it:

"The fuck, Hellerman?"

Sam Hellerman, possibly the last person on earth, and certainly the only person under, like, forty, who still winces at an occasional "the fuck," winced. You'd think he'd be used to it, coming from me, and just about everyone, but Sam Hellerman is a man of tender and unusual sensibilities.

I resisted the urge to pat him on the head.

"This is known as remaining aloof," said Sam Hellerman, his tone implying that a little more aloofness on my part wouldn't go to waste if I knew what was good for me.

The thing we were remaining aloof from, if you haven't guessed, and as I should have realized, and as I soon discovered when I scanned the horizon for things it might be plausible for us to be remaining aloof from—this thing was a girl. I'm sure you guessed, though. Remaining aloof from anything less important than that wouldn't be worth mentioning.

The girl was seated on this low wall in front of the 7-Eleven across the street from our bus stop, sucking her Slurpee and kicking her legs, obviously waiting for someone to come along who just as obviously wasn't us. Bare legs. Little boots. Ski jacket with fuzzy hood because of the California chill, but with a short jeans skirt too. Warm on top, freezing her ass off on the bottom, everything balancing out. And of course, she seemed to be aware of how good she looked.

I squinted through my glasses at her legs from skirt hem to knee, and from knee to ankle, imagining I could make out the goose bumps that were probably running down them and mentally constructing a picture of what everything might look like in the concealed regions. As you do. My guess was it was all in pretty good shape, a well-maintained garden of delights. In other words, she wasn't the kind of girl for whom our aloofness or the lack thereof would register in the slightest. Plus, though she seemed like a nice enough person from a distance, she was almost certainly normal; that is, at least potentially psychotic and without an ounce of kindness or human decency anywhere in her sadistic, corrupted, robotic, petty, nerd-hating soul. Cute, though.

Tearing my eyes away from the legs caused a little part of me to die, but I did, and joined Sam Hellerman in examining the street sign up and to our left. Corte Del Mar Camino Road. "Chop Down the Sea Road Road," if I'm translating it right, and not a bad band name, at that. "Hey, we're Chop Down the Sea Road Road, and this one's called 'Up Yours, Your Majesty (Digitally Remastered Version).' One, two, eat lead . . ." It could work, sort of.

I spend a great deal of my time humoring Sam Hellerman for this or that, and now was no exception. I gave him the look that says "You have my attention."

Whatever it was that we were doing was cut short when a green station wagon pulled into the 7-Eleven parking lot and the jeans skirt girl jumped in. Sam Hellerman clicked the tape off, made a couple of notes on the legal pad, and began to gather his stuff.

"A solid seven point two," he said.

It was harsh grading, though I didn't necessarily disagree, but so what? Sam Hellerman was silent, refusing to answer any questions or even attempt to parry any of my pointed attempts at ridicule. He did ask for "the stuff," but I wasn't dumb enough to give it to him before band practice. The last time I'd done that he'd spent half the practice sprawled on the floor with his head in the bass drum.

It wasn't till late that night, long after returning from band practice, that I realized I had forgotten to ask Sam Hellerman about his letter. My curiosity about it was mild, but it still managed to keep me up half the night wondering about it with a vague, inexplicable sense of dread, because I'm King Dork and that's what I do. I tried to kill time by writing lyrics for a possible song called "Jeans Skirt Girl" but didn't get too far. The chorus was going to go something like "remain aloof, remain aloof, Jeans Skirt Girl, baby you're the proof," but I couldn't get much beyond that, other than to make a note and underline it three times that somehow, some way, I'd have to manage to arrange things so she'd end up on a roof by the third verse.

And you know, I never did wind up finishing that song. I was an artist of a sort, but I was no Salvador Dalí. He'd have figured out a way to get her on the roof.

SAM HELLERMAN'S ASSETS

Band practice, when Sam Hellerman and I finally did arrive, had been less than satisfactory. Celeste Fletcher was there, but so was Shinefield, obviously, as he was the drummer, after all, and moreover, it was his house. I don't know if I've mentioned it before, but in case I haven't, Celeste Fletcher had ditched her sort-of boyfriend, whoever he had been, and as far as anyone could tell was now Shinefield's sort-of girlfriend, though the most I could ever get her to say on the subject was that she "mainly hung out with" him. At practice she had been friendly toward me, but distant, and nowhere near as flirtatious as she sometimes has been, historically. She remained aloof, in fact. But unlike the girl in the jeans skirt, she actually knew us, so any aloofness that was afoot in Shinefield's basement had a whole different feel to it.

This lineup had had several practices since We Have Eaten All the Cake broke up and we rearranged ourselves into the Shopping Centers, before a half-a-practice stint as Ice Cream Gulag, during the second half of which we disintegrated and remelded as Encyclopedia Satanica. So Shinefield was at this point a true veteran with several bands under his belt.

I have to say that everyone at the practice was behaving strangely, even for us. Sam Hellerman, who, like everyone else, it seems, had the hots for Celeste Fletcher and even claimed to have done some messing around with her at one point— not that I ever believed it—was remaining almost as aloof from Celeste Fletcher as he had remained with regard to Jeans Skirt Girl. The thought occurred to me that I could get used to this aloof Sam Hellerman. At least his eyes were on his bass neck and shoes rather than on Celeste Fletcher's ass, which meant better playing and footwork. (It was more than I could say for myself: I found myself unable to resist staring at her much of the time.) As you may have figured out, a little of Sam Hellerman's act can go a long way, and a bit less of it from time to time, whatever the cause, can be a nice novelty. Nevertheless, the weirdness, in the end, overshadowed the novelty, at least for me.

Everyone seemed to be talking past me, sharing some joke I wasn't in on. I mean, more than usual. They kept saying things like "I guess we won't be seeing each other for a while" and "So long, nice to know ya" and laughing. This threw me until it struck me that they were most likely referring, in what I presumed to be a mocking spirit, to Sam Hellerman's Y2K doomsday scenario.

Y2K is an abbreviation for "the year 2000," and worrying about it was based on the fact that the dates of computer systems had been originally designed to show the year as only the last two digits. Once the year 2000 rolled around and you needed four digits, the whole world was supposed to melt down because the computers would all self-destruct in a violent puff of logic and then, somehow, would come to kill us. Sam Hellerman had been predicting Y2K doom for much of the past year.

"I'm just saying," he would intone with solemn confidence and a distant look in his eyes, "convert your assets to gold and other precious metals. It's our only hope."

I would inform him that I have no assets, and ask: "What assets do you have?"

"Considerable assets," Sam Hellerman would reply. And knowing him, I'd say there was a fair chance that he actually had "assets" and had indeed converted them to precious metals in preparation for the coming apocalypse, which I figured would go something like this: this big scary postapocalyptic guy with a chain saw for a hand and a spiky steel mask rides up on a ramshackle motorcycle and says, "Give me your assets," and Sam Hellerman goes, "Okay, sir, let me put these assets in a bag for you." And the guy says, "Thanks for the assets," and drives away. This sensible vision of the future with regard to the topic of assets did not deter Sam Hellerman's favored solution to the end of the world, however.

Now, it seemed to me, and still does seem to me, that people have been saying the world is going to end since forever, and yet, somehow, it never actually does. God, or Communists, or nuclear power, or overpopulation, or the ozone layer, or the environment: they all tried to destroy the world and couldn't manage it. Sam Hellerman was certain the computers would be what finally did it, but I was pretty sure that when the new year rolled around we'd still be here and everyone's assets would be pretty much the way they were before. (And if you will travel forward again, briefly, through the mists of time to when I'm telling you about this, you will no doubt notice that I had the better of this argument. See? Now travel back again, if you please.)

We sounded okay doing "Live Wire." But when it came to our own songs, well, here's something I've noticed about band practices: the first time you run through a song, before anyone really knows it, it sounds rough, perhaps, but kind of great. It has boundless potential, and often there's even a real feeling of true rock and roll energy and spirit about it. Wow, you feel, this is the real thing; this is worth doing after all. And if it sounds this good now, just think how great it'll be when everybody has had a chance to learn it properly and work it all out.

But somehow, the more you play the song, the more it degenerates. The drummer will gradually start to add fancy bits here and there, and soon the fancy bits take over till it's all fancy bits and hardly any beat. The bass player will then be unable to play with the drummer very closely because what he's doing is so unpredictable, so he figures he might as well noodle it up himself because just playing it straight actually makes it sound like he's off compared to the drums. The guitar player hits the chords in what he hopes are the right places, but since the two one-man rhythm sections are contradicting each other, there's no possible way to know exactly where those places are, so he starts meandering as well. After a few practices, everyone is increasingly lost, and soon the song is just *done,* so damaged that it is no use to anyone and no fun to play, and can only be retired and forgotten. We've lost some of my best songs this way. "Live Wire" works because there's an official recording to follow, and for some reason we all seem to participate in an unspoken pact to rein in our excesses, just for those six minutes, possibly because there's a way to prove that you're doing it wrong when you do it wrong. "My Retarded Heart" and "Mr. Teone Killed My Dad" weren't so fortunate, and they bit the dust, as far as I was concerned, in that very practice. I hated to lose songs like that, but that's the music biz, folks.

Now, you couldn't ask for a more amiable guy than Shinefield. Sometimes he seems almost like a young, tall Little Big Tom in his relentless good humor and easygoing-ness. He hadn't minded I Hate This Jar at all, after the initial disbelief had worn off, and he hadn't even been all that stoned, either.

"I Hate This Jar, man," he said with a lackadaisical chuckle. "Where do you guys come up with this stuff?"

And then throughout the day, he started referring to us as "the Jar" and saying things like "Man, that's so Jar. . . ." There was an element of mockery, to be sure, but it was good-natured.

So Shinefield was as cooperative a bandmate as you could ask for. But his drumming was another story. It was . . . what's the word I'm looking for? Atrocious? Loathsome? I almost have it. Ah, abhorrent, that's it. His drumming was *abhorrent.*

The way Shinefield saw it, there was no kick drum hit that couldn't, and shouldn't, be doubled, or even tripled, or even quadrupled; he was a skilled craftsman when it came to slowing down and speeding up, and he sometimes even managed to do both in the same measure. He took the term "fills" quite literally, assuming that the object of the game was to "fill" every available moment with arbitrary, arrhythmic tom-

40

hitting. He was completely innocent of any awareness of the concept of the "rest." Songs would usually finish at a tempo at least twice as fast as the one at which they had started. It was heartbreaking.

"Live Wire" showed that Shinefield was capable of playing a steady beat, with a relatively even tempo. It's only that when it came to our own songs, he just didn't feel like it.

As to how real bands manage to avoid this relentless song degeneration, I've got a theory. And if it's correct, let's just say I've always felt sorry for Phil Rudd, because it was pretty mean of the Young brothers to kidnap his family, tie them all up, and hold them hostage in a basement somewhere on the edge of town in a "play a steady beat or the kid gets it" kind of spirit. But the tragic human toll aside, the results speak for themselves. Go put on SD 36-142 and tell me that the Rudd Family Kidnapping of '75 wasn't worth doing.

The more you work on it, the worse it gets: I think I may have stumbled onto something like a profound principle there. I should try to integrate it into my General Theory of the Universe, or at least write it on the bathroom wall.

As for that Celeste Fletcher, man, what a girl, but she could sure drive you crazy. I am always impressed at how females seem to know what's going on and act like nothing is confusing and what is happening is exactly the way they expected it to be. In a way, they're like the Sam Hellerman of the sexes. They look at everything with this nodding smirk, as though saying to themselves, "Uh, yeah, go ahead and play out your pitiful little script, we're ten steps ahead of you at all times and we all know that in the end you'll wind up doing precisely what we want."

At least, that's how Celeste Fletcher was, sitting against the basement wall at the practice doing homework, or something, and pausing now and then to look up and beam "knowing glance" rays at random targets throughout the room. I was sad that Celeste Fletcher didn't seem to like me anywhere near as much as I liked her but comforted by the fact that she didn't seem to like anyone all that much.

When the practice was over and we were all doing the hug-goodbye thing, she subtly nestled herself into me, a bit more, it seemed, than was required. I was covered in rock and roll practice sweat and my centipede was pulsing, and my all-over body bruise was slightly painful, which only made it that much more awkward.

"Sorry this is so weird," she whispered directly in my ear.

So, there was something—a "this," that was enough of a thing that it warranted the designation "weird." And not just weird, but "so weird." Or not. She was just rubbing herself on people's bruises and saying words. How could anyone know what they actually meant?

At the risk of sounding a little corny, Celeste Fletcher was like a song. That is, the project of trying to figure out what she could possibly be up to was like rehearsing a song: "The more you work on it, the less you get it." Man, that is, unfortunately, maybe the most generally applicable aphorism I have ever come up with. God, I hate being so insightful.

The thing is, we had a lot in common, which I'm not very used to, and I guess it's hard not to get a little carried away with sentimentality when presented with the one person you've ever met in your life who thinks, for instance, that deliberately mispronouncing vocabulary words is funny, especially when she has a pretty nice body.

At the practice, when we had just finished a particularly disastrous run-through of "You Know You Want It," she had looked up from her notebook and said: "Well, that certainly was harminomious and mellifluicious." And then she did this little half smile, directed solely at me. It was what you call a "nice moment." The combination of conspiratorial mispronunciation, sarcasm, and ass was too much for me. I mean, how could you not be in love with that, at least a little?

But I wasn't in love with her, not literally, despite the fact that I once thought I was and even told her so in one of my most embarrassing of moments. If I was in love with anyone, it was this imaginary girl she had portrayed for about two hours one night earlier in the year, basically just Celeste Fletcher in a costume. Fiona: her lack of reality did nothing to diminish her appeal, and possibly enhanced it. Or maybe it was the glasses and the too-small Who T-shirt that did it. I just couldn't get those out of my stupid head.

FIELDWORK

I was thinking how nice it might be to share Sam Hellerman's faith in the end of the world. At least it's faith in something. And the idea is appealing: there will be this big explosion, or flood, or computer glitch, after which everything just stops and you no longer know about anything and nothing knows about you; or maybe life would be simply so changed that nothing that went before is worth caring about. It seems like that would be a tremendous relief, and if I believed in it, I'd look forward to it rather than worry about it.

Little Big Tom's head poked through the door at what seemed like nearly a ninety-degree angle.

"And the weight of the world on his shoulders," he said, with a little mustache twitch. "You doing okay there, sport?"

I guess I'd been looking pensive, if pensive is the one where you're thoughtful about something and you want to sound important.

"Yes . . . chief," I said. "It's nothing. I was just thinking about Y2K."

Little Big Tom had been squabbling with my mom all morning, according to Amanda's breathless report, and he was off his game. He had no jaunty commentary to offer concerning Y2K, though I could see on his face evidence that his brain was trying as hard as it could to come up with something. Finally, he gave up and pursed his lips in defeat, dematerializing mournfully. Now I really felt bad, like, seriously, I felt this ridiculous impulse to run after him and hug him, tell him everything would be okay. Not that my strict codes of personal conduct would have permitted anything like such a display. But I resolved to lob him a softball of some kind at the next opportunity. It's just not fair to spring something weird like Y2K on a guy like Little Big Tom. I'd never seen him give up before, and the spectacle made me conscious of a melancholy void in an area of my chest I hadn't previously known about. Pretty amazing how many of those there are.

I had just returned from another strange session outside of Linda's Pancakes on Broadway, sitting on the bus stop bench next to Sam Hellerman, who was once again listening to his tape, making notes, and remaining intensely aloof from Jeans Skirt Girl, except this time she had been wearing actual jeans. Which looked pretty nice, in the way that jeans look nice when worn by females.

She evidently had a daily appointment in the area that ended around one p.m., after which the arrangement seemed to be that she'd wait in front of the 7-Eleven for her mom to pick her up. It was raining, so she had her hood on and the drawstring pulled tight so that there was a little ring of fur almost completely encircling her face. That, I had to admit, was pretty fucking cute. Sam Hellerman, on the other hand, was not too smooth-looking, huddled under a big black umbrella with his notepad and headphones and the inscrutable eyes behind his thick, half-fogged glasses.

I had asked Sam Hellerman point-blank why on earth he was stalking this poor girl.

"Not stalking," he said. "Fieldwork."

"You do realize, don't you, Hellerman," I said, "that if she ever does notice you spying on her she'll run away screaming and probably call the cops?" I added that he didn't seem to have fully grasped the meaning of the word "aloof." It's not logically possible to remain aloof in any meaningful sense from a person who is unaware that you're there doing it. "And if she does become aware," I concluded, with my eyes, "it can only end in your own humiliation and a possible jail term."

Sam Hellerman didn't answer. While I was dispensing this sensible advice, he was otherwise engaged, snapping a rapid-fire series of photos of Jeans Skirt Girl with his dad's little digital camera.

Once again, I had been so distracted by Sam Hellerman's antics that I'd forgotten to ask about the mysterious letter till I was already halfway home. This was getting out of hand. It was probably nothing at all of consequence, like so many of the other little puzzles that always surround Sam Hellerman like a halo of question marks. But it would remain an ever more irritating irritant till such time as I was finally able to cross it off the list. I got out my Sharpie and wrote LETTER on my hand. Then, just to make sure, I wrote HAND on my shoe. And *then*, just to be absolutely completely certain beyond any conceivable mishap, I wrote SHOE on my other hand (though that was a bit hard to read because I had to write it with my left hand.) That ought to do it, I thought.

It was soggy and muddy outside, and similarly grim in the house. Or maybe it was just my mind that was soggy and muddy and grim.

I was agitated and irritated at no one in particular for no particular reason. Sam Hellerman was off collating the data from his "fieldwork," an embarrassment to himself and everyone associated with him. Celeste Fletcher was sorry it was so weird, but not so sorry about it that she wanted to spend any time with me. Deanna Schumacher was remaining aloof to the degree that she had dropped off the face of the earth. I had inadvertently wounded Little Big Tom by presenting him with a therapy issue to which he had no response. My band sucked. My dad was dead. There was never going to be a lawsuit. I was dreading going back to school at the end of vacation, to face whatever horrors the normal people had in store for me: after all, they tried to kill me, and I just wouldn't get dead like they'd planned, and I could only imagine how mad that would have made them. I was all alone with no one to keep me company but my centipede. I guess there were reasons.

Also, it was Christmas Eve. Maybe you think it's a little strange to mention Christmas only as an afterthought. I guess it is strange. Christmas is a big deal for most people, and probably for you. But not around here. In my house there hasn't really been Christmas to speak of since my dad died. It was put on hold completely for a couple of years after his actual death. Then it gradually seeped back in. But when it did, it was muted, a shadow of its former self compared to how I remember it. I guess my dad had been a pretty Christmassy guy. There used to be a Christmas party every year at my house that lots of neighborhood people and his police friends would come to. One year they even had a band playing jazz or something like that. My parents danced and people clapped, and I watched from the stairs when I was supposed to be in bed: that's one nice memory I have.

Anyhow, nowadays, we all associate Christmas with him, so Christmas just became sad after he was gone, and everyone feels like avoiding it.

Little Big Tom tries. He always sets up a Christmas tree, gets everyone presents, and puts up lights and such, though he doesn't like to use the word "Christmas" for it: he calls it Yule and says things like "Did you know that Christmas was originally a pagan winter festival that the Christians took over and it has nothing to do with Jesus? It's a very cool historical fact." Well, yes, in fact, I did know that, chief, based on the last three hundred thousand times you've mentioned it, the most recent being just fifteen minutes ago. "Okay, then," Little Big Tom's knowing smile seems to say. "I just wanted to make sure you're aware that putting up these lights doesn't mean I'm into the baby Jesus and organized religion and Western medicine and the corporations." Then, when the lights inevitably fall down, Little Big Tom's knowing lowered eyebrow seems to ask the eternal question "Why do these damn things keep falling down?" But that's what it's like living with a hippie. There's just no cheering up the Hendersons on Christmas, is what I'm saying. Don't even try.

I tried to spend some time reading, but I couldn't concentrate. I had finished most of my dad's old books a ways back, and reading anything else now seemed kind of pointless. Those books of his, the books he'd read as a kid, were, in my mind, all about him under the surface, as though reading between the lines allowed me to see him in the books. That had become the main point of reading for me. I wondered if I'd ever be able to enjoy or understand a book he hadn't read. On the other hand, the one of his that I was currently still trying to work through, *The Crying of Lot 49*, was pretty hard going, and I definitely didn't understand it, despite the fact that it was one of his most written-in books. I have no idea what it's about: some conspiracy of competing post offices and crazy drug people who think garbage cans are mailboxes. It was written by a guy named Pynchon, who also wrote this other nine-million-page book about physics or something, which might be good for hitting someone over the head with sometime.

I had too much respect for my dad's teenage library to throw any of it across the room, so I set *The Crying of Lot 49* down reverently and picked up *Dune,* which I had started re-reading to pass the time.

I had no idea if my dad had ever read *Dune.* It didn't have his initials written in it like the others, but it was from a box in the same general area of the basement, and he could well have read it. I decided to pretend he *had* read it and see if that helped. For now, though, I put that book down too, opened the desk drawer, and took out the little square of graph paper containing the Catcher Code, the one piece of physical evidence I had that linked my dad with Mr. Teone. I had made a little case for it by cutting up and taping together a clear plastic seven-inch sleeve. I turned it over in my hand, thinking. At this point, it was little more than a talisman, a souvenir that had already taught me all it had to teach. But maybe if they ever did catch Mr. Teone, they'd want it as evidence. Or if there was ever a lawsuit . . .

As a last-ditch effort at doing something I could actually accomplish, I put on NAR-012 as loud as possible, hoping to provoke someone to get mad and tell me to turn it down, but even that was met with what seemed like utter apathy from the world outside my room.

My mom was in the living room, slouched on the sofa smoking one of her long cigarettes and drinking what I took to be a martini in a regular glass, based on the olives that were in it. I guess she had managed to get that jar open after all, rendering my band obsolete in the process. Ah, well, we'd had a good run. It was a slightly unusual home cocktail for her, and in my current mood, that and the coincidence of the presence of the olives from her most hated jar seemed vaguely ominous.

Now, I think I've mentioned that my mom has an eccentric way of dressing, especially for a mom. She can look like a little girl playing dress-up one day, and then like a crazy lady living on the street the next, and then, on the third day, like an old-fashioned airline stewardess who has fallen out of her plane, landed on a Toys "R" Us, and emerged covered with brightly colored toys. They even called the cops on her a couple times way back when I was a kid when she was picking me up from school: her outlandish dress sense was enough to set in motion an elementary school lockdown and they had to call my dad to come get both of us just to be on the safe side.

It's mostly a matter of strange hats and vibrant, clashing colors. Her outfits have triggered epileptic seizures in the elderly and in cats. This is well known. But even so, I was surprised to find her wearing a kind of Christmas uniform: red-and-white striped socks, green sort of short overalls, glittery boots that Ace Frehley would have been proud to wear, earrings that were little dangling Christmas trees, and a funny green hat like a baseball cap but really puffy on top. As I explained, my dad had been a pretty Christmassy guy. My mom was not, as a rule, anywhere near this Christmassy.

"Work party," she said in response to my questioning look. "So ..." She was distant as usual, distracted by something only she could see, remaining aloof from the entire living room, maybe the entire world. Was it likely that there would be a dress-up work party at the dentist's office on Christmas Eve? It didn't seem too likely to me, but what do I know about Christmas, or dentists?

"Hand," she said.

My look begged her pardon.

"It says 'hand' on your shoe."

Oh, right. By way of explanation, I held up my right palm, the one that had SHOE sloppily written on it, maintaining a deadpan expression. Now, I thought that was funny. My mom didn't see the humor, however, and nodded sadly, as though the spectacle of a son who needed labels to distinguish his foot from his hand, and who moreover got the labels wrong, was somehow a confirmation of some dark, long-held suspicion.

"Mom," I said, finally resorting to words. "Did Sam Hellerman send me a letter recently?"

Her look seemed to say "I don't know, did he?" managing to combine maternal sarcasm, juvenile smart-assery, and her usual mournfulness in the same weird package. But in words she said, "Not that I know of, baby."

She crinkled her brow and sighed out a perplexed jet of smoke.

"Love you, sweetie," she finally said quietly, with just the hint of a shake of her head. That was one of her two ways of signaling that she had no more to say and the conversation was over, the other, less affirmative one being just getting up and leaving the room.

Nice talking to you, Mom, I said silently, by means of placing a gentle hand on her shoulder as I walked past. She patted my hand with the bottom of her glass, and half of her mouth seemed to smile, almost. Looking back at her from the hallway, I thought her eyes might possibly be a little misty. She looked beautiful and shiny in the dim light, a long scroll of smoke spiraling from the tip of her cigarette like an Elizabethan signature.

ALL ABOARD THE OBSESSION TRAIN

SHOE, HAND, LETTER. If nothing else, the awkward conversation with my mom was a reminder to remember to look at my reminders to remember Sam Hellerman's accursed letter. This better be good, Hellerman, I thought. I don't know why I had begun obsessing about the stupid letter. Maybe because I just wanted to cross something, anything, off my list, and nothing else seemed remotely cross-offable at the moment.

Knowing Sam Hellerman, it could be anything: a puzzle, a code, a sly insult, a puzzle that when solved revealed a coded sly insult, an informative newspaper clipping, an uninformative newspaper clipping, a picture of a sexy girl with the caption PHOTON TORPEDOES: TARGET ACQUIRED ... My best guess was that it was something of the photon torpedo type, possibly to do with Jeans Skirt Girl. Or it could in fact be nothing at all, no letter, no nothing, just something Sam Hellerman said for no reason whatsoever. That was my second-best guess.

At any rate, once I jump on the obsession train, there's just no derailing it. I know it's stupid, but the more I try to ignore something, the more it swirls in my mind, till I'm gibbering and laughing hysterically, brushing invisible insects from my arms, covering the walls with crookedly placed newspaper clippings containing the word "letter," and sitting bolt upright in bed in the middle of the night screaming *What letter, Hellerman? For the love of all that is holy, just tell me, WHAT GODDAMN LETTER?"* In that quiet way I have, of course.

Well, I vowed not to let that happen if I could help it; plus, I was going crazy with boredom as it was and I had to do something, so instead of passively waiting till the next time I saw Sam Hellerman and hoping I'd still have HAND on my foot at that point, I decided to take action. A brief tug-of-war with Amanda later, the phone-baby was in my possession, and I was locked in the bathroom tapping in the number of Hellerman Manor.

After many rings, Sam Hellerman's father answered and said, in his scary German-accented voice: "It is the dinner hour, young man, and it is Christmas Eve." He then asked if I was insane. Well, I'm sure I sounded plenty insane, especially when I begged him to put Sam Hellerman on the phone and avowed that it was a matter of life and death. That was taking things too far, I know, but if I've learned anything in my brief time among the inhabitants of this planet, it is that your chances of getting your way can only be improved if the other party believes you're crazy enough to be dangerous. Sam Hellerman soon came on the line.

"I can't talk, Henderson," he said in an exasperated whisper, and I didn't blame him. It had sounded like Herr Hellerman was planning to give someone a nice Christmas beating, and Sam Hellerman was certainly the most likely candidate to receive it.

"Just tell me about your letter, Hellerman," I said quickly, in a tone of voice that added "that's all I ask."

"My letter," he repeated, in the way that someone who was unaware of any letter might say the word "letter" when asked about a letter.

I was pretty sure I had my answer right there, but just to confirm I added:

"So you didn't send a letter."

"No, why would I do that?" he said. "Do you know how crazy you sound right now?"

I was just about to hang up when I heard him suddenly say: "Oh, wait. *That* letter!"

I could almost hear him wince over the phone when I said "Jesus fucking Christ."

"You mean the one from the school district," he said. "It wasn't from me. Did you get–"

But I had already hung up.

There was no mail from Sam Hellerman in the huge pile of barely opened mail on the mail pileup area of the kitchen counter by the phone, but there was lots and lots of mail. Junk mail, bills, bank statements, threats from collection agencies–my family is not very ept at opening and answering mail. The phone and gas get cut off regularly just because no one bothers to open the delinquent bills and pay them, and Little Big Tom sometimes has to drive down to the gas company's headquarters to pay in cash at the last minute when it gets critical.

I wasn't expecting this letter to be anything interesting. And on the outside chance that it turned out to be something interesting, I wasn't expecting it to be anything good. But as I've explained, at this point I just wanted to cross it off my list, and going straight to the source seemed a better approach than trying to tease whatever it was out of a terrified, whispering Sam Hellerman over the phone.

It took some time to find it, but in the end there it was, from the Santa Carla Unified School District, dated a few weeks back. It was a long letter. My eyes scanned it.

"... tragic events ... liability ... district policy ... safety and well-being ... students, staff, and administrators ... appropriate measures ... pending litigation ... law enforcement ... federal investigation ... media scrutiny ... counseling available ... effective immediately ... upon commencement ... close its doors ... offices to remain ... administrative functions ... smooth transition ... academic excellence ..."

Then I read it again, more carefully.

My God, I said, almost out loud. They're closing Hillmont High School.

Well, what do you know? I thought. There was a lot of babble about the welfare of the students and "academic excellence" and so forth, but the bottom line seemed to be that fears of legal trouble and bad publicity and uncertainty as to what else the various investigations might turn up had led the school district's administrators to decide that inviting students back into the Hillmont High School buildings after what had happened would only make them look even worse than they already did and would possibly open them up to further liability. Their solution was to close the school down, effective almost immediately.

I had to hand it to Mr. Teone. He and his hidden cameras had finally managed to achieve what forty years of sucking worse than any high school in the history of high school could not. And it couldn't have happened to a more deserving school, despite being a decade or three late. I doubted anyone would mourn the demise of Hillmont High School.

The Hillmont students were to be filtered into other schools beginning in the spring semester. The end of the letter informed me that following winter break, after doing "Finals" at the Hillmont "campus" (ha, I inserted mentally), I was expected to show up for registration at Clearview High, with classes to begin officially the following week. That was really soon.

It was difficult to believe. I just stood there turning it over in my mind, getting more and more annoyed. I certainly wasn't upset that Hillmont High was closing. I had no delusions that Clearview would be much better, but it could hardly be worse, and I hated Hillmont more than life itself. What was bugging me was my stupid, incompetent family, who couldn't even manage to open the mail every now and then, who showed no interest in participating on my behalf in what appeared to be a considerable orgy of forthcoming litigation against the school, who basically refused to bother to do or know anything about anything. Plus, there was the fact that I was only finding out about it now, when Sam Hellerman and everyone else had already learned of it ages ago.

I was still standing there, letter in hand, when Little Big Tom came up behind me and started giving me one of his trademark unsolicited back rubs, the sort that are supposed to be comforting but actually make your skin crawl.

"Listen, chief," he said in his soothing therapy voice, the one like thick, gentle, alarming syrup. "I know you have deep, deep concerns and anxieties about Y2K. But the first thing to remember is, this is a safe place. . . ."

I started to see bubbly colors like I had seen before I accidentally beat up Paul Krebs.

I wanted to scream. I wanted to punch a baby in the face.

Most of all I wanted to get out from under Little Big Tom's oppressive therapy grip. But what I did was, I tipped up the kitchen table and knocked it all the way over, scattering the mail, dirty dishes, and everything else that was on it in a big clattering crash that made Little Big Tom jump five feet in the air and brought my mom and Amanda rushing into the kitchen at light speed.

"What on earth happened here?" said a Christmas tree who happened also to be my mother.

"The time bomb finally exploded," said Amanda, even as she was tapping in a number on her phone-baby to report the latest to her bureau chiefs at headquarters. Her shoulders raised slightly as though to say "It was only a matter of time."

"Never seen someone so darn upset about Y2K," said a visibly mystified Little Big Tom, dabbing his shirt where a flying open bottle of wine and a tub of butter had landed with satisfying accuracy.

"They're closing Hillmont High School," I said when the colors had receded, rattling the letter.

"Oh, yeah," said my mom. "I heard about that."

I stared at her. My eyes said: "You heard about it and didn't bother to mention it? And that's because why?" And I'm not at all sure that one of my eyebrows didn't add the word "bitch" somewhere in there.

It was the easiest game of Try to Guess What I'm Mad About in the history of the world, but, well, my family really, really sucks at Try to Guess What I'm Mad About.

"Chief," said Little Big Tom, still in the therapy voice, taking my hands in his. "Going to a new high school is a challenging time for any teen...."

I twisted away and left the room, winning.

So, Queerview High School. It had to be better than Hellmont, it just had to be. And while I couldn't go so far as to say I was looking forward to it, I could see some definite pros among the cons. One of the cons was that as awful as Hillmont High was, we'd been there for a year and a half and we knew precisely how things failed to function there, while Clearview's horrors were yet to be discovered. Better the devil you know than the one you don't, they say, but when all's said and done, it's still the devil you're talking about. The devil is bad.

I had no illusions. Closing Hillmont High would do nothing whatsoever to change the senseless, sadistic structure of society and the universe, and I had no doubt that Clearview was crawling with normal people every bit as vicious as those we had known in . . . the other place. But Sam Hellerman and I were pretty good at navigating the beast-infested seas of normalcy, and Sam Hellerman was actually a genius. With his hand on the tiller of our ramshackle skiff, I had no doubt we'd manage. Plus, no Mr. Schtuppe. No Ms. Rambo. No Mr. Donnelly. In a way, Mr. Teone had given us a great and precious gift. The only possible improvement would have been if the buildings were to be razed, the earth salted, and all the psychotic normal perpetrators led away in chains. But let not the horrible be the enemy of the slightly less than terrible, if I have that saying right. Any way you sliced it, there were definitely pros, no doubt about it.

Now, those of you from the future who have already seen *Halls of Innocence* will be surprised to learn that Hillmont High was closed down. At the end of the program, Jake dashes up the school steps and says, "It's great to be back," and there's a freeze-frame on his enormous toothy smile, over which there's a caption that says:

Mr. Cabal fled and has evaded capture.
He is still at large.

Well, of course, no one, not even the worst normal person ever to walk the earth, had ever or would ever actually be glad to be at Hillmont High School, let alone smile at the thought. But the bit about "Mr. Cabal" is true. He was still at large. And that worried me. It worried me a lot.

I didn't get a chance to speak to Sam Hellerman about the letter and our Clearview strategy till the day after the day after Christmas. When I arrived at Toby's Record Hut on El Camino to meet him, he was already there looking through the New Arrivals bins.

One of the few great things about the times we live in is that the normal people of the world have recently reached the misguided conclusion that compact discs are better than vinyl LPs. They're wrong about this, of course, as they are about almost everything. All the great rock and roll recordings were made on analog equipment, and they were specifically engineered to sound right when reproduced on vinyl. Plus, the CDs of those recordings have often been remastered to try to make them match the awful sounds of our contemporary recordings. (For example, go listen to the CD of COC 39105: I promise it will hurt your ears. And not in a good way.) Unless you want, for some reason I can't fathom, to listen to the terrible stuff they're putting out now, you're way better off just putting on the damn Stones record.

But the normal people don't realize this, and they've been

buying their dumb CDs, getting rid of their record players, and discarding their vinyl LPs for years and years now. Result: used vinyl is everywhere, and there has never been a cheaper time to acquire it. You can walk into a place like Toby's with fifteen dollars and come out with six great albums stupidly abandoned by their original normal owners. Sometimes they even leave them out on the street in milk crates. I picked up the entire Alice Cooper catalog on Vista View Terrace Avenue just the other week. Morons.

People from the future: you should have been there. People from now: now's your chance. You can bet it won't last forever.

Sam Hellerman had his headphones on, as he always did lately, but he was still flicking through the records calling out albums and their ridiculously low prices, and putting the good ones aside.

"BS 2607, three fifty," he said. "S CBS 82000, four fifty. ASF 2512, one dollar . . ."

Now, you've probably noticed this thing we've been doing of referring to records by their catalog numbers rather than the titles, and maybe I should explain. Except that there isn't an explanation. It serves no useful purpose. Hence, obviously, it's a thing worth doing. Sam Hellerman started it one day, saying "You know, Henderson, I think I actually might like EKS 74071 better than EKS 74051." I was mystified but went along with it, nodding silently in that way I do, till I figured out from the other stuff he was saying that he was talking about the Stooges. I caught on that EKS stood for Elektra Records, and that he was saying he liked *Funhouse* better than the self-titled debut album. (To which I say: no duh.) So I joined in. It's like a fun, really dumb secret code. We started out with the obvious ones pretty much everyone knows, like BS 2607 or 2409-218. But some of them are really hard, and you wind up having to do a lot of research after some conversations just to find out what the hell you've been talking about. I even take notes sometimes.

Sam Hellerman is way better at this game than I am, of course. The guy seems to know every catalog number of every record by heart. Maybe he prepares a list the night before just to impress me. Either way, it does. Impress me, I mean. Sam Hellerman is like that. He just randomly starts doing something stupid and before too long it becomes a well-established custom and you soon forget that people ever did anything different.

One of the records we found at Toby's that day was APLPA-016, the Australia-only issue of AC/DC's second album, *T.N.T.*, which is perhaps the finest hard rock record ever released. This was the first pressing, with the kangaroos on the labels. I'd never actually seen one. It was five dollars rather than fifty cents, because it was an "import," but it was certainly well worth five dollars of Christmas money. We walked out of there with twenty LPs between us, and we barely spent thirty bucks.

So APLPA-016 got me thinking, and later on the bus I asked Sam Hellerman if he'd ever noticed that Shinefield's drumming when we covered "Live Wire" was much less retarded than it was when we played our own songs. And of course, he had noticed.

We spent the rest of the bus ride engaged in exaggerated, sarcastic mimicry of Shinefield's awful drumming, using our hands as sticks on the seats in front of us and augmenting that by making various drum noises with our mouths. When we were asked to leave the bus and had to get out and walk the rest of the way, we had to use our arms to carry the records

60

instead of using them to mimic Shinefield's eccentric sense of timing and rhythm, but the conversation continued.

Sam Hellerman noted that we had tried to explain the concept of "space," and beats, and regular tempo, and rests, and eighth notes to Shinefield till we were blue in the face, but it never did any good. Shinefield always agreed enthusiastically that good drumming had to be minimal enough so you could detect, say, where beat one was going to fall, and—though this might be pushing it—where beat one stood in relation to all the other beats. And he would say things like "Totally, dude" and flash us a grin that overflowed with eager camaraderie, if "camaraderie" is the one where you're all on the same team saying "Okay, boys, let's get 'em." But then the song would begin and he would be even worse than before.

"The only way to improve his drumming on our songs would be to kick him out of the band," said Sam Hellerman, and he added that in his opinion, Shinefield played "Live Wire" better because it was only a cover and he didn't care enough about it to mess it up by trying to make it all special.

"Wouldn't it be great," I said, "if we could somehow get him to play 'Live Wire' while we played our songs?"

Sam Hellerman stopped in his tracks.

"Say that again, Henderson," he said. Like a scene in a movie where someone says something that turns out to be the key to the big dilemma and another person tells him to say it again so the audience's attention can be drawn to it without any possibility of missing it. In short, there was evidently something to this idea, in the world of Sam Hellerman.

"What?" I said, playing my assigned role as best I could for the moment.

"What you just said. Say it again."

"You mean, 'Fuck you, Hellerman'?"

"You didn't say that," said Sam Hellerman woundedly.

My eyes said, "I know, man, I just felt like saying it for some reason. No offense."

But even though I wouldn't play along with the "say that again" game, Sam Hellerman is a genius, and I could see that faraway genius look in his eyes. And of course he wouldn't tell me his specific plan right then. And of course we had to sit for a while at the bus stop in front of Linda's Pancakes on Broadway pretending not to look at Jeans Skirt Girl. And of course Sam Hellerman was listening to his tape rather than talking to me, making surreptitious notes and swaying from side to side like he was having a fit or something. And of course I sat there too, though I felt like a big idiot, because I was just so curious as to what he was going to propose in the end that I had to stick it out so I'd get to hear it. As with the letter, I was a prisoner of his cockeyed genius, if cockeyed isn't too strange of a thing to call a person's genius. Basically, I just had to know.

Jeans Skirt Girl had climbed into the green station wagon, and Sam Hellerman had switched off his tape player, just as the thought struck: the letter! I'd forgotten all about it in the excitement about APLPA-016. I hadn't yet had a chance to discuss the switch to Clearview High School and compare notes with Sam Hellerman on the pros and cons.

"So," I said. "Queerview."

"What?" he said.

"Queerview."

"What?" he said.

I decided to make my meaning clearer.

"Clearview," I said.

"Stop saying that," said Sam Hellerman. "You sound like a lunatic."

I patiently explained that what I meant was that I'd seen the letter at last and that I had been attempting, using as few audible words as possible, as is my wont, to introduce the topic of how it looked like we'd be attending Clearview High School in the new year. Is it "wont"? I think it's "wont," though that's weird.

"If we're not killed by Y2K, that is," I added with my eyebrows.

Now, I have no idea how astute you, my public, may be. But it occurs to me that some of you possibly will have some idea already of what Sam Hellerman was going to say next. If so, I congratulate you, because I'm obviously not anywhere near as good as you are at astuteness, and it came as a complete surprise to me.

"Clearview?" he said. "I'm not going to Clearview. I'm supposed to go to Mission Hills."

And again, if the astute among you who saw that coming also already knew that my response to this was to sit on the bench, remaining aloof from reality, my blood running cold and sweat bedewing my brow, wishing desperately that there were a kitchen table next to the bus stop just so I could tip it over? Well, you were right about that, too. You're good.

Sam Hellerman and I would be going to different high schools.

It was a con. A definite con.

PART TWO

Y2K

THE BRUTAL CONDITIONS OF THE NORTH AMERICAN KIBBLE MINES

As those of you from the future knew all along, January 1, 2000, dawned on a changed world. Computer irregularities had caused an instant worldwide financial collapse. Huge regions of the western United States were rendered uninhabitable by the failure of the electrical grid and lack of water, while nuclear plants, their automated temperature control systems disabled, quickly melted down and spewed radiation throughout the countryside. The world's great nations, seeing their security endangered, let loose their missiles simultaneously, wiping out all but ten percent of the earth's population. Soon mutant creatures roamed the land, most notably a gigantic fire-breathing lizard and an enormous angry moth: together they laid waste to cities, brushing humans aside like they were so many ants. Now we, the surviving remnant of humanity, live a harsh existence in underground caves, enslaved by a mutant race of superintelligent cats and forced to labor for the entirety of our short lives under the brutal conditions of the North American kibble mines. Only the few among us, the Resistance, continue the struggle to preserve our race, quietly gathering the components with which to assemble a giant laser pointer, a vacuum cleaner, and a spray bottle to distract and drive off our feline overlords and reclaim our ruined planet.

Yeah, no: that didn't actually happen. Too bad, Hellerman. We'll get 'em next millennium.

Not that the real, actual Y2K was any picnic. New Year's Eve was spent at a gruesome party at Shinefield's house where I was the only person not drunk and/or stoned.

Now, there was a time, I believe, long, long ago, when stoner music, or rather, the music stoners liked to listen to, tended to be heavy, bluesy, rock and roll, like Sabbath, Rush, Hendrix, Zeppelin, that kind of thing, plus Pink Floyd for the part at the end where they lay back on the floor looking at the ceiling and talking about how bedrooms were like suitcases for people or how if you had a map that was the same size as the world you could move there and live on it instead, thus solving pollution and overpopulation. But aside from a little Led Zeppelin the music at this party was uniformly terrible, endless formless musician-y "jams" with songs that went no-where, lasted forever, and were so busy and arrhythmic that it made me kind of hate Thomas Edison for having invented the recording technology that would eventually allow them to be put on their stupid CDs and unleashed on an innocent public.

I guess the problem was that Shinefield and his friends were more like skater hippie stoners than regular stoners. You can tell them by their knit caps and stinky white-boy dreads, and the Grateful Dead skulls on their skateboards. Actually, though, the real problem is just that all things nowadays suck so much more than they used to. The only suspense lies in trying to guess the precise ways in which they will suck more, and to what degree. But you could sure see where Shinefield's busy drumming problem came from: the guys on the CDs were all over the map too, though at least they tended to stay at a steady tempo. And unlike Rush, who have the "too much drums" problem too, they were not redeemed by a cartoon-character-sounding vocalist trying to be Ayn Rand. As for what they *were* trying to be, well, if you put a gun to my head I couldn't tell you, nor could I make even an informed guess as to what the songs were supposed to be about.

What I'm saying is, I suppose, that I'd have preferred the kibble mines.

Sam Hellerman was in a state of blissful oblivion through

most of it, courtesy of two Valium with a vodka chaser, so he was spared the terrible music as well as the grim spectacle of Celeste Fletcher grinding all over Shinefield, making out with him like it really was the end of the world and this was her last chance for all eternity to have the opportunity to lick another person's face. Then, when they led each other upstairs, presumably for some apocalyptic ramoning in the bathroom or something along those lines, it really felt like something was breaking inside me, in spite of my most strenuous efforts not to care. The song on at that moment seemed to be about tweezers or some damn thing, but between the lines all I could hear was: worst year ever, coming right up.

Then, when the countdown thing happened on TV, and the jam hippie girls kissed the jam hippie boys happy new year, Celeste Fletcher came up to me.

"Happy New Year, Elvis," she said.

"Fiona," I said, for obvious reasons.

She kissed me Happy New Year lightly but with a bit of a lip bite at the end and didn't recoil when my hand of its own accord somehow happened to wind up cupping her ass under her long coat just as lightly. The hand didn't go too far down, or up, or in, if you know what I mean: it was just on the outside, halfway down and without much pressure, the whole thing designed to seem casual enough that it could be claimed to be accidental if necessary. But, and this is the point, it wasn't necessary. She didn't recoil. I mean, Jeez Louise and all her angels and saints, what was this girl trying to do to me? She then kissed Sam Hellerman's comatose forehead as well, and I suppose the relative levels of intimacy on display here kind of established our precise rankings in the hierarchy of her affections. I win, Hellerman. Kind of.

Little Big Tom picked us up at twelve-thirty as arranged,

and it looked like Y2K hadn't started out all that well for him, either. A Little Big Tom who was fully himself would have tried to counsel Sam Hellerman out of his stupor. But all he said was "Looks like we need to get this cowboy home to bed." Beyond that, there was total silence in the truck on the way back. My thoughts during this silence ran as follows: Man, I should have done just a bit more with that ass when I could, because there's a good chance I'll never have another chance with it, while simultaneously I pledged to myself never to mention that to anyone because it would just make me look pathetic and maybe also kind of psycho. Asses per se aren't supposed to matter that much to a person. What can I say? Asses do funny things to my brain, especially that particular one.

YOU MIGHT WANT TO SKIP THIS PART

Now, I'm about to tell you something that you've probably never noticed before. I only noticed it myself recently, after logging several thousand hours as Sam Hellerman's sidekick on those Jeans Skirt Girl "fieldwork" stalking stakeouts. I feel I should warn you, though, that noticing it will change your world, and that I'm about to make you notice it, and that what has been noticed cannot thenceforward be unnoticed, if "thenceforward" means what I think it does. It is toothpaste that cannot be put back in the tube. Like the A-bomb.

So skip to the next chapter right now if you'd rather not take the risk. For those of you brave enough or stupid enough to forge on despite my warning, here it is:

NEVER MIND

Nope, in the end I just couldn't do that to you. Sometimes you can make the world a better place by just stopping what you're doing before it does too much more damage. And that applies not only to slap bass but to all sorts of other things too, including narration. See, I've made the world better for you, just like that. I am a great American.

THE CURSE OF THE EASYGOING GUY

But I should back up, because I didn't tell you about "Christmas."

So, reading *Dune* while pretending that it was one of the books my dad read when he was a kid was working. I had liked it the first time, but to be honest, I don't think I really "got it." But seeing my dad through its eyes, if a book can be said to have eyes you can see a dead person through, added a whole lot to it, and I was able to plow through to the end almost effortlessly. It's kind of hard to say what it's about, but there's this kid named Paul who is the son of a duke in a space empire where dukes and barons rule whole planets, and they're on this desert planet with these giant worms that produce this spice drug and they ride the worms all over, and it turns out that the main kid is like the messiah of the sand people. And his messiah name is Muad'Dib, which means "a mouse."

Duke Leto reminded me of my dad: authoritative, kind of gruff and brusque, but also pretty gentle and encouraging at the same time. And he really reminded me of my dad when he was murdered by this psycho doctor who implanted a poison tooth in his mouth in a plot to assassinate this great big fat guy named Baron Harkonnen. As for this baron, I find it difficult to believe that the author of the book had never met Mr. Teone, because the descriptions of him were eerily accurate. I mean, Baron Harkonnen pretty much *is* Mr. Teone. No one could mistake it. I should look the author guy up. If it were to turn out that he went to school with my dad and Mr. Teone, back when he was called Tit, I wouldn't be at all surprised.

I was glad to have the distraction too, because things had been pretty rough, even for Christmas. My unexpectedly violent table tipping hadn't made me too popular at home. I may be tense, enraged, and bitter in my secret heart, but on the outside I'm usually a pretty quiet, easygoing person, and I tend to shy away from drama of any kind. On the rare occasions when I don't shy away from it, no one knows how to react. My mom and Little Big Tom spent a lot of time hovering, unsure whether to be mad at me or merely concerned that I was cracking up. The result was a sort of hostile compassion that was hard for me to take and, I would bet, just as hard for them to sustain.

The thing is, if Amanda had tipped the table, no one would have cared all that much, because she always has outbursts and people just expect it and make allowances. Call it the curse of the easygoing guy. No one gives you any credit for being nice, but the minute you stand up for yourself or complain about anything to even the slightest degree, everybody acts like you've just kicked a puppy across the room.

Little Big Tom did his best to be kind and supportive, but he didn't understand what he was up against. Basically, I was irritated because no one seemed to give a damn. My problem was with the whole world. He was trying to address it by reassuring me about how adolescents "go through changes" and how it's "okay to have feelings" and stuff like that.

It didn't help matters that my mom and Little Big Tom were still strifing it up, maritally. Some of it was in the form of whispered arguments you could hear coming from their bedroom, though I could never make out anything they were saying. But mostly it was just a lot of unspoken tension. My mom could be pretty distant to everyone, but it was clear somehow that this time, the focus was on Little Big Tom, and he sure was suffering from it. He was still trying to go through the motions of being his usual jaunty self, but you could tell his heart wasn't completely in it. That's why I tolerated so much more of his counseling misfires than I usually do: it was painful to see him little-lost-lambing around everywhere, and as annoying and ridiculous as he is, your heart just goes out to him sometimes whether you want it to or not.

So, like New Year's, our actual Christmas hadn't been too much fun. As I've said, we don't tend to make a big deal out of Christmas. My mom and Little Big Tom see Christmas gifts mainly as opportunities for social engineering, as an opportunity to try to turn you into something you're not, so as usual I got some sports-related items—a basketball, a soccer calendar, and a baseball jersey and cap—while Amanda received stuff that was supposed to encourage her to be more academically inclined, like books, school supplies, and a calculator. We each got sixty dollars too. I turned around to Amanda, gave her a twenty, and said, "Merry Christmas, sister-type figure." She handed it right back to me and said, "Merry Christmas, *nice-looking boy.*" That's what we always do.

Later that night Amanda claimed to have intelligence on the conflict between Little Big Tom and my mom.

"I think he's cheating on her," she said. "There was underwear in his gym bag."

Now, I had to laugh at this, it was so implausible. Little Big Tom is like a big, dumb, rambunctious little gray golden retriever. His overdeveloped sense of loyalty is one of the things that make him so pitiful and mockable, but without it, you just don't have Little Big Tom. He'll play fetch with you all day long, bounding back repeatedly with a slobbery ball of motivational counseling regardless of your total lack of interest; if you're sad, he will settle himself next to you with the frowny face of sympathy and nuzzle you gently, making plaintive little noises till you reward him with a grudging smile and a scratch behind the ears; if you try to lose him in the woods, he will find his way home and knock you down in a face-licking show of affection and gratitude for letting him back in that will eventually make you decide you can't really bear the thought of rejecting the affections of a creature that goofy after all. And when you mix a raw egg with his food, it makes his coat lustrous and glossy.

What I'm saying is, while I may not be knowledgeable about the full range of factors in "adult relationships," and while I'm hardly an expert in the ways of the world in general, I was pretty sure that any disloyalty in the present situation probably wasn't coming from him. Just give him a bone, or a biscuit, and Little Big Tom will love you fiercely and forever: it's an immutable characteristic of the breed.

"She found underwear in his gym bag," Amanda repeated dreamily.

Merry Christmas to her, I guess.

BOOK ROULETTE

As far as I was concerned, whatever the problem was, my mom and Little Big Tom could work it out, or not, on their own time without any input or interference from me. It's what I would have wanted.

Still, it's hard to spend that much time in a domestic pressure cooker without it affecting your peace of mind. That's why *Dune* had come in handy, for the long stretches of insomnia with no one but my centipede to keep me company. But now that it was over, I either needed (a) to make a new friend, preferably not another silent scar-tissue arthropod, or (b) to choose another book. Choosing a book seemed far more doable. And so, emboldened by my success with *Dune,* I vowed, pretty recklessly, as it turned out, to close my eyes, stick my hand in the basement book box, and read whatever I happened to grab. Call it Book Roulette, or leaving it up to God. Whatever you call it, the result made me blanch slightly when I opened my eyes and looked at what I was holding. *Pride and Prejudice* was the title. From the cover, I could tell that trying to will it to be about my dad between the lines was probably going to be a bit more of a challenge than *Dune* had been. But a reckless vow is a reckless vow. If you start breaking reckless vows, there's no telling where you'll end up.

The first pages consisted of some Pythonesque dialogue between a woman and her husband about how to trick some rich guy into marrying one of their fairly numerous daughters. I think. It was kind of hard to tell what it was really getting at, to be honest. But lots of dirty jokes begin that way, so it possibly had potential. It was going to take some effort to get to the dirty parts, I could tell that right off the bat. Show me what you got, Jane, was kind of my attitude, because the author's name is Jane.

Fortunately, there was a backup. Because besides the afore-mentioned r. v., another idea had been forming in my mind, the vague outlines of a plan, the basic thrust of which was: why not do my own damn lawsuit? Everybody else was doing it. And even though I didn't have any clue how to go about it, I was pretty sure I would be at least as good at doing lawsuits as my mom would have been. Maybe her apathy was a blessing in disguise with regard to lawsuits, in that it left the path wide open for me.

So my centipede and I spent some of our insomnia mak-ing lists and notes and organizing my Catcher Code materials for an eventual presentation to Sam Hellerman. Because I was pretty sure that no matter how good I turned out to be at doing lawsuits, Sam Hellerman was likely to be a whole lot better.

DOING IT FOR HUMANITY

I'm trying to add it up, and I think I've seen Sam Hellerman admit to being surprised by anything precisely three times in my whole life. One was when the end of the world didn't happen as scheduled on Y2K. Another was when I noted that Deanna Schumacher, the fake fake Fiona (not to be confused with the real fake Fiona, Celeste Fletcher), had the same last name as the coroner in the case of my dad's death. And the third was when I revealed to him that I was scheduled to at-tend Clearview High instead of Mission Hills.

It is part of his shtick to act like he knows everything, and to do it in such a way as to leave the impression that he not only knows it all but has somehow had a hand in orchestrating everything down to the tiniest detail. The world is his stage, he wants you to think, and the people merely his puppets. Including me. And you. But as I said, he was shaken by the news about Clearview.

So he hadn't predicted it, much less orchestrated it. But although he was surprised and shaken, he was not, it seemed, anywhere near as s. and s. as I was. What was to me a devastating, intolerable disaster seemed to him the merest inconvenient blip.

Now, I complain about Sam Hellerman a lot. (Have you noticed?) Even though we're bandmates and as close to being friends as I could ever imagine being with anybody, I'm not even sure he likes me all that much. Or if I like him, to be honest. But he is a genius, and moreover, he's all I've got, and the thought of facing a whole new high school fully stocked with its own terrifying supply of awful normal people while attempting to find my way through a whole new set of customs and perils without backup was simply too much to contemplate. How would I ever do it? Could I do it? I really didn't see how.

"Look, Henderson," he had said, "worst-case scenario, it'll only last till the summer, and by that time I'm sure we'll have figured something out." What that "something" might be he left unsaid. Somehow managing to make Clearview or Mission Hills have to close down, so one of us would have to be transferred to the remaining school? If anyone could manage that, it would be Sam Hellerman, but it seemed a slender reed on which to pin our hopes, if indeed reeds of any width can have things like hopes pinned on them, which seems pretty unlikely.

"Can't you get your dad to make them transfer you to Clearview instead?" I asked, a tinge of desperation making my little-used voice squeak just a bit more than usual. I figured his dad, in his capacity as a scary German lawyer, would have some chance of achieving something like that, whereas the very thought of my mom or Little Big Tom being competent, let alone willing, to do that sort of thing on my behalf was laughable. One of the two things my family isn't any good at is official matters. (The other one, of course, is unofficial matters.) Obviously, trying to fight the school district on our own was out of the question. We were up against the entire weight of full-on institutional Normalism: we'd be as likely to prevail in petitioning them, say, to put a stop to the program of the larger people placing the smaller people in garbage cans or gluing their lockers shut or throwing gum in their hair or teasing the fat kid into cutting his arms up or any of the other important programs by means of which the normal establishment tries to keep the world running as it sees fit.

The answer to that question was no, at any rate. Sam Hellerman's father, Sam Hellerman said, was even less likely than my parents to go to any great lengths to make it easier for him. Our parents were all of one mind in this; they seemed to regard discomfort, apprehension, and even terror as important parts of growing up that they could not in good conscience deny us.

"Also," Sam Hellerman added, "he won't be unhappy that we're going to different schools. He sees you as a bad influence."

A bad influence on Hillmont's own scheming-est, manipulating-est, secretive-est and possibly evilest puppet master? *Moi?* It's true I usually don't know what to say, but this took not knowing what to say to a new, as-yet-unmapped and even more silent level. In fact, it's a wonder I ever spoke again.

Sam Hellerman told me not to worry, which is a bit like telling a dog not to slobber. But he had his mind on more pressing matters, and therefore what he required of me was to shake my mind's Etch A Sketch to blankness so he could start to use it for his own designs, unimpeded by what had previously been on it. I did my best, like a good, faithful dog with an Etch A Sketch for a head.

We trundled the new records into my room, and Sam Hellerman immediately dived in and snatched up APLPA-016. I'd had a feeling there might be a bit of a squabble over who was going to be the official owner of that one, though it made little practical difference: Sam Hellerman kept most of his records in my room because his father ruled Hellerman Manor with a fist of iron and forbade the playing of music of any kind but classical or jazz, and even then, he himself was the only one allowed to do it. Any record that failed to comply would be ruthlessly taken into custody and eliminated without mercy. Sam Hellerman had lost too many good records over the years to risk APLPA-016, that's for sure.

So I was expecting him to put forth an argument as to why APLPA-016 should be placed in the Sam Hellerman pile rather than filed into my collection, but what he said instead came as a total surprise.

It was: "Fiona."

Now, Sam Hellerman had engineered the entire fake Fiona operation from its obscure Dud Chart beginnings (about which, see my previous explanations—I don't have the energy to go into it now). Despite that, he had no patience for my continued obsession with the imaginary girl and still tended to bristle when I even so much as said the name. He only ever brought up the topic to tell me not to raise it. But evidently, we had entered a new era of Fiona tolerance on Sam Hellerman's part.

He ignored my puzzled eyes and put the record on, side one, track four: "Live Wire."

"Think of Fiona," he said, holding his finger up as though to say "Wait for it" and seeming to mumble to himself internally as the slow-building intro of the song unfolded. I was mystified but I did as I was told, thinking of Fiona, that is, of Celeste Fletcher in character as Fiona, her glasses, her hat, her too-small Who T-shirt, her yarn jacket, her underwear, that one nipple, her heavy breathing. . . . Though I now knew that the whole thing had been at my expense, an elaborate Make-out/Fake-out designed mostly to humiliate me, the thought of all that still got me going. Is that surprising, or weird? I can't even tell anymore. But I was lost in a world of glasses and nipples, because it doesn't take much to get me lost, obviously.

Sam Hellerman's finger came down at the chorus and he started singing:

"Fiona,
Fiona,
Fiona,
I wanna own ya."

Oh, *that* "Fiona"! It was the chorus of one of my old songs from my Fiona Period, during which I had half written dozens of songs about her being hot and me being sad. It wasn't the right notes, it wasn't the right chords, and it arguably wasn't the right "feel," but it certainly was the right beat.

And of course, I could see where Sam Hellerman was going with this. "Fiona," though unfinished, wasn't a bad song. With a little tweaking, the "Live Wire" drumbeat could certainly be made to work with it, and it would be far better than anything Shinefield would come up with on his own. So we get Shinefield to play the "Live Wire" drum parts to "Fiona" was the apparent idea.

"But we've tried that before," I protested. "Since it's one of our songs, he'll just gradually mess it up like all the others, won't he?"

"Not if we don't tell him," said Sam Hellerman, with his face as close to a grin as anything ever gets on that thing.

I gave him the look that says: "Won't he notice?"

"Not if we're careful," said Sam Hellerman. "Not," he added thoughtfully, "if we're careful."

Sam Hellerman's plan was simple: we would tell Shinefield we were playing "Live Wire" as usual, but while we played it, in our heads we'd be rehearsing the "Fiona" chords and singing the "Fiona" words with the "Fiona" melody. And then, if it ever came time to perform it for an audience, we'd pull the old switcheroo and play "Fiona" outright while Shinefield was still playing "Live Wire." At that point, it would be far too late for Shinefield to come up with any fancy drummer stuff to ruin it. Result: "Fiona" with the "Live Wire" drums, the only way that was ever going to happen.

"And if it works," added Sam Hellerman, "we can do it for all our songs. We just have to find the right song to tell him we're playing for each one."

We spent the rest of the afternoon listening to records with an ear toward finding the appropriate drum parts for each of our songs, with Sam Hellerman taking copious notes. It was not all that long ago that he had refused to participate in any Fiona songs as a matter of principle, but as I said, we had now entered a new era. Because this wasn't about any particular girl or song. It wasn't even about us. We were talking about solving the Drummer Problem, for the world, forever. If this worked, rock and roll would never be the same. We were doing it for humanity.

And best of all, it was far easier than kidnapping Shinefield's family and holding them all hostage in a basement somewhere on the edge of town.

I wasn't sure we could pull it off. But if we could, well, it was so crazy it just might wind up turning out pretty much all right, as the saying goes. A more Hellermanian plan could not have been imagined.

I stared at Sam Hellerman, genius, with the look that says "I'm sorry I ever doubted you."

THE THING

Now, I've decided I'm going to have to tell you the thing that I was going to spare you from earlier, because this other thing happened when Sam Hellerman was over that day and the thing that I was going to avoid mentioning came up during it. But I still advise you to skip it. True, you'll miss out on the explanation for Sam Hellerman's obsessive Jeans Skirt Girl stalking, as well as a pretty good chance to laugh at his expense. But in return, you will have retained the ability to continue your life in blissful unawareness of the thing. It is said that you can't put a price on peace of mind, but in this case you must decide how much your future peace of mind is worth to you. I will tell you, if it helps, that missing out on this bit will only slightly detract from the rest of the story. I'm pretty sure. So the choice is yours. If you'd rather not risk it, skip ahead to page 96. No judging here.

For those who have elected to stay to hear about the thing, here it is.

It's about jeans.

As you may have noticed, a whole lot of people in our contemporary society wear jeans. On a typical day, you see most people, and maybe close to all of them, going about their business wearing them. They are everywhere. Jeans: the American original.

Well, have you ever noticed that jeans have a little diagram of a penis, usually stitched in gold thread, in the appropriate place on the crotch? So all the jeans-wearing people, male and female, are walking around with what are in effect embroidered penises on the front of their pants?

I'm sure the jeans-making industry will tell you it is just a coincidental visual effect of necessary reinforcement stitching or something, but take a good look: this stitching is way too penislike to be an accident. Clearly, Mr. Levi Strauss, the inventor of jeans, if I am correctly informed, was some kind of crazy pervert. Either that or the funniest practical joker since the guy who invented the keytar. Salvador Dalí himself couldn't have done it better.

If you're thinking it's not such a big deal, just go outside and look at people while trying not to notice it. It's like everybody is wearing a penis uniform, with a penis insignia like a crotch badge marking the place where the real-life penis can, presumably, fifty percent of the time, be found underneath. It's weird enough on guys, kind of ridiculous and funny, especially because they're unaware of the fact that there are big golden penises embroidered on their pants as they go around shopping, picking up their kids from school, eating sandwiches, playing golf, and standing in front of a class of teenagers to lecture them about the quadratic formula, STDs, or Holden Caulfield. There is pretty much no activity that is not made sillier, weirder, or more questionable by virtue of being performed by a man with a diagram of a penis embroidered in gold thread on the front of his pants.

But as weird as that is, the girl-jeans penises are just downright disturbing. Girls are, I'm sure, largely unaware of the golden penises on the front of their pants or skirts, even as they stand around talking to each other about whatever girls talk about and trying to look sexy. Granted, they almost always succeed in this (looking sexy, I mean), but when they do, it is always in spite of their gold embroidered penises. What I mean is, the penises aren't helping them in this endeavor. The penises aren't helping anybody.

As for me, I believe noticing this may well have tainted girl watching for me forever. It is just bizarre enough and preposterous enough to distract you from what you want to be thinking about when admiring a beautiful woman. Hint: it's not a great big golden penis.

Okay, so perhaps I exaggerate. Perhaps. It's still pretty weird, though, don't you think? I first noticed it on one of Sam Hellerman's Jeans Skirt Girl stalking photo close-ups, and, if nothing else, it had complicated my enjoyment of the way she looked in that skirt. And it had also complicated the process of writing the song I was writing about her. In fact, I doubted I would ever be able to finish it, and it turned out I was right about that.

OF PIZZA AND METAL

So now that you know about the penises, we can move on.

Sam Hellerman and I had begun to examine the New Wave of British Heavy Metal in our beat-scavenging project, moving from Saxon to Diamond Head, and finally settling on FC 38160, *Screaming for Vengeance.* The Judas Priest catalog had lots of strong contenders.

Sam Hellerman had left to go to the bathroom. And, well, his portable cassette player was just sitting there in plain view where he had left it, on the bed under his jacket, inside the little zip pocket of his backpack. What would you have done, with it staring you in the face like that? Well, just like you would have done, I'm sure, I hurried over, furtively unzipped the pocket, pulled out the device, put on one ear of the headphones, and got ready to push play, keeping the other ear open and an eye on the door for signs of Sam Hellerman's return. I knew I probably had a bit of time: for whatever reason—which I am not at all interested in knowing—Sam Hellerman tends to take longer in the bathroom than your average dude.

I hesitated for a fraction of a moment before pressing play, pausing to consider the possibilities, knowing that once I knew what was on the tape, speculating on it—one of my favorite pastimes, if truth be told—would no longer be available to me as a recreational activity. What kind of music would it be? Could it be secretly recorded demos of songs written by Sam Hellerman himself? If so, what would such songs be about? The mind of Sam Hellerman is dark and obscure, a mysterious and no doubt frightening place, and there was no telling what might emerge from it in song form if such a thing were ever allowed to happen. Would it even sound like music at all? My centipede was twitching in anticipation. But time was a-wasting. I had only a brief window. I pressed play and this is what I heard:

A kind of swirly, pulsing music, with lots of echo, like the sound track of a retro space movie, certainly not rock and roll. So this is what the mind of Sam Hellerman sounds like, I thought, and it seemed to fit. Kind of otherworldly.

Then I heard a deep, resonant Darth Vader voice saying this very slowly:

"You are strong. You are confident. You are in command of the situation. You are respected by your colleagues at work or school. Women like and admire you. They are interested in what you have to say, and you approach them with confidence–"

I heard a footstep in the hall and I quickly ripped the headphones off, wrapped them around the tape player, and shoved it all back in Sam Hellerman's backpack, just as Little Big Tom's trademark shave-and-a-haircut knock sounded on the door. False alarm.

Little Big Tom's head emerged through the doorway at an angle, like some improbable hippie turtle with a gray mustache.

"I heard tell," he said with great solemnity, "that there's some hombres in here who might be interested in a pizza party."

He shouldered his way into my room holding a pizza box in front of him on an outstretched palm, with cans of Coke arranged neatly on top of it. Sam Hellerman followed close behind, lured by the scent of pepperoni as the South American pizza moth (*Lymantria pepperonica*) is drawn to the pizza-shaped flames of traditional Peruvian torches. They got tangled up in each other in the doorway.

"Shall we dance?" said Little Big Tom, which is what he

always says when he is one of a set of people who get tangled up in each other in a doorway.

I'd expected, or rather hoped, that Little Big Tom would deposit the pizza and Cokes on the floor before dematerializing with a quick, parting comment like "Sustenance—what a growing boy needs!" or "Pizza pie—it's like a pie, but made of pizza!" My hopes sank, however, as he came all the way into the room and settled with his back against the wall, emitting a deep sigh.

"Foodstuff," he said. "It's what's for dinner!" Well, my prediction hadn't been far off. But though the words were familiar, it seemed to me there was quite a bit less of an exclamation point at the end than there would ordinarily have been. In fact, I think that poor excuse for an exclamation point was one of the saddest things I've ever heard. Had my mom really found incriminating underwear in Little Big Tom's gym bag, as Amanda had said? I still didn't believe it, but if that was the cause of the marital strife, I really hoped he'd come up with a good excuse, and soon. If "That's so weird, I don't know how they got there" doesn't work, expand your horizons. Send the lady some flowers; tell her you're a secret transvestite and you're sorry but you've got to be you; pass it off as historical memorabilia, some of Isadora Duncan's frilly unmentionables, perhaps, that you won at auction, worth ten times what you paid for them—tell her it's all to finance a holiday in Vegas for her birthday. And then actually take her to Vegas and get her drunk. Failing that, grovel. Because whatever you're doing, little gray stepfather, it clearly isn't working. And I, for one, just couldn't take much more of this moping around.

"Half vegan, half arteriosclerosis," said Little Big Tom, opening the pizza box and popping open one of the Coke cans so that its carbonation's hiss coincided with his third heavy sigh since his arrival. "So, boys," he continued. "What's happenin'?"

Sam Hellerman and I looked at each other. It was hard to know what to say. What was really happening, planning the surreptitious reprogramming of Shinefield's abhorrent drumming, was too complicated to explain. Plus, I had in my head this bubbling pot of "You are strong, you are confident" whose boiling over was long overdue. Holding it to a simmer—that is, keeping it to myself—took all of my strength and concentration. I knew Little Big Tom was lonely and just wanted company, but the timing was really inconvenient.

No one was saying anything, so I said, "Just listening to Judas Priest . . . chief."

"Sounds great," said Little Big Tom, and he made a twirling gesture with his index finger on an imaginary turntable in front of him as if to say "Crank up the Priest, then, ye metal gods."

Sam Hellerman flashed a helpless look my way but got up to do as Little Big Tom's mimed turntable had directed.

There followed the strangest, most uncomfortable, and least likely heavy metal pizza party in recorded history. Little Big Tom was sitting with his back to the wall and his chin on one knee, eating his vegan pizza and nodding to the music intently, examining the screaming eagle on the album cover with serious-minded intensity, while Sam Hellerman and I, our appetites long vanished, looked on in perplexed horror.

"Screaming for vengeance," said Little Big Tom. "What's that they're saying after that? I can't quite make it out."

" 'The world is a manacled place,' " Sam Hellerman and I said almost in unison, and in the same dry, robotic monotone. I don't know about Sam Hellerman, but I was feeling pretty manacled myself at that moment.

Little Big Tom nodded, his face still in a frown, but with his eyebrows raised as though to say "Hey, we've all been there, am I right?" "'The world is a manacled place,'" he repeated. "'Manacled.'" Then: "'A manacled place.'"

Never mind the irony that Little Big Tom had tried to confiscate this very album twice before, on the grounds of its supposed "negativity." That's just typical parental hypocrisy hardly worthy of mention. They confiscate stuff, mostly because they can. But listening to *Screaming for Vengeance* in the presence of Little Big Tom was worse than any confiscation.

It's hard to explain exactly why. I guess all I can say is that I'd become accustomed to a kind of wall of separation between Little Big Tom and Judas Priest. I'd taken this wall largely for granted. Without ever having had the occasion to notice it per se, I suppose I had assumed it would always be there for me. When it was breached, I was defenseless.

When "You've Got Another Thing Comin'" came on, Little Big Tom said "Good beat" and started kind of dancing side to side from the shoulders up. Then he started singing along under his breath with the chorus, curling his lip, and, I kid you not, appearing to play air drums with his index fingers. At this rate, he'd be kicking over the furniture, hitting us over the head with beer bottles, and screaming "Me-*tal*, me-*tal*, me-*tal*" while he banged his forehead to a bloody pulp on the floor before we reached the end of side two. (If it's possible to bang your head to a pulp on shag carpeting. I've never tried it. Anyone?)

Something had to be done, and fast. I reached up to turn the volume knob down and said:

"Have you ever noticed how jeans have a little diagram of a penis embroidered on the front in gold thread?"

Sam Hellerman and Little Big Tom looked at me uncomprehendingly, and then we all looked down at our own individual embroidered penis diagrams. Then we looked up at each other. And the pronounced awkwardness that had seemed just a moment ago like it could not possibly get any worse magically deepened into a vibrantly more vivid shade of awkward. It was enough, like a slap across the face to a hysterical person about to jump off the Golden Gate Bridge. We were effectively, mercifully, moving on to the next scene, and not a moment too soon. Well, golden embroidered jeans penis: at least you're good for something.

"Rock and roll," said Little Big Tom in that resigned way of his, rising to his feet and backing toward the door. He rumpled my hair on the way out, the most despondent hair rumpling of his career.

"You know," he said mournfully, pausing in the doorway, "I'm sure you can get this stuff on CD. Clear you out some space in here. Bonus tracks too."

We looked back at him more in pity than in anger.

"What the heck was that?" Sam Hellerman said.

"That," my eyes said, "is what happens when the wall comes down."

Sam Hellerman gave me the look that says "For the love of God and all that is holy, pray never, ever mention the embroidered jeans penis again in my presence." You know the look I'm talking about. And I knew he had a point.

"You have to admit," I said nevertheless, in words, "that it puts Jeans Skirt Girl's jeans skirt in a different light."

Sam Hellerman was silent. I guess he didn't have to admit it after all.

At any rate, it was clear there would be no more beat mining for the rest of the night. Little Big Tom's reckless behavior had rendered the entire site unsafe; the mine was closed pending the adoption of further safety measures, such as locking the door.

A MANACLED PLACE

"Be right back, Hellerman," I said, hating to leave the matter of the tape hanging but feeling I had no choice. I dashed out the door, brushing past Little Big Tom's trudging, slope-shouldered figure in the hallway. He didn't even ask me where the fire was. This is getting critical, I thought.

Amanda and an unfamiliar girl were sitting on the floor of her room when I burst in, hard at work gluing glitter and maybe rhinestones and leaves and God knows what else to little boxes.

"Don't you knock?" said Amanda with studied petulance, if s. p. means what I think it probably has to mean.

"This has got to stop," I said, knocking on the inside of the door sarcastically. "He just spent the last hour playing air drums to Judas Priest. He thinks the world is a manacled place. A manacled place!" And I sounded only half as hysterical as I actually was.

"My stupid brother," Amanda half whispered in response to her friend's wide-eyed, questioning look. "What are you talking about?" she continued, to me. "Sam?" Then to the girl: *"Sam's the other 'nice-looking boy' I was telling you about."*

Say what you will about Amanda, but whatever her flaws, she's very good at conveying italics with her voice, and here she even managed to convey the quotation marks within the italics. Damn, she's good.

"No, no, not Sam Hellerman. Big Tom," I said, and waited

for her to whisper *"My mom's so-called husband"* before resuming: "His moping around is seriously cutting into my private time, and he's only getting worse."

"I don't know what you expect me to do about it," said Amanda. "It's his own fault." Her friend's eyes widened further as she added: *"There was underwear in his gym bag."* To me, she said, "I bet it's someone from the theater group. And she's super young, I bet, and I bet he's taking advantage of her."

I waved this away. Seriously, what female, young, old, or otherwise, would be interested enough in Little Big Tom to allow herself to be in any kind of position to be taken advantage of by him? I mean, well, except our mom, obviously, but she's a unique case. She won't eat certain tomatoes if she senses that they may have holes in their auras, which should tell you just about all you need to know about her judgment when it comes to whom to allow herself to be taken advantage of by.

"There are a lot of sick people in this world," said Amanda, more or less correctly interpreting the series of facial expressions and eye movements that reflected my train of thought. "Anyway," she added, "it was hot underwear. I saw it."

My attention was temporarily thrown off course, because of the possibly decent band name. Hot Underwear: Jesus the Thong Burglar on guitar and vox, Hellerman Schmellerman on bass and vox, "Phil Rudd" on drums, first album *Wet and Loaded*. The album cover possibilities alone would ... But I digress.

I mean, okay, I don't know what I thought I would accomplish by bursting into Amanda's room like that. Amanda's dislike for Little Big Tom was the stuff of legend, and she seemed pleased enough with the present situation, and her hopes for further disharmony were pretty obvious.

"You know," I said, changing tack, "he invaded our Judas

Priest. He could invade you, too. Don't you understand? The wall is coming down." When she didn't seem to understand the significance of the wall coming down, I added: "He could easily come in with pizza and sit down right there and start trying to help you … do whatever it is you're doing." I tried to make my eyes imply that it was only a matter of time.

"It's called letterboxing," she said with the same studied petulance I described above. But I believe I detected a slight weakening in her resistance. Surely even Amanda preferred a Little Big Tom who issued inane comments only from within his own clearly defined territory. "Maybe there is something I can do after all," she said thoughtfully.

That was a lot more than I'd expected from her. All I wanted was a return to the unsatisfactory situation that had existed before the even less satisfactory situation that had superseded it. How was that too much to ask?

WHAT'S IT ALL ABOUT, HELLERMAN?

Despite Little Big Tom's intrusion, we were off to a pretty good start with the beat mining. We had to keep reminding ourselves that we weren't just picking our favorite songs or bands. Much of my favorite music, like, say, the Buddah Records flavor of bubblegum, was too quirky to be suitable for this purpose. And we had to stay away from good but busy drummers like Keith Moon and John Maher, no matter how great their drumming was in context and no matter how much we liked their bands.

The crucial point in taking Shinefield to beat school against his will and without his knowledge was going to be to make sure the drumbeats we chose were clean, simple, and easily grasped. The arrangements also had to be straightforward;

otherwise they would get in the way of our own arrangements of the songs we would really be playing in our heads while outwardly playing the other ones.

Judas Priest, Thin Lizzy, Cheap Trick, Slade, the Undertones, even some KISS–all had stuff we could use. We could work with the Sweet, too (in their post–"Poppa Joe" phase) and with the Ramones as they appear on SRK 6063. We could use Motörhead for faster tunes. The Cook/Jones bands worked great: "Anarchy in the UK" was almost a perfect match for "Mr. Teone Killed My Dad." To our surprise, no less than three of our songs could be overlaid almost seamlessly on "Cat Scratch Fever," if you set aside the intro: "God Rot Your Bloody Soul," "Meat Tenderizer," and "Sadistic Masochism."

And of course, there was AC/DC's Phil Rudd, the metaphysical ideal of the tamed drummer, if metaphysical means what I hope it does. The plan was to start with "Fiona"/"Live Wire" as a test and, if it worked, to move on from there.

So there we were, still in my room, finishing off the last of Little Big Tom's pizza, listening to PD 5537 in an attempt to restore some balance and sanity to our world. (I'll save you having to go look it up, because I doubt you'd get that one: it's the Pink Fairies, *Kings of Oblivion*.)

I looked at Sam Hellerman. He was strong. He was confident. He was in command of the situation.

"What are we going to do now?" he said.

"You tell me," I replied, pouncing catlike on his mouselike words. "You're strong. You're confident. Women like and admire you." It was like I'd waited my whole life to say it, though I had just recently heard it for the first time. And it fairly came tumbling out of me. I guess in the excitement I hadn't managed to articulate the individual words all too clearly. So Sam Hellerman gave me the look and says "The fuck?" except for

Sam Hellerman it was more like "The heck?" and he didn't react much at all other than that, so I knew he hadn't quite understood me. So I repeated it more slowly, which got the desired result.

If you've ever heard about a person's face clouding over and suspected it to have been a mere figure of speech or the one that starts with "hyper-" that means an exaggeration, I can assure you that it is possible for a face to cloud over. I mean, actual tiny clouds moved in and began to engulf Sam Hellerman's face in darkness, though his eyes retained an eerie, vaguely threatening glow behind them. I believe that at that moment, Sam Hellerman came as close as he has ever come to uttering what he still calls "the F-word."

"What the ... fudge ... darn ... heck ... hell ... ," he said, like a Mormon with Tourette's syndrome.

"Okay, okay," I said by way of apology. I gave him the look that says "Hey, if you don't want people going through your things, you should consider not being so God-almighty mysterious about them all the time." "I just had to know what was on the tape," I added, switching my words to audio mode. "It was driving me nuts."

Sam Hellerman could see my point, it seemed. Plus, now that the preliminary invasion of privacy and subsequent ridicule was out of the way, he seemed to want to tell me what it was all about.

"What's it all about, Hellerman?" I said, egging him on.

And Sam Hellerman began to relate the following tale.

THE SECRETS OF WOMEN REVEALED

Once upon a time, it went, there was a boy who had moved with his family to California from Munich, Germany. At the age of fifteen, he was a stranger in a strange land, misunderstood, mocked, and despised by his new peers. His English was good, because in places like Germany the schools actually teach you things and studying a foreign language means more than just memorizing how to say "I have a lovely box of red pencils" and "Emil, why are you so pale?" and eating snacks. But whereas the language was familiar, the culture was alien. He didn't "fit in," and his accent, glasses, and gaunt features, along with his interest in math and physics and his native intelligence, made him an obvious target for harassment by bullies of every stripe.

Unfortunately for him, the first syllable of his first name sounded to American ears a bit like a familiar term for a person's buttocks, and his country of origin was associated mainly with Nazis–particularly, at the time, with the bumbling prison camp guards depicted in a popular television situation comedy called *Hogan's Heroes*. Accordingly, he was known, in the Hillmont High School Class of 1970, variously as Hiney, Hind Quarters, Shulztie, Das Nincompoop, Colonel Klink, Gay Hiney, Super Gay Nazi Hiney, and even, on occasion, Herr Hitler Hiney, or merely Hitler, a name particularly galling to him, considering what he understood to have been his socialist grandparents' actual suffering during the Second World War. Along with subjecting him to the usual indignities–stuffing him in garbage cans, locking him in lockers, and all the rest– his classmates never passed up the opportunity to draw a mustache on any photograph of him that came their way, in class photos or in the yearbook, or even, on a few occasions, with indelible marker on his actual face.

Now, this was in the late sixties, and teenage bullying wasn't nearly as advanced as it is now. Still, he had had what for the time was a pretty rough experience of high school, and he came out of it hating humanity with a smoldering passion. As one does.

Bullying aside, little Heinrich was, to his own surprise, largely disappointed in America. The America of his childhood dreams—the cowboys and Indians, the fast cars, the trash-talking jazzmen in smoky clubs, the well-dressed private detectives in their fedoras with attractive full-breasted females bringing them martinis and posing seductively, not to mention Hollywood, *Playboy* magazine, the space program, and the abundant candy—simply didn't seem to exist, at least, not in a form that was readily available to a fifteen-year-old of German extraction in Hillmont, California, which, at the time, was even less of a real place than it is today.

Most of all, he was disappointed in the women, or rather, not with the women per se, but with their lack of interest in cooperating with his ambition to couple with them. Instead, they ridiculed him, or almost worse, ignored him completely. So there was to be no "necking" in parked Chevrolets at "the Point," no ass-grabbing slow dances at the "hop," no "Wake Up Little Susie" scenarios at the local drive-in. No love of any kind, at least not for him. He was effectively invisible to those he wanted to be seen by, and at the same time all too identifiable as prey to those who wished to prey upon him.

Thus far, it was a variation on a familiar story, a typical American adolescence, in fact. Most people, outside of a small group of the most severely normal, I suppose, will recognize it instantly and probably see themselves in it to some degree.

But it was at this point that Sam Hellerman's father (for it was he) discovered *The Secrets of Women Revealed: A Guide to Getting (and Keeping) Girls* through an ad in the back of a comic book, and it, according to the story, changed everything.

The Secrets of Women Revealed was a set of ten cassettes with an accompanying book explaining how the most socially unsuccessful person could gain confidence, take control of his life, and get down to the serious business of picking up girls. One side of each tape consisted of general principles and step-by-step instructions, while the other side, a bit of which I had heard, was motivational, designed to penetrate the subconscious mind with confidence-building messages: the more you listened, the more penetration, apparently, which explained Sam Hellerman's recent spate of continual headphoning.

In any case, the teenage Herr Hellerman's transformation, upon receipt of the tapes, was slow but dramatic. Before long he had acquired a circle of friends and another circle next to the first circle of admiring females vying for his attentions. No one drew a mustache on him again, ever. To this day, Herr Hellerman credits the tapes with his eventual success in life, from his triumphs with women to the career he has today as a sinister and filthy-rich lawyer.

This was the tale told by Sam Hellerman. Well, actually, I filled most of it in, using my imagination and my powerful vocabulary. But the bottom line was that Herr Hellerman believed in the tapes and wanted to bestow their bounty upon his only heir when he came of age. So he duly presented them to Sam Hellerman on his fifteenth birthday.

"Dzeez tapes are dzee zecret, viss respect to vimmen," he had told Sam Hellerman in my imaginative reconstruction of the scene, holding the tapes above Sam Hellerman's head and making him jump for them before handing them over. "Use dzem wery visely, young man, use dzem orphan, or dzere vill be dze most terrible consekvenciss, if I make myself cleah. . . ."

And accordingly, Herr Hellerman had added an incentive: if, within a year of receipt of the tapes, Sam Hellerman had not managed to acquire a girlfriend, he was to be severely punished, grounded, deprived of a driver's license for a period of not less than one year, and physically beaten, too, if I didn't miss my guess.

Sam Hellerman was currently at tape three, the second section of which was entitled "Standing Aloof," which explained his Jeans Skirt Girl activities, if not the sense behind them. The idea, according to Sam Hellerman, was that girls, not used to being ignored, are intrigued and ultimately attracted to men who fail to adhere to the expected pattern of following them around like sad, eager puppies. Eventually the female in question seeks reassurance that the ignorer is attracted to her to the degree to which she feels entitled. At that point, the man, that is to say, the Sam Heller-man in the ludicrous fantasy world we're discussing here, having demonstrated that his status is high enough to afford him the luxury of ignoring her, can make a move to escalate the "relationship."

I repeated a previously raised objection, about how standing aloof from someone who isn't aware of you isn't logically possible. People want what they can't have, it's true, but not if they are unacquainted with its existence, and also, I regret to say, not if, in the event that they become acquainted with it, the thing they can't have turns out to be Sam Hellerman. On the contrary, I'd imagine a person in such a situation would experience an overwhelming sense of relief.

"If you think," I said, in a combination of words and facial spasms, "that Jeans Skirt Girl is going to want to be your girl-friend just because you've been watching her from a bus stop under an umbrella but pretending not to, you're more impressively retarded than I ever gave you credit for."

"Thanks," said Sam Hellerman drily. But he stuck to his guns. "It's a demonstration of status."

Yes, I thought. It is. But not in your favor.

"And it will work," he added, with that trademark Sam Hellerman assurance that in almost any other situation might have made me question the evidence of my own eyes and the validity of several deeply held beliefs. Not this time, however. This had disaster written all over it in great big flashing letters.

"Besides," he said on his way out, "I can't stop thinking about her."

Preposterous as this statement was, considering he was talking about someone he hadn't even met, and despite the fact that the English language lacks a word of sufficient intensity to describe just how far out of his league this girl was, there was a desperate pleading in his voice that I recognized from hearing my own voice on those rare occasions when I used it. And though I may have hated to admit it, whether you're crazy about an imaginary girl in the real world, like me, or obsessing over a real girl in la-la land, like Sam Hellerman, it comes down to pretty much the same thing.

Sam Hellerman may be a genius, but love makes you stupid. No exceptions.

"FINALS"

Now, if you were designing a schedule that divided the school year into two terms and you had to work around a lengthy winter break in the middle of it, how would you do it? Have the first term end just before the break, and the second term start right after it? Good, that's how I'd do it too. But for some reason the geniuses of the Santa Carla Unified School District had decided that the way to do it was to pause the first term for Christmas vacation and then continue it for a week and a half after everyone gets back, which is why we all had to return to Hillmont High for eight more days of torture and tedium before heading to our new so-called academic homes.

At Hillmont, it's even sillier because this fall term hangover is called "Finals." Technically you're supposed to use winter break to "study" for some alleged final exams that I imagine a real school might use to test you on what you've learned in the past term. But to my knowledge no Hillmont student has ever studied during this time, and if you've had no unexcused absences, they don't make you take the "Finals" anyway. So the best students—that is, the ones who love school so much that they never miss a day and those with no social life to speak of who couldn't manage to miss a day if their lives depended on it (like Sam Hellerman and me)—are thus exempted. I've never had to take a "Final" in my life for this reason. So "Finals" at Hillmont High School are essentially little more than a punishment for poor attendance. And though I don't speak from experience, I am pretty confident in saying that in practice, they are little different from any detention: you sit at your desk in a room full of other delinquents, head down, for a couple of hours, and you write lines or copy a dictionary page if they catch you looking up or being disruptive in any way.

Sam Hellerman was waiting for me at the corner of Vista View Terrace Court Boulevard and Chop Down the Sea Road Road as usual on the big day. And by big day, I mean the first day of the end of Hillmont High School and the world as we had theretofore known it. It seemed momentous, something to be commemorated, and as Sam Hellerman had his headphones on and was devoting nearly all his energy to being strong, confident, and in command of the situation, it fell to me to deliver a few solemn words to mark the occasion.

"Well," I said. "Well."

There was little conversation on the walk to the oak tree across from the Hillmont High School baseball backstop, the spot where we traditionally paused to gather our resources and brace ourselves for the ordeals to come. With Sam Hellerman's tape motivating him, I was left alone with my thoughts, and though they weren't all that nice to be left alone with, I'd had worse thoughts for company. Contemplating the end of Hillmont High was a bit like the liberating, unfulfilled dream of Y2K: despite whatever terrors might be in store in the short term, you could cling to the comforting thought that, in a world that has effectively ended, none of it would wind up mattering all that much.

Sam Hellerman wasn't smelling so great today, but he was too engrossed in his tape to notice as my raised eyebrow inquired wryly as to the last time he had showered. Well, you have to make allowances for these geniuses, I suppose: a lifetime spent with one's head in the clouds often leaves little room for personal hygiene—that's pretty well known.

Another thing I noticed, upon close examination, was that this unusually pungent Sam Hellerman featured a new accessory: a cell phone, an obvious Christmas present, clipped to his belt in a gay little holster. A few of the rich kids at Hillmont High had been turning up with these monstrosities lately. Amanda had been begging for one for months, to which she had so far gotten little response except a few pointed looks from the parental units, the looks that say: "What, do you think money grows on trees?" Now, as far as I'm concerned, there's no point whatsoever in them: the last thing I need is to be disturbed by unwanted calls when I'm not even at home. And I can think of lots of better things to spend that kind of money on than a car phone you have to carry around with you everywhere in a gay little holster. Like a guitar, say, or a big box of pornography.

For Amanda, whose whole life revolved around being on the phone or being worried about the possibility that someone else's being on the phone might temporarily deprive her of the opportunity to be on the phone herself, such a device made a great deal of sense. For Sam Hellerman, not so much. What imaginary people would he call? What i. p. would call him? It was a bit sad, like Jeans Skirt Girl and the tapes. Not only was Sam Hellerman engaged in a misguided, doomed-to-fail project of seduction, but he also now had a little symbolic representation of his social unsuccessfulness clipped, as a constant reminder, to his belt just next to and slightly above his embroidered gold jeans penis.

Okay, wait, hold on and back up. I've got to rethink this.

Sorry, but I just realized I blew it there by mentioning the golden embroidered jeans penis. You know what? Trying to spare you guys a ways back isn't going to work after all. Basically, there's just no way to tell this story properly without mentioning the gold embroidered jeans penis from time to time. If you're one of the people who skipped from page 82 to 96 earlier, you must be pretty confused, wondering, "What's all this about a golden penis?" So you might as well go back and read that part now. I give up. I just can't make it work. Sorry about that. We'll wait.

Okay, are we all set here? Good, let's continue.

Anyway, as I was saying about Sam Hellerman and what

his cell phone holster and golden embroidered jeans penis symbolized, it isn't that I was in much better shape, social successfulness–wise. But at least I had the saving dignity of not trying. And that counts for a lot.

"It's for emergencies," he said when I pointed to it sarcastically–*God, the phone!* It was the *phone* that I pointed to that was for emergencies, not the golden jeans penis, smart-asses. I pointed to Sam Hellerman's *phone.* Jesus. Anyway, that all only seemed to underscore my point. Somehow.

"Merry Christmas," I said. Then I added: "Any calls?" But watching Sam Hellerman extract the device from the holster, turn it on, wait for it to start up, check it, sigh, switch it back off, make sure it really was off, return it to its holster, buckle the holster closed, and say no with a serious shake of his head–well, it wasn't quite as much fun as I'd expected it to be. The strange feeling I got from it was hard to identify, but there was something Little Big Tom–esque about it. All joking aside, Sam Hellerman was my friend, sort of, and I hated to see his train wreck of a life get even more wrecked. I had to assume he'd feel the same about me and my own train wreck. People without options stick together.

I wasn't sure if they were going to make me do "Finals" or not. On the one hand, while I'd missed quite a few days when I was in the hospital, it didn't seem fair to punish me for that, espe-cially since they themselves were ultimately responsible for the injuries that put me there. On the other hand, life isn't fair, and anything you can say about life generally goes double for Hill-mont, so I figured it could go either way. As it happened, there had been no need to bother even wondering about it, because even though we were explicitly there for "Finals" and pretty much nothing else, according to their own letter, it didn't look like they were making anyone actually take any "Finals."

Because as lax, and poorly organized, and lame, and just generally fucked up as Hillmont High School was before, that was nothing compared to how l., p. o., l., and f. u. it was when it had only eight days to live. The administrators were all going to other schools; the teachers who were being transferred had no reason to care what happened at Hillmont during these last days (and probably hated Hillmont just as much as anyone); the ones who were being let go might not have been happy to lose their jobs, but why should they care either? As for the ones who were taking the school closure as an opportunity to retire early, at, like, twice their regular salary or whatever it was, well, they were practically giddy. The students, even the most virulently normal ones, were in no position to complain. Hillmont High was a hell pit even for the most privileged among them. They had all cared precious little about anything before, and they cared still less now.

The result was a sort of carnival atmosphere, papers flying, open lockers swinging in the breeze, desks overturned, sub-literate attempts at obscene graffiti appearing as if by magic on doors and walls, and even small fires set in trash cans. Of course, just as birds gotta swim and fish gotta fly, normal people gotta be normal. So there was still a bit of the routine harassment of the small and weak that you get wherever normal people gather in large enough numbers to make congratulating themselves over it worth their while. I got slammed into the wall accidentally on purpose by the shoulders of passing goons a couple of times on my way in, and Sam Hellerman was tripped so that he fell in a muddy patch of grass at the edge of Center Court.

"WAGBOG," I said, which means, if you recall from my previous explanations: what a great bunch of guys.

But Sam Hellerman, fortunately in a way, I suppose, was too worried about his precious cell phone to be overconcerned about what a great bunch of guys they were, or even about his own pain, discomfort, and humiliation.

"It's all right," he said, brushing mud off the holster after he had made sure the thing was still able to turn on. "It's all right."

"What a relief," my eyes said. "You're one lucky bastard." Then, in words: "Any calls?"

"No," said Sam Hellerman.

There isn't all that much to report concerning Hillmont High School's final "Finals." There was, however, an assembly in the auditorium, mandatory for all students, according to an announcement during homeroom.

The best thing about this assembly? The three enormous banners that hung above the stage:

CARING
HEALING
UNDERSTANDING

Sam Hellerman's eyes sought mine as we trudged in and took our seats, and both sets of eyes were saying: "Note to selves—must steal banners." If we couldn't construct a band or an album of note out of that excellent raw material, we weren't the rock and rollers I thought we were.

The first speaker was some guy from the Santa Carla Unified School District who recapitulated the contents of the letter announcing the school closure. His remarks can be translated and summarized thus: academic excellence, blah blah blah, please don't sue us, and if you do sue us, please don't sue us that much.

"Never fear, my centipede," I said silently, stroking the little fellow gently but with feeling. "You shall be avenged." If I, that is to say, we, hadn't been out in public like that, I might have risked a sinister laugh, but shrewdly, I kept it to myself. We were going to sue them, and sue them a whole lot, whatever it took; but it seemed like a good idea to keep our cards close to our chests, if that expression means what I think it does, even though centipedes don't have chests and can't hold cards. That's okay. I'll hold them for you, little guy.

Next up was a lady named Dr. Elizabeth Gary, who was some kind of counselor or social worker. Her first words, to my and Sam Hellerman's considerable delight, were: "Caring. Healing. Understanding. Caring, healing, and understanding." Man, there is definitely a song in there somewhere, I thought, and I could tell Sam Hellerman was thinking the same thing. Dr. Elizabeth Gary delivered essentially the same "don't sue us" message that the SCUSD guy had, but with more touchy-feely embellishments—your basic therapy racket shtick, in other words. I was used to this kind of talk from Little Big Tom, so much so that most of it just flew by me without my noticing it to any great degree, as it does when it comes from him. But one of the things she said stuck in my mind because it was so preposterous, yet so representative of the deeply misguided views of normal people and their entire chain of command.

"All teenagers," she said, "want nothing more than simply to fit in, to be accepted by their peers and their society."

Well, I mean, I understand why normal people might *want* this to be the case, and there is no shortage of schemes, well-intentioned or downright sneaky, aimed at brainwashing you into thinking that taking your place in the ranks of the normal ought to be your dearest wish. But it ain't necessarily so, and it certainly isn't the case for me. Normalism is nothing any sane person would volunteer for. It is rotten, corrupt, terrifying, and thoroughly despicable, organized by psychotics, led by fiends, staffed by sadistic, subhuman monsters, and supported by dim-witted enablers like the soppy teenagers Dr. Gary described. When you say "I want to fit in," you are essentially volunteering yourself as a victim, and when the thing you want to fit in with is "society"–well, as "society" is just another word for the government, you're basically begging the government to control you and use you as it wishes for its nefarious purposes, which can be pretty damn nefarious, if "nefarious" means what I believe it means. The fact that they occasionally go around with these big "caring," "healing," and "understanding" banners just makes it that much more insulting.

I have no interest at all in "fitting in" with them or being "accepted" by them. On the contrary, I would very much enjoy their destruction. But failing that, all I want is for them to leave me alone. This, of course, will never happen, because not leaving people alone is the main thing they like to do and pretty much the only thing they're good at.

I only mention this because Dr. Elizabeth Gary's final message was that there was going to be counseling available, at the county's expense, for all those who felt they needed it. And I realized that, in light of what she had said about the supposedly dearest wish of all teenagers to "fit in" at all costs, I now had something else to add to my General Theory of the Universe: in normal-speak, "healing" means submission to authority, and "counseling" is merely a euphemism for brainwashing.

I must warn the others, I thought. But there was really only Sam Hellerman other than me, and I had a feeling he already knew.

But in case you're not already normal, here's your warning: if they try to "heal" you with a little "counseling," head for the hills. Never surrender. Because it's a trick, you see.

NO ASS-GRABBIO

The one further thing I'll mention about the Last Days of Hillmont High School is what happened in Mr. Schtuppe's class. Mr. Schtuppe, if you'll remember from my previous explanations, is this big, bald, pink, buffoonish English teacher of a man easily identified by his plentiful ear hair and his talent for mispronouncing practically any word in the English language with breathtaking ease. In view of the fact that he has had the audacity to grade decades' worth of students on their ability to replicate these mispronunciations, you could say he's pretty much a one-man indictment of our educational system. And yet somehow I wound up being fond of him in the end. I've learned more from him than I have in any of the other god-awful classes at Hillmont High School, that's for sure. Fine mispronunciation, like a fine cigar, has first to be endured, then explored, and only then savored. (Actually, I've never had a fine cigar and wouldn't know the first thing about what to do with one if I had one, but I imagine it's something like that.) I have said before that I owe much of my success with women to mispronunciation skills, and I'm not even exaggerating all that much, so I feel rather indebted to Mr. Schtuppe, whether he intended it that way or not.

Plus, he was the one who introduced me to *30 Days to a More Powerful Vocabulary,* the only truly useful book I've come across in ten years of being forced to attend school. If you like my powerful vocabulary and find my playful mispronunciation of words drawn from it to be inexplicably sexy (and I'm sure you do), you have Mr. Schtuppe to thank or blame for it.

On this particular day, Mr. Schtuppe was in a mood that he himself might have characterized as ebullient ("ay-byoo-LYE-ent"). He was one of the teachers taking early retirement, and he was clearly glorying in the prospect: you could practically see actual dollar signs spinning in his retirement-crazed eyes. At one point, I thought he might go so far as to do a little jig, which is a dance done by leprechauns, mainly. He didn't, but he had a definite jig look about him, nonetheless. I could hardly blame the guy: "teaching" "English" to barely sentient ("sen-TEE-ant") Hillmont "students" year after year must have seemed like a long, slow death sentence for which retirement with a lavish pension was an unexpectedly acceptable reprieve.

Even though there were no "Finals," Mr. Schtuppe had to give us something to do, so he handed out sheets of paper and said "Write something" in the tone someone might use to say "Scram, will ya?"

As I may have mentioned before, Celeste Fletcher was in Mr. Schtuppe's class as well. We sat together and wrote out phonetic mispronunciations of all the words we could think of. The likelihood was that these papers would simply be thrown in the trash as soon as we handed them in, like most assignments you do at Hillmont High School, but on the off chance that Mr. Schtuppe was actually going to read any of them, it seemed like a nice gesture, a way of showing him that, if nothing else, he had "reached" at least two of us.

"So," said Celeste Fletcher at the end of the class. "I guess I'll be seeing you at Queerview."

"Really?" I said. I mean, I had already known she was one of the ones going to Clearview with me, but it was the "I'll be seeing you" part that seemed to offer more than it said. God, she smelled nice.

"Really," she said, like it was nothing and like I was dumb for asking.

Damn. Shinefield was going to Mission Hills with Sam Hellerman, though he was planning to graduate early and apply to MIT. (Apparently he was some kind of math genius, somewhere in that fuzzy, stoned head of his.) But this whole Clearview thing wasn't sounding too bad at all, in view of that "really": just me and Fiona, alone in a strange new school with no competition and only each other to cling to for warmth and protection. It is in such situations that true affection can take root and grow.

As I leaned in for the customary goodbye hug—I don't know how or when this became standard in our tiny social circle, but, hey, I'll take it—she stiffened a bit like my mom has recently started doing with Little Big Tom.

"No ass-grabbio," whispered Celeste Fletcher. Got it, Fiona, I conceded silently. Not in public. Our love, such as it was, would remain a closely guarded secret. That was the deal.

I didn't know what to think, but that was pretty much par for the course, meaning that if my life were a golf course, not knowing what was really going on, particularly where girls were involved, was equivalent to the number of strokes ordinarily required to make it through to the end of the game and not lose embarrassingly. And that, my dear friends, is called optimism.

THE SWEET FRUIT OF TRUE ROCK AND ROLL

It seemed that whatever coolness Sam Hellerman and I had acquired from our band's performance at the Battle of the Bands during the last term had mostly dissipated over Christmas vacation. While my centipede and my slightly weird shorter haircut attracted a few looks, people seemed to take little notice of me. Giving the occasional girl a "hey, remember me, I'm in a band" look had no effect at all, if you can believe that. Rock and roll is a proven aphrodisiac, if "aphrodisiac" is the one that makes everybody horny for you, but its effects are fleeting. You're only as good as your last disastrous performance, and our l. d. p. was quickly fading from public memory.

Well, their minds—I'm referring to the public here—were understandably on other things. But as being seen to be in a rock and roll band was the key—the only key—to what success with girls we were ever likely to have, there was no time to lose: we had to jump-start our career, and fast. In other words, the time was ripe for a comeback.

With this in mind, we put everything we had into our first practice since Sam Hellerman came up with the "Fiona"/"Live Wire" gambit.

Now, I don't know if you've ever tried this yourself, but playing one song out loud while playing an entirely different song in secret in your head is pretty difficult. Both Sam Hellerman and I made a lot of mistakes, playing bits of "Fiona" out loud by accident, or, in my case, at least, thinking bits of "Live Wire" when I should have been think-playing "Fiona."

Fortunately, the lyrics didn't matter too much. I was singing into a cheap microphone plugged into a half-fried channel of the old Hillmont High Jazz Band Polytone amp that I was also using for the guitar. Sam Hellerman was plugged into this

amp as well, because he hadn't yet replaced the Magnavox/
Fender Bassman Frankenstein amp that had been wrecked at
the Battle of the Bands. Point being, no one could hear what
I was singing, not even me, and moreover, Shinefield didn't
seem to care, so I just sang the "Fiona" lyrics, with no one the
wiser. However, Shinefield did notice when Sam Hellerman or
I would slip into the "Fiona" chords too obviously. When that
occurred, he would give us this perplexed yet good-natured
"what just happened there?" look, which we would return
with shrugs and what we hoped were smiles that said "Whoa,
that was weird, but never mind, let us carry on, my good man,
you're doing just fine."

Nevertheless, one thing was absolutely clear as soon as we
did the first verse the first time: it sounded fucking great.

Like, I don't even have words to describe how great it
sounded, other than "fucking," and I imagine even Sam Hellerman would have agreed. How great was it? Fucking great,
that's how great it was. Even while having to hold the two
things in my head at the same time, I could feel the realness
of the rock and roll shining through on the important half. It
was louder. It was tighter. It was heavier. And that's despite
our terrible equipment—the worst rock and roll had ever seen.
Half of it was just in my head, it's true, but I could tell. I just
could.

It was clear from Sam Hellerman's trembling hands and
wild eyes that he had felt it too. During one of Shinefield's
smoke breaks, Sam Hellerman quickly whispered his new
plan: we would accidentally on purpose play one full verse and
chorus of "Fiona" in the middle of doing "Live Wire" and pass
it off as a mistake. If that worked and if Shinefield went along
with it, we would, at the very end, during the run-through-the-
set-one-last-time part, simply play "Fiona" all the way through,

come what may. That was risky, but as Sam Hellerman said, now that we had tasted the sweet fruit of true rock and roll, we could never go back to the way it had been, to the bitter herbs of everything just being lame and kind of stupid. I'm paraphrasing. Anyway, either it worked or it didn't.

We got the perplexed, smiley look from Shinefield during the one-verse "mistake" experiment, but it was easily shrugged off. The final full "Fiona," however, was harder to pull off, to say the least.

"What the hell just happened?" he said after it was over. But he was laughing. This is probably the one situation where having a stoned drummer can actually help rather than hinder you. "Wow, that was weird!" he continued, starting to emit a chuckle that verged, if ever so slightly, on out-and-out giggling. "What was that?" It turns out there are more ways to express "What just happened?" than we ever knew, and Shinefield ran through them all, laughing harder and harder all the time, saying we were crazy and asking what had gotten into us.

We started laughing too, saying we didn't know, that it sure was weird, wasn't it? But all the while we were looking at each other, gloating. The full "Fiona" had ruled, exceeding every expectation. How much had it ruled? Well, put it this way: it was nearly impossible to believe it was us playing it and not some real band.

Our two pairs of eyes met through the haze and over the semi-stoned what-just-happened laughing and babbling. Come on, the eyes were saying. Feel the noise.

AND THEY SHALL KNOW US BY OUR MONIKERS

So rock and roll was back and, with any luck, here to stay, and it felt pretty good. We had a difficult road ahead, however. Now that we were committed to it, we had to come up with a real list of other songs to tell Shinefield we were covering while playing our own songs to them in our heads. Then we would have to practice them relentlessly on our own, till playing them became something we didn't have to think about and it would thus be easier to switch "modes" at will. Sam Hellerman said he'd make Shinefield a tape of the final list, and since his dad's turntable had a vari-speed slide on it, he could even alter the tempos to some of the songs to match ours better, to a very slight degree, anyway.

Now, not that I'm one to talk here, but I could see the clear signs of delusions of grandeur beginning to display themselves in Sam Hellerman's shining eyes. You have to understand, we'd been used to sucking so bad and so hard for our entire rock and roll lives that the prospect of participating in something that did anything other than suck, or that sucked even just a bit less than usual, was simply intoxicating.

"The publicity campaign starts now," he said. "But what's the name going to be? We need a name to stick with for at least a little while."

This was hard. We'd already gone through three band names since I Hate This Jar, and I was particularly fond of the current one, Buddy of Christ. At the same time, the idea of sticking with one band for any extended length of time felt extraordinarily oppressive, and it was something we'd never been able to manage before.

"How long does publicity last?" I said.

"Long as it takes" was the reply.

That could be a long, long time, I thought.

We spent the next four hours saying names at each other and rejecting them.

"Caring Healing Understanding?" said Sam Hellerman. "We've already got the banners." True to his note to self, Sam Hellerman had managed to swipe the Hillmont High brainwashing banners: they were rolled up neatly in his closet.

"Not much of a band name, though," I said glumly. I had my standards.

Sam Hellerman suggested simply the Understanding, first album *Caring Healing,* but with pictures of bloody dismembered corpses on the album cover. Which wasn't bad, but also wasn't quite as exciting as you'd want a name that was going to last as long as several weeks to be. Plus, to make it sound like it was as cool as it was, you'd have to take the time to explain the album cover, losing the vital element of surprise. We needed something with a less complex path to greatness.

"Adolf Oliver Nipples?" Sam Hellerman suggested, which was obviously as great as band names come, but unfortunately, as I had to remind him, we'd already used it. You can't repeat band names: that way lies madness.

I thought of Dr. Elizabeth Gary. There were possibilities in there somewhere: Dr. Elizabeth. Therapy Bomb. The Grief Counselors. The Therapy Counselors from the Planet Stupid, first album *Healed, Feeled, and Congealed.* Or was that almost *too* good?

"How about," I said at last, "the Teenage Brainwashers."

It was less bad than all the others. So Teenage Brainwashers it was.

HELLERMAN AND HELLERMAN, ATTORNEYS AT LAW

I was over at Sam Hellerman's house because I believed it was the best place to explain my ideas concerning lawsuits, the sadistic structure of reality, and my General Theory of the Universe. It seemed like a bad idea to discuss such matters when Little Big Tom was liable to break in at any moment saying "Let's hear some more of that Jesus Proust, boys."

I had been building what I thought was a pretty good comprehensive case against Matt Lynch, Paul Krebs, Mark McAllister, Rich Zim, Mr. Teone, Mr. Donnelly, the Hillmont High School administration and student body, the Santa Carla Unified School District, the State of California, and the United States of America for conspiracy, murder, grievous assault, violent misuse of a public school band instrument with intent to maim or kill, educational malpractice, extortion, censorship, racketeering, obscenity, torture, discrimination, civil rights violations, human rights violations, and crimes against humanity.

Now, as my friends looking back from the future mists of time will know, *Halls of Innocence* barely scratched the surface of the greater conspiracy I've tried to outline here. According to *Halls of Innocence,* all "Mr. Cabal" did was put a few pinhole cameras in the girls' bathrooms and locker rooms and walk around saying disturbing things like "Get to class, young lady—I'll be seeing you later!" Not that that isn't accurate, or disturbing enough on its own, but it's the stuff beneath the surface that truly matters in the case.

My apologies to those who already know all this from my previous extremely clear and easy-to-follow explanations. I know I've been over it before and you're all saying, "Yes, yes, we know all that, you've already made it abundantly clear and presented the case with utter and complete persuasiveness and coherence, so why bother to rehash it now?" Hey, I said I was sorry, didn't I?

Anyway, for those who have missed my p. e.'s: the key to the whole sick, twisted affair was the Catcher Code, a creepy encoded square of slanted text, in backwards French, that reveals the remote origins of Mr. "Cabal" Teone's criminality, as well as his connection to my dad, going back to when they were both students at Most Precious Blood College Preparatory in San Francisco in the sixties. As the code and its associated materials indicate, the young Mr. Teone, known at the time by the acronym Tit, had already been involved in creepy perverted skullduggery at that school. ("Skullduggery" means illicit or underhanded activity. It doesn't necessarily have to involve digging up any actual skulls, but it could, and in the case of Mr. Teone, I wouldn't be at all surprised if it did.)

For reasons not yet clear, Mr. Teone had also arranged for the fake suicide of a fellow student named Timothy J. Anderson, otherwise known as the Dead Bastard. Later on, when the grown-up Mr. Teone had become the assistant principal at Hillmont High School, he returned to his old perverted tricks. But my dad, now a police detective, had known too much, and Mr. Teone had murdered him, staging the murder as a fake suicide just as he had done with the Dead Bastard so many years before. Then, when the songs we played at the Battle of the Bands seemed to indicate that I knew too much as well, Mr. Teone tried to have me killed too, delegating the task to a group of ultra-normal teenage subhuman replicant thugs. How he would have made a tuba wound seem self-inflicted had this attempt on my life been successful, I cannot say, but I'm confident he would have managed it: Mr. Teone's depravity and ingenuity had few limits, if d. and i. mean what I must assume they mean.

Mr. Teone had done more than just set up cameras, and he hadn't acted alone. He had sold his illicit videos on the underground market and had recruited like-minded normal students to help with the operation by setting up their classmates to be unwitting stars of the videos, and enforcing the silence and cooperation of the student body and administration by means of violence, subterfuge, and intimidation. To the extent that this silent cooperation amounted to participation, the conspiracy went right to the top, which was why I ultimately named the United States of America in my indictment.

Underlying it all was the sadistic structure of society and its organizing principle of Normalism, reflecting in turn the sadistic, essentially evil structure of reality itself, i.e., the Survival of the Cruelest and the Dumbest at the Expense of the Nice, the Decent, and the Moderately Intelligent. But I couldn't very well indict the universe. Or could I? No, I had to draw the line somewhere, and for the purposes of my lawsuit, I had elected to draw the line at the United States of America. The universe could wait.

"You don't really know what a lawsuit is, do you?" was Sam Hellerman's response after I had given him this brief outline of my plans.

"Well, no," I replied to the response, after a brief pause. "I guess I don't." But, my eyes implored, *you* do. Or failing that, somebody does. "That's why I'm asking."

Sam Hellerman did seem to know a bit about lawsuits, as I had anticipated, but he was hardly encouraging. I guess I'd thought of it like a court version of a citizen's arrest, where people do something to you and you catch them, take them to court, get to tell your story about how bad what they did was, and get lots of money from them, and then they go to jail.

"So let me get this straight," said Sam Hellerman, simply for the sake of reveling in my absurdity rather than from any true desire to get anything straight. "You want to do a citizen's arrest on the United States of America." Well, yes, I did. After all, it was largely their fault.

Sam Hellerman wasn't even sure I could file anything or sue anyone without a parent or guardian doing it on my behalf. They look at your age on the form, and if you're not at least eighteen, they throw it away without reading it, just like they do with your assignments at school. And according to Sam Hellerman, you can't bring a lawsuit against someone just because he's a bad person. If they ever caught Mr. Teone, it's possible I could be a witness or give some evidence in the criminal trial, and maybe even get money in a separate action if I could prove I had been injured. Which wouldn't present much of a problem. But to hear Sam Hellerman tell it, the opportunity to put my centipede on the stand was not likely to come about. As there were no criminal charges against the school, or against anyone but Mr. Teone himself, there would be no trial unless they caught Mr. Teone, who was probably safely in South America by now, living as a gentleman farmer with a new identity, protected by former Nazis and the Venezuelan government and other bad guys like that.

Such was Sam Hellerman's view. He really made it seem like it wasn't worth doing at all. Moreover, I got the impression that he didn't particularly care for the idea of my doing it. Well, his mind was on other matters, like Jeans Skirt Girl and the publicity for the Teenage Brainwashers, it's true.

But the most disheartening thing of all was Sam Hellerman's dismissive attitude toward the Catcher Code. This was galling, because my General Theory of the Universe as it applied to Mr. Teone and the Catcher Code was largely based on the analysis of Sam Hellerman himself, presented in the immediate aftermath of my hospitalization. In fact, I had been hoping for a little more clarification from him on certain points that were still extremely fuzzy and confusing. But as I said, he just waved it all away.

"Forget about this," he said, jabbing a disdainful finger at the Catcher Code and the assorted secondary documents I had neatly assembled in a binder, some of which he himself had produced in his Sherlock Hellerman phase. "It's all circumstantial. It doesn't prove anything."

Well, that's not what you said when you explained it all to me just a month ago, counselor, I said in my head. But what I said, in words, was: "Well."

I snatched the polyethylened Catcher Code square and secured it in my jacket pocket, because it looked as if Sam Hellerman might grab hold of it and tear it to pieces before my eyes. Such was his newfound disdain for the Catcher Code. But the Catcher Code meant a lot to me. The least I could do was ensure that it be treated with the reverence it deserved.

"Bathed lately?" I asked in words, when my wrinkled nose and raised eyebrow proved unequal to the task of posing the question in a way Sam Hellerman could understand.

His aroma was particularly biting on this day, and it was interfering with my powers of concentration.

Sam Hellerman raised his arm and sniffed his armpit, nodding as though satisfied with the results. I suppose that was a kind of answer. Sam Hellerman came with several drawbacks, obviously, and here was yet another, and by no means the worst of them, was how I chose to look at it. You take your geniuses as you find them.

✳ ✳ ✳

Of course I wanted a second opinion on the legal matter. It took over an hour of pleading and cajoling along with a bit of outright whining to persuade Sam Hellerman to allow me to present the matter to his father. After all, Herr Hellerman was an actual lawyer. Moreover, as the story of *The Secrets of Women Revealed* had seemed to indicate, he had once been one of us. He might have clawed his way into normalcy, but he certainly hadn't been normal at our age. Perhaps there was still, buried in that dark, villainous, normal shell, a spark of humanity that could be kindled into a generous, helpful flame. Sam Hellerman wasn't buying it, but one of many important lessons I'd learned from Amanda is that the easiest way to get people to do what you want is to make them feel that just about anything would be a relief if only you would shut up for five minutes. And though I am certainly no great talker, this I endeavored to do, with, as it happened, complete success.

"All right, all right," said Sam Hellerman at last, in the tone that I imagine the bullied boys of yesteryear used to use when saying uncle. He coughed and suppressed a shudder. "It won't be nice, though. He's not a nice guy. He can melt the skin from your face with a single glance." But I was undeterred. If I wound up with a bit of melted face skin, so be it, was my attitude.

There was a long silence. This gave way to another, even longer silence.

"You're going in too, right?" I said, just making sure.

Sam Hellerman looked at me, startled. He hadn't considered that to be part of the deal. But he reluctantly and shudderingly agreed. Ultimately, it seemed, Sam Hellerman would do anything to help out a pal. Even talk to his own father. That meant a lot.

There were several more long, uneasy silences, till we finally heard Herr Hellerman's car snap, crackle, and pop its way onto the gravel of the Hellerman Manor driveway. Sam Hellerman recommended we give him twenty minutes to settle in with his predinner martini before attempting to solicit an audience with him.

"Make it thirty," I said, blanching slightly and mindful of my mom's own after-work cocktail schedule.

In response to Sam Hellerman's discreet knock, we were invited into Herr Hellerman's study. Herr Hellerman was at his large, unnaturally tidy desk, a martini glass before him in its center. He waved us forward, and then made a "have a seat" gesture.

"Now," said Herr Hellerman pleasantly enough. "What can I do for you young men?"

"Tom has a, a legal question matter, sir, a legal legal, a legal . . ." That was the best Sam Hellerman could do under the circumstances. My heart went out to him.

Herr Hellerman turned his skin-melting eyes on me.

I stood up and gave him a brief summary of my lawsuit plan, with some nervousness but thankfully no stuttering. I displayed my centipede and my documents, including the Catcher Code square, and read the list of indictments as clearly and as distinctly as I could, beginning with conspiracy and ending with crimes against humanity. I realized halfway through the reading of this list that I didn't have a specific question. I just wanted it to happen somehow.

"So," I ended a bit lamely, reseating myself. "What do you, you know, think, and whatever?"

Remember that string of uneasy silences I referred to just moments ago, when we were waiting for Herr Hellerman to arrive? Well, that was nothing compared to the uneasiness of the silence that followed the delivery of my comprehensive indictment of Normalism in the thoroughly unsettling presence of Herr Heinrich Hellerman, Esq. Sam Hellerman was twitching. I was willing my face not to melt, long ago having failed in my initial resolution to retain eye contact with Herr Hellerman, surely the most unnerving entity I'd ever encountered at such close range.

His eyes behind their steel-rimmed spectacles darted methodically from one of us to the other, back and forth, lingering longer each time.

Finally, he spoke.

"Get out of here," he said.

Well, you can bet we got out of there, scrambling over our chairs and each other and whimpering like drowning kittens, I mean, like drowning kittens seem like they might have whimpered if I'd ever drowned any.

"Satisfied?" said Sam Hellerman when we had fled to safety, his voice sounding almost "Crimson and Clover"–y, that is to say, shaky.

Well, "satisfied" wasn't exactly the word, but for better or worse, I did have my second opinion. "Get out of here" says it all, really. And if nothing else was clear in this notoriously murky world, it was this: Herr Heinrich Hellerman had no concealed spark of humanity waiting to be kindled into a flame of warmth and generosity; he was, on the contrary, normal through and through. It was a bit sad, but mostly simply alarming, because if it could happen to Little Hitler Hiney Hellerman, it could happen to anyone. Even us.

PART THREE

Queerview

SAINT ASS

Queerview High School. It's harder to describe than I expected it to be. In some ways it's quite different from Hellmont High, but in other ways it's not too different at all. One thing I can say without reservation is that, for whatever reason, Clearview is not in as advanced a state of degeneration as Hillmont was, probably because Hillmont's s. of d. was very advanced indeed, leaving the degeneration of all other regional high schools in the dust.

In Hillmont's final phase, during which I attended it, the benign façade of the traditional American high school had long since fallen away. All the niceties—the clubs, the activities, the sports, the school customs and institutions, and most especially the "classes"—stood brutish and naked, revealed as nothing more than an organized schedule of feeble pretexts for harassment, hazing, and other senseless savagery. Even the highest-ranking normal people didn't bother with the euphemisms and pretty lies anymore, and the teachers and administrators gave them no more than the most cursory lip service. Where once the "Math Club," say, was claimed with a straight face to be a gathering of the mathematically inclined that by pure coincidence happened to attract the brutal attention of the occasional bully or hopped-up delinquent, now it was simply known as a convenient corral, clearly labeled and scheduled, where the most defenseless members of the student body would be herded for the convenience of any normal psychotic who might like to practice his skills upon them. And if the aforementioned normal psycho might wish, on a given day, to incorporate a bit of bizarre homoerotic sexual humiliation into his routine, he had only to consult his class schedule and pay a visit to the boys' locker room, once, it was claimed, merely an innocent place for showering, but now revealed as little more than a corral similar to the "Math Club," except that everybody in it is, by order of the state, naked as well as helpless.

But at Clearview, well, they still pretended that the Math Club was actually a math club, and that the showers were really there for people to take showers in. This appeared to be true from top to bottom, throughout the school. The teachers still pretended they were there to teach people things, the drama department actually put on plays, and the marching band, so it was rumored, really marched. At Hillmont no one, and I mean absolutely no one, not the principals or the teachers or the students of any rank, not even the "athletes" themselves, cared to any degree at all about the football team or the football games, and you could say the same about the "cheerleading" or the "career counseling" or the "dances" or whatever they happened to label each successive pretext for preying on the defenseless and smoking dope. But in the halls of Clearview, on the contrary and to my genuine surprise, there was everywhere a frankly nauseating miasma, if "miasma" means what I think it does, of "school spirit."

This is why, in my first homeroom period as a Clearview student, the girl seated in front of me (the person in the Sam Hellerman position, alphabetically speaking) said, first thing:

"How does it feel to be a badger?"

I was stumped, mystified, and, what's the other one, with the "f"? Flummoxed. I think that's it. I was stumped, mystified, and flummoxed. And my s. m. and f. status must have been visible on my face, because she shook her head in an "oh, what's to become of us?" way and pointed to her shirt, which said "Clearview Badgers" in big cursive letters and had, near the right shoulder, a little puffy image of what I supposed was a badger, which is evidently some kind of animal.

I'll tell you what I replied, but stop for a moment and think about this. This was just a regular person, not normal to any great degree, as far as I could tell, wearing a school shirt on the first day back at school, apparently of her own free will. Not only that, but she went around referring to herself as a Badger with no sarcasm or mockery, and assumed that all the other students, even new ones from other schools, thought of themselves primarily as Badgers too. I was to learn that this bizarre behavior was quite usual at Clearview High School. At the orientation assembly later that day, at which our old friend Dr. Elizabeth Gary had given a repeat performance of her now familiar Caring, Healing, and Understanding speech, sans banners, of course, the principal of the school, one Dr. Tadich, affectionately (I kid you not) known among the student body as T-Dog (I kid you not), jogged onstage and bellowed "Helloooooooooooo, Badgers!" I kid you not. And unlike at Hillmont, where such a thing would never ever occur in any of its particulars by the wildest stretch of even the most vivid imagination, the student body erupted in thunderous applause, fervent cheering, whistling, and a deafening chant of "Badgers! Badgers! Badgers! ..." I kept looking for the sarcasm and failing to find it. It was deeply unsettling, even while I had to acknowledge that I felt physically quite a bit safer. Hillmont may have been something of a concentration camp, it's true. But this, this was Nuremberg.

Anyway, what I said to the badger girl was:

"I don't know."

Then, because Badger Girl seemed to expect more from me, I added: "How do *you* feel?"

"Great," she said with disconcerting sincerity. She actually meant she was feeling, literally, great. About "being a Badger."

"We've got a great team this year," she continued, "and

we're going to really kick some saint ass." Well, after a bit more of me being s. m. and f., it was revealed: she was referring to the Mission Hills Saints, Clearview's "rivals." I resisted the urge to invite her down to the soda fountain for a malted and to tell her to make sure to bring Skippy, Squirt, and the Big Moose along because later we were all going to the sock hop and we were going to ... you know.... It's like the fifties, the way you're being, don't you get it? The fifties, like you're all fifties, you know, zombies, for God's sake. Doesn't anyone realize what's happening here?

Well, that's one urge I'm glad I resisted, anyway.

I still couldn't get my mind around the idea that anyone in the real actual world cared about this kind of thing. I mean, yes, you see it in movies and old TV shows, this "school spirit" and eagerness on the part of high school students to try to "fit in" by doing every single asinine thing that was expected of them, but I'd never expected to encounter it in real life. It was like I was talking to Marcia Brady without the short skirt and overall hotness. So right, this chick was some kind of school spirit sports girl. I'd never met one in the wild, but okay, I don't get out much. I guess they exist, and I don't care one way or the other. But I'm not kidding when I say she was not identifiably normal. She was a bit nerdy, a bit freckly, a bit small, a bit spindly, a bit patches-on-the-backpack-y. If any of the normal person's standard-issue cruelty and hostility lurked within, she certainly kept it well hidden. They'd have made mincemeat of her at Hillmont High, just chewed her up and spit out the bones and danced around them in gleeful abandon before leaving them scattered in the grass on Center Court as a grim reminder: BEWARE OF THE NORMAL GIRLS. But here she was, seemingly unminced.

She said her name was Roberta Halloran.

"Ah," I said. "The female Robert."

"Oh," she said, after a pause, and I thought I'd possibly offended her. But then: "Yes, the female Robert. I *am* the female Robert!"

I gave her the look that says "Settle down, now," and I told her my name too, when prompted.

"I had a cat named Thomas," said the Female Robert.

And at that point there really didn't seem to be much more to say.

It had been a deeply disturbing exchange, in its way, but I suppose I had also passed a sort of test. Strange as they were, these Queerviewians, it was possible to walk among them. I had a brief flash of an alternative future, one in which I would learn their ways, feign enthusiasm for their customs, and thus manage to make it through the next two and a half years unscathed and in one piece. Every time I was hassled by normal people, I would shout "Badger! Badger! Badger!" and they would leave me alone. I would, in essence, become a Badger, hiding my true self deep, deep inside. I doubted I could pull it off, what with having a personality of my own and hating everything they stood for and all, but it was beginning to seem like the least worst option.

"Yay, school. Yay, sports," I said to myself, trying it out. I had to admit, it needed work.

Of course, I had no illusions. My inability to spot the normal people at Clearview didn't mean they didn't exist. It just meant that there were different cues, different identifying behaviors, and that I would have to identify them and try to evade the most threatening among them. I needed to learn the code.

My brief conversation with Roberta the Female Robert had been an eye-opener. If the world I'd glimpsed through her eyes was indeed real, a world of school spirit and team rivalries and sincerely attended pep rallies and "varsity," whatever that was, well, maybe the old representations of teenage life that I had always dismissed so casually might reflect reality as well. If this received wisdom, the validity of which I hadn't even considered believing in just moments ago, was anything to go by, the most vicious normal people in this kind of environment would turn out to be the "jocks." These "jocks" would mainly attack the "nerds." The "hoods," on the other hand, might be dangerous but frequently had hearts of gold and would defend a worthy "nerd" on occasion from the predations of the "jocks" if he be true of spirit. But surely it couldn't be that simple, or that weird. I resolved to make a study of them, the major texts: *The Brady Bunch, Archie* comics, *Happy Days, Grease, Revenge of the Nerds, Carrie, Straw Dogs* . . . I was sure there were others. I would have to do some serious research.

Sam Hellerman's genius would have penetrated these mysteries without nearly as much trouble as I was probably going to have. And yet, though it was decidedly unpleasant to be out there on my own, my first day at Clearview persuaded me that I was in little immediate danger. There was sure to be senseless brutality lurking in hidden corners, s. b. that was possibly all the more brutal for its being hidden, but it was beginning to look like these hidden brutal corners would be easy to avoid. Moreover, as puzzling as these strange creatures and their unfamiliar ways were to me, it was a safe bet that I was just as puzzling to them. That is, whereas at Hillmont I had had "victim" written all over me, the Clearview normal people couldn't read my cues. They were bound to figure me out eventually, but for the time being, I was golden.

You could see it throughout the school grounds. The Hillmont transfers in the student population were easily spotted, the normal as well as the decent, stumbling in bewilderment, trying to figure out their place in the new pecking order. It amused me to no end, thinking how it would gradually dawn on the former Hillmont normal psychos that entering the top tier of sadistic tormenters in this brave new Clearview world would entail doing things like wearing gay little "letterman" jackets, going to pep rallies, calling each other Badgers, and learning to confine their student-on-student violence and psychological harassment to hidden, out-of-the-way nooks and crannies rather than carrying them out in plain sight under the approving eye of teachers and administrators. Slow-witted as they were, this bitter realization would no doubt take some time to hit them, but when it did, well, you know, it couldn't happen to a nicer bunch of guys.

Now, if you people from the future have spotted the fact that the Clearview High School I have described sounds and looks quite a bit like "Millmont High" from *Halls of Innocence*, well, good for you. It sure does. That's what I'm saying: it was so obviously fake and ridiculous that you'd never believe it if you saw it on TV, and yet here it was in real life, and at the time it sure was hard to believe it wasn't some kind of elaborate hoax.

Any hopes I might have had that the Alphabet Gods would see fit, in their wisdom, to provide me with a suitable Sam Hellerman substitute for use during this Clearview ordeal were dashed on the rocks of homeroom's roll call. As I explained, the person before me in alphabetical order—in the Sam Hellerman slot—was the Badger girl: nice enough, but hardly a genius. If I ever happened to need any advice on how to get "pumped" and "psyched" for the "game," she'd be the one to consult. Otherwise, I couldn't see how she'd be much use. The student behind me was a guy named Bill Henderson, no relation, and he looked as slow-witted and normal as they come. He was wearing one of those "letterman" jackets that still looked like a costume to me, and had that typically normal air of vapid peevishness, which means always being pissed off for no reason, I think. But he made no threatening moves. It was like he was on hold, a subhuman psycho machine on standby, yet to be activated by headquarters. At least he couldn't call me Hender-queer. But that was the best that could be said of him, I was sure.

Now, anyone who has followed my previous explanations might well be wondering: where are all the Clearview drama mods? Couldn't I make friends with them?

It's a good question. I wondered about it too. My experience at that Clearview party (the one where I met "Fiona") had certainly left me with the impression that the drama people at this school were a mod subculture, much like the hippie subculture that had infested the Hillmont drama department. But I had been mistaken. That had been nothing more than a mod theme party, and in real life, the Clearview drama people looked and behaved just like all the other Clearview students. They were not, it seemed, particularly dangerous, but neither were they "my people," as I'd dared to imagine all those months ago. Which should come as no surprise. My "people" are Sam Hellerman and ... well, that's pretty much it.

But even if the place had been crawling with mods, I don't see how that would have helped. It wasn't like I was going to sign up for drama and try out for plays. It wasn't like I was going to walk up to the first asymmetrical haircut I saw and say, "Hey, you must like Northern Soul, am I right?"

I couldn't expect a subculture to save me. In fact, it was extremely difficult to detect any subcultures within the Clearview student body. To the untrained eye, these people all looked pretty much the same. And a large number of them, statistically speaking, would probably turn out to be mostly harmless. It was the harmful ones that were the worry, and those were maddeningly difficult to identify.

I only had one class (English) with Celeste Fletcher, but it was a doozy.

First off, there was the teacher's name. Again, I had the impression that someone was "putting me on," as Little Big Tom might say. I mean, if you tried as hard as you could and if your life depended on it, could you possibly come up with a better, less probable name for a teacher than Mrs. Pizzaballa? Mrs. Pizzaballa, I kid you not.

The other point in Mrs. Pizzaballa's favor, as if the name weren't enough, was a kind of, I don't know, whimsical sense of humor that resulted in her delivering these deadpan clichés that had absolutely nothing to do with whatever they were supposed to be commenting on. They were not all that different from Little Big Tom's weird little sayings, I guess, but in LBT's case, at least it's clear that he's trying, on some level, to make what comes out of his mouth relate to reality. With Mrs. Pizzaballa, though, reality didn't enter into it, not even slightly. She was a regular Salvador Dalí without the mustache—or mostly without it, anyway—her class a piece of performance art: a portrait of the artist as an absurdist educator.

For example, when the handouts Mrs. Pizzaballa was handing out slipped from her grasp and scattered all over the floor in front of her, she paused and said with a faraway look in her eyes: "Garbage in, garbage out." And when this girl raised her hand and said she needed to go to the bathroom, Mrs. Pizzaballa said, "Famous last words." And when the girl came back, instead of saying "Everything come out all right?" as Little Big Tom might have said, Mrs. Pizzaballa simply shook her head and intoned a solemn "Michael, row your boat ashore."

I couldn't help thinking that Mrs. Pizzaballa and Little Big Tom should get together sometime. They'd certainly have some great conversations. Maybe if things didn't work out between my mom and Little Big Tom, and if Mr. Pizzaballa were to meet with an unfortunate accident, I could introduce them. She could tell him she had an itchy trigger finger and he could counsel her about it.

Anyway, I took to Mrs. Pizzaballa almost instantly. I couldn't say the same for her handout, a big annotated list of books with *Catcher in the Rye* at the top of it, followed by all the same other books they make you read in every single English class. I'd tell you what they were, but I'm sure you already know. At least I wouldn't have to worry about having to do any homework for Mrs. Pizzaballa's class: I had done it all before, many, many times.

As for my plans for huddling with Celeste Fletcher and bonding over shared new school anxiety, I had to admit, it wasn't looking all that good.

I love Celeste Fletcher to pieces, as you know, but I'd be the first to acknowledge that while she was not outright normal, she had a tendency to flirt with Normalism and sometimes veered much closer to normalcy than I was comfortable with. She was pleasant enough in Mrs. Pizzaballa's class and when I encountered her in the halls, but I'm not stupid: even though my status had yet to be solidified at Clearview, I could tell she was taking no chances and was clearly trying to maintain as much distance as she could, in case anybody was watching and taking notes for future use against her. We did eat lunch together that first day, but the entire time she was scanning the horizon for other, presumably better, lunch partner opportunities, and halfway through she got up "to say hi" to some girls from her homeroom and never came back.

I'm enough of a realist to have understood, when I zoomed out mentally to view the scene from above and saw a boy and his centipede seated on a bench sans Fiona with a wide zone of empty space on all sides and little groups of happily chatting, potentially hostile and dangerous kids clustered all around, that this was most likely a pretty accurate picture of the future. Clearview wasn't Hillmont, it's true, but it wasn't going to be any kind of picnic, either.

ONE-THIRD OF A LIFETIME SUPPLY

The Teenage Brainwashers' set was coming along. I was getting the hang of playing one song while thinking another, and we'd managed to alter the arrangements so they matched our own songs more closely with less trouble than I'd expected. Even Shinefield, as a math guy, could understand that we had to shorten all of these six-minute songs if we wanted to do more than five of them in a thirty-minute set, plus two for the obligatory encore. We got rid of most of the nonessential bits of "Live Wire" till "Fiona" was a short, sharp blast of concise mooning over an imaginary girl, just like it was supposed to be. But I decided I couldn't resist keeping Bon Scott's "Oh stick this in your fuse box"–that really fit in, if you know what I mean. (If you don't, it has to do with sex.)

One thing we hadn't anticipated, though maybe we should have, was that Shinefield eventually noticed that our whole set was, as far as he knew, covers.

"Let's play some of our songs," Shinefield would say,

meaning my songs, little knowing that that was exactly what we'd been doing all along. "They're actually pretty good." My eyes said, "Gee, ya think, stoner boy?" but fortunately Shinefield was not much of an eye-reader.

The whole thing almost blew up in our faces when it came to convincing him to play "Cat Scratch Fever" three times in the same set, and twice in a row, without the guitar intro. Even the dimmest, most stoned-out-of-his-skull hippie skater in the world would have smelled a rat there, and Shinefield was not nearly as dim as he was cracked up to be. I knew we were pushing it, but Sam Hellerman had insisted. "Which one would we cut?" he had asked me. "'Sadistic Masochism'? Be serious."

He didn't have to convince me to be serious about "Sadistic Masochism," but Shinefield was another story.

"Well," said Sam Hellerman, when Shinefield's disgruntlement had risen too close to the surface to push it back under all that easily, "I didn't want to tell you this till it was for sure, but see, there's a show. Well, not a show. I mean, it is a show, but it's also kind of a contest...."

"Another battle of the bands?" said Shinefield, his eyes lighting up. He had loved the Chi-Mos' terrible Battle of the Bands performance at Hillmont High School last year (about which, see my previous explanations, and laugh all you want to: it was the best we could do at the time, and plus, what terrible B. o. t. B. performances have you done lately?). He was always bringing it up and saying things like "That's how I first got into you guys," and he had made it very clear that he'd like nothing better than to experience some of that terribleness himself one day.

Yes, Sam Hellerman had explained. It was kind of like a battle of the bands. Sort of. But more like a real show, too, where bands were supposed to do covers, and the band that

138

got the biggest audience response would win ... this really great thing. Sam Hellerman apologized for not having all the details committed to memory, but as far as he could recall it included things like a small amount of money and possible studio time at a, you know, studio. And, Sam Hellerman thought he remembered, hats, maybe. Oh, and also a lifetime supply of Mountain Dew.

"Are you *serious*?" Shinefield sounded almost giddy. "A lifetime supply? For each of us?"

"No," Sam Hellerman had said with a slightly worried tone. "Between the three of us. Still, that's pretty good."

And Shinefield had readily agreed: one-third of a lifetime supply of Mountain Dew was pretty good. But of course, Sam Hellerman had added, the real benefit was the opportunity to show off how good our band was before a receptive audience, not to mention all the free publicity we would get.

But Sam Hellerman had had Shinefield at "lifetime supply of Mountain Dew." He was, in an instant, the compliant and cooperative drummer once again. For a bit of Mountain Dew, it seemed, Shinefield would play "Cat Scratch Fever" all you wanted till the cows came home. It was kind of weird, actually. But what can I say? The guy just happened to like Mountain Dew. A *lot.*

Could this possibly end well? It was difficult to see how. But the songs were sounding so good, and I was, as ever, Sam Hellerman's faithful and obedient servant, so I really had no choice but to roll with it and leave everything in Sam Hellerman's capable, if slightly sinister, hands. God help us all.

At first I had half wondered if there might have been any basis at all to the story Sam Hellerman had told Shinefield, because you never could tell with that guy. For all I knew, there really could have been some kind of covers contest Mountain Dew show with free hats. But it had soon become apparent that he was making it up as he went along.

"What are we going to do," I asked Sam Hellerman afterward, "when Phil figures out there's no show?" Because we had started calling Shinefield "Phil" in honor of Phil Rudd, his kind of patron saint.

"Oh, there will be a show," said Sam Hellerman, his eyes shining with an unearthly light behind his glasses. "Of that I can assure you."

And that was how I learned that Sam Hellerman, having inadvertently talked his way into the concert promotion and soft drink public relations business, intended to go through with it. But where? But how? But who? He wouldn't give me any details, as usual, and I think it pretty likely that he didn't know any details himself at that point. But I could as good as see the machinery grinding in his odd but retardedly brilliant little head, and I knew better than to interrupt a genius at work. Plus, he said the thing that always silences further discussion.

"Leave it to me, Henderson," he said.

And of course, as always, I left it to him as directed. I was all too happy to have someone to leave it to, and it might as well be him. And really, what choice did I have?

SAM HELLERMAN'S CAMELOT

Sam Hellerman wasn't having an easy time at Mission Hills High School, if his puffy eye and the slightly scraped side of his face were any indication.

"What happened to you?" my look said, mingling curiosity, sympathy, and relief that it wasn't me.

"What do you think?" said Sam Hellerman's look in response, adding a hint of bitterness and a dash of casual thirst for vengeance to the communal pot of c., s., and r. Oh, I remembered it well.

There was little more to say. A puffy eye in the first week: it wasn't unprecedented, but it sure wasn't a good sign.

"Never mind," he said, in words. "Two months from now, I'll be running the place."

Part of me had enough faith in Sam Hellerman's fractured genius to consider the possibility that he might be right about that, but the other part, the bigger part, looked at Sam Hellerman with his stinky Iron Maiden T-shirt, off-kilter glasses, scraped-up face, puffy eye, and sad little phone holster and knew pretty much beyond doubt that Sam Hellerman's "running" with regard to Mission Hills High School in any sense other than "fleeing to evade capture" was just some mad dream. Those confidence-building tapes had done their work all too well, it seemed: someone was liable to get hurt. Even more so, I mean.

I didn't have the heart to tell him about Clearview's relatively benign bizarrely Brady Bunch brotherhood of benevolent blockheads. I did mention the "letterman" jackets, though, and he gave me a look that said something like "Gee whiz, Scooter."

At any rate, Sam Hellerman's mind was on publicity, not jackets. And the main thrust of his publicity plan was this: (a) he would call radio stations, TV stations, record stores, nightclubs, music stores, libraries, and places like that; (b) he would say "The Teenage Brainwashers are coming" in a soft, growly, threatening voice; and (c) he would hang up the phone. He'd been doing it for hours when I arrived at Hellerman Manor that day, and he was ready to take a break.

Now that there was a show in the offing, and "the publicity" was afoot, Sam Hellerman had changed his mind about my lawsuit. A public trial, even if doomed to failure, he reasoned, would be as a good a way as any to draw attention to the Teenage Brainwashers, the equivalent of dozens of crank calls. And if the case was big enough and splashy enough to "become a thing," as Sam Hellerman put it, well, we'd be household names before the first chords of "Fiona" even sounded.

So the purpose of our rendezvous at Hellerman Manor that day was to work on the lawsuit as well as to continue practicing our think-playing. Sam Hellerman was still irritatingly dismissive of the greater case against Normalism and its institutions, and when I pulled out the Catcher Code he gave me a surprisingly intimidating look, like he was going to slap it out of my hand or something.

"Forget about that," he said testily. "It has nothing to do with anything. Focus on the assault and battery." Well, as I didn't want things to develop into fisticuffs, which is an effeminate form of punching that they used to do in Sherlock Holmes, I thought it prudent to comply, at least outwardly.

Sam Hellerman's view was that the quickest and easiest way to a publicity-generating public spectacle was to target each of the kids who had directly participated in the tuba attack and related incidents. It's a good story, he said, to which my eyes replied, "Thanks, I found it engrossing myself."

There was Paul Krebs, and Matt Lynch, of course, and Rich Zim, who had actually struck the blow with the tuba, as far as I knew. Then there were the kids who had carried me through the halls, banging my head hither and thither as they went, and Mark McAllister, who had initially knocked me senseless in the PE boxing ring while the others held me down ... and

142

Mr. Donnelly, the PE teacher, who had overseen it all, and Mr. Teone . . . but Sam Hellerman stopped me there: no teachers, he said. And certainly no Teone. It didn't make much sense to me, but Sam Hellerman stood firm. If I wanted his help, I had to play by his rules, and for some reason one of those rules was that mention of Mr. Teone in relation to the tuba attack was forbidden. I reluctantly and perplexedly agreed.

I had to admit, just making a list of the kids who had been involved was challenging enough. It included, potentially, the entire PE class, and some kids from band, and perhaps others. And maybe even my parents, too, since their uncooperative attitude toward my lawsuit plans had really gotten in the way of my lawsuit plans.

"Can you sue someone to force them to sue someone else on your behalf?" I asked with my eyes, but Sam Hellerman refused to dignify that with a response.

He did, however, pull out last year's Hillmont High School yearbook, *The Camelot*. My assignment was to go through the class pictures one by one and make a list of the sueable among them. But it was hard to focus on that because, well, Sam Hellerman had completely covered these pages with tiny, meticulously scribbled, detailed, and thoroughly distracting notes. The girls were all ranked on what appeared to be the standard one-to-ten scale with neat little numerals inscribed in the bottom right-hand corner of their pictures, and there were notes in the margins next to the photos providing what looked like more detail on the rankings, as well as addresses, phone numbers, favorite colors, favorite foods, unusual interests, astrological signs, and psychological attributes like "loyal," "mean," "adventurous," "generous," "dumb," "nice," "prude," even, I kid you not, "shrewd" and "sex-positive." How he thought he knew all this stuff about these girls was beyond me, but it was clear that compiling it had involved many, many hours of careful, misguided research, even though the things he was researching were, I would bet, only his own fantasies. Even weirder, most girls had an additional number, a decimal fraction, of which I could make neither heads nor, even especially, tails. And even weirdest, some of the *guys* also had rankings, though they only seemed to go up to five.

Whatever else it meant, one thing was clear: Sam Hellerman had made stunning progress in his long-cherished dream of reducing love to math.

Well, this was weirder and creepier than I'd bargained for. I wanted out. So I shut the yearbook with a loud clap that made us both jump.

I gave Sam Hellerman a look. And he looked back at me like "... ?"

Some time went by.

"Do I really," I finally said, in words, "have to ask?"

"It's a simple confidence-building exercise," said Sam Hellerman patiently, as though explaining to a grandparent how to turn the computer on.

Well, I might have known it had to do with those confounded tapes. According to *The Secrets of Women Revealed,* Sam Hellerman explained, careful, objective, detailed ranking and evaluation is merely a way of demystifying sex appeal and leveling the playing field, which is ordinarily stacked against "men" from the get-go. Training yourself to replace romantic daydreams with cold analysis makes "dating," and women themselves, less intimidating. A man who is in command of the facts, unswayed by sentiment, is a confident man, a capable man, and ultimately a successful man.

The guys' rankings were intended to identify the other "men" who needed to be eliminated or neutralized, or, failing that, sucked up to and made into allies. Sam Hellerman assured me that it "worked," though I couldn't help noticing that as of yet, he had not succeeded in anything beyond acting like an idiot at a bus stop and defacing a school yearbook in such a way as to suggest to anyone who wasn't prepared to give him the most generous benefit of the doubt that he was a disturbed and possibly dangerous nut.

"Besides," he added defensively, "they do it too. Don't kid yourself."

Well, if he was talking about ranking and evaluation, he certainly had a point, about which I wouldn't dream of kidding myself. As I've explained in my other explanations, Sam Hellerman and I, along with Hillmont High School's other socially unsuccessful males, had ourselves been the target of a malicious, elaborately charted Make-out/Fake-out program of ranking and evaluation designed specifically to engineer our humiliation. We had, of course, had extremely low rankings, and hence a high value in the Hillmont High game known as Dud Chart. But as elaborate and sociopathic as Dud Chart had been, I was pretty sure Sam Hellerman's annotated *Camelot* had it beat.

During all of this, I hadn't failed to note that Sam Hellerman had, rather gallantly, I thought, given Celeste Fletcher what amounted to a kind of honorary 10, the only one in the book, and had refrained from analyzing her further as he had with most of the other girls. I mean, I love and admire Celeste Fletcher beyond all reason, but a 10 ranking, if it exists at all, is properly reserved only for stratospheric ideals of womanhood like porn stars and underwear models, that kind of thing. Well,

Sam Hellerman's regard for Celeste Fletcher was evident. The bastard. But I knew what he meant. That girl is dynamite, if not, strictly speaking, an actual 10.

But what's the other number, the one in 0.x form? I asked. It was less a case of wanting to know than needing to know.

"WHR," said Sam Hellerman. "Waist-hip ratio. Zero point seven is the ideal of female beauty. It's the only metric that truly matters, far more accurate and more useful than the highly overrated BWR." BWR, Sam Hellerman patiently explained, was the bust-waist ratio. The WHR was a standard developed by the World Health Organization, he added, which seemed like it couldn't possibly be true, but when I looked it up later, it turned out it was.

I said Sam Hellerman had reduced love to math, didn't I? With a little help from the World Health Organization, it seemed, anything was possible. It was disturbing and, kind of, I don't know, inspiring at the same time. Because, yes, I could see how the WHR might be more "useful" than the BWR, though I'm going to go out on a limb here and say that, as I like big butts and I cannot lie, I'm probably more of a 0.66 man myself. But I digress.

"What's Celeste Fletcher?" I ventured to ask.

"Zero point seven," said Sam Hellerman dreamily. "On the dot."

And Jeans Skirt Girl?

"A solid, respectable, zero point seven three six," said Sam Hellerman. That's what I'd have answered too. I was getting the hang of this game. "She'll get closer to point seven in a year or so," Sam Hellerman added, defending her honor. He had, he assured me, developed an algorithm for that.

Well, maybe I wasn't quite getting the hang of the game after all.

In all the excitement, I had lost track of the lawsuit and my yearbook assignment. I looked at Sam Hellerman, who now had an old Mission Hills yearbook and a calculator in hand and was hard at work scribbling.

"Any calls yet?" I asked.

"No," said Sam Hellerman.

DOIN' THE HILLMONT RAG

The thing about music is that to get good at it, you have to put in a lot of effort.

But it's possible to put only a little effort into it and still manage. This is rock and roll's great advantage. If it's loud enough and enthusiastic enough, and if it goes by quickly enough, you can be quite awful at playing and nobody will notice all that much. Sometimes people even prefer it that way. But Shinefield's abhorrent drumming had got me thinking. Truth be told, my guitar playing was rather abhorrent too. Rock and roll depends on a solid, "together" rhythm section, which is a tall order, to be sure. But once you have that, the guitar player can pretty much do whatever he wants, and even sloppiness and ineptitude can sound kind of cool against the competent backdrop. It's *better* if you're good at playing. But it's not absolutely necessary to be all that good, is what I'm saying.

Much as I love rock and roll, and I do, with everything I've got, now that the Teenage Brainwashers were sounding alright—well, it was starting to feel a little bit like cheating, on my part.

There was this guy at Clearview High School lunch period one day who had this fancy nylon-string guitar and was playing this impressive classical music thing, a Bach fugue or something like that. He played it flawlessly, and didn't seem to be concentrating too hard on it, as he was carrying on a conversation with a couple of other guys about where to score weed all the while. Now, see, you could tell by his conversation that this was a pretty dumb guy, more stoner than normal, though there is certainly such a thing as a normal stoner. It's so hard to tell these things at Clearview, because, normal or otherwise, this guy was wearing one of the Badgers shirts—that's right, at Clearview, even the stoners had school spirit. It was nauseating.

But anyway, dumb and quasi-normal as he was, he was light-years better at playing guitar than I could ever be, no matter how hard I tried, especially because, as I hope I've explained well enough, I am more or less constitutionally unable to try all that hard, if "constitutionally" means what I think it means. And while tricking your drummer into playing like Phil Rudd certainly has its place, part of me couldn't help but fantasize about a theoretical world where a guy like me could just pick up a guitar and start playing and it would sound great all on its own, and people would hear it and say "Boy, that kid can really play." If I just sat down with a guitar, not distorted to cover up the ineptitude, and without a hoodwinked drummer herded by a bespectacled rock and roll mastermind bass player, and played "I Wanna Ramone You" or "Sadistic Masochism," no one would be impressed. They'd throw tomatoes and cabbages and possibly call the cops. I actually think my lyrics aren't all that bad, but no one, almost literally no one, cares about that.

Now, playing fugues by Bach wasn't really my thing, but in my fantasy world where I could actually play guitar, the thing that was my thing, or that I wanted to be my thing, is this kind of music that they used to call ragtime, like, eons and eons ago. It's played on the piano, mostly, but it can be done on a guitar, and when it is, it's just mindfuckingly magical. Regular guitar playing like I do in the real world is just: you put your fingers in a chord position and hit the strings with your pick hand as hard as you can and then slide the chord fingers up and down the neck. But with the fantasy-world magical good guitar playing, each finger is, like, playing its own little part, and one guy with one guitar sounds like a whole band.

People back then would gather in a barn and actually dance to one guy playing the guitar standing on a barrel or a wagon. And at the end of the song the girls would bend over and show their underwear, kind of being sassy. So that was legitimately cool, pre–rock and roll music that might as well have been rock and roll, and you didn't even need to trick a drummer into doing anything. In fact, you could just send him out for burritos, for all it would matter, because your own fingers were the rhythm section.

Back then it was played by cool-looking black guys with bowler hats and, for some reason, hair scrunchies on their arms, and they were playing guitars they had made themselves out of a box and some wire. These days the guys who can play the guitar like that tend to be pudgy white sixties guys with little gray mustaches and maybe a bald-guy ponytail who want you to call them Big Skillet or Rib Eye. "This is an old country blues tune, name of 'Grandma's Kitchen,'" they'll say, and then unleash hell on the strings. It's not the same without the cool black guys and the scrunchies and the wagon and the skinny girls and their underwear, of course, but it's still impressive.

It occurred to me that maybe Little Big Tom could play the guitar like that. He was from the sixties. And with the

"Big" in his name, and the mustache, he was already halfway there.

I had been looking for something to talk to him about that didn't involve Jesus Proust for some time. The guy needed cheering up.

He didn't seem to be around at the moment, but it was a safe bet that it wouldn't be long before he ambled in, and that when he did he'd head straight for the den, where his Mac lives, to put away his shoulder bag and coat and check his email and message boards before beginning his evening rounds. So I took my Melody Maker and practice amp with me and settled down with my back against the den door to wait for him and read the reckless vow book while I waited.

It was a pretty weird book. The people in it all spoke in this formal, stilted way that was basically so elaborate and polite that it was difficult to tell what they were getting at half the time. Everything they said was like a code, and the point of the code was for everyone to hide what they really felt from everyone else. But the main point, underneath it all, was for the girls to figure out which guys had the most money and then try to marry them. It was easy to tell who the best girl was (the smart, witty one) and it was easy to tell who the best guy was (the guy with "ten thousand a year," which was apparently a lot in those days), so there didn't seem to be too much suspense as to how it was going to end. It was odd, not quite like a real story, but more like a dramatization of how these weird old English people organized their finances. Girls seem to see this book as this tender, super-romantic love story, but I sure didn't get that. There was hardly any emotional content in it at all, and the characters weren't so much people as personified bank accounts.

I had resigned myself to the fact that it probably wasn't

going to have any sexy parts. It was a bit slow going, but not as slow as *The Crying of Lot 49*. Now, that one's really in code. I was fortunate not to have made a reckless vow about that.

PAT O'BRIEN AND HIS HONOLULU LOU

Soon enough, as I'd predicted, Little Big Tom ambled up. He saw me sitting there, mimed as though the surprise of seeing me in such a position was going to knock him over backwards, and said:

"You mind very much if they smoke! Oh, brutal."

The first sentence was in reference to my little battery-powered practice amp that was made out of a cigarette box; the second was directed at *Pride and Prejudice* and was accompanied by a hand drawn melodramatically across his brow, expressing sympathy for my having to read it. I suppose he must have thought I was being forced to read it for school rather than just reading it for "fun" because of a reckless vow.

I put down the book and asked Little Big Tom if he, by any possible chance, knew how to fingerpick like all the other hippies in the sixties did, and if so, could he show me how.

I wish *30 Days to a More Powerful Vocabulary* had powerful enough words to describe the alarming yet touching smile that blossomed, in slow motion, under Little Big Tom's mustache as it gradually dawned on him that I had come of my own free will to ask him for a bit of fake fatherly instruction. For a moment there I thought he might actually start to cry. It's good he didn't, because if he had, I would have had to do something far more wounding than necessary, just to escape. But in the end, Little Big Tom regained his composure enough to pat me on the shoulder and reach for the guitar.

"I'm a little rusty," he said, testing the strings and frowning at the brittle, distorted sound coming out of the cigarette-pack amp. "But I think I may know a thing or two."

A horrifying thought struck me. Please, I prayed, don't play "Stairway to Heaven," please don't play "Stairway to Heaven," please don't play—

Would you be at all surprised if I were to tell you that it was at that point that Little Big Tom started to play "Stairway to Heaven"? I didn't think so.

I made the buzz-alarm sound, signaling that he could stop that right away. My face said: "What else ya got?"

Little Big Tom frowned. It seemed beyond his comprehension that anyone would veto "Stairway to Heaven," his unofficial anthem. But he regrouped and tried something else. It was hard to make out what it was through the fuzz, but it was clear that whatever it was, he kind of knew what he was doing. Finally, he identified the song as "Dear Prudence." Okay, that was better, and I'd like to learn how to do that too, but it wasn't quite what I'd had in mind. I explained about the cool black guys with the derby hats and the arm scrunchies and the skinny girls and their underwear. Little Big Tom got a strange, distant look in his eye.

"Well," he said. "There is something, maybe, that I was taught by a great man long ago. I'm not sure you'll like it. I don't know if I can even remember it, but it's the only other one I really know. . . ."

Then Little Big Tom started to play, and sing, what was perhaps the stupidest song I had ever heard. He had a surprisingly good voice, and even though he kept forgetting the words and stumbling over the chords, and despite the terrible fake Irish accent he was trying to sing in, I got the gist of it. It was about this Irish guy named Pat O'Brien who goes to Hawaii to try to seduce a hula girl, but because he can't speak her language he just shouts gibberish at her, things like "begorrah hickey doola" and other nonsense, hoping she'll understand him and let him ramone her. But of course the poor girl can't understand a word, though he keeps trying and trying, like a big idiot. In other words, this guy is kind of like Sam Hellerman with Jeans Skirt Girl, or face it, kind of like just about every guy with just about any girl. A tale as old as time, I think it's called.

"That song is almost a hundred years old," said Little Big Tom when he had finished, obviously proud that he had been able to remember something so old. And I agree, it was impressive. The oldest song I knew how to play was only from 1955.

Anyway, I hated it, mostly. It wasn't a song I could imagine the hair scrunchie guys with the underwear girls doing, not at all. It was as uncool as it's possible for a thing to be. But I found myself inexplicably drawn to it at the same time. It was kind of catchy. And without understanding why, I knew that I wanted to be able to play it. Maybe I could pull a kind of Shinefieldian switcheroo on it, changing the chords around and rewriting the lyrics so they'd be about Sam Hellerman and Jeans Skirt Girl instead of the Irish dude and his Honolulu Lou. It seemed like a pretty good plan to me.

Unfortunately, while Little Big Tom wasn't all that bad at playing it, he was terrible at teaching it. He would play a bit and then say "You just–" and instead of saying what it was that you do, he would mime it and then do it again. Still, I figured if Little Big Tom could do it, I probably could manage it eventually. I made him do it very slowly and took down the lyrics in my notebook. I'd have those skinny dancing girls showing their underwear if my life depended on it.

GOING STEADY FOR GOOD

Well, that didn't take long, did it? I'm referring to this: by the end of the second week of classes at Clearview High, Celeste Fletcher could already be seen around the school wearing this jacket with a letter on it that was two sizes too big for her.

"What the hell is that?" I said, when she flounced into Mrs. Pizzaballa's class, swimming in the *Bye Bye Birdie* dating symbolism of yesteryear.

But Mrs. Pizzaballa cleared her throat and said, "We're not in Kansas anymore," which, in this context, meant that we weren't supposed to talk during our vocabulary test and that if we kept it up we'd get Fs and possibly detention. Because at Clearview, they actually do grade the tests and give you failing grades if you talk during them enough to look like you might be cheating.

Celeste Fletcher took advantage of Mrs. Pizzaballa's test and her warning about it to avoid having to tell me what the hell it, whatever "it" was, was. If you follow me.

I passed her a note that said: "Did you really get pinned?" But she just rolled her eyes at me, not getting or failing to acknowledge the reference and refusing to dignify my sarcastic note with a reply.

Forty-two minutes later, soft piano chords began to play on the intercom–that's what Clearview has instead of a bell, because we Clearview students are far too precious to have our tender ears assailed with a jarring buzzer while being enfolded in the warm embrace of Learning. At the chords, Celeste Fletcher bounded up without a word to me and handed her paper in, rushing out the door, 0.7 waist-to-hip ratio and all.

Now, Mrs. Pizzaballa had this habit of delivering what I had begun to think of as Life Lessons at the end of many class periods. She would introduce them by saying something like "Children, if I can teach you nothing else, I hope at least that you walk away from here understanding that ..." (And yes, she always called us "children," which made me feel kind of, I don't know, Amish or something. But I preferred it to "men and women," which was the usual preposterous way of addressing students at Clearview.)

Her Life Lesson on that day was typical.

"Children, please remember that school is hokum," she said, a sentiment with which I found myself in full agreement once I looked up "hokum," which is another word for bullshit. "One day you will have to get a job, and whatever that job is, you'll find you'll be much better at it if you simply learn what is expected of you and do it with no nonsense." I believe the implication was that we were to think of her class as a kind of practice run. Then she added: "Hope is the thing with feathers."

You know, it was nice to hear someone being honest about things for a change. I had no doubt that the true objective of education really was to condition people for a future of mindless obedience, and that the attempts to dress it all up with encouragement to "think for yourself" and "draw your own conclusions" were just hokum. No one has ever been rewarded in any way, that I know of, for drawing his own conclusions. Quite the contrary.

Find out what is expected of you and do it with no nonsense. I'm sure it's pretty good advice. This was in fact precisely what I faced in the developing Clearview ordeal, and it was helpful, if hugely depressing, to have it spelled out with such clarity. I was trying the best I could to *look like* I was doing what was expected of me, but it was touch and go. One false move would reveal my true King Dork nature, sending me straight to the bottom and into the torture hopper, despite Clearview's benign school spirit façade. I didn't see how I could sustain this for much longer. But Celeste Fletcher seemed to be doing just fine at figuring out what was expected of her and doing it with no nonsense.

Man, I felt low.

They didn't actually call it "going steady" like in the movies of antiquity, if "antiquity" means what I think it does. They called it "going." Skippy's "going" with Peggy Sue. Hey, says Marcia to the Big Man on Campus, I like you, wanna ask me to "go"? Are Jughead and Veronica "going"? No, they're just hanging out, but he really wants to "go" with her. Too bad she's "going" with Archie.

This going, it seemed to me, meant "going together," like clothes that match, or wine paired with the right entrée, or alternatively, like people embarking on a journey together, "going" somewhere, to the Orient, or Bakersfield, or the grave, or what have you, except instead of actually going to Bakersfield, the place the "goers" wind up "going" is, essentially, walking around and around this central area called the Quad. A couple of Badgers can manage to do seven laps during the thirty-minute lunch period if they "go" continuously, though stopping to talk to other "goers" or to make out can impede their progress. If they do begin to make out, Clearview custom dictates that everyone in their immediate proximity has to yell "PDA," which stands for "public display of affection." PDA is by legend forbidden on school grounds, but this rule is rarely if ever enforced. I've even seen Principal "T-Dog" trot over and "high-five" a couple of frisky Badgers who'd been caught PDA-ing, and everyone cheers, "Go, Badgers!" It's that kind of place.

Of course, it's all a euphemism for ramoning, like so much

else. And we had a similar set of customs at Hillmont, though we said "hanging out" or "hooking up" more often than "going," and the lovers' laps were done around a "Center Court" rather than a "Quad," and while we didn't have the thing of chanting "PDA" every five minutes, there were other similarly dumb things we chanted, probably. But the jackets and the insane school spirit somehow made it all so much stranger and more depressing and, well, basically, I just can't get over the damn jackets, okay? What kind of sick, twisted, jacket-oriented motherfuckery had I stumbled into over here? I ask you that most sincerely.

So Celeste Fletcher, apparently, was now "going" with the owner of the jacket, one Todd Dante, a big, dumb guy on a sports team of some kind and almost certainly, irredeemably, virulently normal. Wearing the jacket was her way, in accordance with custom handed down by the Clearview elders from time immemorial and embraced by her without a moment's hesitation, of signaling that she was "taken." That was more commitment and loyalty than I'd ever seen from her toward any guy she had "hung out" with in all the years I'd known her. I guess she just hadn't met the right jacket before. I don't know where that left Shinefield. But I knew where it left me. And that's Nowheresville, daddy-o. King Dork strikes again.

TOM, GET YOUR HORN UP

There was nothing I could do except marinate in my own bitterness and, perhaps, commemorate this marination with lyrics composed specially for the occasion. This I endeavored to do—in a lively number I intended to call "King Dork Strikes Again." But Clearview High School had a method of discouraging that sort of thing—by which I mean creativity and self-expression—in its own caring, healing, and understanding way.

Because I have to tell you about Band, the class. It was, like pretty much everything else, way, way different at Clearview than it had been at Hillmont.

At Hillmont High, the whole point of Band, from the students' perspective, was to try to drive the Band teacher insane by means of constructive sabotage. Essentially, the students would all de-tune their instruments just slightly so that when the Band teacher, Ms. Filuli, would count in, the resulting cacophony would send her reeling in dismay and pain. When you have perfect pitch, like Ms. Filuli, even a slight deviation from in-tune-ness is like the world's largest set of nails on the world's most gargantuan chalkboard. And we deviated. Boy, did we deviate. She would try to be patient, and would spend entire class periods attempting to teach the class how to use the strobe tuner, and the class would play along, remaining more or less in tune when playing concert C in unison to exhibit the results of all this effort at tuning. But then, just when she thought she'd made progress, the first notes of "Stars and Stripes Forever" would come out just as bad as before, because everyone was playing their notes a different fraction of a tone sharp or flat from everyone else. What can I say, it helped to pass the time. But there was no Hillmont teacher more grateful to be put out to pasture than Ms. F., I can tell you that.

You could tell right away that Clearview band class was going to be different. For one thing, the band teacher, Mr. Matthew "Matt-Patt" Pattinson, was kind of a cult figure, not despised but in fact sincerely beloved by the students.

He would jog in every day and yell "How're my Badgers today?!" And the students would whoop and holler and sound off their instruments in between spirited bouts of chanting "Matt-Patt! Matt-Patt!" (As an aside, can I just point out how weird it is that so many Clearview teachers and administrators seemed to think it was part of their job description to run around punching the air and high-fiving everybody? Except Mrs. Pizzaballa—she was the only non–air puncher on the faculty, and I respected her for it.)

Anyway, then Matt-Patt would click his heels, salute, and count off with "Ah one and ah two and . . ." and everyone would launch into "Louie Louie," their standard opening number, and not just play it, but dance and march in place and do their best to mirror Matt-Patt's insane, over-the-top enthusiasm.

I had long ago given up trying to discern any hint of sarcasm, or mockery, or even mild irony in this sort of behavior at Clearview High School: there really wasn't any. These people, as crazy as it seems, really were this into it, and the "it" that they were into, believe it or not, was simply high school. Damnedest thing I ever did see.

There were a few Hillmont refugees in the class besides me, including the rotund yet nice Yasmynne Schmick and Pierre Butterfly Cameroon (though he had renamed himself Peter in an effort to "reinvent" himself for the school switch), plus a normal girl with a pretty nice WHR named Trina de los Santos, as well as a couple of normal guys whose names I refused to know as a matter of principle. Our collective bewilderment was obvious. None of us knew how to go about being in a band class where you were expected to play actual music, all in tune and everything. And not only that, but you were expected to do so with deranged, melodramatic fervor and a straight face. It was easy to read the look in the eyes of the refugees, the decent and the normal alike: a whole semester of this will surely kill us.

On that first day, Roberta the Female Robert, who was also in the class in her capacity as a strangely competent clarinet player, had kept looking over at me encouragingly and also doing these upward nods of her head and clarinet. I'd soon realized what she was getting at, because it wasn't long before Matt-Patt started barking out "Tom, get your horn up" every time he noticed my trombone slide extending at anything less than a ninety-degree angle. Which was all the time. Have you ever tried to hold a trombone all the way up for forty-two minutes? It's simply not possible.

But this became a recurring theme during Band, with Matt-Patt starting off the count by saying things like "One, and two, and Tom, get your horn up. . . ." Not every single time, but often enough to be worrying. Even if it was only Band, it could still endanger my precious status of neutrality and reveal my secret identity if it became a catchphrase that leaked into the general population. I'd had way worse things shouted at me in my career as a socially unsuccessful person, but it was something to be avoided nonetheless. So, much as I hated to let the bad guys win like that, I did what I could to get my horn up, at least a bit, trying to shake the troubling suspicion that it is in small concessions like this that the process of becoming one of them begins.

But the truly alarming thing about Band was only revealed later during that second week, when at the end of class Matt-Patt said the cryptic words "Now, I want you Badgers RTP on the dot at three-thirty" and added something about how the project of kicking St. Keister would involve giving him a hundred and ten percent of something.

"What was that about three-thirty and a dot and kicking St. Keister?" I asked the Female Robert afterward, because it seemed like she, if anyone, would probably know, and because I didn't have anyone else to ask.

"After-school practice" were the dread words she uttered in response. "'RTP' is 'ready to play.' At three-thirty. For our routines for the rallies and the games. So we can help our Badgers to beat the Mission Hills Saints." She gave me the look that says "I don't know how I could possibly make this any clearer." I was feeling faint. I mean, it was starting to look, a bit, like they were going to make us dress in little *Sergeant Pepper's* outfits and march around a football field. But that couldn't be. They wouldn't go that far, surely.

"Not *football*, Thomas," R. the F. R. said, shaking her head when I had murmured words to that effect. "Basketball. Badger Basketball." Football, basketball, what did I care? Either way, it was just a bunch of normal meatheads chasing a ball. I wanted no part of it, and certainly not if it involved staying after school to work on "routines." My time was valuable.

"'Keister' means 'ass,'" she said helpfully. "Anyway, we have to practice. What did you do after school at the other place?"

Well, the answer is, I went home. I listened to records. Or played the guitar, wrote lyrics, watched TV, ate cereal, read books, looked at naked ladies, you know: the building blocks of a life.

So that's what I mean about Clearview discouraging creativity. When was I supposed to write my lyrics about how awful everything was? But perhaps that was the point: prevent all lyrics from being written by filling every available moment with inane activity and everybody will just fall obediently in line. It actually seemed like it could work.

But it didn't seem right that they could force you to stay

161

at school after school was over. I mean, hadn't we already paid our debt to society for the day? But they could, and they would, and as it happened, they did. I was thinking that once my Indictment of the Universe lawsuit was done, there'd certainly be a case for a lawsuit against making you stay after school to do "routines." Now, that's a crime against humanity if I ever saw one.

MY CHARIOT

So that, babies and gentlemen, is how your illustrious narrator found himself in a gym, after hours, trying to play "Louie Louie," "On, Wisconsin!" and "Don't Stop Believin'" on the trombone instead of working on his own actual stuff with his own actual band that played his own actual real songs. He was in a pretty foul mood about it too, let me tell you. They made him stand in the bleachers, point the slide part of his trombone upward, and move it from left to right and back again in time to "streetlights people"; they made him run onto the court in a procedure they called scattering and then dance in place with the trombone held above his head during rests, in a move they called freestyling. To his great relief, he was informed that he would not be required to wear a *Sergeant Pepper's* outfit while engaged in "scattering" and "freestyling." But his relief turned to ashes in his brain upon learning that he would need to purchase a pair of white pants and an orange beret to wear instead.

Poor guy. It's hard not to feel sorry for him. Hey, wait a minute: that's me!

Anyway, you want to hear something really weird? When Badgers talk about the Clearview High School "fight song," what they mean is "On, Wisconsin!" I don't know why; maybe it's that there's a certain Milwaukee-esque-ness to Clearview because it looks like you could have filmed *Happy Days* there. Could you make that up? Could anyone?

In the aftermath of this gruesome episode I was sitting on the steps at the west edge of the front of the school under the overhang trying to work on my lyrics while waiting to be picked up by Little Big Tom—because Clearview is just a little too far to walk to from my house, and it was raining pretty hard—when Roberta the F. R. and this other girl from Band walked up and plopped down cross-legged in front of me. The girl with her was a saxophone named Pam Something. I'd noticed her before because she was not bad-looking, for a band Badger, with a fairly decent WHR and an even better BWR, from what I could tell, though she also had a funny look about her—super smiley but with a distracted eye, like she was seeing disturbing things off in the distance that no one else could see. They were a funny pair, side by side like that, because of their relative sizes, the tiny, spindly Female Robert and the comparatively more substantial Pam Something.

The Make-out/Fake-out sensor in my gut tingled warily, as it always does in the presence of more than one female, but only slightly. It was obvious that these girls meant no harm. So I tamped down the paranoia. What were they up to? Probably an attempt at Badger camaraderie. After all, Badgers need to stick together and give a hundred and ten percent if they're ever to stand a chance of kicking St. Ass clear to the other side of Shrove Tuesday. That said, I couldn't think of one thing to say to them. So I just did a little salute and gave them the look that says: "Ladies."

"See, Thomas?" said R. the F. R. "That wasn't so bad, was it?"

163

"I don't know," I said. "I was only giving about forty-five percent." They both gave me the look that says: "Yeah, we could tell."

There followed some largely incomprehensible conversation between the two of them about basketball and, specifically, about basketball players, that I was no more able and willing to follow at the time than I am a. and w. to summarize it for you now. My brain is immune to varsity talk. It just doesn't penetrate.

"I have a question for you, Thomas," said Pam Something, turning to me.

Was this "Thomas" business some kind of subtle mockery? My wariness-o-meter bumped up an eighth of a tic. But I looked at her with what I hoped was a neutral expression to signal my consent to being interrogated. She was looking off into the distance, though, kind of how my mom does when she's mad at someone, but she didn't look mad. We all waited.

"Oh," said Pam. "Oh. Yes. I was wondering. . . ." She paused again. Then resumed: "Oh. I was wondering what happened to your face?"

I had grown so used to my centipede that I'd almost forgotten that other people could see it. Its legs had mostly dissolved by this time, though there were still a few spots where traces remained, but it was still very much there.

"Tuba wound," I said.

"No, really," said R. the F. R., "what was it really?"

"Really," I said, "somebody hit me in the head with a tuba."

After a quick pause both girls started laughing wildly, their mouths wide open. Now, I knew from my experience with Amanda and her friends that this sort of laughter doesn't always mean that they think something is funny. It can just be a reaction to something being weird and their not knowing what

164

to say about it. It's similar to my own reaction when something is weird and I don't know what to say, except in my version, it mostly involves just sitting there and not saying anything.

"But ... *why?*" said Roberta the F. R., finally, when they had regained control of their faculties.

I considered explaining about Mr. Teone and the Catcher Code and my General Theory of the Universe. But I didn't: it would have taken forever, and I was pretty sure these girls couldn't handle it.

"Long story," I said instead.

Roberta the F. R. was pulling at my notebook because she'd seen me scribbling in it. I had subtly tried to slide it under my trombone case, but not subtly enough, it seemed.

"What are you working on?" she asked, looking at it before I yanked it back from her.

"Just some lyrics," I said as her eyes widened.

"For Pizzaballa?" she said, skeptical. Outside of the reading journal, about which I will say more by and by, Mrs. Pizzaballa's class was well known for consisting only of diagramming sentences and rapid-fire reading and vocabulary tests, no creative writing of any kind assigned or allowed. I explained that it was just something I was doing on my own. Both girls looked incredulous, and I believed I was beginning to catch on here. It seemed that in the weird, school-loving atmosphere of Clearview High, the notion that anyone would do anything at all that wasn't for credit or part of an assignment was more or less unthinkable. What's the point of doing something, they reasoned, in my imaginative dramatization of their probable line of thinking, if you're not graded for doing it or penalized for not doing it? It seemed to me like a vaguely totalitarian state of mind, but freeing the minds of Roberta the F. R. and Pam Something simply wasn't my job, so I let the matter drop.

I did explain that I was in a band, a real band, the sort of band that is not "for credit." I mean, boy, is it ever not for credit. And here I will note, as I have so many times before, the strange, inexplicable power that just saying you're in a band can have when it comes to certain females. It wasn't like they suddenly climbed on top of me or anything, and it also wasn't like that was something I was angling for–though I suppose I wouldn't have minded too much in the case of Pam Something, with all her ratios, weird eyes notwithstanding. Anyway, it wasn't anything that extreme. It was just a slight but notice-able uptick in their interest in me, not much more. The Female Robert leaned in, invading my personal space ever so slightly, and Pam Something, I swear to God, sat back on her hands like she was yawning, pushed out her breasts, and licked her lips, like a kitten. I kid you not. I don't think they even know they're doing it. You say "band" and they get hot. Simple as that. KISS knew it.

It was disconcerting to find, when R. t. F. R. asked what kind of music it was and I said "Rock and roll," that neither of them seemed all that familiar with the term. ("Is that like rock?" said Pam Something. My look said, "Yes, it's a little like rock.") But I explained that we were going to be doing this big Mountain Dew show coming up and that I was working on some songs for it. And I showed them the logo.

"It used to say 'Encyclopedia Satanica,'" I explained. "Then it said 'I Hate This Jar.' But now it says 'Teenage Brainwashers.'"

I think they were more impressed with the Mountain Dew than anything, and I had to concede that it was possible that as powerful as rock and roll may be as an aphrodisiac, adding a lemon-flavored caffeinated beverage seems to make it even more potent. At any rate, the Mountain Dew seal of approval

166

seemed to count heavily in the Teenage Brainwashers' favor with these two. I guess our imaginary Mountain Dew endorsement deal had, in effect, given us "credit" that the Clearview mind could understand.

Roberta the F. R. wanted me to tell her what the song was about, but I deflected that. I mean, talk about a long story.

"You know what I love?" said Pamela Something.

I looked at her, bracing myself for more varsity talk, while Roberta the F. R. said "What?"

"I love how Thomas is all 'yeah, whatever' about pep band when he's actually a pretty good bone."

Now, a "good bone" is a good trombone player in band-speak, but while there's always a possible hint of a sexual meaning in the term, I really couldn't tell if the one here was intended or not. I couldn't tell what was intended with this conversation, period. These girls were an unfamiliar breed of nonnormal semidecent fringe varsity "background," like they were extras for the crowd scenes in a propaganda film that celebrates Sports Normalism. They used to call such people "collaborators" during World War II. I tried not to think too much about Vichy France, however, because even though the system that had earned their misguided support was evil, well, they knew not what they did. And they were pretty nice.

"Well," R. t. F. R. was saying, "you know what *I* love? *I* love how the Hillmont Badgers just don't give a single fuck about anything."

I noticed Pamela Something doing a slight but decidedly Hellermanian wince. She hadn't liked the swearing. You could tell.

"But you know what I really, really love?" continued R. t. F. R. We both looked at her as she grabbed the pen out of my hand and made a motion as if to write something on my notebook cover.

Then she held up the pen and shouted: "This pen!"

Well, I had thoughts that I could express here as comments. But before I could do much thinking about them, Little Big Tom pulled up in his truck, stuck his head out the window at one of his trademark improbable angles, and called:

"Your chariot awaits, my liege."

The girls started doing the don't-know-what-to-say laugh again.

"Gotta go," I said, pretty embarrassed but trying to gather my stuff with a bit of dignity. Little Big Tom means well, no doubt, but a single "Your chariot awaits, my liege" from him can puncture and deflate a person's hard-won rock and roll credibility in seconds flat.

I was trundling my trombone and backpack into the truck's behind-the-seat compartment when Little Big Tom called out once again, this time to the girls, who were still on the steps under the overhang:

"Can we give you two a lift?"

My heart sank as Roberta the Female Robert and Pam Something ran down the muddy slope with their hoods up and their instrument cases banging against their legs.

It took some doing to get into the truck, because there wasn't enough official room for that many people. So Pam Something got the main passenger seat, while I was next to her in the middle, with Roberta the F. R. sitting with her legs splayed, kind of on both our laps.

"A little cozy," said Little Big Tom with a mustache twitch. "But we're all friends here. They call me Big Tom."

"They call her Pam," I said. "And they call her Roberta."

"The Female Robert!" shrieked the Female Robert. There was low-level laughing almost all the way to whomever's house we dropped them off at, up on Santa Carolina Pine Road Terrace, not too far from Hellerman Manor.

It was an awkward position. I didn't know where to put my hands, though there were lots of interesting possibilities available. And I don't know if I've happened to mention it before, but I am always at least a little bit horny. So a couple of girls practically sitting on me, even if their ratios wouldn't necessarily get the best grade in the Sam Hellerman ranking system, and even with Little Big Tom sitting right there next to me—well, let's just say, I'd be kind of surprised if R. t. F. R., at least, wasn't able to gauge with pretty good accuracy the precise level to which my horniness had elected to express itself underneath my embroidered golden jeans penis, if you see what I'm trying to get across. I just had to hope the laughing wasn't directed at me or, God help us, at *that*, but you really couldn't tell. Ever.

The girls got out of the truck and retrieved their instruments.

"See you in the band room," said Pam S. before they scampered off.

"I'll be the one wearing the yellow carnation," I said, and I was relieved when they laughed. But then, just to make sure, I asked why that was funny.

"That's a flower, right?" said Pam S.

I sighed. The carnation joke was dead.

As they were leaving, R. t. F. R. had slid a note, a thickly folded little envelope of notepaper, in my front pocket. When girls give you notes, it's always at the last possible second before they rush off, have you ever noticed that? Like you're an unpredictable device and they don't want to be in the vicinity when you read them, just in case of . . . something? Well, to me that seems precisely backwards: I'm a thoroughly predictable device, as I've outlined above.

"Spreading it around, I see," said Little Big Tom. "The little one, the female . . . robot?" He raised an eyebrow. "I think she likes you."

But that is a conversation I was just not going to have with Little Big Tom. As for the note, well, I don't know what to say about it. I mean, it pretty much had to be seen to be believed.

GODZILLA VS. DEODORANT

"The thing I don't understand," Amanda was saying while we were trying to choke down some of Little Big Tom's vegan slop, "is that you *love* the eighties. Aren't you always saying everything sucks now and it was way better back in the good old days before CDs and solid transvestites and the alligator snares?"

She was responding to my complaints about Clearview High School and its strange existence as an alternate *Grease* sound track/fifties dimension, symbolized by the jackets. She was a little confused, though: to her, anything more than a few years old was "eighties," and she had evidently absorbed my complaints about solid-state transistors and the awful gated reverb sound of eighties snare drums.

"The *music*," I said. "The rock and roll of the fifties was great, obviously. I'm not complaining about that." Of course the music was great. And the movies and books, too. And the less content-free educational system and the less advanced, less brutal Normalism. And the cars. And, like, bathing beauties or whatever. And *Brown v. Board of Education,* that was pretty cool. The hats weren't too bad. But *not* the jackets and the school spirit and all that stuff.

But I suppose Amanda had a point, in a way. Because maybe you couldn't have had rock and roll in the first place if you didn't have all that as the background: you know, all that "Gee whiz, we're going steady at the soda fountain, Potsie" and "Well, golly, Peggy Ann, our team is just swell this year, I really hope you can come to the game and watch me score the winning points." There could even be, possibly, a connection between the non-sucky educational system they used to have, the one that actually taught you stuff, and the weird school spirit society that contained it, though if so, Clearview had managed to retain or re-create the second with no noticeable effect on the absence of the first.

But those battles had been fought long ago, and I didn't see why we had to relive them. You can appreciate the music without taking it literally. For example, digging the Beach Boys without necessarily being true to your school is totally possible, and preferable. Basically, Sam Phillips recorded Bill Haley, Johnny Cash, and all those other Memphis guys; Chuck Berry played the top two strings; Elvis appeared on *The Ed Sullivan Show* above the waist; the Beatles made all the girls squirm by singing about wanting to hold their "hands"; Ray Davies got lost in a sunset; Pete Townshend smashed his guitar; Brian Wilson heard magic in his head and made it come out of a studio; the Rolling Stones urinated on a garage door; and then (skipping a bit) you've got Joey Levine and Chapman-Chinn and Mott the Hoople and Iggy and the Runaways and KISS and the Pink Fairies and Rick Nielsen and Jonathan Richman and Johnny Ramone and Lemmy and the Young brothers and Cook and Jones and Pete Shelley and Feargal Sharkey and Rob

Halford ... and Foghat. You get what I'm saying. It didn't happen in a vacuum, but it did happen, and now here we are in the aftermath. I see no need to try to re-create the conditions that made it necessary to invent rock and roll in the first place, and I certainly see no earthly reason why we should have to go to school in those conditions. Our forefathers fought and died so we wouldn't have to, is kind of how I thought about it.

But Amanda had finished her slop and was on her way out before I could get much of this across. At least I believe I managed to explain that the eighties were not the fifties. I mean, I couldn't have her going around saying I liked the eighties. The eighties were crap, a terrible time to be alive, as far as I could tell.

"Don't you want to watch *Revenge of the Nerds* with me?" I called out, because I'd checked it out of the library, along with a few other materials, as part of my quest to understand Clearview High School a little better and to be able to spot the dangerous normal people with greater accuracy. Amanda's empty chair was an eloquent answer. She had been sitting next to me and conversing, it's true, but mainly, as it turned out, she was only in it for the slop.

"Great slop ... chief," I said, turning to Little Big Tom, but before he could respond, my mom had drifted in and he did a kind of insta-fade into the background, resuming the walking-on-eggshells posture he had developed in the face of the recent marital strife at 507 Cedarview Circle, Hillmont, CA 94033.

My mom was wearing a big, fuzzy, black and purple striped sweater that came halfway down to her knees, with a shiny belt of enormous sequins around her waist and a–was it a cape? Yeah, it was a kind of cape, nearly floor-length and made of some dark velvetlike fabric, thrown back around her shoulders and secured at her throat with the biggest sequin of them all. She was Super Mom. Or a wicked queen.

She stood before me, balanced her cigarette on the edge of the table, and took my hands in hers.

"Baby," she said, after a lengthy pause during which she looked into my eyes with unnerving earnestness. "Tom told me about today, and I just want you to know, I am . . . we are . . . so, *so* proud of you. I know you've had a tough time at the new school, but it's just so nice that you've been able to make some . . . normal friends, nice, normal friends at last. . . ."

Oh, for God's sake. You'd think a lifetime of embarrassing parental moments would exhaust your embarrassment capacity at some point, but if so, it was a point I hadn't yet reached. I was conscious of a hot sensation in my face, and my centipede began to twitch up a storm. Why does talking about girls out loud in the presence of parents make you so embarrassed? And these weren't even particularly noteworthy ones, just some girls from "pep band" who randomly happened to get pulled in by Little Big Tom's largely indiscriminate tractor beam. But you can't help your physical reactions, inconvenient as they may be. Your physical reactions just happen, like in the truck with Little Big Tom and . . . Oh, God.

I felt, somehow, that it was expected that I say a few words, a kind of acceptance speech, so I said:

"I don't know." And added, with my eyes, "This is indeed a great day for us all."

My mom made it clear that if I needed anything in order to cultivate and nurture these tender shoots of a budding, non-unacceptable social life, I had only to ask. This was a little bit different than the standard spiel that goes: "I'm surprised to learn that you're not gay, though if you were gay, I'd be totally pleased and into it that you are, no judgments here." Partly, it was directed against Sam Hellerman, who they both thought was a bit of an odd duck, if I have that expression right. (They're not wrong about that, I concede, but still, I must ask, what business is it of theirs what kind of duck Sam Hellerman is? Oh yeah, it's not their business at all.)

Sam Hellerman aside, though, I guess Little Big Tom's report to my mom had left the impression that here could be seen my first dainty steps into normalcy, a prospect that pleased her for some reason. But seriously, if my mom, as currently constituted, were reverse-aged to fifteen years old and tossed into a tank fully stocked with normal people, what did she think would happen? The tank's waters would churn red with her blood within a few seconds, that's what. They'd make short work of Little Big Tom as well. I felt like shouting at them: "Hey! Parental units. Don't you get it? *You're not normal!*" I wouldn't wish the shark tank of Normalcy on them, no matter how irritating they may be, and it was pretty galling that a stint in that tank was their fondest wish for me.

In other words, my parents' sense of normalcy was in desperate need of recalibration. Pam Something and the Female Robot (to use Little Big Tom's memorably mistaken term) might not have matched Sam Hellerman's abnormality, it's true—who could?—but no one would describe them as normal, though Pam S. could maybe pass for near normal with a bit of a makeover. It was a stretch, though, is what I'm saying.

But Little Big Tom wasn't done with me yet. After my mom had said "Night, puppy" and drifted off with a heavy emission of exhaust and a bit of a shoulder squeeze, he zoomed in and took his place in the chair formerly occupied by my sister.

"Revenge of the Nerds," he said, riffling through my library

materials. "Good flick. Not quite reality, though, is it?" Well, I thought, you tell me. I'd assumed not, until I'd darkened Clearview High's doorstep, but now, as I've explained, I wasn't so sure.

"You know, sport," he continued, "I think you just might find that the modern age does have something to offer, if you know where, and *how,* to look." He scooted his chair toward me, getting dangerously close to unsolicited back rub proximity, and as his voice was taking on that therapy tone, I thought it prudent to scoot my chair away from him just as quickly. He had evidently heard my conversation with Amanda and had some wisdom to impart about not living in the past, hanging on to your dreams, and having an open mind but only about certain prearranged topics.

"If you keep an open mind, you just might find that you have more in common with people than you think." Unable to execute any massage plans he may have had, Little Big Tom resorted instead to a rather gruesome wink. "And it never hurts to try a new thing every now and then. I think you'll find the results could surprise you."

I suppose what he was getting at was that maybe, if I were to change my whole personality and replace everything I like and am interested in with stuff that other people like and are interested in, well, then my life would be this wonderful picnic where I had lots in common with everyone and we would all skip merrily down the lane hand in hand. But what if I didn't want to change my whole personality? Not that I liked it all that much, but at least it was mine. Inconvenient as it was at times, I kind of wanted to keep it. And to be honest, skipping merrily down the lane never held much appeal for me anyway.

"I just prefer Godzilla to deodorant," I said.

Now, I meant this as a cryptic conversation ender. There

was no way Little Big Tom would have any clue what I meant by it, so what could he say in response? But I might as well explain it here.

See, okay: there was once this guy named Kurt who was in this really big popular rock band. A ways back he blew his head off with a shotgun, and it was really sad and everything, et cetera, et cetera. So his band's big hit song was basically Blue Öyster Cult's "Godzilla" with the lyrics replaced by this semicoherent, artsy drug poetry about deodorant. Now, it was a fine enough song, and believe me, miles and miles better than most of the other garbage that was popular at that time. Still, I mean, you've got to say, when it's Godzilla vs. deodorant, Godzilla wins, right? Why would I deliberately choose to play the deodorant guy's version, when there's Blue Öyster Cult sitting right there on the turntable? The question answers itself. (Though it occurs to me now that it's possible that the deodorant band might have been using a similar technique on its drummer that we were using on Shinefield, pretending they were playing "Godzilla" till the last second to trick him into playing a steady beat. If so, I'll say this for them: it seems to have worked. Well done, guys.)

Or there's this other big group that is pretty much dedicated to rearranging Beatles recordings into their own "new" songs. Again, it's orders of magnitude better than most of what's popular. Still, if I want the Beatles, first I go to the Beatles; then I go to all the legitimate Beatles imitators of the sixties and seventies; then I might sing "I Am the Walrus" in the shower or put on a Cheap Trick record or something. Only then, having exhausted all the other possibilities, would I resort to last year's fake Beatles. The same can be said for all those fake punk bands with suburban guys whining about how hard it is to find a girlfriend. I mean, I get it, and I can obviously relate, and I wish them all the luck in the world. I might even choose to listen to them now and again. But not when I have SA-7528, UAG 30159, SRK 6081, or SEEZ 1 on hand. Would you?

And that's just the good stuff: the music most normal people like is simply beyond redemption, or comprehension. If you like that sort of thing, you deserve each other.

Anyway, Little Big Tom just gave me the old sympathetic yet taken aback "get a load of my oddball stepson" look and rumpled my hair. In other words, it worked as planned.

"How's the song coming?" he asked, meaning how was I doing in my attempt to learn how to fingerpick the song about the Irish guy and the hula girl.

"'O'Brien Is Tryin' to Learn to Talk Hawaiian'?" I said. "Okay."

Actually, it was going terrible. Even though I grasped the concept (your thumb has to do alternating bass notes with runs back and forth, while your other fingers "roll" in the spaces and play notes and partial chords), I couldn't make it happen, no matter how hard I tried. My right hand was made for hitting, not plucking, and it didn't look like I'd ever be able to instruct it to make the h. to p. transition. The Chet Atkins book I'd checked out of the library only made things worse by spelling out and comprehensively cataloguing all the things I would never have a prayer of doing. What guitar playing ability I did have seemed to erode with each page.

Perhaps sensing the frustration behind the word "okay" despite my efforts to mask it, Little Big Tom had one more bit of wisdom to impart.

"I think you'll find," he said, with lips slightly pursed, "that if you keep at it, there will be one moment where you suddenly realize you're doing it without even thinking. That's how it works in the old brain box." Then he added, with a thumbs-up, a nod, and that little clicking sound he makes with his tongue on his upper molars: "The human head: check it out."

Well, that exhausted my daily ration of patience for hearing about things that Little Big Tom thought I would "find," so I saluted him and sauntered off with my research materials. I was still embarrassed from before, and my centipede was still twitching, and I ached for Fiona, and I was still mystified and futilely angry about the whole jacket thing, and I still knew in my heart of hearts that I'd never, ever be able to play "O'Brien Is Tryin' to Learn to Talk Hawaiian"–but I had avoided an unsolicited back rub, and that's what really matters.

I had a lot to think about, that's for sure. I headed upstairs to take a long, soothing shower and get my thoughts together. I do a lot of my best thinking in the shower. And by thinking, I mean masturbation.

BOOK READER

Now, Little Big Tom had said, or rather mimed, that *Pride and Prejudice* was "brutal," and I knew what he meant, but in the end, I found I didn't quite agree. I mean, I could not be less interested in the trials and tribulations of silly families trying to marry off their silly daughters to silly rich guys in silly olde England. But once you got used to their strange way of talking, it was actually pretty funny in places, like the author was kind of subtly making fun of the characters and their weird, awkward, money-grubbing world. Most of all, though, there was something impressive and, I don't know, satisfying about how the sentences would go off in all sorts of different directions and then manage to land everything safely and with a kind of unexpected neatness right at the end. This chick was a good writer, better than a truckload of Pynchons and Salingers. If only she hadn't chosen such a lame subject. If she had written about, say, spies, or juvenile delinquents, or ghosts, or hobbits, or space worms, or even about paranoid druggies who think garbage cans are mailboxes, there'd have been no stopping her.

Seeing my dad through this book's eyes, or even imagining he had read it, wasn't happening, obviously. I didn't even try. This definitely put the book in the second tier as far as I was concerned, but you know: they can't all be *Brighton Rock*.

So yeah, not my thing, really, except for the sentences. But as I've said, females seem to like it a lot, as I learned when the book fell out of my backpack during lunch on the Quad with the "pep band" people, and the girls around who saw it kind of shrieked and started mumbling "Mr. Darcy, Mr. Darcy," like they couldn't help themselves. That's what they always do when this book is mentioned. Try mentioning it around some girls sometime and see. (Mr. Darcy is the name of the ten-thousand-a-year rich guy who's kind of a dick.)

"Why are you reading *that*?" said this near-normal girl named (kidding you not) Blossom van Kinkle, in an accusing yet mildly amused tone. That was unfortunate, as she was probably the second- or third-hottest girl in the "pep band," and truth be told, I'd been hoping I could, somehow, take advantage of my current neutral status and apply the secrets of women revealed in such a way as to induce her to enter into a ramoning-type situation with me. I could feel my precious neutral status, and any chance at ramoning anyone, draining away rapidly as it began to dawn on all in the vicinity, band people though they were, that I was some kind of book reader.

This was not good, the most King Dork moment I'd had since my time at Clearview began.

I guess it's a pretty unusual book for a guy to read, but it's unusual for a guy to read any book at all. You can get away with doing it, but not if you look like you're enjoying it too much: that enrages normal people like almost nothing else. Openly flaunting enjoyment of a book at Hillmont High would mark you as a target for an immediate game of involuntary "smear the queer" with the book as the "ball" and a subsequent lifetime of extra physical and psychological abuse. True, I have used books to shut out the world and deter human interaction, but in a high school environment this tactic must be used sparingly. If word gets out, rest assured, they will hunt you down. Then you can kiss your book, and possibly your very ass, goodbye. I had been careful to conceal my book-reading habit as much as I could at Hillmont, but I suppose the relatively lax atmosphere of Clearview had made me sloppy.

They were staring at me. I didn't know what to say.

It could have been ugly. But in the end I was saved by the Robot.

"Oh, it must be for Pizzaballa's list," she said, and I believe I noticed her wink at me, though I could have been imagining it.

There were sympathetic groans and all was suddenly back to the way it had been before. Mrs. Pizzaballa's "reading journal" list was notorious, evidently, and all appeared to have been forgiven in the wave of empathy caused by the very thought of it. Blossom van Kinkle was even smiling at me now, which I'd never noticed her doing before. Thanks, Jane. I owe you one.

Sam Hellerman would have advised, I'm sure, remaining aloof from Blossom van Kinkle, but remaining aloof on purpose just ain't my bag, baby.

"I play guitar," I said. "In a band." "And," my eyes added, "I should deem it an honour propitiously fulfilled indeed were my esteem to meet with reciprocation in your tender, discerning heart."

180

And I couldn't be sure, but I believe those words kindled a little extra light in Blossom van Kinkle's delicate amber eyes. At least, she didn't turn away or spit on me or anything, which was good, and she wasn't all the way across the street like Jeans Skirt Girl either, which was even better.

I mentioned Mrs. Pizzaballa's list already, that big handout she distributed on the first day of class. It turned out to be more than a simple reading list, as I'd initially assumed. It was instead an annotated list of what seemed like just about every school-approved book there was, with a little paragraph describing each one and a score from one to ten on each as well, representing how important or difficult Mrs. Pizzaballa thought it was. The assignment was to select and read a given book and write a brief review or comment in your "book-reading journal," which she would collect and grade at the end of each week, giving you some portion of the book's total points, depending on how much she liked your review. The problem with the whole thing, and the reason for all the groans from the "pep band" people when the Robot mentioned it, was that she was a very harsh grader if she didn't like what you wrote, and to pass her class you needed to have accumulated at least 100 points by the end of the term. A few weeks and eleven "reviews" in, I had a grand total of zero points. I had no idea what she wanted, but it wasn't the usual three sentences about how Holden Caulfield was the voice of a generation and a genuine authentic personality that exploded off the page fully formed just waiting for you to worship him.

"Passing a class" at Hillmont had been a mere formality requiring no particular effort, but they seemed to take it a bit more seriously here, so I wasn't sure what to do, or what would happen if I kept getting zeros.

After that first week of zeros, I'd stayed after the piano-bell and asked Mrs. Pizzaballa for a little clarity as to what she expected in a book-reading journal review.

"The worms crawl in," she replied. "The worms crawl out. The worms play pinochle on your snout."

That was, of course, absolutely no help. But I was glad she said it nonetheless. Applying any attention at all to schoolwork was unfamiliar territory for me, but here was a puzzle, a question for the ages: what did Pizzaballa want? I began to set about the business of racking my brain for an answer. Perhaps, I thought, there's something important about books that school could teach me after all, and Mrs. Pizzaballa's methods, unorthodox as they are, will ultimately lead me there. Perhaps I will look back on this time as the moment when literature came alive for me, thanks to the teacher who made a difference. I sincerely doubted it, but, you know, it was a thought nevertheless.

But if you've noted how petty, how superficial, how downright *minor* this is as a high school worry, well, you're not wrong. Because by and large, Clearview High was a cakewalk. Sure, maybe you'll have a tough time figuring out what a given teacher wants, and you certainly have to endure an atmosphere thick with noxious "school spirit" jacket-varsity fumes, and perhaps having to pretend to be something you're not each and every day will eventually take its psychological toll. But it's hard to describe what it feels like just to sit on the grass at lunch without having to brace yourself for a savage, life-threatening attack. I had a circle of sort-of friends to eat lunch with, including a few I could almost say I genuinely liked, and I didn't have to worry about any of them ever trying to kill me. Which, frankly, was more than I could say for Sam Hellerman with complete confidence. The normal people at Clearview were comparative pussycats. Even PE wasn't too bad, and I'm not even exaggerating all that much.

I could get used to this, I thought, though thinking that made me hate myself a little. I was maybe halfway used to it already, if truth be told.

SCIENCE BE DAMNED

The sudden absence of Celeste Fletcher from her former spot in the red beanbag in Shinefield's basement during our band practices was a source of unspoken tension. At our second practice without her, Shinefield finally ventured to break the silence and ask me about her.

"Chi-Mo, my man," he said, because he said things like "my man" and Chi-Mo was one of my old nicknames, as you'll know if you are acquainted with my previous explanations. "What's the deal with Celeste?" According to Shinefield, he had seen her only once since the semester had begun and hardly talked to her at all; most of his many calls to her had gone unanswered. When he had reached her, she had informed him that she was busy with school and had a lot going on in her life, and when he'd pressed her on the matter, she'd told him not to flatter himself and that she needed space.

"Do you think she's messing around with some other guy?" he asked plaintively.

Well, Einstein, I thought, what do you *think* it means when a girl says she "needs space"? God, these math geniuses can be dumb. I was in a bit of a quandary, if a quandary is what I think it is. On the one hand, I did have information that Shinefield wanted, perhaps needed, and I was, technically, his sort-of friend. But on the other hand, we were engaged in a delicate experiment in drum conditioning in which he was the subject, and I didn't want to introduce data that could complicate the results. This was a matter of Science. But now you have to imagine that I have another hand growing out of my forehead, say, or perhaps we could just use one of my centipede's feet, because on the third hand, I was pretty pissed off at Fiona all on my own, so in the end I said "Science be damned" and threw caution to the wind.

"Science be damned," I said, to Shinefield's puzzlement, though Sam Hellerman had seemed to follow my train of thought and twitched warningly. I plunged in, however, and told Shinefield about Todd Dante and the jacket.

"Jesus," said Shinefield, powerfully affected, and if I was reading his face correctly, his expression said something like: "A 'letterman' jacket? Seriously? What kind of terrible *Bye Bye Birdie/Grease* sound track/*Happy Days/Revenge of the Nerds/ Leave It to Beaver* place are they running over there?"

These were good questions. Shinefield was looking wounded.

"Radio silence," said Sam Hellerman, out of the blue, sparking yet more puzzlement, this time from both of us.

He went on: "That's the only possible way to salvage a relationship with a girl who says she needs space." He said he was serious: no calls, no messages, no contact whatsoever. Give her time to figure out that she misses you and make her wonder what you're up to. Then, he continued, when the thing with the jacket guy crashes and burns—which it will—and she's feeling sad and vulnerable just like you are right now, wait for her to come to you begging for comfort, reassurance, and attention, which she probably will. "At that point," he concluded, "it's up to you how to proceed. But if you have another girlfriend when it happens, and you manage to leave the impression that you like the new one more, you'll basically have her for life. If you still want her."

It was the tapes talking. But Sam Hellerman, to one's surprise, sounded like he made a lot of sense, and both Shinefield and I stared at him in a kind of wonderment. Because that was pretty fucking Machiavellian, we were thinking. And to see and hear such Machiavellianisms emerging from the mouth of the slight, bespectacled, cell-phone-holstered, eminently socially unsuccessful Sam Hellerman, well, it was a curious and arresting experience, to say the least. Remain aloof, the tapes said. It was inexpressibly dumb with regard to Jeans Skirt Girl and Sam Hellerman, but with Celeste Fletcher and Shinefield, it seemed to have a bit more oomph.

The thing about Celeste Fletcher was that she had seen the lay of the land, so to speak, at Clearview: she had realized that for her, there was no real downside to going full-on normal in this environment. As I've said, she had always flirted with normalcy, ever since I'd known her, though she had kept her options open, through her involvement with the subnormal Hillmont drama-hippies and not least through her association with me, Sam Hellerman, and Shinefield. That was a dangerous game, but she could get away with it because, well, mostly because of her ass, let's be honest; if you're a girl and you're sexy enough, you really don't have that much to fear from normal people, even when they're the extreme variety of normal featured at Hillmont High School. To the degree that the shifting sands of her personal philosophy could be interpreted on the basis of her choice of guy-she-mainly-hangs-out-with, Shinefield had been a good choice for the circumstances. He was normal enough not to arouse the senseless anger and resentment of the normal establishment, but not normal enough to threaten or frighten off any of her less-than-normal associates. But things change, and at Clearview High, boy, did they ever.

As far as I could tell, status at Clearview, as elsewhere, was pretty straightforward for girls: basically, it was based one hundred percent on looks. If you arranged them all in a line, the prettiest ones at the top, progressing downward from there—maybe aided by some of Sam Hellerman's metrics—you'd have a fairly clear picture of where any given girl stood, status-wise. There were cutoffs, obviously, a line dividing the normal girls from the subnormal, and another one dividing the subnormal from the abnormal. It was those lines that were hard for a non-native Clearviewian like me to draw.

Occasionally, it's true, a given girl could move beyond her station, by being especially mean, or loud, or funny, or by sucking up to the higher-ranked girls. But there was a limit, and such upgrades in status were usually no more than temporary. It was kind of like you were on probation: one false move and back down the ladder you went. I'd add that trying to be attractive to boys seemed to be only a tiny part of this system. Many of the most important markers of "prettiness" go largely unnoticed by any guy, and some of them are actually actively disliked (flip-flops, the pulled-back hairstyles, and some of the more substantial clothes, for example). Of course, "getting guys" was part of it, but only a part of a bigger game the girls seemed to play largely among themselves. The worst thing a normal girl can say about another is "She's not even that pretty."

For guys at Clearview, status seemed to be mostly a matter of size, though as at Hillmont, being especially cruel or dumb could raise your stock considerably in the eyes of the normal masses. Behavior mattered, much more than it did for girls. Being cool, funny, or especially mean or violent could bump your stats way up. So could having a nice car, or, a car. If you ranked them by size, however, you'd still get a broadly accurate picture of where everyone stood, though you'd have to filter out the fat guys and some of the freakishly tall, beanpole-geek types, obviously. Not too different from Hillmont, in other words, with this difference: pretty much every dude above the normalcy cutoff was some kind of sports guy, and the entire student body, all the way down the scale, was solidly in favor of them. Hillmont High, as an institution, if it stood for anything, stood for raw, naked, senseless brutality; at Clearview you had a more refined version, a kind of institutional sports cruelty, supported by everyone, even its victims, with improbable, unfathomable enthusiasm. I mean, look at the Female Robot: what did a girl like that, well outside the main scale of normalcy, possibly think she could achieve with her embrace of a status quo that sought only to demean and marginalize her? I would never get that.

Celeste Fletcher, on the other hand, had a lot to work with. All she had had to do, evidently, was to signal her willingness to join the system by securing the jacket of one of the larger boys and then just waltz right into her place near the top. Even Shinefield couldn't cut it up there, much less Sam Hellerman or I.

In any case, I needn't have worried about Todd Dante's jacket having a damaging effect on the Phil Rudd experiment. Quite the contrary. Shinefield, thinking of Celeste Fletcher and the jacket, had never hit the snare harder or more solidly. And it was ironic, and, I felt, rather poignant that unbeknownst to him, the song he was playing with such decisiveness was in fact about Celeste Fletcher, in her guise as the sexy, imaginary fake-mod girl Fiona. It gave the song a whole new energy.

"I don't get it, though, Hellerman," I said, when we were on our own afterward. And what I meant was, it was kind of strange how he was doling out Machiavellian advice on the best way for Shinefield to win back the affections of a girl he himself, it seemed, still had the hots for. I kind of felt that way myself. If it worked out as Sam Hellerman predicted it would, and that seemed possible if not probable, I wasn't sure I felt all that warmly about the idea of Shinefield "having" Fiona "for life" if he "still wanted her."

"Oh, don't worry," said Sam Hellerman. "He'll never actually manage to do it. Hardly anyone can."

DOWN WITH THE UNIVERSE

It turned out that Sam Hellerman already had a fully formed position on *Pride and Prejudice,* almost even before I brought the subject up. Of course females perceive it as a romantic story, he said, because that's what they think they're supposed to like and what they feel good about liking, but what they're really responding to, on an unconscious level, is the money. Nothing has changed since the days of Greedie Olde Englande: females still seek the highest-status males, and money equals status, and always will. But since mating is largely a mechanical process based on behavioral cues and smell, a little knowledge can turn this state of affairs to your advantage. If you mimic the conduct and attitude of a wealthy or powerful person, even if you're not wealthy or powerful yourself, women will find themselves drawn to you without quite knowing why because they're programmed to respond to those cues. Also, it helps if you smell a little funky. (Well, there was one mystery solved, anyhow: the Case of Sam Hellerman and the Increasingly Infrequent Showers.)

"That's why they find just being in a band to be such a turn-on," he added. Because on some unconscious level guys in bands remind them of real rock stars who are rich and culturally powerful, and their bodies respond accordingly without their even being aware of it.

But, I objected, if that were true, we could just as easily get girls by mimicking smelly computer programmers or unusually aromatic investment bankers.

His response startled me.

"I don't know, Henderson," it ran. "Have you ever worn a suit and tie to school? You'd be surprised at the response."

"You're not seriously trying to tell me," my look said, "that you wear a suit to school?"

I could almost picture it, in fact. But being a suit wearer was even worse than being a book reader, or it seemed like it would be. I mean, I'd never actually seen it done before. Sam Hellerman's only response was to give me the look that says "I have so much to teach you, little lamb." You know the one I mean.

I still felt that the principle of Survival of the Cruelest and Dumbest offered a better explanation for who wanted to mate with whom in this stupid universe of ours, but Sam Hellerman delivered his analysis with such offhand confidence that it was hard not to be swayed by it at least a little. It was exactly how someone who actually knew what he was talking about might speak about the thing he knew about, and I suppose the fact that it worked on me to some small degree on that basis alone was a kind of confirmation of the general point he was making, though just speaking for myself, the smell wasn't helping in any way.

When defeated by "O'Brien Is Trying to Learn to Talk Hawaiian," I would usually shift to working on my own stuff, and it was around this time, after a particularly finger-busting "O'Brien" session, that I began to come up with a tune I thought showed a bit of promise. It went:

> *I hate reality*
> *I hate normality*
> *There's really nothing worse:*
> *Down with the universe. . . .*

My mom, fulfilling the Little Big Tom role in a surprise, unbilled cameo, heard me singing the chorus and materialized in my bedroom doorway, nodding.

"I like it," she said, expelling a lungful of exhaust in an admiring manner. "Oh, Tom, baby, that's really, really beautiful."

I couldn't think what she was getting at, as this was not her sarcastic voice.

"People forget that the universe is what connects us all," she continued, making it clearer. "We're all part of it, so we better be good to each other if we want our planet to survive. I'm down with the universe too, so . . ."

She kissed me on the forehead and retreated, a barely perceptible, decidedly atypical spring in her step. Because of course, there's another sense of saying "down with" something that means almost the opposite of the other meaning. My mom speaks so infrequently that it's easy to forget sometimes that she's such a hippie, and also, evidently, a bit more "street" than I'd ever have given her credit for.

I was glad I was able to cheer her up, however slightly and under whatever false pretenses, but it did make me wonder if, to avoid confusion, I should change the title, which I was reluctant to do.

Not that "Death to the Universe" didn't have a nice ring to it.

SPACE: THE FINAL FRONTIER

"That's a nice-looking boy," Amanda would say, each time one of the "nerds" in *Revenge of the Nerds* came on-screen. Basically, you could tell them by their glasses; by their calm, if often bizarre, demeanor; by their intelligence; by their bumbling behavior in social situations; and by the hatred of them that lurked in the hearts of society at large. So that part was true-to-life enough. Sam Hellerman and I have most of that. Still, it hadn't taken long for "that's a nice-looking boy" to get on my nerves. Their snorting laughs were annoying too, and had no basis in reality as far as my experience goes, but these laughs were made even more annoying by the fact that Amanda quickly figured out the snort-laugh technique and kept doing it along with them, looking at me meaningfully.

"Stop being so normal," I said, but she gave me the look that says "This shall I never do" and hit me with a couch cushion.

The nerds in the movie were basically your usual collection of misfits with the misfit characteristics exaggerated and played up for laughs, but it wasn't too hard to see me and Sam Hellerman in there somewhere. The normal people were the "jocks," represented by this football fraternity, along with their pretty but mean girlfriends: again, it was exaggerated, but nevertheless not all that far from the Clearview High reality.

And they had the jackets. What was missing was any depiction of the neutral population, much larger at Clearview than it had been at Hillmont: that is, the people who hadn't yet been sorted into their respective normal and victim piles, who walked among the normal in a state of limbo waiting to be identified by squawking, finger-pointing normal zombies. Like me, so far.

The worst thing about the movie, though, is that it could well have been written by Dr. Elizabeth Gary. The "nerds" and other misfits all seemed to come precounseled and prebrainwashed: their response to their own abuse and torture was simply to try as hard as they could to "beat them at their own game," which meant, in essence, participating in the normal people's ludicrous institutions and activities and trying to "win." And what winning meant was "fitting in." In other words, losing. At one point one of the nerds said they should just blow up the football guys' house in retaliation for some gross indignity. That was rejected in the script by the fitter-inners, but in my opinion, it would have made for a far better, more satisfying film. In fact, as I watched it, I imagined this better ending in my head, and much like thinking "Fiona" while outwardly playing "Live Wire," it kind of worked.

Now, unless you count the recent family awards ceremony for being seen with two girls who appeared to be slightly less eccentric than Sam Hellerman, there hadn't been a good, full-blown classic Henderson-Tucci family discussion in quite some time.

I mean, there was the time when Little Big Tom found the Jerusalem Bible I had checked out of the library (to help research a quote related to the Catcher Code) and got all worried that I was turning into a dangerous religious nut.

"We just feel," he had said, with my mom nodding beside him, "that this kind of . . . material is not such a good influence on your sister." And, he'd added, if I felt the need for spiritual fulfillment there were lots of other, less damaging self-help options available, like yoga, the Landmark Forum, or this great book called *Jonathan Livingston Seagull.*

"I've known a lot of guys," he had said, "who fell into the Jesus thing because they were lost in their lives. You may think Christ is the answer, but it's a heavy trip. A *very* heavy trip." He managed to leave the impression, with his frowning eyes and face, that this was a "trip" that didn't tend to turn out so well.

I was able to promise him that I had no intention of taking such a "trip," no matter how bad things got.

"I have found everything I require," I said, "in Satanism," deftly managing to reassure him in the least reassuring way possible. I'm still pretty proud of that one.

And then there was the time, briefly alluded to earlier, when they wanted to let me know that if I was gay, it was totally okay and they would love me and respect me and my choices because it's who you are inside that matters; but if I did happen to be gay, just for the sake of argument, it would be most convenient for them if I would "come out" before their couples retreat the following month, because there were resources available and they knew several couples in a similar situation with whom it might be useful to compare notes about effective strategies for making me feel accepted, boosting my self-esteem, and helping me deal with the terrible but unfortunately very real social opprobrium, if "opprobrium" means what I'm pretty sure it means.

Anyway, if you think I didn't respond to that one by saying "Thanks, but I have found everything I require in Satanism," well, you don't know me as well as you probably thought you did.

So yeah, as you can imagine, we were due for a family discussion. And as it happens, when it came, it came during *Revenge of the Nerds.*

I heard my mom come in through the back door while *Revenge of the Nerds* played on. I heard her lighting a cigarette on the stove, and then I heard the first heavy exhalation of smoke, always the loudest one, it seems. Then I heard the characteristic sounds of my mom fixing a drink in the kitchen, and then the clink of her ice moving closer and closer down the hallway till we could see her standing in the living room doorway, with Little Big Tom bringing up the rear, as the saying goes, looking grim and serious.

"I think the nerds can wait," said Little Big Tom, taking up the remote and pressing pause. And fortunately or unfortunately, depending on how you look at it, the frozen frame he had happened to stop on was a close-up of one of the naked sorority girls in one of the hidden spy-cam scenes. Moreover, fortunately or unfortunately, Little Big Tom just happened to lean back, half sitting on the TV, little realizing that between his splayed legs, just under his embroidered golden jeans penis, could be seen a picture of a blonde kind of cupping her slightly weird-looking, though still inherently interesting, naked breasts.

Amanda and I looked at one another. It was distracting, to say the least.

My mom took a drag on her cigarette and clinked her ice, signaling to Little Big Tom to get on with it.

"Now," said Little Big Tom. "Now ..." It was the therapy voice but with a little something extra, something that reminded me of something. "The first thing," he continued, "that we want you to understand is that none of this is your fault."

Amanda's hand gripped my forearm excitedly. There was suddenly not much suspense over where this was going.

"Your mom and I care about you both very much." His voice sounded strained and frayed, almost breaking just a little. The thing it reminded me of was Shinefield's voice when telling me about Celeste Fletcher's final phone call to him. Amanda's hand clenched tighter. "And that is never going to change, no matter what happens. I will always—"

Now, it was at this point that the naked sorority girl between Little Big Tom's legs sprang back into action, the pause button's duration period having expired, and a voice from the TV interrupted him.

"Pan down," it said. "I want bush. Let's see some bush."

Well, sir. This was tough. Because, face it: any way you slice it, it was hilarious. On the other hand, it was just about the least dignified and saddest interruption of a Little Big Tom heartfelt declaration as is possible to imagine. No, wait, that's actually pretty much the same hand.

I quickly pressed the mute button, though the movie continued to play between Little Big Tom's legs: we'd tried "pause" once before, with disastrous results, after all. Little Big Tom sighed and had that look about him, the one that says "The moment has passed." But he soldiered on.

"Your mom," he said, "and I . . ." He paused. Amanda retained her grip on my arm, but this was getting excruciating, even for her, I would bet. "Your mom just needs some space," he concluded.

"We still love each other," said my mom, in a kind of monotone, as if her mind were far, far away. "Just in a different way. So . . ."

Now, this sounded like quite a bit more than simply "needing space," especially if you didn't know what "needing space" really means, and it seemed to hit Little Big Tom like a slap in the face. "Space: the final frontier," he seemed to be saying with his eyes. Where no one can hear you scream.

Little Big Tom explained the rest with a pained expression. He would be moving into a motel "for a little while." He wanted us to know that we could talk to him any time and he wanted to make sure, just in case, that we really, really understood that neither of us was to blame and that we shouldn't feel guilty.

Then he said something I'd heard from him many times before, but never in such a weary tone, or with such huge implications.

"Everything happens for a reason," he said as the jocks between his legs ran silently back into the locker room, clutching their burning crotches.

PART FOUR
Naomi

QUESTIONS

Sam Hellerman showed me the flyer he had been working on. It looked like this:

Mountain Dew Presents

A Benefit Concert
for Recycling
Don't Miss This Rock-and-Roll
EXTRAVAGANZA!

featuring:

THE TEENAGE BRAINWASHERS?

and

TBA

and

TBA

location: TBA

admission: $10

(all proceeds to go to the International
Ted Nugent Center for the Promotion of Recycling)

Well, I don't know about you, but I had questions.

"A benefit concert for recycling?" I said, first off.

"People love recycling," said Sam Hellerman. "People would kill their *puppies* if they thought it would help recycling."

Well, it's true: people do love recycling. And Sam Hellerman added that holding the show as a benefit would mean that we didn't have to pay the other bands, which would help the bottom line quite a bit. This led to Question 1 (b), which I had to get out of the way before charging on to Question 2.

"What are the other bands?"

"Working on that," said Sam Hellerman.

Which was fair enough. But then Question 2 was upon us:

"Why the question mark after our band name?"

Answer: it turned out that Sam Hellerman's crank-call publicity campaign had been all too successful, and he suspected that the lady at the Salthaven Recreation Center, where he hoped to be able to hold the show, had recognized his voice and had grown weary of the band name, becoming inexplicably irate every time she heard it. Therefore, he thought it would probably be prudent to consider changing the name after all.

"But what about the publicity?" I said, thinking primarily of my lawsuit, on which we had made little progress.

"There are other ways," said Sam Hellerman darkly.

This led to Question 3:

"The International Ted Nugent Center for the Promotion of Recycling?"

I asked Question 3 with a Little Big Tom–style raised eyebrow.

"That's just the name of my production company," said Sam Hellerman, adding that the words "Ted" and "Nugent" were in there for creative purposes, and also as a way of explaining to Shinefield, if the subject ever came up again, why we wanted him to play "Cat Scratch Fever" three times in the set.

"Is that," I said, broaching Question 4, "you know, legal?"

Sam Hellerman waved this away. It wasn't like Ted Nugent or Mountain Dew were going to find out about the show and come looking for us, his look said, and we certainly couldn't be hunted down and killed by Recycling itself. I guess he had a point. Then he gave me the look that says "And if Ted Nugent or Mountain Dew do sue us, well, that's publicity that money can't buy."

Okay, then. I was convinced, all my questions satisfactorily answered.

Sam Hellerman had to hide the flyer under his shirt when Shinefield came back into the basement more suddenly then we'd expected. We both felt it would be better to present him with the flyer and the plans for the show only when all the details had been sorted out.

"I was just wrestling with a skunk," he said, and started laughing. Then he said: "Oh. Yellow."

Because while he had been out skunk-wrestling, a girl had arrived and was sitting in Celeste Fletcher's former spot in the big, grubby vinyl beanbag in the corner, looking kind of hard to miss with her shorts and cowboy boots and legs and breasts and everything.

I introduced them to her: "This is Shinefield. And you know Sam Hellerman." The girl emitted a slight sigh, the usual way, the universal sign, really, of conceding one's acquaintance with Sam Hellerman.

"Are you going to play my song, sweetie?" she said. I winced with a weird combination of embarrassment and a kind of perverse, guilty pride. But of course I said "Yes."

But I've got to back up quite a bit to explain how and why what was going on here was going on.

A PRETTY GOOD BONE

I suppose I should start with Roberta the Female Robot's note. Well, "note" is really an inadequate way to describe it. Missive. Epistle. Dispatch. Disquisition. Monograph. Just going through my powerful vocabulary here, trying to come up with a suitable term, but there really, really isn't one. For one thing, it was *long*, six whole binder pages of close handwritten text, both sides. For another, it was vibrant, with what I'd estimate to be around a dozen different colors running into each other at the points where she had switched pens. For a third thing, the right edge of the last three pages was stained a mysterious dark brownish color, making a substantial number of the words, mainly those written in yellow, practically indecipherable. And for a fourth, but by no means final, thing, it was ... My powerful vocabulary is failing me once again here, but I'll just put it out there nonetheless.

For a fourth thing, it was: just incredibly boring.

```
My Dearest Thomas,
```

it began.

```
I'm in English toodle-lee-oo. This is the
same desk I had last simester, it still has
my gum on it! At least I hope its mine!
Ewwwwww! Gross! Are you enjoying Pizzaballa
or do you think she's a witch or a bitch
```

or a glitch? Look how small I'm writing!!
I don't know why! Ewww God this is boring,
I'm sick of thesis statements just bring
on the fucken porn!! Just kidding! I got
the porn right here! Just kidding!!! What
sports do you play? I'm in cross country
and Mr. Gamma-ray is such an asshole but
he works you hard so I guess its good.
Ewww but I had shinsplintz yesterday,
ouch. So, Tommie boy, which is it Coke or
Pepsi, boxers or briefs, umquiring minds
want to know! [indecipherable] I can write
big too. Now it's small again. English
be over! English be over! It's not over.
(sigh) I'll be seeing you in band soon.
Tom get your horn up!!! Will you say hi to
me? You better! Or I'll knock your block
off! Just kidding . . . or maybe? Not?
[indecipherable] [indecipherable] Pammelah
says you are a pretty good bone and I've
known many bones in my industrious career
(wink wink) NOT REALLY!!! Shirts are
weird. . . .

Now, if you think that's maybe a little charming, I'd probably have agreed with you up till about halfway down the second page, but, trust me, eventually this type of thing overstays
its welcome. I skimmed much of it, scanning for some indication that there was actual information or a message of any
import, but honestly, there was none. I don't know what I'd
expected, but it wasn't this: the Female Robot had just pretty
much written whatever happened to be in her head, ripped the

pages out, folded them into a tight little square, and handed it in at the end of the day.

So maybe you spotted the one bit where it was revealed how Pam Something spelled her name. Pammelah. I present that without comment.

And I sure didn't know what to make of, or do with, Roberta the Female Robot's letter. I took out a sheet of paper and wrote: "Dear Robot, look how small I'm writing . . . ," but that's about as far as I got and I soon gave up trying.

I'd expected I'd have to say something about the note, or at least excuse the fact that I hadn't written a detailed account of every single moment of my entire night in response, when I saw her in homeroom the next day. But the subject didn't come up because she simply handed me a new tightly folded packet—an even longer letter, to judge from the heft of it.

"Thanks?" I said.

"De nada" was her reply.

Why couldn't I just play the damn song? I'd been doing everything right, growing the fingernails on my right hand so they could pluck the strings more effectively and practicing for hour upon tedious hour, but "O'Brien Is Tryin' to Learn to Talk Hawaiian" was still refusing to come through my fingers. In fact, I seemed to get worse at it the more I practiced doing it, which shouldn't have surprised me too much. After all, it is an axiom that forms a powerful thesis among the many theses of my General Theory of the Universe, as I have outlined above: the harder you try, the worse it gets. Nevertheless, lots of hippies could do it. What was their secret? Drugs?

The Henderson-Tucci household without the Tucci was a pretty sad place to be. My mom was the same as ever; that is, a silent, barely present presence in her vibrant clothes, coming home from work and drifting from room to room with her bourbon on the rocks and cigarette, lost in thought, or at any rate, lost in something. But I, for one, found I missed the Little Big Tom pop-ins quite a bit. I mean, silly and annoying as they could be, they did keep things moving. Without them, and without the sights and sounds of Little Big Tom making his rounds, monitoring each room with doglike diligence, everything felt empty, stagnant, boarded up, like the soul had gone out of the building. And quiet, so quiet you could hear yourself think, which is never a good thing.

I may be projecting here, but I kind of had the impression that Amanda might have been missing him too, in her own way. Of course she was outwardly exultant. Ever since my mom had brought Little Big Tom home with her so long ago, Amanda had had no dearer wish than to see that situation reversed. But she can't have enjoyed the emptiness and silence, not really, and there were even times when I believed I saw as much in her hunched shoulders, occasional sighs, and aimless wandering of the grounds with her phone-baby dangling all but neglected from its antenna in her seemingly weary hand.

I'll say one thing: whatever it had meant, if my mom had really wanted space, she had it now. Nothing but, in fact.

HAPPY BIRTHDAY TO ME, HAPPY BIRTHDAY TO ME

Your humble narrator turned fifteen on a cold, wet day in January, wearing an orange beret, white pants, and an orange and white shirt that said "Badger Power," prancing around and playing "Don't Stop Believin'" on the trombone in front of a crowd of school-spirit-addled, bloodthirsty normal people.

Okay, other stuff happened on that day too, but I'd say that's a pretty bad way to start off such an important year, wouldn't you? An ill omen. When once upon a time a father might have taken his just-come-of-age son out to teach him to shoot guns or drive a car, to get drunk, or to lose his virginity at a local brothel to a plump, merry, blushing, gregarious, ample-bosomed, redheaded lady named Big Griselda, there I was, fatherless twice over, holding a trombone above my head, doing a gay little dance, and playing a "pep band" arrangement of what has to be one of the worst songs ever devised by man. "Streetlights people." The corrosive idiocy of it all was going to leave permanent scars on my soul, and I could almost feel it happening in real time.

I'm not a big birthday guy, so it didn't bug me too much that my mom and Amanda hadn't remembered it. They had their minds on other things; plus, I was spared the awkwardness of having to respond to whatever half-assed commemoration they would have thrown together at the last second by saying "Oh, you shouldn't have" or something like that. Once again, though, I missed the nonsensical words of wisdom Little Big Tom would undoubtedly have assembled to mark the occasion: I missed having the opportunity to roll my eyes at them, anyway. We both used to enjoy that, probably.

As it turned out, Little Big Tom had slipped a birthday present into my backpack—no idea how he had managed that. Had he been secretly returning to the house at 507 Cedarview Circle in the small hours, roaming the all but empty rooms like a silent, ghostly caretaker, placing a birthday present here, a vegan cheeseburger there, guarding his former domain, vow-ing to return one day? It was a disturbing yet strangely comforting thought.

It was CDs. Ugh. Best-ofs. I know, ugh. Good stuff, though, all fingerstyle guys–Bert Jansch, who's the guy Jimmy Page stole all the Led Zeppelin acoustic instrumental arrangements from; another dude named Big Bill Broonzy; and perhaps best of all, Blind Blake, who was to become something like my idol in the months to come, though at that time I hadn't heard of him yet. What is it about these blind guys that gives them the improbable superhuman power to play guitars like pianos? Something beyond nature, without a doubt (disproving atheism conclusively, if you ask me). Little Big Tom seemed to know his stuff, I reluctantly conceded. The sight of the familiar yellow Post-it note, LBT's preferred form of communication, caused a brief welling-up of sentiment, not so much for what was written on it, but because of the bittersweet recollection of all the other Post-its he'd left me over the years. This one said: "Let your fingers do the walking!!!–Big Tom. P.S. Come see me sometime."

I winced at the notion of coming to see him. It was the least I could do, but man, how awkward would it be to visit your mom's estranged husband in his motel room? I almost wished he hadn't given me the CDs, but not really.

This is what my life had become:

```
Are you excited? Go Badgers! Go Badgers!
I can't believe you've never done pep band
before. I bet you wish you could play your
guitar instead! Maybe Matt-Patt would let
you but he wouldn't because your a bone.
Bones are bones. At least your not a
```

trumpet! I almost slept through the alarm
today but then I didn't. Do you like milk?
I guess I do. Pammelah has pretty eyes.
What kind of eyes do you like? I totally
hafta pee, like right now. Ewww this chick
Janice just breathed on me. She smells like
Chinese food. . . .

I already had a stockpile of several unread notes from the Robot kicking around, set aside for when I had time to catch up on my reading, so I simply added this to the pile. Being acquainted with her was a big job. Fortunately, it didn't seem to matter to her whether or not I did the reading.

I would say that of all the indignities associated with being in the Clearview High School "pep band," and there were many, the absolute worst one was that they made you wear the little outfit all through the school day on the days when you were supposed to play at the games. And yet, while the school spirit at Clearview was just about the most irritating thing in the world, it also functioned as a useful protective force field. Being in the band certainly marked you as a second-class citizen compared to actually being a sports psycho, but because you were part of the general project of promoting the Badgers and celebrating the breathtaking awesomeness of the fact that guys wearing gay little shiny orange shorts were pretty good at prancing around and playing with balls, everyone left you alone. There seemed to be no dissenters, no misfits, no one who wasn't with the program. Except me, semi-secretly, and some of the other Hillmont refugees, though most of them had by this time learned that the easiest way to assimilate was to pretend to be just as enraptured by the Spirit as everybody else. If I had shown up at Hillmont High wearing white pants and a beret, they'd have been scraping my remains off Center Court within seconds. But at Clearview, I was serving the designs of the normal psychos, so I was golden, protected by the Spirit.

Because now that I'd been there long enough, I'd seen a bit of what happened to people of the second tier and lower who were not protected by the Spirit at Clearview, and though it wasn't anywhere near as bad as it had been at Hillmont, it wasn't pretty. Since it wasn't happening to me personally I didn't feel it nearly as keenly, but the normal psychos preyed on the defenseless at Clearview High just as they do anywhere else.

I don't know if you recall from my previous explanations, but there's this narcoleptic kid named Bobby Duboyce who has to wear a helmet all the time to protect his soft skull. At Hillmont the normal kids knew just what to do with a Helmet Boy: they would wait till he was asleep and then descend upon him and write obscenities on his helmet, or do things like roll him in the mud or carry him to strange allegedly amusing locations so that when he woke up he would be in a state of confusion, embarrassment, or terror. And they'd do it right out in the open, under the approving, or at least willfully oblivious, eyes of the teachers and administrators. Now, as one of the Hillmont refugees, he no longer has to worry about that kind of public humiliation. Instead, the normal Clearview guys, and even some of the girls, I believe, just randomly, and with a kind of cheerful attitude, subtly knock him on top of the helmet throughout the day with their books or knuckles as they walk by. That's all. I'm sure it's irritating, but I guess it's the sort of thing you get used to after a while. His parents probably think it "builds character." It's not nice, but for a guy like Bobby Duboyce it must have felt kind of like winning the lottery.

Or there's this chubby Asian kid named Pang. He's kind

of weird, but he isn't harming anyone. When I take over the world, I'll institute a strict policy of leaving the fat kids, and maybe especially Pang, alone: he'll get a free pass to sit wherever he wants just being himself, unharassed. But till then, the normal psychos at Clearview High will have their fun with him, and the way they do that is to make him run back and forth all around the Quad and down the hallways till he is about to collapse from exhaustion. "Pang, give me a dollar," one of them will say, and when he produces it, they send him running across the Quad to give it to another subhuman psychotic normal goon, who promptly sends him running off in the other direction. They make the game last throughout the school day, and they say things like "Come on, work off some of that blubber." It's in the interest of physical fitness, after all, so I guess it's just fine; even good for him, maybe. I hate physical fitness myself, but there are those who swear by it.

I mean, thank God it's not me. But maybe, I found myself thinking, it's not such a bad thing for the normal people to have these relatively benign ways of letting off steam, considering the damage they could do otherwise. When I take power, I'm going to be the best, sanest dictator ever, protecting not just the fat, but the gay, the shy, the short, the freakishly tall, the redheaded, the handicapped, the smart, the spastic, the meek, the cheese makers, the stutterers, the mumblers, and the readers. I'll even protect the sporty and the normal in my beneficence, if b. means what I think it means. But everyone has to leave everyone else alone, and the instant they start hassling anyone, for any reason, the penalty is instant vaporization by my roving surveillance robots. Thanks for playing. Problem solved. But till then? Well, Clearview isn't exactly nice, but it sure could be a whole lot worse.

Even though I couldn't do anything about the white pants, I

buttoned my jeans jacket all the way up to hide the dumb shirt and put the beret in my pocket for most of the day, because even after all this, I still had some standards left.

Now, one of the other terrible things about Clearview High is that they don't have open campus for lunch. That means that, unlike at Hillmont, every single student has to eat lunch either in the cafeteria building or in the grass in the middle of the Quad. Basically you're on display at all times, and it's hard to find a private space of your own of any kind. I think the technical term for the thing I'm describing is a "panopticon," which is a kind of prison where you're being constantly watched, exposed to your jailers one hundred percent of the time. I was sitting with the "pep band" in our panopticon on the grass at lunch, beretless, my tiny gesture of rebellion in full view. And when Principal T-Dog walked by and pointed at me, saying "Where's your Badger beret, soldier?" and tried to make me high-five him, and actually stood there till I put the beret on *and* high-fived him, and then led the band and assorted on-lookers in a little round of applause at my expense—well, that's about as low as low gets in the First World.

"We have to support our Badger men," said Pammelah Something, scrunching down her own beret.

It was possibly the weirdest thing I'd ever heard anyone say out loud in my entire sorry life.

About the game and "Don't Stop Believin'" and "On, Wisconsin!", the less said the better. The whole time I was conscious of little more than my shame and Celeste Fletcher's jacketed presence in the bleachers. It was bad enough to be seen in such a state by people I didn't know, but when it came to Fiona ... I'll just say I was almost crying literal tears of humiliation and leave it at that. I'll tell you what, Sam Hellerman's escape hatch, that is, a couple of illicitly acquired tranquilizers swallowed with a large glass of bourbon, wasn't looking too bad. For the first time, I felt I understood.

"We" won, by the way. By which I mean, the Clearview normal psychos had managed to throw their little ball through the hoop more often than the normal psychos from whatever the hell the other high school was called. It was indeed a great day for America.

Everyone was happy, anyway. As the triumphant Clearview student body tramped off to celebrate, setting things on fire and beating up orphans or whatever they do to express joy and pride, we band people stayed behind to gloat amongst ourselves, congratulating each other on a job well done supporting our Badger men.

Pammelah and the Robot and the always fetching Blossom van Kinkle were sharing a big energy drink bottle that turned out to contain red wine.

They started to sing:

"On, Wisconsin,
suck my johnson
lick my hairy balls. . . ."

Now, okay, *that* was pretty funny. Because they were mocking everything they believed in. Plus: balls. I honestly hadn't thought they had it in them, so to speak.

"Here's to ya," said the Robot, handing me the bottle and another note. Here's to me indeed, I said to myself, taking a big swallow and putting the note in my bulging pocket with the day's others.

I couldn't believe she was going to make me read all of

these, for no grade or credit. That certainly wasn't the Clearview way.

HOT UNDERWEAR

Little Big Tom's motel was down on the northeast edge of Hillmont by the railroad tracks. It was an easy bike ride from my house after I'd dropped off my trombone and changed out of the stupid Badger shirt. But it was still raining and it started to rain harder on the way, so, well, much as I hate to do it, I feel I must tell you that to get an accurate picture of this fateful bike ride, you have to know that I wound up putting on the orange beret, because it was all I had. With my old hooded army coat, the rain would have been no problem. This thought, in turn, brought to mind my unfulfilled lawsuit dreams, so by the time I arrived at the El Capitano Motor Lodge, not only was I looking ridiculous in a soggy orange beret, but I was in a pretty foul mood as well.

"Thanks for the CDs," I said, when Little Big Tom opened the door to my knock, words I'd never believed I'd utter.

"Come on in," said Little Big Tom, smiling widely, obviously glad to see me. "Wring out your hat and stay awhile!"

Now, Little Big Tom was still a bit of a mess, it's true, but not nearly as big a mess as I'd expected him to be. I wouldn't want to say he was his old self again, not by any means, but he did have, it seemed to me, if only to a slight degree, just a little of that old spark, the Little Big Tom Classic that I'd learned how easy it was to miss. I suppose after weeks of fretting and bracing himself for the "I need space" blow to fall, it might have been something of a relief when it finally came. And maybe he was finding that hell wasn't such a bad place to be. I sometimes had a glimmer of that feeling with regard to Celeste Fletcher, when I realized she was irrevocably lost to normality and that I might as well face it and move on. There's a kind of freedom in failure, once you truly grasp that the cause is lost.

On the other hand, though, this wasn't me and Celeste Fletcher we were talking about here. It was my mom and Little Big Tom. And whatever else you might say about my mom, she was certainly not "lost to normality." Far from it. And Little Big Tom, the bounding, slobbering, gray golden retriever whose fondest dream, I knew, was to return to the good old days of wandering from room to room with a tennis ball in his mouth spouting inane aphorisms and nuzzling everyone's tears away? I had to think there was still some hope there, despite any underwear that may or may not have been found in that notorious gym bag of his.

"Had dinner yet?" he asked, patting the spot on the bed next to him where he wanted me to sit. "I've got a hot plate and a microwave: tacos and pumpkin chai, what a growing boy needs."

Soon we were eating these semidisgusting microwaved vegetarian tacos and drinking this weird tea out of paper cups that said "El Capitano" on them in slanted script.

"I hear you guys won a big game today," said Little Big Tom.

Oh, for God's sake. I gave him the look that says "Yes, thank God 'we' won, now I can die happy."

"At this rate," he continued, "you'll make the quarterfinals before you know it."

Something snapped.

"Look," I said. "Stop trying to make me be normal. I'm not normal. I'm never going to be normal and I don't want to be normal. I don't care about the quarterfinals or the sock hop or

214

the, like, jackets, or the 'spirit' thing the school spirit the pep spirit or whatever, or the, you know, junior prom or the . . . the junior varsity . . . or the senior varsity or any, really, any variety of varsity whatsoever."

I was sputtering and I knew I sounded hysterical. Plus, saying this many words in a row out loud was a rarity, and my doing it had shocked us both. Little Big Tom was taken aback, clearly worried that at this rate I'd be flipping tables and kicking puppies in no time.

"Sorry," I said, deflating myself with a sigh. "It's just been a rough day."

Little Big Tom nodded sympathetically and put an encouraging arm around my shoulder.

"I hear ya, chief," he said. "I hear ya. I guess it's going around. But you know what I think? I think it wouldn't hurt to give people a chance sometimes. Sure, it can be a little silly, the things people do, the things they say. But it's all just a means of communication, and that's important in life. Underneath it all, they're just people. And I think you'll find—"

"Jesus," I said drawing a breath and reinflating, cutting him off. Because I couldn't let this stand either. "Just . . . no. Stop telling me what you think I'll find. You don't know what I'll find. Everything you always think I'll find is not remotely anywhere near what I actually find, ever. You have no idea what I'm capable of finding. And if you knew the kind of stuff I *do* . . . find . . ."

Well, I ran out of steam there and deflated again, trying and failing to summon the words to express the idea that if he knew what was really in this little head of mine he'd probably be shocked out of his complacent, cheerful, therapy-hippie "brain box."

"Sorry," I said. "It's been a rough week."

Which didn't work nearly as well as it had the first time I'd said it moments before. Little Big Tom was looking heartbreakingly wounded.

"Seriously," I said. "I'm sorry . . . chief. I do appreciate the advice."

And I ventured to attempt a little encouraging tap-squeeze on his shoulder like the ones he does. I wouldn't say it perked him up, exactly, but he looked at me with this combination smile and frown and nodded, as though to say: "Hey, we've both been there."

"How's your mom?" he said, in a mournful tone that instantly persuaded me he hadn't found getting used to the Final Frontier nearly as easy as I'd imagined.

"Okay" was all I could say.

"I miss you guys," he said, still mournful. "I miss her." Man, this conversation was getting difficult. Little Big Tom explained how he was trying to keep the lines of communication open and making sure he was always available to work things through but that my mom hadn't been returning his messages and didn't seem to want to talk. Well, there's a surprise, I thought. When had she ever "wanted to talk" in her life?

I wasn't sure how much more of this weird conversation I could take. I mean, he should have been commiserating with a bartender or a rabbi (of yoga or whatever, not Christianity, obviously) or, like, writing a letter to an advice columnist. But not me. I'm the chick's son, remember? The sympathetic expression I was trying to hold on my face began to harden and I was worried that soon it would simply shatter and clatter to the floor.

"Look . . . chief," I said. I couldn't believe I was going to do this. I chose my words with care and delicacy.

"Radio silence," I said. "That's the only possible way to salvage a relationship with a woman who says she needs space. I'm serious. No calls, no messages, no contact whatsoever. Give her time to figure out that she misses you and make her wonder what you're up to. Then, when ..." I paused and took a breath. "When," I resumed, "she's feeling sad and vulnerable just like you are right now, wait for her to come to you begging for comfort, reassurance, and attention, which she probably will. At that point, it's up to you how to proceed."

Now, I had never, ever in my life seen, on any face that I could recall, and certainly never on Little Big Tom's face, the expression with which he looked at me after I had delivered this Hellermanian sermon. It was actually a rapid series of expressions, as though his face were a chameleon that had happened to find itself sitting on the lens of a giant kaleidoscope operated by a kid with ADHD. And now I knew there were two things, at least, that could reduce a man like Little Big Tom to speechlessness, the other, of course, being Y2K.

I pushed on, though, not really sure why I was doing it.

"But it's not really about the underwear," I said. "Is it?"

Oh man, that ADHD kid was really spinning the kaleidoscope like crazy now.

"Underwear," Little Big Tom repeated, sounding mystified and, I don't know, shell-shocked. "Underwear ... What are you talking about, underwear?"

"I mean, the panties in your gym bag," I said. "You know."

"Gym bag," said Little Big Tom, in a dumbfounded manner. "I don't even have a gym bag." Well, now that he mentioned it, I'd never actually seen him with a gym bag, and the idea of him going to a gym was pretty outlandish.

"You mean," I said, in a "let me get this straight" tone, "that this whole thing with my mom isn't because she found"–I quoted Amanda–"'hot underwear' in your gym bag?"

217

The kaleidoscope stopped spinning and just kind of snapped into place, and the chameleon expression it landed on was easy to read this time. "Are you," it ran, "out of your freakin' mind?"

My look said, in return: "Yes, evidently, sorry I brought it up."

Little Big Tom wouldn't tell me what it really was about, however. Which was fine with me. I didn't want to know.

"Radio silence," I repeated, channeling Sam Hellerman again. "It's the only way." I had no basis for Sam Hellerman's confidence, but I just knew, like how you know the sky is blue, that it was true, that it would work. Well, it's frequently blue. And I wanted it to work.

All in all, it was probably the weirdest Little Big Tom conversation of my life, and that sure is saying something.

He gave me a lift home after it was all over and dropped me off down the block so my mom wouldn't see the truck and feel awkward.

"You know, kemosabe," said Little Big Tom, pretty generously, I thought, considering the content and tenor of our previous conversation, if "tenor" means what I think it does, "you're a good guy, a good *person*, underneath it all."

Underneath it all, yes. Underneath it all, we're all just people.

NAOMI

Now, if you've had enough of Little Big Tom at this point, I can't say I'd blame you, but, if so, I'm sorry to inform you that something else happened with Little Big Tom at the El Capitano Motor Lodge that night that I have to tell you about.

It was after we had kind of, somehow, with our eyes,

reached an unspoken gentleman's agreement to forget the "hot underwear" conversation had ever occurred, with the important corollary that neither of us would ever bring up the topic of "hot underwear" again, no matter what, "hot underwear" now having become a forbidden term, like "mailman" or "actress" or "Eskimo"; but obviously, it was before he dropped me off at home, when we were still in his motel room.

And it started like this:

"I think you'll find–" Little Big Tom began, then corrected himself, making me feel a bit guilty: "I think you'll *like* Big Bill Broonzy. He's the best there was." Such statements from a guy like Little Big Tom always raise my skeptical hackles, if hackles can be skeptical, and actually, what are hackles, exactly? But in this case, looking at the CD, I had no doubt he was right. I could tell just by looking at the guy and the way he was holding his weird little guitar that it was going to be something extraordinary.

Little Big Tom asked me how the fingerpicking was going, and I admitted that it was not going well at all, and that no matter how hard I tried I couldn't get my fingers to "roll" in such a way that it sounded like anything at all, and that the more I worked on it, the worse it seemed to get. I asked him if he'd ever noticed this phenomenon, that the harder you try the worse you do, adding that it seemed to apply to pretty much everything there was in the world: guitar, women . . . well, guitar and women, anyway, and that's a lot.

Little Big Tom didn't answer, thinking what appeared to be deep, faraway thoughts.

"Well, chief," he said, after a good stretch of this, standing up suddenly. "I think it's time you met Naomi."

He told me to "wait here" and dashed out the door. Then I heard his truck start up, followed by the sound of the Little

Big Tom mobile skidding off through puddles, bound for God knows where.

Naomi. Maybe I was going to lose my virginity to a plump, merry, blushing, gregarious, ample-bosomed, redheaded lady after all, except her name was going to be Naomi instead of Griselda. That was pretty unlikely, I admit, but it was the least unlikely explanation I could come up with. I'd be okay with that, I decided.

I waited in Little Big Tom's motel room for quite some time. There was nothing of interest on the television. I'd had all the weird tea and semiedible tacos I could stand. I considered taking a shower, but I wasn't sure how long it would be before Little Big Tom returned and I sure didn't want him walking in on *that*. The seconds turned into minutes, and the minutes turned into larger sets of minutes, and these larger sets of minutes eventually gathered steam and turned into what seemed like forever.

So basically, what I'm saying is that there was pretty much literally nothing else to do, other than pull out Roberta the Female Robot's letters and get to work on my reading assignment. And this I did.

It was rough going, as I'd known it would be. But now that I was actually reading rather than skimming, I realized that, buried deep inside them, among the items in the inane, seemingly endless lists of every single thing she had done or thought during whatever period of time it was that she was writing them, there were some really . . . I don't want to say interesting things. Striking? Alarming? Flabbergasting? Something like that. There were strange bits, is what I'm saying, and there turned out to be a lot of them.

Here's an example of what I mean:

. . . I really like these socks, you know
the ones? They have stripes and diamonds.
And you know, I hate bandaids sometimes. I
wasn't feeling well enough to eat breakfast
but then I had an apple. Yay apples!
Nutrition. Now I have a question for you,
my dear Thomas: what shows do you like?
I bet you like Malcom in the Middle, it's
the best!! You remind me of the kid Malcom
mostly but Pammelah says your cuter. (wink
wink) Hey, she wants him, maybe you should
get in there boy! JK!!! Do you ever feel
like hurting yourself, like really bad?
Sometimes its like, nobody cares about me
and I almost don't even really exist and
when the last person forgets to notice
me I might find out I'm actually dead.
[unintelligible] [unintelligible] with a
knife or something. Tra la la. Kittens are
the best. Ah, bus drivers. They can be syko
(sp?) don't you think. I'm taking drivers
ed but I just want a scooter not a car.
I wonder what it would be like to be a
shelf. . . .

See? What was going on with this Robot? I mean, there was
so much dark, disturbing stuff buried in there that it made my
own idle morbidity seem like amateur hour. And I can't even
bring myself to quote the craziest stuff because it would feel
like too much of a betrayal of confidence. You'll just have to
trust me that it was pretty extreme. I wasn't sure what to do.

There was also in the most recent letter something not at all like that but very extraordinary that was to have a big effect on this thing I'm telling and that I will get to shortly. But just as I had read the thing in question and begun to shake my head over it, I heard keys in the motel room door and saw Little Big Tom come through it, smiling.

I looked up.

"Tom Henderson," he said. "Meet Naomi."

He threw the door open and stepped aside. And standing there, just outside the motel room door, dripping wet, was a grossly obese bald man with a fringe of orange hair ponytailed at the back, a big ZZ Top beard, and a grubby "Coke: It's the real thing" T-shirt that barely covered his belly; and on that belly was resting the tiniest guitar I'd ever seen.

Well, as it turned out, Naomi was the guitar, not the fat hippie. The hippie's name, I was told, was Flapjack. The head-stock of the guitar said NIOMA on it. It was all slowly becoming clear. Sort of.

Flapjack entered the room and Little Big Tom closed the door behind him, smiling like a great big idiot and pointing to him as if to say "Flapjack and Naomi—pretty cool, right?" It was a look I'd know anywhere, that unholy *Catcher in the Rye* glow that lights up the eyes of authority figures whenever they manage to force you to stroke the nose of one of their cherished sacred cows. It is a look of aggressive enthusiasm, accompanied by a trembling, desperate smile reflecting an expectation that is almost by definition impossible to live up to. You know it when you see it. I've most often experienced it with *Catcher*, but I've also seen it done with Dylan, *Apocalypse Now*, even with the album that has the Blue Öyster Cult Godzilla drug poetry song about deodorant that I mentioned before. And now it was happening with Flapjack.

Nothing triggers my fight-or-flight response like the *Catcher* look. However, as the only means of egress was at the moment being blocked by nearly four hundred immovable pounds of solid hippie, neither f. nor f. was remotely possible. And when you realize that "egress" is a fancy-pants word for "exit," you'll see my point, I'm sure. I was caught in a Flapjack trap, not to mention a hippie sandwich, and I had to make the best of it.

Flapjack cleared his throat.

"'The Maple Leaf Rag'" he said, in a deep, reedy, emphysemic voice. And then he commenced what was easily the most amazing guitar playing I had ever seen in person. It was super fast and he did it pretty much perfect in every way, playing the main melody line and bass and backup rhythm plus all these crazy embellishments and harmonics, and at one point even reaching his right hand over to the tuning pegs to slide a note up and back down again with a little wrist flip and a wink. His fingers were a blur. It almost made me want to do a little dance or something, but of course I didn't. I just stared.

Little Big Tom was nodding at me with this "hey, what'd I tell ya" look, though in fact he hadn't told me anything. But he had shown me something, and what it was, was magic.

When "Maple Leaf Rag" was finished, Flapjack did this little salute-like downward nod. Then he raised his head and started to play again. And the song he played was "O'Brien Is Tryin' to Learn to Talk Hawaiian."

Now, I told you I'd hated the song at first, and I really had. But by this time, it had grown on me till it was almost my favorite song. Partly it was just the tune, which was pretty catchy. But also, I had really started to identify with this guy

O'Brien, trying to speak a language he doesn't understand to communicate with someone who just doesn't get him at all. I mean, I've been there, brother. And then he goes ahead and does it anyway, just barreling in, making his ignorance work for him. I thought that was, maybe, something to aspire to.

Flapjack didn't sing the song in an Irish accent like Little Big Tom had, but it sounded just as great as an instrumental as "Maple Leaf Rag" had, and he did a whole new set of crazy, inventive, unexpected embellishments on it.

I wanted to be able to do that more than anything in the world, except maybe going back in time to ramone the young Jane Birkin. Or to ramone Celeste Fletcher right here in our own time. Or basically to ramone pretty much anyone. But what I'm saying is, I wanted it.

When Flapjack was finished with "O'Brien Is Tryin' to Learn to Talk Hawaiian," he paused, then handed the guitar to me.

"Play," he said, just before his voice dissolved into a series of scary coughs.

If it's possible for a person to be shaking and petrified at the same time, well, that person was me. I knew I couldn't get out of playing. This guy outweighed me by hundreds of pounds. So with trembling hands I played my own horrible attempt at "O'Brien Is Tryin' to Learn to Talk Hawaiian." And it was bad, though Naomi sounded pretty nice even through the badness. When I finished playing my lame-ass version of the song, hardly recognizable as a song, really, Flapjack stared at me for a long, unnerving stretch.

"One finger was good enough for Travis," he finally said. "One finger was good enough for Broonzy. So one finger is good enough for you."

He was commenting on the fact that I'd rigidly positioned

my index, middle, and ring fingers on each of the top three strings, like my Chet Atkins book advised.

"Atkins," said Flapjack, when I tried to explain, "is a pip-squeak."

Then he took the guitar back and showed me, playing very slowly, how you could do the thumb picking and the finger roll with mostly just the index finger and thumb. He said not one additional word during this, but he was a way better teacher than Little Big Tom. I still couldn't play it, but at least I kind of got what you were supposed to do a little bit better.

Flapjack handed the guitar back to me, gave Little Big Tom the three-fingered Jerry Garcia salute, and tramped out amid another cascade of coughs.

"Flapjack," said Little Big Tom.

Apparently Flapjack not only was a buddy of Little Big Tom's, but also had been some kind of famous hippie guitar guy way back when. Little Big Tom was acting starstruck, to be honest, and seemed vaguely distressed that I hadn't heard of him. He said Flapjack had told him he'd be willing to show me a thing or two if I ever wanted to come visit him on his houseboat in Fenton City. I could tell this was supposed to be a big honor, so I did my best to nod reverently. I wasn't sure I ever wanted to meet Flapjack again, but I was in awe of his playing and grateful for what he'd taught me.

As for Naomi, it, or she, was Little Big Tom's guitar from when he was a kid. Part of why he had taken so long is that he'd had to go to his storage space in Santa Carla to retrieve it. It was of the type known as a "parlor guitar," the kind that a lot of old blues guys played; whenever anyone tried to play ragtime music on a guitar back in the eighteen hundreds or whenever, they would have done it on something like Naomi.

It looked, and sounded, about as cool as I could have imagined, even in my clumsy ham hands. Little Big Tom was going to let me borrow it to learn on, he said, but he made me promise to look after it.

"She's always been my baby," he said creepily.

Little Big Tom had provided me with my Melody Maker, too, if you'll remember from my previous explanations. He was a dependable guitar supplier, if nothing else. The thing I've learned is, when people give you guitars all the time, it's pretty hard to hate them actively. You try it.

LULGUAYVIAN EVENTS AT THE ALADDIN ARCADE

Before I tell you the other significant thing that was buried deep in one of the Female Robot's letters, I have to relate the surprising events that transpired when I went to meet Sam Hellerman at the Salthaven mall a day or so after Naomi day.

"Happy birthday," Sam Hellerman said, handing me a sloppily wrapped gift that was obviously an LP. KSBS 2021, he said it was, and he made me try to guess its secret identity before letting me open it. I couldn't guess, of course, but it turned out to be the Flamin' Groovies' *Flamingo,* the 1971 repress without the gatefold cover and with the pink labels. Still pretty nice, though.

Sam Hellerman hadn't told me why we were meeting at the mall, but it became painfully obvious when we settled down on a bench near the mall entrance across the corridor from the Aladdin Arcade and he got out his notebook and put on his headphones without another word. More fieldwork: we were remaining ineffectually aloof once again.

Soon, as if on cue, Jeans Skirt Girl came along, wearing not a jeans skirt this time, but rather a kind of dress thing, which, because of the golden jeans penis, was a bit of a relief. (She would always be Jeans Skirt Girl to me, though, whatever she wore.) She was with two other girls, pretty normal, they all seemed.

Now, the Aladdin Arcade had seen better days, but it was still a social hangout for the kids of Slut Heaven and the surrounding areas, and a lot of them tended to congregate outside of it because if the management noticed you weren't actually playing, they would kick you out till you were ready to play again. It was to this congregation of kicked-out kids, loitering in the mall corridor, that Jeans Skirt Girl and her friends were headed.

Sam Hellerman explained, patiently enough, a little more about Jeans Skirt Girl after I snatched the headphones off his head and told him I would refuse to give them back till he provided some answers to my pointed questions. She was a student at Mission Hills High School. Sam Hellerman had picked her out of last year's MHHS yearbook as his fieldwork subject once he'd learned he would be attending that school. He had certainly done his research on her. His algorithm had told him that by the time he turned sixteen and the sands of his father's ultimatum ran out, her WHR would be just about ideal; she also was the child of parents who had had an acrimonious divorce when she was a little girl, which for some reason, according to Sam Hellerman, made her more likely to be receptive to being "got" and "kept" by a guy like Sam Hellerman. And she had been raised Catholic, which also apparently made her more likely to be r. to being g. and k. by a guy like S. H. Make of it what you will. I didn't make much of it, I can tell you that.

Now, I had been on quite a few of these stakeouts by this point, though never one at this mall. If I'd known that that was what this was going to be, I'd have brought a book. Currently, I was reading this one called *Flow My Tears, the Policeman Said*, pretending that my dad had read it, and it was going pretty well, though it had a distinct *Crying of Lot 49*–ishness about it. It made me feel just slightly disoriented, another example of that Salvador Dalí feeling I've mentioned. Actually, maybe it was a good thing I didn't have that particular book with me on this stakeout: if I had been at all disoriented and Salvador-y during what happened next, I wouldn't have known whether to trust my own eyes when they took it in.

Because, as I was saying, the usual pattern for Jeans Skirt Girl fieldwork was, we'd show up and watch her while pretending not to watch her, with Sam Hellerman listening to his tapes and taking notes and the occasional photo till she left, when we would pack up and head home in a state, in my case, at least, of embarrassed self-loathing. But this time, around fifteen minutes in, to my astonishment, Sam Hellerman suddenly yanked off his headphones, handed them to me, and stood up.

"I'm going in," he said.

As you know, I like to think I have a pretty powerful vocabulary. But how does one go about describing the degree of astonishment that comes with witnessing the most flabbergasting, mind-scrambling thing the world has ever seen? The word hasn't been invented. I must invent one. "Lulguayvian" is the one I have chosen. Because what happened next was way beyond astonishing, so lulguayvian that even "lulguayvian" doesn't quite come close to getting it across. Hyperlulguayvian, that's better.

So imagine, my friends, my hyperlulguayvia when I watched Sam Hellerman stride boldly across the corridor toward the

Aladdin Arcade, stumbling once, and then, smoothing down his hair, walk straight up to Jeans Skirt Girl. Imagine the thoroughly hyperlulguayvian spectacle of Sam Hellerman actually engaging Jeans Skirt Girl in conversation, during which she begins to smile and laugh. Well, my skeptical friends, maybe you're like me, and Jeans Skirt Girl laughing at Sam Hellerman might not strike you as being quite as lulguayvian as advertised. I'm with you, believe me. Fair enough.

But imagine my hyperlulguayvianicity, dear reader, when I saw Sam Hellerman lean in and actually kiss Jeans Skirt Girl. On the mouth. With her arms around his slump-shouldered Hellermanian back, and his hands gently, almost gallantly, I would say, around her tender 0.736 WHR. Now, understand me: it wasn't quite "making out." I wouldn't go that far. There was no face licking, no lip biting that I could see, maybe even no tongue. And no discernible ass-grabbio. It might not even have merited a Clearview High PDA chant, though, then again, it might have. Still, it was perhaps the most stunning case of lulguayvia I'd ever experienced in a career of pretty significant lulguayvian episodes.

When the kiss was over, Sam Hellerman trotted back to our bench while Jeans Skirt Girl and her friends waved good-bye and giggled, and there was scattered (sarcastic?) clapping from the other kids standing around. But Sam Hellerman was holding a slip of paper in his hand like a trophy—her phone number, I had to guess.

"Wave to them," he whispered. I was still staring, frozen, unable to control my movements. He reached out like he was going to lift my arm up and make me wave it, but I managed in the end to execute a feeble wave of my own with what I imagine must have been a pretty weird-looking, thoroughly befuddled half smile. Sam Hellerman smirked and did a much more confident-looking salute-wave, gathered his stuff, and led me to the door. I was still in a daze, mouth open, walking in slow motion. The world had suddenly ceased to operate by the laws of nature that I had known and trusted all my life. The thought throbbed in my bewildered brain: this can't be happening. But it was.

When we had emerged from the mall and were safely out of range of Jeans Skirt Girl and her friends, Sam Hellerman stopped and turned to me, an expression on his face that clearly said: "Well?"

"Gimme those tapes," I growled.

THE HOTS

I am strong. I am confident. I am in command of the situation. I am respected by my colleagues at work or school. Women like and admire me. . . .

See, it just wasn't true. I was trying, but honestly, I never felt less s., c., and in c. of the s., much less r. by my c. at w. or s. Maybe you had to have a genius-level lack of self-awareness like Sam Hellerman to will yourself into the kind of idiocy that would allow your brain to permit you to believe it enough for these accursed tapes to work.

"What is it?" said Roberta the Female Robot, plopping down next to me on the Quad lawn at lunch and noticing my headphones. "Is it . . . *'rock 'n' roll'*?" She made this balancing gesture with her hands when she said "rock 'n' roll," like she was surfing. She and Little Big Tom had a bit in common, it had to be admitted, in their capacity as mimes.

"No, and you wouldn't be interested," I said, quickly taking the headphones off. The Female Robot shrugged. One thing that was nice about her was she never pressed or pried when someone didn't want her to ask about something. She just moved on to the next topic, which, for her, could be anything: tables, eyebrows, the weird texture of spaghetti, who invented mayonnaise, how cars look like they have faces, why we have snaps, how gross feet are, daisies, kittens, suicide, self-harm....

I looked at her intently.

"Are you ... all right?" I said. She hadn't been in homeroom today, and it was the first time I'd seen her since discovering the unlikely but fairly worrying darkness lurking in the depths of her scattered little soul.

"Yeah," she said, in an offhand way. "What?"

Haltingly, I explained that I'd been reading her letters and that she seemed a bit ... troubled.

"Oh, that," she said, waving it away. "That's just letters. Jeez, you sound like my mom! I overslept today and she thought I'd taken pills—not I, said the Roberta!"

She leaned in farther, with a conspiratorial nod. "But what," she whispered, "did you think about the Pammelah thing?" Her face communicated a pretty good face version of a question mark, her lower teeth up against her upper lip slightly and her eyes narrowed.

Well, see, that's the other aspect of the letters that I haven't gotten around to mentioning yet. Throughout them there had been lots of mentions of her sax-playing friend "Pammelah," mostly in the form of questions to me: did I think she was pretty, did I think she was nice, did I think she was sexy, did I like her eyes, did I like her hair, did I like her butt? (I kid you not: "... can we say, thumbs up to Pammelah's butt? I think we can!! I'm sure you'll agree Mr. Thomas boy burger. I wish I had a good juicy butt but my butt's a late bloomer. But (!!!!) you like it don't you? ←P's butt. Best in the west! Why don't birds have hands? ...") Maybe you see where this is heading, though I didn't till I did my Robot homework in Little Big Tom's motel room. But after all these hints, some of which were quite strong indeed, the latest note began:

My Dearest Thomas: Can I tell you a secret?
I will anyway! Somebody likes you. Somebody
in this room. And its: Pammelah! She thinks
your smart and funneee and likes your
dark eyes. How romantic! [illegible] (Man
of mystery!!) She wants to have your eyes
babies. Not really!!! . . .

There followed several drawings of hearts in different colors, and what looked like what I believed she would have probably called boobs, though they might have been infinity symbols with dots in them. Then:

But she's nice, right? Nice bod fun at
parties boobies like boys like. OK!?! Your
a bone and she likes bones!! JK . . .
or . . . . . . ? So, you didn't hear it
from me DON'T TELL HER IT WAS ME but I
think if you like her and you asked her to
go she would. (wink wink) SHHHH. Secret!!!!
I have to pee so bad its not even funni.
Do you think red paint tastes better than
white paint. . . .

So, it was "boobies," not "boobs." Euphemisms make the world go round.

"So," the Female Robot was saying, still in a whisper, looking around. "You have the hots for Pammelah. Am I right? Am I right?" She raised and lowered her eyebrows rapidly.

I didn't know what to say.

"I don't know what to say," I said.

"You do or you don't," she said. "Or do you like Blossom van Kinkle? Because Pamm was worried you might. That would be so sad. But come on, who do you like, Blossom or Pammelah? You can tell me, I won't tell." The Robot poked me in the ribs, mouthing the two names with that question mark still on her face, Blossom, Pammelah, Blossom, Pammelah . . .

Now, look, see, this is actually one of the hardest and easiest questions there is, best answered by Sam Hellerman once when I asked if he had the hots for Celeste Fletcher. "I have the hots for everybody," he had said. And so do I, for pretty much every girl I see who is even slightly in the ballpark of halfway decent and who hasn't given me any reason to dislike her actively—and even then, I'd probably still have "the hots" for her. You can't control "the hots." You don't say, like, oh, I would ordinarily like this girl's ass, but now that I know she's a Republican or likes the Doors then I suddenly don't. It doesn't work like that, at least not for me. And it's true the other way too: things like accomplishments or abilities don't much matter like people seem to think they should. "Well, Gwendolyn, now that I know you came in second in the spelling bee, I suddenly inexplicably want to ramone you." No, not so much. An ass is an ass is an ass. You either like it or you don't, and spelling bees don't enter into it, so to speak. But honestly? I usually do like it.

Because my standards are . . . generous. I just like girls. In general. Not just their asses, don't get me wrong here: their tits, too, and, I mean, pretty much all that stuff they got. Is that so wrong? Because I know some people think it is wrong somehow, but what are you supposed to do about it if it's, you know, the case? Just pretend it's not "the case," I guess. So okay, I'll pretend if you want. But as the Robot might whisper: *It's still the case.* I even got turned on by the Robot's bony ass when she was half sitting on me in Little Big Tom's truck. Her WHR and BWR wouldn't get the Sam Hellerman seal of approval, I can tell you that right now: I'm pretty sure both would be not all that far from 1.0. But I don't see how anyone could deny that there were "hots" during that uncomfortable drive in the truck. Sometimes "the hots" just happen.

Now, of course, out of the enormous field of people for whom you might have "the hots," the number of them with whom you will ever actually have an opportunity to express your "hots" is going to be a whole lot smaller, and sometimes, sadly, it could even be zero. I happen to think I haven't done too badly there, in view of my considerable limitations. But maybe what the question "Do you have the hots" for someone really means is something like: "Do you feel you can get away with making an attempt to express your 'hots' in the context of this particular person?" And the ones where you want to express your "hots" but don't feel you can get away with it? Well, those right there are your "secret hots," really probably the overwhelming majority of all the world's "hots," let's be honest.

Well, I mean, basically, I'm not an idiot: I knew I was being offered Pammelah on a silver platter here, in a plan obviously cooked up between the two of them, good cop/oblivious cop style, if o. means what I think it does. In other words, it seemed like something I could probably definitely get away with. So whatever "hots" I had for Pammelah, it didn't look like they'd have to be "secret hots." And I was, frankly, getting pretty tired of secret hots. Pammelah was no Celeste Fletcher, and Blossom van Kinkle was the hotter of the two by a wide margin, but I wasn't being offered any sort of deal concerning them. And the one I was being offered was pretty cute and quite sexy, far beyond what I could have reasonably expected to "go" with on my credentials alone. The Robot was right: she had the "boobies like boys like," and even her WHR wasn't too bad. She did exhibit some unusual behavior, and maybe the crazy eyes. But she was available, available as they come. There was no doubt that she was the smart one to say I had the hots for, and it wasn't even all that untrue.

Yet somehow, despite having what can only be described as a "sure thing" on my hands, I found the prospect of actually following the Robot's crystal clear, step-by-step instructions in real life to be extremely daunting. I wasn't sure I could go through with it. And I also found I couldn't manage to will myself to know what to say to the Robot about the matter either.

"I don't know," I said finally.

"You know," said the Female Robot, "you don't know more often than anyone else I've ever known."

I knew.

MEANWHILE, I WAS STILL THINKING....

Later on, on the bus back from the Slut Heaven game, while Pammelah was "otherwise occupied," Roberta the F. R. asked me what kind of girls I liked, and when I said I didn't know she shook her head and said "Oh, Thomas, oh, Thomas..." But then she added:

"Who's the girl in the song?"

After some confusion, I realized she was talking about the little bit of lyrics she had seen in my notebook way back after our first "pep band" experience, the beginning of the "King Dork Strikes Again" work-very-much-in-progress.

There are things I'd like to get across to you, my dear
Approximate emotions I believe you ought to hear
hey hey hey, little calendar girl
before you disappear
I'll try to make myself at least approximately clear....

"You say she's your 'dear,'" said the Robot, remembering pretty well.

I didn't see any reason not to tell her about Celeste Fletcher and how we used to be, kind of . . . close. She was incredulous.

"Celeste?" she said. "Going-Out-with-Todd-Dante Celeste? That's your ex?"

Well, now, "ex" was maybe pushing things, if she meant ex-girlfriend, which she did. I'd made out with Celeste Fletcher a couple times, signed her tits once, got a drugged-up hand job from her in the hospital–at least, I think I did–and managed casually as if by accident to touch her ass a few times thereafter. Not the deepest or most "meaningful" relationship in the history of the battle of the sexes by any stretch. And if you had ever called her my girlfriend in her presence she'd have hit you with a tire iron. I mean, if she'd happened to be holding a tire iron at the time. I doubt she'd actually make the effort to go out and find a tire iron just to hit you with if she didn't already have one. But she'd be mad.

Anyway, I suppose I said I didn't know in the "yes" way rather than in the "no" way.

The Robot was staring at me in awe. Celeste Fletcher had clawed her way to the upper midrange of the Clearview girl hierarchy, and Todd Dante was a big-deal football or basketball guy, worshipped by one and all among the general population of the school, which, as I've noted, tilted heavily normal. Sam Hellerman had explained that a guy could raise his stock dramatically among females if they saw him associated with pretty girls, particularly those above their own status. It seemed to be what was happening here. I guess merely being the "ex" of someone who is the not-yet-"ex" of a popular sports guy confers a little of the sports guy's allure. Chalk up another one to Sam Hellerman and the Hellerman tapes. They were running around four–zip, by my calculations.

When Pammelah returned from the front of the bus, the Robot moved to make room for her next to me, but not before doing some hurried whispering directly into Pammelah's ear. Telling her about Celeste Fletcher? I imagine so, because Pammelah's off-kilter eyes instantly began to take on the same look of astonishment and awe.

Meanwhile, I was thinking: I've got the chance and I ought to take it. And the way I saw it, there was no reason this whole thing couldn't be accomplished without resorting to the terrifyingly extreme tactic of exchanging actual words.

So I tentatively put the very edge of my hand so it was just touching Pammelah's leg. Her hand found mine. And, in secret, hidden underneath our two pressed-together thighs, my slender one and her quite a bit more substantial one, we rubbed our fingers all over each other the whole way, while the Robot chattered on and on and the kids on the bus sang "On, Wisconsin, suck my johnson. . . ."

It was a nice moment.

"What's the song about?" the Robot said at one point.

"I think it's about getting a blow job from the University of Wisconsin at Madison," I said.

"No, *your* song!" she said, and her eyes added: "Idiot."

What *was* my song about?

"I don't know," I said. But I gave her the look that says: "I think it's about how it's difficult to explain how hard it is to figure out how to go about trying to express how difficult to explain everything is."

Sam Hellerman had advised, in the aftermath of the Jeans Skirt Girl operation, that the best way to kiss a girl the first time is, contrary to popular belief, just to zoom in and do it with little preamble. Talk to her first, of course, to ensure her comfort with you, but don't waste time trying to "set it up." Just do it. And whatever you do, don't ask if it's okay. Girls, apparently, hate it when a guy goes "I really want to kiss you, would that be all right?" and they instantly lose respect for any guy who does it.

"Just make eye contact and lean into her," he had said. "And if you can organize it so you can push her up against a wall as you do it, they love that too." Kind of tragic, if so, when you think about how the Aladdin Arcade had had no available walls. Or maybe it was not tragedy but merely poor organizational skills.

So meanwhile, I was still thinking. I was sure I could organize things better than that.

I waited for my moment, and when circumstances allowed, I pushed Pammelah Something up against the wall–well, the shelves really–of the band room, made contact with her eyes, and then made contact with her mouth. Well, what can I say? It was maybe a bit awkward because of her being bigger than me. But it was kissing a girl and it went as well as it could have, in my estimation, except for this one part halfway through where I started to wonder if I was failing to be interesting enough in there and to worry that my tongue may have, in fact, over-stayed its welcome and to consider the possibility that my best course of action might well be to cut my losses and run from the room sobbing, never to be heard from again. But then she looked at me and said, I kid you not, "Mm, I'd like another one of those." Essentially, Pammelah Something (whose actual last name had turned out to be Shumway, of all things) responded with wild passion, just as the Robot had hinted and as Sam Hellerman had confidently predicted. And I had to hand it to the Robot on another matter as well, concerning the ass-grabbio: it was a pretty good butt, if not, perhaps, literally the "best in the west."

HEY, I'LL TAKE IT

So that, my dear friends, is how your illustrious narrator, through no fault of his own and largely by accident, wound up with a girlfriend. And they said it couldn't be done.

I didn't even have to ask her, in so many words, to "go." Which I'm glad about, because the practice runs in my head hadn't gone well. I mean, it's pretty much impossible to say "Do you want to go?" and have it not sound sarcastic, no matter how hard you try. But in the event, the kiss (Hellermanian method, against-the-shelves variation) was all it took. We were going.

And that's how Pammelah Shumway wound up in the red beanbag in the Celeste Fletcher spot at our band practice, looking all sexy, calling me "sweetie," and asking if I was going to "play her song." By "her song" she meant the half-finished "King Dork Strikes Again," though she didn't know it by that title. I'm afraid I must admit that the title under which she knew it was "Pamm's Song." This is because, after hearing the Robot refer to it a few times, she had said:

"Is it about me?"

The look I gave her was one of surprise mingled with indignation and slight amusement at this presumptuous question. I'm not so cavalier with my songs, young lady, if "cavalier" means what I think it does. My songs are sacred. But Pammelah Shumway, being just about the worst face-reader I've ever come across in a lifetime of making people try to read my face, had taken that as a solid yes. Then, well, I guess I just kind of ran with it, because I didn't know what else to do. And I was staring at her breasts, which distracted me at the crucial moment when I might have figured out a way to say "No, it isn't, actually." Not that I'm convinced there would have been one, practically speaking.

So I guess I am pretty cavalier with my songs after all.

But that brings us to the other matter, that of Pammelah Shumway's sexiness. Almost as soon as we had reached the state of "going," she had started dressing better, by which I mean sluttier. The skirts got shorter, the shirts got tighter and lower, and the shoes got higher. Sam Hellerman was fairly—and in another sense kind of unfairly—critical of Pammelah's WHR, but he was encouraging about this development. It shows that she cares enough about you to try to look good for you and to make you look good in front of other men, raising your status accordingly, he said. Well, all due snickers and snorts to that other "men" bit aside, of course I liked it. I mean, that was the point, wasn't it? Liking things about each other, I mean?

As for what she liked about me, well, honestly, I can't help you there. All I had to go on was stuff the Robot had said, that she liked my eyes, my hair, and my supposed resemblance to the kid on *Malcolm in the Middle,* and that she thought I was "cute and funny." She liked my teeth. I kid you not, there was apparently something intoxicating about them, something that couldn't be put into words. In fact, I'd pardon you for wondering if this whole thing might not have been a slow-building, meticulously planned Make-out/Fake-out. I had that thought myself but had rejected it for two reasons: (a) Pammelah Shumway, though moving up in the world of sexiness, to be sure, was nowhere near high-status enough to attempt a classic Make-out/Fake-out on me, especially since I was, as far as anybody at Clearview knew, in a neutral zone between normalcy and decency, and a fellow "pep band" member to boot; and (b) the Robot, whatever else she was, was unquestionably genuine. Everything she was, and every waking thought she had, was voluminously documented, in a form that would be simply impossible to fake.

But you know my philosophy. Oh, you don't? It's called the Hey, I'll Take It philosophy, and it goes like this: "Hey, I'll take it." I'd stumbled into Pammelah Shumway, and right or wrong, I was going to roll with it.

Having a girl with large breasts on your team comes with all sorts of benefits, one of which I'll illustrate by explaining what happened when Shinefield, hearing Pammelah ask about "her song," began to look puzzled and perturbed, being under the impression, precarious though it may have been, that we were practicing only covers in the run up to the Mountain Dew show. And what happened was this: nothing. He was too distracted to notice much of anything in any way that mattered. Never underestimate the power of loveliness. It can move mountains, or at least make you forget that there was a mountain there in the first place, which is just as good. Maybe better.

241

Sam Hellerman motioned to me to start the strum intro of "King Dork Strikes Again" and directed Shinefield to play "Cat Scratch Fever."

Well, I wasn't finished with the lyrics, but it sounded pretty decent, though maybe on the quick side, tempo-wise. As for my girlfriend, she seemed to like the idea of there being a song about her. But it was clear that, for whatever reason, she just didn't get it—the music, the song, just rock and roll in general. She would smile, but her basic attitude seemed to be one of total bewilderment with a tinge of, let's face it, boredom. She had one of those car phones you carry with you everywhere, though mercifully she didn't wear it in a holster like Sam Hellerman, and she kept going out to take calls while we were practicing. I tried not to be offended, but, you know, this was my rock and roll we were talking about here, and I was singing a song that I was pretending was about her, though of course, outwardly it still sounded like "Cat Scratch Fever." But she could at least turn the phone off and give it some attention, it seemed to me.

The Robot showed up later, having come straight from her cross-country race or whatever it was, still dressed in her orange and white Badger running gear. She had a big bottle of iced tea, which turned out actually to contain bourbon, and when the girls began to pass it back and forth, my girlfriend loosened up quite a bit. She liked the way I looked with a guitar, I could tell—once she'd had a few drinks, anyway.

And what about Naomi? Well, Naomi, Bert Jansch, Blind Blake, Big Bill Broonzy, O'Brien, and I were getting along just great. I still couldn't play to save my life, and listening to Big Bill Broonzy made me kind of embarrassed that I'd ever tried to call myself a guitar player. My attempts to play like Blind Blake were an absolute fiasco. I even tried blindfolding myself while trying to do "Diddie Wa Diddie" just to see if it would help. (It didn't.) But sighin', cryin', and tryin' to learn to play "O'Brien Is Tryin' to Learn to Talk Hawaiian" wasn't going *all* that badly, even if it wasn't quite . . . flyin'. And even my own little songs were nice to play on Naomi–they had a warm, "real" feel to them that my cigarette-box amp just couldn't equal. I even found I had some success willing "King Dork Strikes Again" to be about Pammelah Shumway instead of Celeste Fletcher. After all, my real girlfriend was a lot nicer than my old fake imaginary girlfriend, but that didn't mean it was any easier to explain stuff. Quite the contrary, really.

My girlfriend. It sounded so strange to say it. It still sounds strange to say it, as you will surely hear if you go back to the beginning of this paragraph, pretend you're me, and read the first sentence of it out loud.

PART FIVE

Prom

FONZIE

At home, very little had changed since Little Big Tom had moved to the El Capitano Motor Lodge. My mom had been going out more, always saying she was headed "to therapy," but with my mom, the difference between her being out and not being out could be difficult to spot. Amanda and I wound up eating more delivered pizza and frozen food, which some people would complain about, I guess, but it's safe to say that such people are coming from a place of never having experienced Little Big Tom's big pots of vegetarian slop.

I visited Little Big Tom from time to time, when I could. It was almost unbearably depressing in that motel room, but he was always so relieved to see me when he opened the door that I felt I just couldn't deprive him of what seemed like the sole bright spot in his otherwise grim existence. He seemed to spend most of his time actually in the room, typing away on his laptop. When I asked what he was writing he said:

"Memoirs."

Well, that sure sounds like an interesting "read." You can't make this stuff up, you really can't.

Of course I had gone straight to Amanda with the news about the Case of Little Big Tom and the Nonexistent Gym Bag.

Her reaction had been "Well, of course he'd say that." But she hadn't seen the unquestionably genuine look of utter confusion on Little Big Tom's face when I brought it up.

Let's find this gym bag, I thought, and rummaged through the dark, silent house, till at last I located, in the master bedroom closet, a duffel bag that contained, in each of two side pockets, a pair of ladies' panties, one pink and the other powder blue. Kind of strange, I remarked to Amanda, that Little

247

Big Tom hadn't taken his gym bag with him to the El Capitano Motor Lodge. And even stranger, I continued, that Little Big Tom's gym bag happened to have a Santa Carla Police Department seal on it and closely resembled our dad's old police bag.

To my mind, this pretty much wrapped up the case of the hot underwear in the gym bag. Whatever the interparental-unit conflict may have been about, the underwear in the bag was completely irrelevant to it.

"Would I be all that far off in speculating, mademoiselle," I said, going all Hercule Poirot on her ass, "that it was you, Amanda Henderson, who planted the underwear in this bag, under the mistaken impression that it belonged to the suspect, with the intention of ensnaring *le Grand Tom* in a clever plot to force his vacation of the premises? Is it not that that is the case?" Or words to that effect. My Belgian accent rules, have I ever mentioned that?

Amanda looked back at me with a serene expression, as though to say "I couldn't possibly comment, and even if I did, what does it matter? It worked, didn't it?"

I gave her the look that says "No, it didn't."

Her response look of "Oh yeah? Then where is he?" was quickly followed by one that said, if I'm not mistaken, "You're such an asshole."

Amanda's gloating didn't fool me: I could tell she wasn't a hundred percent pleased with how things were turning out around here. I mean, how could she be? A weird impulse made me ask if she'd like to come with me to visit Little Big Tom at the motel sometime, but her exaggerated eye roll seemed to be a "No, I'd rather drink lighter fluid."

I had to leave it at that. Little Big Tom could sing its praises all he wanted, but "communication" isn't always all it's cracked up to be, and quite often it gets you precisely nowhere.

Basically, with Little Big Tom gone and my mom either away or hardly present, and Amanda pretending to be pleased with herself but trudging around from room to room with her phone-baby like a patient in a mental hospital, this house was pretty much dead. All I had left were my records, Naomi, my lawsuit files, and my research project on the jacket-fifties-varsity version of normalcy on display at Clearview High School. This last project had stalled a bit as I'd learned more about Clearview firsthand, but when there was nothing else to do, I would sometimes return to it.

One of those cable channels that feature blocks of reruns of old TV shows had *Happy Days,* which is this program from the seventies about the fifties concerning a teenage guy, his family and friends, and this character called Fonzie, who is a "hood" with a heart of gold. Basically, it is pretty much in line with the central fallacy presented in *Halls of Innocence:* the normal kids, jacket-varsity people one and all, are the good guys, whereas, in reality, this combination of decent and normal is so rare that it might as well not exist. So either the show is lying, and off-screen Richie and Potsie are spending most of their time persecuting the weak and asking each other "Who you calling homo, faggot? Who you calling faggot, homo?" or they're the off-screen victims of actual normal people who just don't make it onto the main show. Neither Richie nor Potsie would have lasted even one day at Hillmont High School, I can tell you that, and I doubt they'd have fared much better in the subtler but still senseless and brutal Clearview environment—not for long, anyway.

Potsie did kind of remind me of a larger, less bespectacled, better-looking Sam Hellerman. He was always coming up with schemes that landed Richie in trouble, and showing him how to do things like surreptitiously undo bras and practice kissing by making out with bathroom stalls and stuff like that. He's not half the evil genius Sam Hellerman is, and frankly, I think the show would have benefited from a bit more evil as well as a bit more reality. But you know, it's just a show. When they would get into scrapes, Richie would always be rescued by Fonzie, who was a motorcycle-riding juvenile delinquent in a leather jacket, except he looks about forty-five. At the end, Richie would learn a valuable lesson, and Fonzie would comb his hair and say "Hey."

Point being, in real life, there ain't no Fonzie.

RAMONING MAKES THE WORLD GO ROUND

But here, let me tell you about sex.

Got your attention there, didn't I? Good old sex. You can't beat it.

First, though, I should mention that the Female Robot's letters didn't stop coming when I became Pammelah Shumway's boyfriend. On the contrary, their frequency increased, to sometimes as many as three a day. Pammelah sent me notes too, but hers were, as Gandalf said of the lesser rings, mere essays in the craft. The Robot's, on the other hand: they were perilous.

As pointless and random as the Robot's letters were, she had a style all her own and, I'd venture to say, a kind of warped way with words. Pammelah's vocabulary was not very powerful at all, and moreover, it didn't seem like her heart was in it. But the Robot certainly picked up the slack. Her letters were now filled with detailed notes on Pammelah's thoughts and state of mind as well as her own, plus many, many questions. Was I mad at Pamm, did I like her shoes today, did I know that she said I was a good kisser, didn't I think her skin was pretty, was I going to "molest" her after school in the band room today, did I know that she liked my arms and that she wanted me to take her to the girls bathroom at the Slut Heaven Rec Center and do terrible things to her.... The Pammelah of the Robot's letters sounded quite a bit more interesting than the one presented by Pammelah herself. I wondered about that Pammelah. She sounded fun. The real Pammelah never said any of that stuff to me. I had only the Robot's word, though I had no real cause to doubt it, that she had actually said any of it at all.

It was, however, a convenient aid to managing my "relationship." A Robot letter would inform me in homeroom what Pammelah was mad about, and by second period I could take action to correct it; by fourth period, I would learn from another Robot missive whether the action I had taken had been successful. It beat the hell out of Try to Guess What I'm Mad About. I couldn't help thinking how unfortunate it was that there wasn't a robot in Little Big Tom and my mom's marriage. It can be a real labor-saving device.

Now, one of the things I'd always liked about the Robot was her unapologetic vulgarity. Especially in context with all the stuff about kittens and socks and candy, it was arresting and kind of unexpectedly charming. At least, I thought so. Well, this increased both in intensity and frequency now that I was her best friend's boyfriend. The mentions of Pammelah and me got sexier and sexier. I'll give you one example:

```
. . . naughty boy Thomas dum de dum de
dum. How's the bone, my dear bone? My
fuzzy blanket with the catapillers is the
cutest thing, but it kinda smells like
```

251

salad. Do you like cuddles with Pamm under
a blanket? You can use mine! Just don't
get gross stains on it eewww. Are you tow
lovebirds gonna get naked and have sexy
times tonight? Curiosity! You can do "the
shocker"! ha ha! Scandalous! (wink) What's
moss made of? . . .

So, if you don't know what "the shocker" is, I didn't either. I don't ask about everything, but this one I had to ask. And when the Robot told me what it was, with that impish little nose crinkle, I mean, you know, I talk a good game, but I'm really a tender soul deep down, and honestly I found "the shocker" a bit, well, shocking. Plus, I like to be the most vulgar person in the room—that's well known—and I hated being upstaged.

"You know 'the shocker,'" the Robot said. She held up her hand with the ring finger folded down. Now I'd been seeing the Clearview kids, especially the girls, doing this hand sign all over the place ever since I'd started there, and, silly me, I thought it was the Jerry Garcia salute that they got slightly wrong. (Basically Jerry Garcia had his middle finger chopped off with an ax, so hippies sometimes salute each other this way. If you'll remember, Flapjack did it to Little Big Tom.) But no. The Robot continued: "'Two in the pink, one in the stink'?" Then she scampered away laughing like a crazy person. It took me till halfway through fourth period to get it, and I imagine my perturbed expression in reaction to getting it lasted semi-frozen pretty much throughout the rest of the day.

And also no, I didn't, as it happens, do "the shocker" on Pammelah Shumway. As you shall see.

Ramoning makes the world go round, everyone knows that.

But have you noticed how in movies and TV and books, the girls never seem to be as interested in ramoning as the guys? You know what I mean: the guy tries to put his arm around the girl casually and gradually inch his hand toward her breast and she realizes and takes the hand off her chest and puts it back on her shoulder with a kind of "behave yourself, Buster" attitude? Or, as in *Happy Days,* the guys are trying to learn how to unhook the girls' bras behind their backs so they can get them off before the girls notice, and once the girls notice they get mad and say they're not "that kind of a girl"? Or maybe it's not so old-fashioned as in *Happy Days,* but more modern: nevertheless, the girl is still trying not to "give it away" and the guy has to try to get around her defenses, and it's like, by doing it with her he's kind of taking advantage of her, regardless of whether she's into it?

Well, I don't have a lot of experience with girls, maybe, but in what experience I have had, that just has never been my, you know, experience. True, it's difficult and certainly rare to get to the point where they like you enough or are interested enough in you to want to make out with you, as Sam Hellerman's tapes and the clear need for them indicate. But however you get there, if you do manage to get there, my experience has been that girls tend to be, like, just as into it as you are. In fact, usually more so. And they get mad if you don't or can't keep up with them. I never had to resort to skullduggery to unhook Deanna Schumacher's bra. Basically, a girl likes you, the bra comes off. Pretty simple. So I have always thought of the whole notion of the reluctant female ramoner as some kind of myth, or maybe it's the way it used to be long, long ago, from when people were weird and uptight about sex in a whole different way than the way we are w. and u. about it now. Another weird jacket-varsity-type thing, in other words.

But here's the point: Pammelah Shumway was exactly like that, just like in *Happy Days*. She really liked kissing, it's true. And she really liked my hands on her while we were doing it, and she would grope me too, often and with great enthusiasm. But when I tried to do the next thing, like go down her pants or up her shirt or whatever, she would take my hand with her hand and put it back where it was before. Or she would say "Don't do that," and I would of course recoil and feel mortified, thinking "Oh no, what have I done wrong?", but then she would start kissing me again, like the "don't do that" never happened.

The weirdest part, though, was she would do all of this with this kind of seductive attitude, posing in a sexy way and saying sexy things like "Can I interest you in some of the merchandise?" She wasn't shy at all. But she seemed to want to keep her clothes on at all costs.

So, for example, we would be kissing and rubbing on each other and saying things like "Oh baby" like you do, and she would lean into me and say, "Mm, feels like you have something special for me there." So I don't know about you, but to me that made it seem very much like the time for the blow job part to begin had begun. It was exactly the sort of thing Deanna Schumacher would say right before pouncing, if you know what I mean. So I would lean back, like you do, but unlike Deanna Schumacher, Pammelah would shake her head and say, "I'm not doing that," with a little grimace. The first time, I stupidly thought she meant that undoing my pants was the thing she wouldn't do, for some reason, so I started to undo my belt buckle and she shook her head again, making it pretty clear that I should just buckle the belt right back up. Well, okay. I did.

"So," I said. "What should we do, then?"

And she leaned back and winked and pushed her breasts out and said: "I don't know. What did you have in mind?"

Well, you know, it was pretty obvious what I'd had in mind. And of course I didn't want her to do it if she didn't want to. I mean, obviously, I *did*, but I wasn't going to press the issue. And if you've managed to pick up on how shy and unconfident I am in general as a person, you'll probably understand that I'm not exaggerating when I say that I really didn't. Press the issue, that is. Actually, the whole ramoning thing had started to terrify me in a way it never quite had before. I did indeed have "something special" for Pammelah Shumway. Why didn't she want it, exactly? Was there something wrong with it, some defect she could feel through my pants that I wasn't even aware was a defect? When you have something special like that, it doesn't take much to give you a complex about it, and I was well on my way to developing one.

Now, I realize that everyone's different. And sometimes you have to work up to things, I know that. And I was patient as can be, with the patience born of self-loathing and sheer terror, which is the best, most effective kind of patience there is. But over time it became pretty clear that no matter how much making out we did, no clothes were ever coming off and no actual ramoning, by even the most generous definition, was going to happen.

The point here is ... well, no, the main point is the lack of ramoning, let's be honest. But the other main point, if you didn't get it, is this: here was yet another example of the fifties-varsity-oh-gee-Penelope-Anne-did-you-really-get-pinned-let's-get-burgers-down-at-the-sock-hop-jacket phenomenon at

Clearview High School, if "phenomenon" means what I think it means. In other words, just call me Potsie, I guess. I hear the Hooper twins neck on the first date. I mean, they're, like, fast, daddy-o.

If you'll remember from my previous explanations, I once imagined that being part of a couple would be like forming a Sex Alliance Against Society, the two of you against the world, ramoning away, and facing the terrors and predations of society at large with a great big "Fuck you, world, we have each other and we don't need you anymore." I have to say, "going" with Pammelah Shumway fell a bit short of this ideal. But I've never been too big on idealism. It was what it was, and I was willing to work with it.

The thing is–and you can believe me or not, I don't really care–I didn't mind the ramonelessness all that much, once I had grasped the situation. Until things started to get out of hand a little later, I was still having fun. I could always take a shower and think about Fiona if anything ever got to be too much for me. And it was definitely a fun novelty having a girl-friend, even without the ramoning. At first.

SHIRLEY TEMPLE, THE YOUNGEST, MOST SACRED MONSTER OF THE CINEMA IN HER TIME

Pride and Prejudice aside, the thing I liked best, I think, about the books I was pretending my dad had read was also the thing I liked least about them. *The Crying of Lot 49* and *Flow My Tears, the Policeman Said* and even *Dune* each depicted a world where nothing made sense, and the main guy is utterly confused and disoriented and tries, largely without success, to figure every-thing out, to make some sense out of the mess he has found himself in. Unfortunately, the reader is also confused about what's going on, and I often found myself pretty lost, and maybe a little paranoid as well, suspecting that my own world, as confusing as it is, might have yet another layer of sinister confusingness to it that I hadn't yet taken enough drugs to perceive.

That said, I could really relate to these characters, and despite their crazy features—the replicants, the sand worms, the W.A.S.T.E. baskets—their worlds still looked a lot more like mine than, say, the quaint, old-timey version of New York City presented in *The Catcher in the Rye*. I suppose Holden Caulfield is a bit confused about who he is and where he is and so forth, but it occurs to me that one of the reasons I have had such a hard time being all in love with his story like everyone else— besides the fact that they make you read the dumb book over and over and try to force you to like it—is that his confusion just isn't state-of-the-art enough for me.

Because *Flow My Tears, the Policeman Said* is way more how I felt about Clearview High School than anything J. D. Salinger ever dreamed up. (Salinger is the *Catcher in the Rye* guy, a very bad person who has caused the world untold misery.) In a way, I *am* like Jason Taverner, waking up with no identity in a mysterious hotel room, not knowing how much of the parasitic life form my girlfriend infected me with is still in my system, and the world outside is a scary police state where I don't know any of the rules. Although I guess I knew the rules, really. They were the rules of *Happy Days* and *Revenge of the Nerds*. I just didn't want to accept it.

I was telling Roberta the Female Robot about *Flow My Tears, the Policeman Said*. Well, I was trying to explain it but failing, and she was looking at me with appropriate puzzlement.

"That's really in the book?" she said, all agog, if "agog" means what I think it means.

I assured her that yes, yes it was. I'm certain her only exposure to literature of any kind was to books you got credit for reading, meaning, basically, highlights from the books on Mrs. Pizzaballa's list: *The Catcher in the Rye, A Separate Peace, Lord of the Flies, The Grapes of Wrath, The Scarlet Letter,* and possibly *A Tale of Two Cities.* So it's not surprising that *Flow My Tears, the Policeman Said* was something of a shock to her. It had been to me, even after reading all those real, noncredit books in my dad's library.

The Robot said it all sounded warped and surreal, like Salvador Dalí.

"Who?" I said.

"Salvador Dalí," she said.

"Who?" I said, trying to narrow it down.

That was when she told me who Salvador Dalí was.

"Oh, that Salvador Dalí," I said.

So that was two things the Robot had known about that I hadn't, the other being "the shocker." What else was in this girl's head? I wasn't sure I wanted to know.

I had heard from Pammelah Shumway a little bit about Roberta the F. R.'s rough childhood, her troubled home life, her brother's overdose, her suicide attempt, her occasional and continuing self-destructive behavior. It was strange because, other than the little bits of darkness that would pop up from within the dense text of her letters, she was such a cheerful, sunny little goofball. It kind of made you wonder about what might be lurking inside all the other cheerful, sunny people in the world who don't write letters. Maybe Little Big Tom's memoirs would be worth reading after all. I mean, you never know, do you?

"She's never had a boyfriend," Pammelah had said, "and I've known her since kindergarten and I've only ever been to her house twice. Do you think your friend Sam would like her? Maybe he should ask her to go. But oh my God, Thomas, does that girl ever like to drink!"

Well, there was that, it's true: the Robot always had a can or a bottle with the original contents poured out and replaced with some kind of alcohol, apparently stolen from her parents' liquor cabinet and from other peoples' parents as well. She never seemed drunk, though, at least not to me, which was surprising, because with her being so little you'd think it would have affected her a whole lot more. Pammelah Shumway, though a bit of a drinker herself, like every kid at Clearview, nevertheless had to take care of the Robot sometimes when she would get too sloppy. I'd had the same kind of relationship with Sam Hellerman for years, though he preferred his pills. In a way, I guess, the Robot was Pammelah Shumway's Sam Hellerman, the vulnerable mastermind. Lord, what kind of tapes was *she* listening to? It was a strange thought.

Raising the issue of "fixing up" the Robot and Sam Hellerman was a well-known girl move that you may remember from my previous explanations, though of course Sam Hellerman had his hands full with Jeans Skirt Girl (and God only knows what else) over at Mission Hills. It wasn't going to happen. But though it wasn't something I particularly noticed at the time, her raising it at all reflected something about how she felt about the Robot, in that it was basically, in a subtle backhanded way, intended as an insult to Sam Hellerman. Which wasn't very nice, when you think about it, to either of them.

"I'm glad she has someone to talk to now," Pammelah had continued, meaning me, and she displayed what I thought was surprising honesty by admitting she sometimes saw the Robot as something of a burden and didn't know how to deal with her and had no idea what to say to her most times. It was almost like she was relieved to be passing her off to someone else, or at least to have someone to share the burden. I didn't think it was all that burdensome, really, but then again, I didn't know what to say either. I figured just asking her if she was okay from time to time was both the least and the most I could do. She always said yes.

At any rate, it was pretty convenient to have easy access to a brain-deadening agent–the Robot's alcohol supply–though I didn't overdo it by any means. I've never been a big drinker, but it was really pretty much impossible to take Clearview High's weirdness without some help.

Later that day, in the band room, the Robot came in holding a big book close to her chest.

"You like books," she said.

I nodded warily. I trusted the Robot, but this was a sore spot. I didn't want just anyone tagging me as a book reader, as I've explained.

"I think they're okay," I said, hoping she could read on my face that "okay" was a euphemism for really, really, really terrific.

"I think they're okay too," she said.

There was a pause.

"I liked *How to Kill a Mockingbird*," she said. "Do you like art?"

My look said that I didn't know much about art, but I knew what I liked, which was basically naked ladies, so I guessed the answer was yeah, it's okay. She understood, and nodded. Boy, was this conversation awkward. I honestly preferred to do this in written form, where I'd read ten insane pages and then respond "I don't know" to everything later at my leisure.

At long last, the Robot got to the point, showing me her

book, which was a book of Salvador Dalí art from the library. That's where I first saw the picture of him with the sexy desk-woman. That photo made a powerful impression on me, but there were paintings of interest as well, including one called *Shirley Temple, The Youngest, Most Sacred Monster of the Cinema in Her Time*, and another called *Dream Caused by the Flight of a Bee Around a Pomegranate a Second Before Awakening*, which had a naked lady in it. These would have made fantastic album titles, and covers, and the ladies were decent as well. Impressive guy. It was kind of too bad he lived before rock and roll.

"And here's one about you," said the Robot, turning to a page featuring a painting called *The Great Masturbator*. Her voice dissolved into a storm of giggles, but I was nonetheless taken aback: however did she know? But then I realized: yeah, that's pretty much everyone, isn't it? I mean, isn't it? Anyway, I guess setting up that "joke" had been the whole point of the conversation. Most amusing.

At that point, Pammelah came into the band room and said, "Excuse me, Roberta, I need to talk to Thomas about something."

The Robot said "Bow chicka wow wow" and scrammed. And Pammelah Shumway stuck her tongue in my mouth.

NEW BAND NAME

How to Kill a Mockingbird.
 Guitar and vocals: the Great Masturbator
 Bass and lobsters: the Good Masturbator
 Drums and ennui: the Halfway Decent Masturbator
 First album: *The Ghost of Vermeer of Delft Which Can Be Used as a Table*

261

WOMEN!

Sam Hellerman had been dead accurate in his prediction that having a sexy, not-too-bad-looking girlfriend would raise my status at Clearview High School. "Other men" seemed impressed, and girls also seemed to be friendlier, or at least less hostile, than I was used to. You'd think that my official choice of Pammelah Shumway would have dampened things considerably between me and Blossom van Kinkle, but in fact, Blossom van Kinkle still, it seemed to me, had that unholy light in her eyes when she looked at me, and she began to flirt with me quite openly and as never before. This, in turn, seemed to give the wider population of girls the impression, mistaken though it undoubtedly was, that there was, perhaps, a little more to me than met the eye. It was like the Hellerman tapes had come to life before my eyes. The secrets of women had been revealed.

There was one time when Pammelah was dressed particularly sexily, in a little skirt and long socks and those high-heeled boots with fur on them, and this normal guy walking past told me I was "da man" and fist-bumped me. (I've still never quite gotten used to that, as I tend to see every approaching fist as a developing punch, but I recovered enough to do the bump in the end, if only just barely.) But how often does King Dork get told by some random guy, even a big dumb normal lug, that he's "da man"? Answer: not often. But it happened once. It was hard not to enjoy that, at least a little.

"You know," I said, only half joking, "if you keep dressing like this, some normal guy is going to take a liking to you and decide to stomp me into the ground till only the stones remain."

"Aw, thanks, Thomas," Pammelah said, with a look in her

weirdly distant eye that left the distinct impression that to her way of thinking such a course of events might well have its silver lining. "You're so sweet."

Silly as it seems, I took the precaution, when walking around the Quad with Pammelah Shumway, of invoking the protective Spirit of the Clearview Badgers by wearing my orange Badger beret, pulled down tightly around my ears. Surely you wouldn't stomp a card-carrying, beret-wearing Badger in good standing into the ground till only the stones remain, was the message I hoped it communicated. It may not have been much, but sad to say, the Spirit was pretty much all I had.

My having a girlfriend even had an effect on Celeste Fletcher, who had mostly shunned me since becoming a jacket girl, refusing to acknowledge my existence despite sitting right in front of me in Mrs. Pizzaballa's class. Not that she was all that nice, mind you. But I had moved up in the world enough to where she evidently felt she could get away with being seen conversing with me without damaging her reputation too much. (Incidentally, I had recently learned that Celeste Fletcher had joined drama and was currently set to star in a school production of ... *Grease*. Sometimes you can actually hear the universe laughing behind your back.)

"How's your girlfriend?" she said once, after the piano chords had signaled the end of Mrs. Pizzaballa's class.

"She's fine," I said.

"I'm sure she is," said Celeste Fletcher with enough of an eye roll to suggest that one or the other of us had just been insulted, though I had no idea about what. "Oh, and by the way," she continued even as she set off down the hall, "could you tell your *drummer* to please stop calling me all the time? My dad wants to get a restraining order."

"Nice talking to you," I said. Even her walk, though nice to watch as always, looked peeved and hostile. Oh, she was normal, all right.

So Shinefield hadn't taken Sam Hellerman's radio silence advice, just as Sam Hellerman had predicted, and his failure to follow the radio silence advice was working out about as predicted as well. My heart went out to Shinefield almost in spite of myself, because I had an inkling of what he was going through, but it also occurred to me that he was, in part, suffering from the curse of being seminormal and optimistic and confident enough to do ill-advised things like make an ass of himself phone-stalking an estranged girlfriend. A single rebuff is usually enough to turn me into an antisocial, hyperventilating, lovelorn lyrics generator, shunning contact with the outside world and lovingly caressing my enemies list. All in all, that's a much better way to handle the situation, it seems to me.

As for Sam Hellerman's love life, if such there were, it remained mysterious, and he remained his characteristic inscrutable self in response to any questions about it.

"How's Jeans Skirt Girl going?" I asked one time when I met him at Toby's to look through the new arrivals. Jeans Skirt Girl had never made an appearance at band practice as I'd half expected, and he hadn't mentioned her since that fateful day at the Aladdin Arcade.

"Cynthia with a 'y,' you mean," he said. So he knew her name. That was progress.

"But wait a minute," I said. "Doesn't 'Cynthia' normally have a 'y' in it?" What was the need to specify?

"The 'y' is in place of the 'i' at the end," said Sam Hellerman, "and there's an 'i' instead of the first 'y.' And there's an 'x' instead of the dot on the 'i'.'" He spelled it out for me: C-I-N-T-H-Y-A.

"So it's Cinthya with a Y, X above the I?" I said, clarifying.

"Exactly," said Sam Hellerman.

We gave each other the look that said: "Women!"

THE REPTILIANS

I still hadn't given up on my lawsuit idea, though it was seeming less and less likely to come about anytime soon, and Sam Hellerman's interest in using it as a way to generate publicity for the Mountain Dew show seemed to have dwindled to just about zero. But whatever you do on your own, he cautioned, keep the Catcher Code out of it. It was hard to see why he should care, but the ways of the boy genius are unfathomable to mere mortals like me. I told him what he wanted to hear, but of course the Catcher Code was integral to my case, the linchpin of the whole thing, and I wasn't going to leave it out. I wanted teams of investigators combing through the archives, digging up the grounds of schools, diagramming Mr. Teone's associations and movements looking for patterns, exposing the whole rotten mess. But failing that, I at least wanted an opportunity to make a public declaration that Mr. Teone had killed my dad and that the normal world had conspired to cover it up and had facilitated the attempt on my life as well. If that resulted in general moral condemnation of Normalism itself, as it certainly should, well then, so be it.

I had a feeling, though, that Sam Hellerman was right to the extent that as a minor I'd need the participation of a legal guardian to get anywhere with this plan. And that meant Little Big Tom. I knew it would be a long shot, but I gathered up my files and took them over to the El Capitano Motor Lodge for an informal consultation.

He was pleased to see me as always, but he was looking pretty rough, still in his underwear and leaving the definite impression that he hadn't shaved or bathed, or even left the room, in days.

"How's the radio silence going?" I asked. In response, he stared at me glumly, saying nothing, though if I'd learned anything from Sam Hellerman on this topic it was that it was probably not going all that well. Radio silence in the face of romantic trouble takes an iron will that few possess. And it didn't seem very likely that Little Big Tom would turn out to be one of the few who did.

Anyway, with those pleasantries out of the way, I launched into my carefully prepared argument for the indictment of Mr. Teone and the United States of America for murder, conspiracy, and crimes against humanity, including as exhibits all the necessary documentation, from my dad's old copy of *The Catcher in the Rye* to the Catcher Code, the marginal notes in the books from my dad's teen library, my medical charts, everything I had. It was my best presentation of the case thus far. And I ended it with a simple, heartfelt plea: will you help me?

Little Big Tom took off his sunglasses and rubbed his eyes vigorously. He opened his mouth to speak and shut it right back up again no less than four times before seeming to give up on the idea of speaking for good. Then he just stared at me for what seemed like a long, long time.

In view of this reaction, if he had said "Get out of here" like Herr Hellerman had, I wouldn't have been all that surprised. But instead he said:

"Karma ..." Then he was silent again. "You know, chief," he

continued eventually, "there's an old saying that you reap what you sow. It's the old eastern idea of karma, really a very cool philosophy. When people have wronged you, the best thing to do is to turn the other cheek and not sink to their level. I think you'll find that a life lived in negativity like that will have its effects. I understand that you're angry, angry at those kids and … at other … various … things. But trust me about the karma. I promise you they're not going to have an easy time, living with that kind of energy. The best revenge is not to wallow in their darkness but to seek the light. Clear a path for justice, and then let it happen. And it will. You see?"

Yes, I saw very well: it was a brush-off.

Now, it should go without saying, really, that Little Big Tom didn't know what he was talking about. His knowledge of eastern philosophy was based, I'm certain, on a vague familiarity with *Sergeant Pepper's Lonely Hearts Club Band,* a bumper sticker he had once read while stuck in traffic behind a minivan painted like an eggplant, and possibly some mushrooms he once ate.

As a matter of fact, I didn't, and still don't, believe in justice, other than the kind you make for yourself. If justice were real, there would be no Normalism. The normal people would all have gotten their comeuppance long, long ago and died out by natural selection, leaving the world to the decent and the nice to rule in their place. But I wasn't about to argue philosophy with Little Big Tom. And anyway, it didn't look like he'd be up to any courtroom appearances anytime soon.

I was gathering up my materials dejectedly when Little Big Tom roused himself.

"If you do want legal advice, though," he said, to my surprise, "there's someone who might be able to help."

We were driving on the freeway in Little Big Tom's truck. He still seemed pretty out of it, but at least he'd had the presence of mind to put on pants. I admired that. And even if this supposed legal advice turned out to be a dead end, which I considered highly probable, at least it was getting him out of the house, or the motel, rather. My questions about where we were going and who we were going to see were waved away.

"Sit tight" was all he would say.

I sat tight.

It was yet another silent ride. I suppose that was partly owing to my having freaked him out with the Catcher Code, but also it was clear that Little Big Tom wasn't doing so well in general. He even passed a trucker without doing the hand signal to try to get him to sound the horn, and he went by the ramp for Filibuster Road without even saying "Filibuster? I didn't even know her." It was almost like he wasn't the same guy.

Eventually we exited the freeway and drove down a frontage road along the bay, finally edging in toward a little line of houseboats moored to a small dock. I almost literally slapped my forehead.

"Flapjack?" I said.

"Flapjack," said Little Big Tom. "He has a law degree."

"Wonderful," I said. This ought to be good.

Flapjack answered the houseboat door with a shotgun in his hands, totally naked except for a grubby bathrobe that barely closed around his enormous belly and failed completely to conceal that which was in urgent need of concealment.

"Oh, it's you," he said, motioning us in with the gun.

268

"Flapjack doesn't like visitors," whispered Little Big Tom reassuringly.

"Wonderful," I said.

I had never been on a houseboat before, and I was surprised at how unboatlike it really was. Once you got down the stairs, it was like being in a compact, damp room. If a fastidious person had lived there, it might have been kind of a cool setup, everything stowed in a neat series of cleverly designed drawers and cabinets; pieces of built-in furniture doing double or triple duty, like the table-counter-desk; polished brass whatchamacallits; the sound of the shorebirds and the lonely whistle of the freight trains in the distance. Well, that was the ideal. The reality of Flapjack's houseboat was quite different. It was a filthy, chaotic collection of little piles of junk and trash that were at various stages of joining together into larger piles of junk and trash. It smelled a bit like the girls' restroom at the Salthaven Rec Center, the one with the broken lock. I was afraid to touch anything, lest I disturb any of the animals that were, in all probability, nesting within.

Several layers deep, poking out here and there through the grimy thicket of refuse, could be seen evidence of a once thriving and obviously pretty interesting life. I mean stacks of LPs, moldering books, guitars, electronic equipment, and quite a few large paintings leaning in careless clumps, apparently Flapjack's own work. Some of them, despite the absence of naked ladies, seemed pretty good. I was looking at the wreck of a human life, a wreck that genius guitar playing and a supposed law degree hadn't managed to salvage.

Little Big Tom looked at me meaningfully as Flapjack motioned to us to sit on a small benchlike sofa while he settled himself on the floor, or deck, I suppose you'd say, across from us in what I think is called the lotus position—an impressive contortion for such a fat person—with the gun across his knees. Fortunately, his belly hung all the way down to the floor, restoring his modesty. Like the Buddha. We stared at each other.

Little Big Tom motioned me to begin. So I presented my indictment against the Universe, in all its particulars, for the fourth time, handing over the documents to Flapjack at the appropriate points, telling it all as carefully and clearly as I could. I was getting pretty good at it, with all this practice. Flapjack appeared to be engaged and following me closely but made no comment till I was finished.

Actually, he stared at me for quite some time after I'd reached the end, an unreadable expression on his face. I was used to that. It was a lot to take in all at once, I knew.

Finally, he started laughing. It began as a quiet chuckle and built to a boat-shaking thunder of deep, resonant belly laughs, punctuated by the occasional ghost of a cough, and in the end dissolving into the by-now-familiar emphysemic hacking that was his signature sound effect. He wore a wry expression.

"You'll never manage it," he said. "Not in a thousand years." He began to laugh again, and to elaborate on why I'd never manage it in a thousand years, waving my documents for emphasis. They got Eisenhower, he said, and Kennedy, and they got Nixon, too. The key to the whole conspiracy is a code written into the United States Constitution that, when properly deciphered, reveals that all articles and provisions contained in it are really to be understood to mean the exact opposite of what they say literally. Presidents and other leaders who resist when informed of the code are destroyed by scandal or assassination, and regular people who begin to piece it together, if detected by the Reptilians, are either instantly vaporized or closely monitored by biological microchips rigged to superheat the brains of those who get too close to unraveling the mystery. The biochips are introduced into the host subject by means of tiny darts shot from the robotic surveillance insects that monitor our cities. The only way to tell if you've been infected is if you see faint streams of code and Reptilian characters racing across your peripheral vision: a quick suicide is your only option then, since removing the biochip would entail the removal of the entire brain and spinal column. That's what happened to Ambrose Bierce, Jack Parsons, and Bishop Pike, and to Jimi, Janis, Lenny, and possibly Kurt, too. And that's how we got Vietnam, McDonald's, credit cards, the designated hitter rule, and the Reagan presidency. Lyndon Johnson was himself a Reptilian in disguise, and in our contemporary world, the actor Keanu Reeves is perhaps the most powerful Reptilian of them all. The world's population is enslaved by brain manipulation, mechanical insect surveillance, and credit card debt, all controlled at the Federal World Government Headquarters in deep caverns hidden in the Colorado Rocky Mountains.

Then Flapjack showed me a bloody spot on his arm where he had managed to dig out a surveillance dart before it was able to deposit its parasitic biochip into his bloodstream. He nodded knowingly.

"So you see," he concluded with a warm, ironic chuckle, "you'll never fight them with *this*." He waved my papers derisively. "They'll melt your brain before you get within ten miles of any courtroom. But if you want my legal advice, here it is: when you see them coming, shoot to kill. It's your only chance."

"Wonderful," I said.

We were silent yet again in the truck on the way back to the motel. I had certainly gotten Little Big Tom's message, which was: it is, in fact, possible to be too paranoid. And if I didn't want to wind up like Flapjack, I'd have to try to recalibrate my paranoia to a more acceptable level.

My lawsuit days were over. Flapjack had scared me straight. "Thanks . . . chief," I said. Of all the lessons he had ever tried to teach me, this was perhaps the only one that had worked, or even been comprehensible.

Little Big Tom rumpled my hair and smiled wearily. I left him with Sam Hellerman's motivational tape, because if anyone needed artificially induced self-confidence these days, it was Little Big Tom. It hadn't worked too well for me, as far as I could tell, but who knew? It was certainly worth a try.

ON BEING A BOYFRIEND

"I've been thinking about it," said Pammelah Shumway, "and I've decided that from now on I'm going to wear only leopard print and drink only vodka drinks, and no underwear ever."

"As long as you've got a plan," I said. That wasn't snide. It was way more of a plan than I'd ever had. But maybe I didn't need a plan. Just letting things happen hadn't turned out all that badly, at least so far.

Time passed. And then more time passed, predictably. My home life still sucked, but my personal life had never seemed so "on track," despite the Clearview jacket-varsity confusion. Walking among the normal people and avoiding detection by cloaking myself in the Spirit wasn't the worst way to live. My band was, finally, pretty good. (We had gone from How to Kill a Mockingbird to Lobster Telephone, then to the Rimjobs, then to Salvador Dalí's Hot Underwear, then back to Lobster Telephone, then to just Lobster, finally settling on the Reptil-

272

ians, Thomas "Rock" Henderson on guitar-vox, the Hell Man on bass and spacecraft design, Lovelorn Phil on drums, first album *FAQ on the Removal of the Brain and Spinal Column*. Our illegible logo was really getting a workout.)

Moreover, I had a girlfriend, something I never thought in a million years I'd ever have. I even had a kind of nonthreatening social circle in the "pep band." I hated the games and the routines, and spent a great deal of my time trying to will the basketball team to lose so we would have fewer games to go to. But I never had to worry that a band person would try to beat me up. And even though they found my lack of Spirit perplexing, the band kids were quite accepting in the end, seeing me, I believe, as a kind of lovable rogue. I'm sure making out all the time with Pammelah Shumway, who easily had the largest breasts in the whole music program, enhanced my standing even among my seminormal band comrades, as it did among the normal population at large. After all, they didn't know that my girlfriend was in effect permanently locked down. I must seem like quite an impressive guy to them, I imagined, and it might even have been sort of true.

Nevertheless, I began to be conscious of a vague but growing sense of dissatisfaction.

Because having a girlfriend was not at all how I'd imagined it would be. I liked her a lot, and I found myself daydreaming about her and writing songs about her, and suffered bouts of crippling anxiety about whether she really loved me and what she was doing and with whom when we were apart: you know, all the hallmarks of true love. I told her I loved her with the precise required frequency, aided by the Robot's helpful letters: once a day was too little, four times a day was too much. We talked on the phone to say good night to each other every single night. I meant it all too, at least to the degree that a person can be sure of genuinely meaning anything. In other words, this was my one, perhaps my only, chance at having a non-imaginary girlfriend, and I was trying my hardest to do it well. That part, the liking each other and being nice to each other and being on each other's team, wasn't difficult at all.

And yet . . . being "had" as a boyfriend turned out to be a pretty stressful, anxiety-ridden affair, very unlike, as I said, what I'd expected.

For one thing, it involved quite a lot more walking than you'd think. Not only were there the obligatory laps around the Quad during lunch, but there were similarly organized laps around the mall in off-hours, plus a good deal of walking just out and about on the street and in parks and such, because there really wasn't anywhere to go and at least at the park you could find some semiprivate place to make out. But other than the walking around and making out, we didn't end up doing a whole lot alone together, just the two of us. When we weren't kissing or groping or walking in an arm-in-arm clinch, there didn't seem to be a whole lot to say, so when we stopped, there would be a kind of uncomfortable pause till we would just relieve the tension by starting to make out again. Most of the conversations we did have revolved around administering the "relationship": where we were going to go, who we were going to see, what she was going to wear, whether I still thought she was cute, et cetera.

But the most difficult part for me was the endless array of social obligations that came along with being Pammelah Shumway's boyfriend. Until you have been the boyfriend of a girl with "school spirit," you have no idea how much non–making out activity it involves.

Now, you may not know this about me, but basically, I don't like people all that much. One on one, I'm fine, if the other one is halfway decent and at least sort of interesting and, most importantly, not trying to kill me. A trio, if everyone is nice and not too normal, I can handle. But a big group of kids, jabbering and chattering and whooping and hollering about their damnable school activities, their GPAs, and the terrible music they liked, and ranging in type from quasi-decent to full-on normal psychotic? That's not my scene, baby. Just not my scene. I mean, you have no idea how many school-sponsored events there are on the calendar. It's unreal. And I was obligated to go to pretty much every one—the games, the track meets, the plays, the dances, the gymnastics, the fund-raising bake sales, everything, and that was on top of the "pep band" stuff I already had to do. I felt like I was spending nearly all my waking hours participating in some school-sponsored activity, which is basically everything I stand against. I would come home from some event, look in the mirror, and say, "Who *are* you?"

The only break I ever had from this relentless socializing was on Tuesday nights, when Pamm would attend her Latter-Day Saints Youth Group meetings. (That's three things I detest all in one: youth, groups, and, you know, meeting.) I never thought I'd have cause to thank God for not making me a Mormon. But it was the one thing I wasn't forced to go to, and I came to look forward to Tuesday as a precious little island of freedom set in a sea of oppression.

Now, when I'm with a big group of normal people I withdraw into my own head. A defense mechanism, I guess it's called. It's either that or I explode; at least, that's what it feels like. Or I manage to slink off to some corner and lick my wounds, or make some excuse and flee back home to where there are no people, only records and guitars, and a sort of family.

But when you have a girlfriend, you can't leave. And you can't withdraw into your head either, not if you don't want her to get mad at you and take it out on you for days. (My girlfriend expressed her anger and disappointment chiefly by walking slower. We would be walking along as usual and I'd suddenly notice she was back there going at a slowed pace, her head down. So I would scamper back and try to recalibrate, attempting to match her step, which would in turn get even slower. Sometimes she would just stop in the middle of the street altogether, head down, till I went back and grabbed her by the arm to pull her out of the way of the oncoming traffic. It was the most challenging game of Try to Guess What I'm Mad About ever.)

I mean, I guess I get it, because in the dynamic, glittering social scene of drinking Coors Light, smoking dope, and blasting "booty music" down by the reservoir, a silent, pensive boyfriend is just an embarrassment. If it had been just Pamm, the Robot, and I, like how it started out, it would have been nice, even fun, maybe. But in the greater semi- to full-on normal world, I wasn't cutting it as a boyfriend. And I knew the other girls were all saying things like "What's the matter with your boyfriend?" and "He's weird," and even "He's creepy." I suppose I should have known it would only be a matter of time before this exposure of who I really was would be my undoing. But I was naive. Free girlfriend, I thought; what could go wrong? But as the saying goes, there's no such thing as a free girlfriend. And as a philosophy, or at least as a practical guide to how to conduct your romantic affairs, the "Hey, I'll Take It" philosophy isn't quite the be-all and end-all of philosophies that I'd imagined it to be.

Now, you'll have noticed, perhaps, that Roberta the Female Robot's name is largely absent from the explanations I have just given. That's because R. the F. R., though a school spirit girl herself (and how), was largely excluded from these wider social activities. Edging her out had been a gradual process that I only noticed after it was already well under way. My main contact with the Robot was through her still-frequent letters, a ten-minute briefing/debriefing in homeroom, and the conversations we would have at lunch or in the band room or on band trips at those odd times when I didn't happen to have a second tongue in my mouth. But Pammelah Shumway's circle of friends had been gradually widening, and in a place like Clearview, that meant that it—the circle, I mean—was becoming increasingly normal.

It was not at all surprising to me that the rank and file of Clearview High normalcy had rejected the Female Robot. She was as eccentric as they come, and clearly not normal material any way you sliced it: basically, she was one of those kids with nothing whatsoever to offer to the normal people of the world other than to serve as a target, a servant, a doormat, or a punching bag. The Clearview Spirit protected her from the worst of it, as it had thus far protected me, but that was as far as it was going to go. It infuriated me—still infuriates me, in fact—that she accepted this fate, welcomed it, even, with such bland goodwill. She should have been on my side, declaring total war on Normality forever. She was either oblivious to it or simply liked being marginalized by her favorite people in the world. That was incomprehensible to me, but it was her problem, not mine. The surprising part, at least at first, was that while the Robot clearly admired Pammelah Shumway almost to the point of idolatry, and whereas in my preboyfriend experience of the two of them in only "pep band" situations Pammelah had seemed like a nice enough friend to her, in the outer world and behind her back she was actually quite mean, and was in fact becoming nearly as bad as any normal person.

"Roberta's so weird," she would say. Okay, so Pammelah Shumway doesn't exactly have a powerful vocabulary and you have to read between the lines. "Weird" covers a lot of ground, but I knew it was the third-worst thing she knew to say about anyone, right behind "creepy" and "not that cute": it meant, your existence is embarrassing; it meant, you are beneath contempt. It sounds silly, I know, but translate it from normalspeak and put the whole weight of the psychotic universe behind it and it basically amounts to a death sentence.

Well, it was a slow-developing eye-opener. And all this, along with one other thing that I'll tell you about in a minute, is why I decided before too long that I would have to break up with Pammelah Shumway. Like Celeste Fletcher, she had basically turned normal before my eyes. And unlike the Robot, I found I couldn't just let it slide and play along.

All I had ever wanted was a Sex Alliance Against Society, and I had been quite willing to overlook the sex part in the interests of maintaining the alliance. But now it was turning out to be not much of an alliance, either. And it certainly wasn't, in any meaningful sense, "against" society. Quite the opposite, in fact. Having a girlfriend, contrary to the conventional wisdom, kind of sucked. I wanted out.

Love was dead.

A WELL-ROUNDED NUT

In the midst of all this, I solved the Puzzling Case of the Perplexing Pizzaballa Papers by accident, which should be no surprise, as that is the only way I've ever solved anything.

My second attempt at playing book roulette in the basement book boxes had yielded a challenge to a reckless vow like no other: *Naked Lunch*. It's about . . . well, I defy anyone to say what it's about. It starts with a drug guy on the run from the cops, I think. Beyond that, I really couldn't tell you, and since there's no story in there, at all, it's hard to see the point of someone's having written it. Or of reading it. You know, it really seems like all those sixties people were just so proud of all the drugs they took that every single one of them felt like he had to write at least one incoherent book to demonstrate it, or prove it, or celebrate it. This was one of those.

I guess you could say that the *Flow My Tears* writer, a guy by the name of Philip K. Dick, was part of the same general drug writing movement, but with his stuff there was a story you could follow, and a whole lot of interesting ideas, and it was possible to tell that the ideas were in there because the writing didn't suck. Plus, it was frequently hilarious. I had the suspicion too that Philip K. Dick was possibly literally crazy, which made the relative coherence of the books seem like a stunning feat. Great writer, one of the best, right up there with Jane and Graham.

I had been reading another of his, *Clans of the Alphane Moon*, about this psychiatric space colony where each different psychological disorder was its own separate community-like clan, when Sam Hellerman and I stopped by to visit Little Big Tom at his motel on the way to practice one day. (As for these clans, I'm pretty sure I would have been an Ob-Com, though there've been times when I was a definite Dep, and maybe sometimes a Pare. . . . Oh hell, I could have been in every one of them. I may be a nut, but I'm a well-rounded one.)

Little Big Tom noticed and nodded with that appreciative half frown he has.

"*Clans of the Alphane Moon*," he said. "Very cool book. Wild stuff. I've always liked Dick."

Sam Hellerman and I looked at each other. I tried not to say anything, I really did, for at least a brief little bit of time.

"Can we," I said, with unfortunately perfect timing, "quote you on that, chief?"

Well, that visit didn't end well, though possibly the joke had been worth it. But it got me thinking that maybe walking around with a bunch of Dick books wasn't the smartest thing to do, considering the precarious state of my neutral status at Queerview and my near miss with Jane Austen.

So instead of another one of those, or another reckless vow book, I decided to try to read a book from Mrs. Pizzaballa's list. And I mean actually read it, rather than just fake it based on my memory of the three thousand other times I'd been forced to read most of those books.

It was *A Farewell to Arms*. It was by a man named Ernest Hemingway.

And it made all the difference.

Now, before any English-teacher types who might be in attendance get too excited, let me make something clear: it wasn't actually reading the book that made all the difference. It was *deciding* to read it that made the difference. And in fact, I didn't actually have to read it.

Here's how.

A Farewell to Arms is a love story set during World War I, and this Hemingway guy was a seriously famous writer. He won the Publishers Clearing House Prize for Literature, so he's obviously a really big deal. He's known for being an adventuring tough guy who was in a lot of wars, and a no-nonsense writer of simple phrases made up of very short words connected with each other into sentences by frequent use of the word "and," something that was controversial at the time but ended up being so influential that now it just seems standard. Also he is known as a guy who blew his head off with a shotgun.

The book was on Mrs. Pizzaballa's list. I got it out of the library and started to read it, and it was indeed some great writing. I could very much see my dad reading it and even being in it. He was in a war too, you know. But I realized that there was still no way of knowing what Mrs. Pizzaballa was looking for in a review. I'd really thought I'd hit the bull's-eye when I'd diagrammed one of the great sentences in *Pride and Prejudice* and wrote about how it's more of an economics story than a love story. That seemed like a serious kind of thing to write, and it had the unusual distinction of being something I actually did think, about a book I actually had read, but it came back a zero like all the rest.

That was when, in desperation, I finally looked at Mrs. Pizzaballa's descriptions on the book list, which I guess I should have done in the first place. The one about *Farewell to Arms* wasn't even about the book at all. It was about how this guy Hemingway was mean to women because his mother dressed him up as a girl when he was a baby, turning him secretly gay, and how his suicide was the cowardly act of an entitled, impotent brute in denial of his own sexuality. ("Impotent" means you have trouble ramoning, more or less, and Mr. Schtuppe would have been pretty confused about how to mispronounce it, since the only way to get it right is to try to do it wrong.) Anyway, I don't know if that's true or not, or if it even could possibly be true, but even if it is, how did it have anything to do with the book? No wonder I couldn't figure out what she wanted. It turned out that all her descriptions were like that, personal attacks on the authors for being bad people. They were racist, or sexist, or homophobes, or colonialists, or rich people who mistreated their servants or who abandoned their mentally handicapped children or who happened to live in countries that did bad things, or just plain old drunks who cheated on their wives and evaded taxes. Nothing in the descriptions required any knowledge of the books themselves. In fact, it was looking very much like the author of the list (Mrs. Pizzaballa herself, I had to assume) was the one who had figured out a way to get out of doing the reading, not me. And if so, I didn't blame her. If I were an English teacher, I'd want to put in the least possible effort too.

I started to write something in my journal to the effect that I wasn't sure that the Hemingway description was quite as politically correct as she seemed to think it was, but then I crossed it out, because I had just remembered one of Mrs. Pizzaballa's own Life Lessons.

"Anyone who isn't the president has a boss," she had said, "and anyone who has a boss has to do what their boss says, to the letter. And you're not the president." Something clicked in my mind as I realized that most of Mrs. Pizzaballa's Life Lessons had been along those lines.

Armed with the knowledge that I was not the President of the United States and based on the premise that Mrs. Pizzaballa was, for the purposes of this class, my boss, I copied out her irrelevant descriptions for ten of the ten-point books, word for word, to the letter.

The journal came back with a perfect score of 100 along with a smiley face with an x for one of the eyes (a wink, I believe) and the sublimely Pizzaballian message: "Smoke 'em if you got 'em."

And indeed I felt as though I had learned something important, and awful.

✳   ✳   ✳

So I didn't have to read *A Farewell to Arms* after all, though I probably will one of these days. That was easily the most work I'd ever had to do to avoid doing work in a class. I guess maybe that's what they mean by rigorous academic standards. I have no doubt that Mrs. Pizzaballa's most important Life Lesson was right: in school, in social situations, in love, and in life in general, the way to succeed is to figure out exactly what is expected of you and do precisely that, nothing more, nothing less, while keeping your big mouth shut. And I guess that's probably why I'm so terrible at all those things, like anyone else who can't follow instructions and who isn't the president.

CARRIE

I tried to break up with Pammelah Shumway four times before it "took," and the way it went down when it finally did, well, a tale lies in there, as I think the saying goes.

If you've never tried to do it yourself, you probably don't know that it is virtually impossible to break up with a girl who doesn't want you to break up with her, even if you're not getting along, and even if she kind of hates you. I mean, I suppose you could do it by just leaving a note on her windshield or locker saying "Bye, toots, it was fun" and then never call her and never answer the phone or return her messages and, if necessary, change your identity and move to Cleveland. That's actually how girls do it sometimes—if you'll remember Celeste Fletcher's breakup procedure with Shinefield, it kind of went that way, except she didn't go so far as to move to Cleveland.

But if you're like me and you want to have a conversation about it that ends with the acknowledgment that breaking up is the thing to do, possibly with a friendly mutual concession that it's best for everybody and a pledge to remain on good terms, well, you can just forget it. It's never going to happen.

Try this one: "You know, honey, it seems like you're always kind of mad at me, and it's clear that you're not happy with our relationship and my personality and how I think and behave–which is perfectly fine, I know I'm an acquired taste–and moreover we don't like to do the same things and when we do each other's 'things' neither of us has a good time, so maybe we should just acknowledge that we're not the most compatible couple and move on to other relationships that might be more satisfying to us both."

How'd that work out for you? I'll tell you how it worked out for me. My girlfriend told me not to flatter myself, and that everything would be just fine if I would stop being such a dick to her friends and learn to have a little fun sometimes and not be so weird. Then, somehow, she made it into this thing about how if I thought I could do better then go right ahead if I don't think she's pretty enough for me. Well, I couldn't look her in the eye and tell her she wasn't pretty enough for me. I just couldn't. And that was all that seemed to matter to her.

Sometimes she would say she didn't want to be my girlfriend if I didn't want her to, but she clearly was only saying that to sound reasonable, because it was obvious by how difficult she was making the whole thing that that was pretty much exactly what she wanted. Sam Hellerman's take on it was that she probably wanted to be the one to break up with me rather than the other way around to avoid a loss of face, and that seemed pretty plausible, so I experimented with lying low and biding my time, waiting for her to give me the "it's not you, it's me" talk I've heard so much about, or simply to disappear to Cleveland, which, frankly, would have been my preferred option. But it never happened, not even close.

Admittedly, after all the stress of these conversations, it was a relief to back off from them, act like their failure was a resolution, pretend things were okay and that we'd "worked it out," and just go back to making out. Sometimes it's nice just to be able to stop talking.

It all came to a kind of head, if I'm putting that right, because of . . . well, I'll show you a bit of the Robot's letter that first alerted me to the matter. And yes, the Robot's letters continued their function as a relationship facilitator even after Pammelah Shumway and her normal friends had shunted her aside. Indeed, it was almost as though providing me with passive-aggressive marching orders was the Robot's one remaining use to her. Anyway, as to the relevant bit of the letter, it ran:

```
    . . . what do you think is smarter, trees
or plants? You know what Pamm said? You
give her "girl wood"! Are you still mad
at her? I hope not. I don't like when
she's sad. Come on Thomas, think about the
makeup sex! (wink) [unintelligible] ugh
[unintelligible] When are you gonna ask her
to prom? Get off your ass man! JK!!! She
showed me a picture of her dress and what a
knockout, I think you'll like her ass . . .
etts! ha ha. get it? (wink) She'll make it
worth your while. Did you ever eat too much
licorice? They should put rugs on walls so
you can vackyume them (sp?) . . .
```

Now, "prom" is short for "promenade," and I think it has its origin in the big debutante balls that slave owners used to have for their stuck-up daughters in the South before we won the Civil War. In modern-day high schools, it is pretty much the ultimate normal institution, involving all the worst characteristics of Normalcy: Pointlessness? Check. Embarrassingness? Check. Cruelty? Well, in the sense that it is a huge competition designed to make those who lack the status or money to join in feel debased, worthless, and inferior? Check. You dress up in a rented tuxedo, and the girls make their parents buy them gazillion-dollar dresses, and they book limos and sometimes hotel rooms for the binge drinking, ecstasy, and cocaine use that happens after the so-called dance part. And parents take pictures of their daughters with their dates and say things like, aw, how cute, they're acting just like grown-ups. (As if actual people ever behaved like that at any time since the War Between the States.)

Not only that, but it is also the ultimate staging area for, and possibly the origin of, the classic form of the traditional Make-out/Fake-out, with people being asked to go "as a joke," or the nonnormal people who are foolish enough to dare to attend ridiculed and condescended to relentlessly by sadistic drunken normal people high on their own power. Just see the movie *Carrie,* if you want it spelled out for you.

I hope that I would never knowingly participate in any activity, particularly one involving jumping through multiple hoops, whose chief objective is to make adults and normal people look at me and say "How cute." The only good I ever saw in the "prom" was that it gathered all the normal people in one convenient location if anyone wanted to blow it up or lock all the doors with psychokinetic powers and burn everyone inside to a crisp.

Now, it's true, ramoning is part of the tradition as well, and it should go without saying that I fully support ramoning's rich tapestry. It's one of the main reasons kids look forward to the "prom" with such intensity, and fair enough. Hence the promise dangled before me that Pammelah would "make it worth my while." Well, despite my deeply held principles, that might possibly have swayed me once, but as you know, the most that would happen there would be a sort of warp-speed *Happy Days,* the usual schizophrenic teasing, but in an expensive dress this time. Plus, as much as I cherished the dream of ramoning a nice-looking girl one day, I actually think I might have drawn the line anyway. I'll endure a lot of humiliation for love, as you well know, but the "prom" was a bridge too far.

I wasn't going to the "prom." No way in hell.

Nevertheless, my clear orders, transmitted from headquarters by means of its Robot messenger service, were to get off my ass and ask headquarters, that is, Pammelah Shumway, to go to the "prom." As is my usual custom, I procrastinated and avoided the subject as long as I could, but the pressure soon escalated to the point where it was impossible to avoid it any longer.

I knew explaining the way I was feeling in an honest, sincere way and trying to make my girlfriend see my point of view enough to respect my wishes had no chance of success, but I tried anyway. She just ran circles around my logic, taking advantage of my nervousness and tied tongue and basically just wearing me down till I was so exhausted by the conversation that I had to back off and say we'd talk about it later. She took that as surrender, and it was, but on the big matter my resolve was firm, even if I couldn't quite express my position, to anyone's satisfaction, in words.

"But," I said, trying one last time, "why do you even want

to go with me? You know I don't want to, and you don't even like me all that much."

Even she couldn't deny that very convincingly, but her attitude seemed to be that she'd invested so much time and effort in being my girlfriend that the least she was entitled to was to be able to go to the "prom," even if, as was certain, we were guaranteed to have an absolutely terrible time. She repeated the promise to "make it worth my while," but she said it in a quite remarkably angry tone, and even had I believed it, at this point, I have to say that the prospect was sounding increasingly gruesome. And yes, I still can't believe I'm saying that.

So I tried explaining to the Robot why I didn't want to go. Like this:

"Ever seen the movie *Carrie?*"

She hadn't, and what was more, she wasn't interested in trying to use the magic of cinema to decode my sentiments, which were, to her, incomprehensible. The Robot couldn't understand why I didn't want to participate, and I couldn't make her understand. She just kept cajoling me, by letter and in in-person arguments, with the refrain: come on Thomas bone you know you want to just ask her Thomas just ask her. . . .

As my resolve became more apparent, my girlfriend and the Robot proposed a compromise: all three of us would go to the prom together, "as a joke," just to mess with everybody. I could even wear my Chucks with my tux, and we would defy convention and be deliberately weird, and dance all crazy with each other. And the pictures would be cute. It was the closest any Clearview person had ever come to grasping something of the spirit that animated me, and I was well aware that it was a big concession on my girlfriend's part. But it didn't address the issue. You can't fight back by surrendering and joining in, even if you say you're doing it as a joke. As I tried to explain:

"Ever seen *Revenge of the Nerds?*"

The Robot just told me to stop talking about movies all the time.

"Well, why don't the three of us do something fun together that night," I suggested. "Can't you ever do anything not sponsored by the school?" Like going to the beach and having a bonfire, or getting drunk by the tracks and talking about deep, important things, or going to a show in the city. Now, that actually sounded pretty nice to me, and I would have done it in a second. I looked fondly on those days back in the beginning, where it was just Pammelah, the Robot, and I, before my girlfriend turned evil and all the normal people came in and swamped our quirky, semihappy little world. "Why," my eyes added, "does it have to be some contrived, humiliating 'activity' organized by the state in order to normalize and control everybody?"

This didn't make any sense to either of them, not that I expected it to, and in fact, it just made them madder, not that I expected it not to. It had to be the "prom." But it wasn't going to be the "prom." It just wasn't.

On the day it happened, I was in a foul mood from all the tension. Everyone was irritated with me, it seemed, and it was certainly reciprocal, if "reciprocal" is the one where you do it right back at them.

I was coming out of third period when I saw Celeste Fletcher heading down the hall toward me, with Todd Dante, the jacket guy of her dreams, in tow. I wasn't sure how I was supposed to act around her, but since we'd had a couple of conversations recently, I didn't feel I could just pretend she wasn't there, so I kind of nodded my head up in a cursory greeting as I walked past.

Todd Dante grabbed me by the shoulder and pushed me against the Language Lab door.

"This the guy?" he said to Celeste Fletcher, kind of sputtering.

"No," said Celeste, just as Todd Dante's fist slammed with inexpressible force straight into my nose. There was a cracking sound as my nose broke, a hot sensation in my face as the blood rushed up and out, a pounding sound in my ears from the adrenaline, and a feeling of being unable to breathe from just, you know, being unable to breathe. Rushing blackness subsumed my field of vision, and I was gone for a while.

PART SIX

Halls of Innocence

ZERO TOLERANCE

I think all people, men, women, children, and otherwise, should get punched in the face at least once, just so they will know what it feels like so they can grasp how important it is to avoid placing themselves in situations where it might happen and make their plans accordingly. For instance, if I had had the experience before being hit by Todd Dante, I would have known as soon as I saw him and Celeste coming that the most prudent thing to do would have been to turn around and run, not walk, in the other direction. I'm sure there would have been a broom closet or an empty classroom in which I could have cowered till the danger had passed. But no, I naively thought that nodding slightly in the direction of Celeste Fletcher when her normal psycho jacket provider was around was sound policy.

I had, I realize now, been lulled into a false sense of invulnerability by the Clearview Badger Spirit. But there were limits, and nodding at Celeste Fletcher had crossed one of them.

When I came to, I was in the hospital, and it was déjà vu all over again. As my eyes and ears and brain took in my surroundings, I saw Celeste Fletcher, still wearing the accursed jacket, standing in front of my little bed thing, saying "Tom, Tom, Tom . . . ," trying to wake me up. Which was déjà vu all over again all over again. Was she going to ask me to sign her tits and give me a hand job? I kind of doubted it, but you know, one lives in hope.

"I'm so sorry," she said, once she had my attention. "Todd thought you were Shinefield. But you really shouldn't have said hi to me. Where's your girlfriend?"

I ignored the question, because I didn't know, and also because I kind of had an instinctive suspicion that I actually didn't have a girlfriend anymore. I told Celeste that she should tell her primary jacket provider that when you ask "Is this the guy?" it is customary to wait until hearing the answer before hauling off and pummeling the person in question in the face with your enormous frozen brisket fist.

"I know," she said. "I keep telling him that." Then she added, in a tone you might use to say someone has nice eyes or a dazzling smile: "He's got a temper."

Indeed. Isn't he dreamy. Good old violence. The chicks have always loved it, and always will.

But there was to be no hand job or cleavage signing today. The world had moved on from hand jobs and cleavage signing, and we had moved with it, some voluntarily, some less so.

As nasal fractures go, mine wasn't too bad, and I was told it would heal by itself, leaving no more than a bump. See what I got you, I told my centipede. A nice little bump to keep you company. The only reason I had wound up in the hospital rather than the nurse's office at school was because I had hit my head when I'd fallen and then kept losing consciousness every time I came to and saw my own blood. You'd think I'd be used to it by now, wouldn't you? My own blood, I mean.

My mom picked me up from the hospital and was as sympathetic as she had it in her to be, but she kept shaking her head and saying "Oh, Tom" in a way that seemed to express puzzlement as to why I kept getting myself into such situations, as though it were some kind of choice on my part.

Amanda took one look at me when I came in the door and said:

"What a nice-looking boy."

Todd Dante and I were to receive the same punishment, I was told: two days' suspension, but it was stressed that it was a much worse penalty for him because it would cause him to miss a game. They hoped I was proud of myself, they seemed to imply. This one, I had to say, really didn't feel like it was my fault. But Clearview High School, like Hillmont High before it, had a policy of "zero tolerance for violence." Think about that. If you are not laughing your head off at the very thought of it, well, my friend, you have either failed to grasp something essential about the meaning of the word "tolerance," or perhaps you have grasped it all too well.

STUPID EYEBALL

Sam Hellerman called to make sure I was going to be recovered enough to play the Mountain Dew show, which was coming up in a little over a week. Well, of course I was going to play the show. The show must go on, and if anything, I'd look even cooler onstage with a banged-up face. Sam Hellerman seemed to admire my derring-do, if "derring-do" means—well, okay, I don't even know what the hell "derring-do" is supposed to mean, but whatever I had when I said I'd play the show with or without a broken nose, Sam Hellerman seemed to admire it.

I told him about a song I was working on about Jeans Skirt Girl and sang it to him over the phone:

Jenni with an I, Lysa with a Y, Gwladys with a W,
K-Y-double-M, doesn't trouble them,
so why should it trouble you?
If you have any messages to send,
just address them to Pammelah with an H on the end . . .
Cinthya with a Y, Cinthya with a Y,
X above the I, Cinthya with a Y . . .

"We must," Sam Hellerman said, "do this song. We must."

I was kind of proud of it, to tell you the truth. (On the lyric sheet, I was planning simply to spell the names, so it would go "Jenni, Lysa, Gwladys, Kymm. . . .") But I warned him that it was yet another "Cat Scratch Fever" tune, and we already had three in the set. Four would really be pushing it, even for all the Mountain Dew in the world. But Sam Hellerman was willing, finally, to ditch "Sadistic Masochism" for it. That's how much Sam Hellerman cared for Cinthya with a Y, X above the I.

Sam Hellerman had informed me that he had nailed down the venue and the lineup for the show. It was going to be at the Slut Heaven Rec Center, and we were playing with a couple of bands from Mission Hills High.

"Don't worry," he said. "They're terrible." Which was a relief. It simply wouldn't do to be upstaged at our own show.

He also said that the name the Reptilians, cool as it was, didn't look right printed out, so he had made an executive decision, and basically, he was sorry not to have told me sooner, but the name of the band for the show was now irrevocably going to be Stupid Eyeball, because it was already on the flyer.

"Stupid Eyeball," I repeated.

"Yes," said Sam Hellerman.

"That's the name?"

"Yes," said Sam Hellerman.

"Really?"

"Yes."

There was a pause.

"Fair enough," I said. We'd had way worse names than Stupid Eyeball. Stupid Eyeball was actually one of the better ones, to be honest.

Returning to my room, feeling like I had nothing left to lose, I picked up Naomi, and something happened. Remember how Little Big Tom told me that if I kept trying, eventually I would find that I suddenly could play the fingerstyle pattern? Well, that's exactly what I found. For once. Maybe being punched in the face had granted me the spirit of the Irish Ragtime Blues. They do call it the school of hard knocks, after all, and I'd been knocked pretty hard.

I spent the rest of the night playing "O'Brien Is Tryin' to Learn to Talk Hawaiian" over and over, till my fingers were killing me. It wasn't rock and roll, but it was enough.

KING DORK STRIKES AGAIN

I entered Clearview High School on my first day after the Todd Dante incident and saw before me a changed world. Being punched and publicly humiliated by Todd Dante had cost me pretty much every perk I had enjoyed in my former position as a neutral pep band member with a pretty girlfriend. The Spirit had abandoned me, offering no more protection. And the magical veil of the gentler, less dangerous Clearview social structure had been abruptly torn away.

Where once I had seen a puzzling array of relatively benign "school spirit" *Happy Days* tolerance with only an occasional or hidden undercurrent of senseless brutality, I now beheld a view that reminded me strongly of the Hillmont High School I had left behind. There was Pang running for dear life, terrified out of his skull, trying to please the jeering president of the student body; and there was Bobby Duboyce getting a good, solid helmet thumping from the girls of the varsity field hockey

297

team; there again was Yasmynne Schmick being taunted about her weight and pushed around by a semicircle of normal girls. And there were half a dozen other scenes straight out of Hieronymus Bosch that I'd simply never noticed at Clearview. It's really true that you're oblivious to the suffering of others till it happens to you. Think about that next time you're feeling strong and confident and in command of the situation. Someone out there is crying the tears you've managed to avoid, and it's only luck that prevents you from having to join in.

Walking through the halls myself, I was pushed, tripped, jeered at, and hair-gummed. In PE someone tried to close my gym locker with my head in it. And remember Bill Henderson, the normal jacket guy I knew alphabetical-orderically? Well, it turns out he wasn't at all averse to calling another Henderson "Hender-queer" if the feeling moved him.

My secret was out. I was back on the bottom. King Dork strikes again.

Well, I said. I'm back.

I had prepared a little speech for Pammelah in my head, a final attempt to explain, as kindly and as gently and as positively as possible, that I just couldn't be her boyfriend anymore and that I was truly sorry. But I needn't have bothered. Her interest in being my girlfriend had been strained more to the breaking point than I had known by my antiprom activism and had vanished completely as soon as I had been exposed as King Dork by Todd Dante's Fist of Revealing.

And what about the Robot? Well, if I had expected things to go on as before with the Robot—the letters, the goofy conversation, the secret, conspiratorial sips of vodka from emptied-out Evian bottles—then I was in for a rude surprise. Because the Robot seemed to have become just as hostile as everyone else, or if not absolutely hostile, at least aggressively distant and totally uninterested in anything I had to say.

"Thanks, goodbye," she would say coldly before scampering off. Or when she had to be in my presence somewhere, like in homeroom or Band, she would just refuse to look at me. I was invisible, untouchable, hated and despised, the wretched of the earth. Even Blossom van Kinkle, always my backup plan and once so unapologetically flirtatious and seemingly entranced by the Regency Period eloquence of my eyes, responded to my silent plea for sympathy with hard, cold indifference. And, predictably perhaps, it was at just about this precise point, as it dawned on me that there would be no further letters from the Robot nor sly winks from Blossom van Kinkle, that my dumb brain decided to start missing Pammelah Shumway. Stupid emotions. They're no help at all, are they?

I always say I just want to be left alone, and I basically do, but I have to admit, this pretty much sucked.

So now I was in the same boat as Little Big Tom, exiled from the world I had known and loved, or at least rolled with. And I was also in the same boat as Amanda, wandering around the empty house with an idle phone-baby, pushing away the idea that my empty world was largely of my own making, but knowing deep down that, had I wanted to, I could probably have managed to sustain a status quo that, while unacceptable, had certainly felt a lot better than the alternative I was experiencing now. And I was also in the same boat as my mom, because . . . well, okay, you know what? I honestly don't have any earthly idea what kind of boat my mom is in, ever. But what I'm saying is, there were an awful lot of boats floating around my house, and I was somehow in most of them.

At least I had my rock and roll. For maybe the first time,

though, I wasn't all that sure it was going to be enough. "O'Brien Is Tryin' to Learn to Talk Hawaiian" was my only refuge, though it also seemed to level a kind of accusation at me. I mean, why *couldn't* I just try to learn to talk Hawaiian, so to speak, instead of remaining clumsily silent and just hoping people would somehow get me, and then despising them when they didn't? I'm a hard guy to get. And I make myself even harder to get by refusing to learn the rules and follow them even slightly. I mean, it's because I hate the rules and I think they're stupid, obviously. And, don't get me wrong, they are. But conducting myself that way, I had to admit, had left me with not a friend to my name except for Little Big Tom and Sam Hellerman. And in a way, Sam Hellerman had been learning and following rules from his dad's tapes and was pretty much leaving me in the dust. I'd ridiculed those rules, and look where it had gotten me. Mrs. Pizzaballa had had the solution all along, if only I had been perceptive enough to see it and humble enough to accept it: find out what is expected of you and do it with no nonsense. It would have worked with my girlfriend, with school, with life. And now it was too late.

I was even deprived of one of my favorite jokes at Sam Hellerman's expense when I pointed to his cell phone and asked, at a practice, whether he'd had any calls. Sam Hellerman had checked his phone and pushed several buttons as though scanning through a multitude of possibilities. "Oh, wait," he had said. "I need to get this one." And he had hurried outside to talk privately to whoever it was, Cinthya with a Y, X above the I, or someone else equally more interesting than the nobody I and Shinefield were getting calls from. Man, we'd had some fucking morose practices, I can tell you, despite Sam Hellerman's bouncing off the walls and chirping like a, well, like the kind of bird that chirps a lot, an owl or a vulture or some damn thing.

If you've never experienced mopey, melancholy Chi-Mo before, you're lucky, and I'll spare you any more of the gruesome details. Just picture day after day of me being hassled and ostracized at school and feeling resentful and sorry for myself at home, with joyless band practices in between. And I didn't even have Little Big Tom to amuse me with inept efforts to cheer me up or give me advice. You know you're low when you find yourself wishing your hippie stepfather would pop his head through the door and say "This is the first day of the rest of your life," but then again, I was low, man. I mean, I was practically subterranean.

Now, "Queen Jane Approximately" is a song from Bob Dylan's CS 9189 album. A lot of people will tell you that this song is a harsh put-down of a frivolous, superficial person, and maybe it is, but I've always seen the main point of it to be something else: basically, he's telling this girl who has this complicated life of hustle and bustle and who lives in a world of her own making that once she has finally exhausted all other possibilities, she should come see him and they can just sit there not worrying about talking or figuring anything out. Whether or not that's true about the song, it's always been something I've wanted someone to say to me. Leave everything behind, and don't worry about trying to explain anything or engineer anything or account for yourself. Don't ruin it by saying anything. Don't try at all. Just come here and look out the window with me and see what happens.

I guess no one's good at that. I'm sure not. But thinking about it in my morose mood and everything, well, it's embarrassing to admit, and whatever you do, don't tell Sam Hellerman because it pretty much breaks every rule he ever laid down, but I was just going nuts and almost without even thinking I snatched Amanda's phone-baby out of her hand, locked myself in the bathroom, and dialed Pammelah Shumway, not knowing what I was going to say. And when she answered, what I said was that I missed her. And when she started to laugh and said I was amazing–or maybe it was "unbelievable"–I for some reason said maybe I could go to the "prom" with her after all. And when she laughed again and hung up on me, I wrote some more of the song I'd been calling "King Dork Strikes Again" but decided to retitle it "King Dork Approximately" because of Dylan and Queen Jane and because honestly, I didn't feel I even knew who I wanted to be anymore, but King Dork was the closest I'd ever come to specifying an identity. And because I've only ever been able to sort of feel anything and kind of know what I think about it.

The bridge went:

crying on the telephone, hanging on the line
my world is misery, a soggy valentine
but I know everything will almost be approximately fine
when it's approximately clear that you're approximately
mine . . .

Thank God she didn't say yes, to any of it. It was maybe the stupidest phone call I have ever made. Because now I can see it wasn't really about her at all. It wasn't even about Fiona. It was about a feeling–the feeling of wanting to look out a window with someone and have them get it.

ELMYR DE HELLERMAN

They happened to broadcast *Halls of Innocence* on the same night as the Clearview "prom," one of those coincidences that seem significant but actually probably really aren't. I had been looking forward to it for ages, and in my mind I had pictured a cozy scene of watching it at my house with my mom and Little Big Tom and Amanda, Sam Hellerman, Pammelah Shumway and the Robot, and maybe even Celeste Fletcher, if she could be persuaded to leave Todd Dante and the jacket behind. In reality, though, it was just Sam Hellerman, Amanda, my mom, and me, and it was more depressing than anything.

Sam Hellerman arrived with flyers and handbills for the show, saying that he had blanketed the area and he expected at least half the Mission Hills student body to attend. I confessed that I wasn't the most popular guy at Clearview High School these days and that I doubted I'd need anywhere near that many flyers. Sam Hellerman shook his head.

"Too bad you couldn't hang on to that chick with the boobies," he said. "She was your ticket." Despite his "man of the world" pretenses these days, he still couldn't bring himself to use regular words for things. It sounded weird, like Hugh Hefner doing baby talk.

"Pammelah Shumway," I said, just kind of drawing a line under her with my voice. She was the past now. And there had been good times somewhere in there, I supposed.

But Sam Hellerman just looked at me and said, "Shumway? Her name is Shumway? Why didn't you tell me she was Mormon?" I guess the name Shumway is some kind of dead giveaway of Mormonism that I didn't know about. Sam Hellerman said it explained everything. "Mormon girls never put out," he said. "Never. Ever. I know. I'm Mormon. Well, Jack Mormon."

It was true that Sam Hellerman's mom was Mormon and Sam Hellerman had been raised as one till his family went off the reservation, so to speak. "It was doomed from the start," he said finally.

"Tell me about it," I replied. "Aren't we all?"

And to that he had no answer.

I've already told you about *Halls of Innocence*. There was lots to laugh about and lots to groan about. My mom just sat there saying "That's terrible" every time anything at all happened, and, yeah, it sure was terrible, but not always in the way she meant it. The jacket-throwing scene got the biggest reaction. Man, I wish you could see Amanda's reenactment of it. It's top-notch.

I found myself kind of daydreaming that there would be a knock on the door, and that my mom would get up to answer it and return with Pammelah Shumway and the Robot, still dressed in their "prom" getups. The fantasy wasn't clear on what would happen then, but it was vaguely along the lines of everyone telling each other that everything was going to be okay.

It didn't happen.

Back in my room afterward, making some last-minute notes and preparations for the set the following day, I told Sam Hellerman about my latest line of thinking on the Catcher Code and my indictment against the Universe. The lawsuit plan was all over, I assured him, but it had occurred to me that the whole thing could make a pretty good book. I mean, think about it. It has everything: sex, drugs, rock and roll, suicide, dad-icide, attempted tuba-cide. I asked Sam Hellerman if he knew anything about publishing.

Sam Hellerman had gone a bit pale as I was speaking, and his eyes flashed with the usual annoyance.

"No," he said. "You can't write that book. No one would be interested at all in a book like that."

Well, I certainly didn't agree, so I tried again. It could start all the way back at Most Precious Blood, and it could show Tit writing the Catcher Code and hatching the whole sordid plot, and then zoom forward in time to Hillmont and my dad and then finally to us and our rock and roll. In fact, now that I was narrating it, it seemed more like a movie than a book. Yeah, a movie. Close-up of Tit's chubby hand filling in the graph-paper squares, chuckling softly, then a cut to Timothy J. Anderson hanging in the gym by a rope. . . .

"No," said Sam Hellerman. "It can't be a movie, either." Sam Hellerman paused and then seemed to make up his mind about something.

"Okay, Henderson," he said. "I'm going to tell you something now, and I don't want you to freak out." He made me promise, dumb though that was, that I would not freak out before he would continue, and of course I promised.

"I hereby solemnly swear that I will not freak out, so help me Satan," I said.

"I don't know who killed your dad," Sam Hellerman continued, "if it was Mr. Teone or someone else, or if he was even murdered at all. I don't think anyone will ever know, and I don't know if it's even possible to figure it out, *especially* from the Catcher Code. And you should stop obsessing about this because . . . because it's going to ruin your life if you keep it up."

I was taken aback. That was the most earnest thing I'd ever heard Sam Hellerman say. It didn't sound like him. Since when did he care whether anyone's life got ruined? I guess our little guy is growing up, was my main thought about that, and I wasn't at all sure that I liked it. Still, it was just a variation on what Little Big Tom had said, and I wouldn't say I even disagreed with it. Maybe it already had ruined my life, in a way. But I didn't see any reason to freak out to any extent over it. I reassured him on that, but I had to point out that I still felt the Catcher Code was important.

"After all, Tit wrote it. It's the earliest evidence we have for his state of mind at that young age, and of his relationship with my dad."

Sam Hellerman sighed and rolled his eyes.

"You're not listening, Henderson," he said. "Here's the thing. I've been feeling bad about it ever since you started heading off into crazy town on this thing about Tit and your dad and I should have told you a long time ago. Tit didn't write the Catcher Code."

What was he talking about? Of course Tit wrote it. It was right there in the code itself, internal textual evidence, the best kind there could be.

"He didn't write the Catcher Code," said Sam Hellerman. "I know it for absolute certain."

"Well, okay, then, if Tit didn't write it, who did?"

Sam Hellerman laughed.

"I did," he said.

I looked at Sam Hellerman. Then I kept looking at him. I knew it was the truth as soon as he said it. The whole thing had had Sam Hellerman written all over it from the beginning, really, if I had only thought to think of it. But I kept staring at him, not knowing what to say. He stared back at me, wondering what I was going to say. Then I knew, and so did he a moment later.

"Get out of here," I said.

THEY CALL IT THAT OLD MOUNTAIN DEW

So the Catcher Code had been a Hellerman forgery. I could easily see how he might have managed it. And knowing Sam Hellerman as I do, it wasn't that much more difficult to imagine a host of possible reasons why: he had wanted to give me something to focus on as a distraction from his schemes-in-progress, or he had merely wanted to see if he could pull it off, or it could even have just been that presenting his Sherlock Hellerman explanations and stretching them out over time had been a good opportunity to acquire an additional supply of my hospital tranquilizers. I wasn't going to ask him. I knew that would get me nowhere. But I suppose it did explain why Sam Hellerman had been so negative about the Catcher Code during our lawsuit discussions.

To be honest, it was a bit of a relief not to have to think about the Catcher Code anymore, irritating and embarrassing as it was that running around in circles over it had cost me so much grief over the past year. The only thing that truly irked me, when I really thought about it, was the desecration of my dad's book. (Look up "desecration." I just did, and it definitely means what I thought it meant.) There was no excuse for it. Sam Hellerman could have easily accomplished whatever he had wanted to accomplish without resorting to that. I had accidentally beaten up Paul Krebs for the same sort of thing when he had poured Coke in one of my dad's books, and I knew that if I dwelled on it there was a good chance that the flashing colors of rage would once again start to blot out my vision and I'd wind up accidentally beating up Sam Hellerman. I can't say for sure I wouldn't have enjoyed that, on some level. You never know till you try, do you?

As for what I was going to do now, well, we had a show,

and I wasn't about to miss it just because of being pissed off at Sam Hellerman. After that, I didn't know, but all that meant was that I had to add it to the huge list of other things I didn't know—as usual, but possibly even more so.

Sam Hellerman had been startled enough by my "Get out of here" that he had fled from me like a cat from a jar of clinking pennies. Maybe I had reminded him of his dad and struck momentary terror into his soul. I hoped so. But in the interests of show business and rock and roll, I knew it would be a good idea to tell him I was still planning to show up and play the next day. I called him on his holster phone and had to listen to him fumble with it, drop it, scamper after it, and finally pick it up to answer.

"Tomorrow we rock" was all I said.

"Good man," said Sam Hellerman.

And I had to hand it to Sam Hellerman. He had managed to produce a fake Mountain Dew–sponsored show to benefit recycling that was almost exactly like you might imagine a real one would look like, if your imagination was a bit gullible and your natural skepticism a bit leaky. Along with the CARING, HEALING, and UNDERSTANDING banners from school, he had painted banners that said MOUNTAIN DEW PRESENTS, complete with logos and everything. Unless you examined them close up, they looked almost unquestionably authentic, and no one, that I knew of, ever thought to question them. He had also enlisted some of his classmates from MHHS to staff tables and sell what was apparently Mountain Dew from big fountain tanks, wearing little Mountain Dew uniforms of Sam Hellerman's own design. It was the hats that made it work: they looked too stupid to be fake. It wasn't genuine Mountain Dew in the tanks, Sam Hellerman told me, but similar-tasting discount generic soda he had managed to acquire somehow at a fraction of the cost. He also had placed free pretzels and other salty snacks in little buckets around the room to make people thirsty enough to buy the soda, and had set the thermostat at a high temperature for the same reason.

"If this sells out," said Sam Hellerman, "we're going to make a fortune in concessions alone."

He had arranged for a back line too, drums and amps as well as the PA and monitors, to make the set changes go more smoothly and also because, as I've explained, our own equipment was total crap. And he had instructed the sound guy, who was basically his employee for the night, to reduce the volume of the opening bands' mixes and to sabotage their sets subtly to make us look better, just like they do to the opening acts at real professional rock and roll shows.

Finally, he had had pamphlets printed up extolling the virtues of recycling and asking for donations to the International Ted Nugent Center for the Promotion of Recycling, along with envelopes to put the money in and slotted boxes in which to deposit them.

"How'd you pay for all this?" I asked. It must have cost a fortune.

But Sam Hellerman told me not to worry my pretty little head about it.

"We'll make it all back and then some," he said confidently. And I believed him. Sam Hellerman had always claimed he had assets, and it looked like by the end of the night, he was going to have even more.

If nothing else, Sam Hellerman's elaborate preparations had impressed and successfully deceived their primary target. Shinefield was over the moon.

"I can't believe this is really happening," he said.

I wasn't sure how to answer because, one, I couldn't believe it either, and two, it wasn't actually really happening.

When Sam Hellerman gave the signal for the doors to open at eight o'clock, it was clear that while he might have overestimated in his claim that half the Mission Hills students would attend, he hadn't overestimated by nearly as much as I'd figured. There were hundreds of paying customers. We were out of the red on the hall within the first ten minutes, he gloated.

By this time, Sam Hellerman had gone backstage to change and had reemerged wearing an ill-fitting suit and tie, and he was acting very much the host and master of ceremonies, greeting many of the people as they came in and pointing them toward the concessions and donation bins.

"Salvation Army," he said out of the side of his mouth, repeating his advice that I should try wearing a suit sometime. "Chicks love it."

It was clear that whatever methods Sam Hellerman had been using to bump up his popularity and status at MHHS, they had had some success. His fellow students all called him Sammy and were high-fiving and fist-bumping him, and he responded in kind, calling them "my man" or "young lady" as the case warranted. If you'll recall, Sam Hellerman had predicted that in two months he'd be running the place. Well, I didn't know about that, but he did indeed appear to be "respected by his colleagues at work or school," which was borderline amazing. However, there did not seem to be any hint of an actual girlfriend, or even any obvious romantic interest that I could see. The girls he was talking to were friendly, but they seemed to be treating him more as a sort of mascot than as a man who was in command of the situation. I believe I even saw one of them reach out to pat him on the head. Which, honestly, is something I've been tempted to do from time to time myself.

At any rate, Sam Hellerman the entrepreneur and rock concert impresario was in full effect; Sam Hellerman the womanizer had yet to be demonstrated.

Still, seeing him in action in his little suit, frolicking with his little Mission Hills friends, provoked an unsettling thought: this was Sam Hellerman's "prom." How cute. Someone should have taken some photos for the mantelpiece.

I noticed my mom and Amanda drift in and was disturbed to see my mom head straight for the donation boxes and start writing a check.

"Mom, don't," I said. But she shushed me, saying it was for a good cause, so . . . Well, I guess it was a good cause—that is, Sam Hellerman and, kind of, me.

Little Big Tom came in a bit later, easy to spot because he was accompanied by Flapjack, who was wearing cutoff overalls, big rubber boots, and an enormous cowboy hat. And if you think you have seen a weirder sight in your life than the two of them winking and shooting finger guns, I would humbly submit that you cannot possibly know what you're talking about. I couldn't resist responding by flashing them "the shocker," because I'm mischievous and vulgar like that.

I was still in a melancholy mood, however, and I was having difficulty getting into the spirit of the affair. Sam Hellerman kept gliding past and saying things like "She's just a chick" and "Plenty more out there, my man" that were meant to be encouraging and, I didn't doubt, to take the focus of my agitation off him, but in fact, they were really just depressing. It wasn't like I was going to see some Jeans Skirt Girl and walk up and kiss her. Some guys, including even Sam Hellerman, as I'd seen with my own eyes, can do things like that, but I sure wasn't one of them. I suppose I had this secret hope that I'd look up and see Pammelah Shumway and the Robot walk in and all would be forgiven and we could go outside and drink spiked fake Mountain Dew and talk nonsense like we used to do back in the beginning. But of course, practically nothing was less likely to occur, so I wasn't genuinely hoping for it: rather, I was just imagining it in a "what if" and "wouldn't that be weird" kind of way that would, just by coincidence, have been really nice too. I guess my fantasy from the *Halls of Innocence* night had never really ended, sad as that is to admit.

One person I did unexpectedly run into was my old secret girl ... associate, Deanna Schumacher, whom I hadn't seen since before Christmas vacation. Deanna Schumacher said she only had a minute to talk because her boyfriend and her dad were there, and it probably wouldn't be good for my health to be seen talking to her. But she wanted to say hi, because, well, some things never change, I guess.

"I'm sorry this is so weird," she said, like they all do, though she didn't look all that sorry.

"Thanks," I said.

"What happened to your forehead?"

"Tuba," I said.

"Oh yeah," she said. "I remember. What happened to your nose?"

"Fist," I said.

Now, during this conversation, I have to admit, I was pretty distracted by what Deanna Schumacher was wearing. And what I mean is, well, it's not like I *wanted* to stand there staring at the great big penis embroidered in bright gold thread on the front of her short, navy-blue jeans skirt, but once I noticed that it was there, it was impossible to unnotice it. Trying not to look

312

at it with all my strength just seemed to make my eyes stray back to it against my will, with the result that I spent most of this brief exchange staring at Deanna Schumacher's crotch with what I can only imagine was a fairly distraught expression on my face.

"Oh, Tom Tom," she said wistfully, noticing my anguished gaze but clearly misinterpreting it. She raised her hand to touch my cheek and said, "I'm sorry, but it's not going to happen."

Well, as that made it quite clear she wasn't going to invite me somewhere for some discreet oral sex like she might once have done, and as I certainly didn't want to risk another "this the guy?" incident by prolonging the conversation, and as I was still haunted by her disturbing jeans penis, there didn't seem to be much more to say.

"Say hi to your mom for me," said Deanna Schumacher, flouncing away. Somehow, I'd known she was going to say that.

He could have found some old, weathered graph paper somewhere and used it for the code square, then folded it up and applied pressure for an extended period of time to make the creases look real, and possibly treated it with something like lemon juice to create the brownish age spots. He could have consulted a French teacher or other French speaker to help with the translation. He could have found out details about Tit and my dad by discreetly interviewing my mom. . . .

I shook these thoughts from my head, knowing there was no point in dwelling on them, and as I was doing so, I spotted the one and only Jeans Skirt Girl with a group of friends leaning against a wall at the back.

"Cinthya with a Y, X above the I?" I said.

She gave me the look that says: "The same."

I could tell she was trying to place me, and I was about to reveal my identity with a suave "Tom Henderson, guitar and vox," but before I could get it out she said:

"Oh, you're the guy! The guy from the mall."

Yes, I conceded. I was indeed the guy from the mall.

"Well, how did you like the show?" she said.

I was puzzled because the show hadn't yet started, and as I was playing in the band it wouldn't have been appropriate to say whether I'd liked my own show, but obviously she was talking about some other unspecified show. She said I'd sure looked surprised, and I realized the "show" she was referring to was one in which she was the costar, that is, the notorious incident where Sam Hellerman had brought weeks of dedicated fieldwork to completion with an unlikely kiss. So it had been a show?

Well, folks, I can smell a rat as well as most people, and this had the definite odor of some variation of the subfamily *Murinae*. So when I came across Sam Hellerman during one of his laps around the floor, I pulled him aside and said I'd bumped into Jeans Skirt Girl.

"Cinthya with a Y, X above the I?" he said. "Good, I'm glad she made it."

I looked at Sam Hellerman with narrowed eyes, thinking about the Aladdin Arcade kiss in all its particulars.

"You gave her twenty bucks, didn't you?" I said finally.

"Ten," said Sam Hellerman.

Well, I might have known.

He had done it, he said, partly to impress me and to persuade me to give the tapes a try myself because he thought they could help me. But mostly it was a ploy to enhance his reputation by being seen kissing a girl above his status by other MHHS students. As my own experience had shown, this can work, and it seemed to have worked for Sam Hellerman, if his evident popularity among the student body of MHHS was any indication. He had told Jeans Skirt Girl and her friends that he wanted to impress me and play a practical joke, and that he had made a bet that he wouldn't be able to get a kiss in front of the arcade. It was kind of pathetic, it's true, but I also had to acknowledge that on some level it had indeed taken genuine self-confidence and real social skills to pull it off. I couldn't have done it.

Another group of girls walked by and called out "Sammy!" Sam Hellerman was looking sheepish, if not guilty, and I knew him well enough to make a pretty good guess as to why.

"Jesus, Hellerman," I said. "You paid those girls ten bucks too?" I asked him how much money he had spent on artificial status enhancement through hired kisses.

"No more than a couple hundred," said Sam Hellerman, adding that that was one reason we needed the concessions to do well.

"You're never going to get a girlfriend that way, Hellerman," I said. And he gave me the look that says "I know."

Well, I didn't know what to think. On the one hand, it was funny and maybe even almost cute, these antics meant to create the impression, but not the reality, that Sam Hellerman was a success with girls. On the other hand, it was genuinely reassuring to learn that the magic of the tapes hadn't managed to bend the laws of nature in Sam Hellerman's favor after all. I was back on the solid ground I knew so well, though it must be admitted, it was ground I pretty much hated.

But on that third hand growing out of my forehead, well, it went something like this: the arcade kiss was fake; the tapes were, if not fake, certainly not what they were cracked up to be; the Catcher Code was fake; love was fake; even the very

315

show at which all the fakeness was being revealed was itself fake. I felt pretty fake myself. Was anything real? Only Todd Dante's fist and my own melancholy, as far as I could see. Beyond that, I just couldn't say.

CARNAGE

So how did the Stupid Eyeball set go, in the end? If you're halfway intelligent and have been paying attention, I think you know the answer already. But if not, just imagine the worst show you can possibly imagine and then try to imagine it being around ten times worse.

One problem right off the bat was that my nose hadn't yet completely healed from Todd Dante's punch and my voice was sounding pretty strange, nasal and also not all that loud. Hearing it in the monitors freaked me out, and my singing was about as awful as singing ever gets.

However, the house was packed and the crowd was in a pretty good mood, ready for some actual entertainment after the sabotaged sets of the opening bands whose names I have now completely forgotten. (Sorry about that, dudes. You seemed like pretty nice guys.) I had figured we'd manage to do at least two songs before Shinefield would notice something was wrong that was systematic and engineered rather than the result of us just not being very good. Then it was anyone's guess what he'd do. Be good-natured and continue the set? Storm off like Todd Panchowski had at the Hillmont High Battle of the Bands? Something in the middle?

In fact, Shinefield managed to last an impressive four and a half songs. This was partly because Sam Hellerman had told the sound guy to turn off the drum monitor so he'd have a harder time hearing what we were doing; it was partly, perhaps, because he was high and didn't have his wits about him; and possibly it was partly also because of his good nature and willingness to roll with things—always his best quality.

It turned out to be a lot more confusing and disorienting to play the switcherooed versions of these songs in the auditorium setting than it had been in Shinefield's basement. But "Fiona" to the drums of "Live Wire" still sounded more or less like an actual, if shaky, song, as did "Down with the Universe" to the drums of "Cat Scratch Fever." With "King Dork Approximately" (also to the drums of "Cat Scratch Fever") things were basically still on track, but getting ragged. I noticed Celeste Fletcher drifting into the venue halfway through that song, which kind of jumbled me up and made me make some mistakes. I was glad she got to hear some of it, though, somehow.

By the time we got to "Cinthya with a Y," it had finally begun to sink into Shinefield's dope-fuzzed, good-natured brain that this whole set had been a deception, and possibly even a joke at his expense. And on "Caring, Healing, Understanding" he did some sabotage himself by returning to his old abhorrent technique for the duration of the song, making it almost incomprehensible, and then he threw his sticks down, walking into the crowd. Maybe we should have kidnapped his family after all.

Now, Sam Hellerman remembers it differently. He claims that Shinefield was okay with playing the songs and was even smiling while it was happening. But then he saw Celeste Fletcher in the audience and decided that being in closer proximity to Celeste Fletcher was more important to him than continuing to play the set. Either way: drummers, right?

At any rate, we were stuck onstage without a drummer, and with a restless crowd already booing because the last song had sucked so bad. And because we're us, despite this thoroughly predictable state of affairs, we found we had absolutely no plan whatsoever.

Sam Hellerman tried to appease them by reminding them why they were there in the first place, saying, "Come on, people, let me hear you say it: recycling! Can I get a 'recycling'?" And while there was indeed a surprisingly responsive "recycling" chant, pandering to their rabid love of recycling wasn't going to hold this crowd's interest forever.

My next decision was a pretty bad one, in retrospect. But I felt I had to make some noise, and the only nonband noise I was capable of creating was "O'Brien Is Tryin' to Learn to Talk Hawaiian." This I attempted to play. But as bad as my feeble attempt at Irish novelty ragtime blues fingerpicking had sounded through my cigarette-box amp in my room, that was nothing compared to how bad it sounded coming through a heavily distorted Marshall JCM 900 and a kind of crappy feedback-prone PA system, with my fingers hyperclumsified by stress and nervousness. The look on Flapjack's face, as I glimpsed it in the crowd, was really something, and I stopped abruptly as soon as I saw it. It had only been a few seconds, but the damage had been done. We were officially sucking even worse than the mediocre sabotaged bands that had gone before us.

It was at this point that things got really strange.

Sam Hellerman tapped me on the shoulder and I turned around to see that Little Big Tom had climbed onstage and was heading toward the drum kit. I could see what was happening, almost in slow motion, but I was paralyzed and powerless to stop it. By the time I got control of my faculties, Little Big Tom was already seated at the drums. And by the time I finally found enough voice to scream "Nooooo!" it was too late.

"Well, boys," said Little Big Tom. "'Screeching for Vengeance'?" And no sooner had he said that than the stick click count-in was upon us and I pretty much had to join in if I didn't want to be a dick. In other words, there we were, Stupid Eyeball, the future of rock and roll, the Great Masturbator on guitar and quiet nasal vox, Sam Hellerman on bass and suit and tie, and Little Big Tom, yes, Little Big Tom, on drums and inept parenting. Covering Judas Priest's "Screaming for Vengeance."

Now, I wish I could tell you that Little Big Tom turned out to be this great drummer, and that his stepping in at the last minute saved the day and rescued the set. I wish I could tell you that I was able to sing like Rob Halford. I wish I could tell you that the song we played sounded anything remotely like "Screaming for Vengeance." I wish I could tell you that it sounded like anything in particular. And I wish I could tell you that it sounded even vaguely like a song.

But in fact, as you can probably surmise from the way I have framed this tender chain of wishes, it just didn't happen that way. Little Big Tom's drumming, such as it was, was not simply abhorrent. It was, rather, incomprehensible, like drumming from another dimension where they have a different kind of math and a different concept of time. Or maybe he was just hitting as hard as he could at random, hoping something useful would come out. Playing the drums is harder than most people think. You can't just sit down at the drum kit for the first time, hit stuff, and hope it comes out all right, as in finger painting or making soup. But that, it seems, was precisely what Little Big Tom was doing. It was the same approach he took to making a big pot of vegetarian slop. And actually, "slop" is as good a way of describing his drumming as anything else.

When things go wrong onstage, your impulse is to over-compensate in reaction. A string breaks, you scream louder. The bass cuts out, you turn the guitar up. Well, I'm no Rob

Halford, even in the best of times. But singing "Screaming for Vengeance" on top of a band that sounded like a natural disaster in progress made me work that much harder, trying to scream for vengeance in a way nature had never intended my dear little voice to do. And I suppose that somehow, in the process of doing that, my still-healing nasal fracture refractured itself. I heard a loud pop in my head and blood started flowing like wine out of my face, except it was a lot more like blood than wine.

Sam Hellerman, well known for his special talent of being able to make his own nose bleed on command, was unable to prevent a sympathetic nosebleed of his own.

So both of our noses were gushing blood all over ourselves, all over the stage, and all over the mics, while the song was still going, after a fashion, sort of. The sound guy, worried about his mics, cut the power and rushed up to wrestle them away from Sam Hellerman and me. Little Big Tom, seeing me knocked to the floor by the angry sound guy and having my back, leapt from behind the drums and attempted to tackle him. At least, I think that's what he was trying to do. But the stage was now slick with blood, and he lost his footing, missing his target and winding up face-first in the steel grating of the floor monitor. When he picked himself up, it was revealed that he too had blood gushing from his nose and running all over his face and down his shirt.

The chaos and carnage onstage had reduced the crowd to stunned silence. And it was at that point that I heard, drifting from somewhere in the front of house, the now-familiar voice of Todd Dante saying "This the guy?" followed by a thud and a sickening crackling sound. And I knew without even looking that he had punched Shinefield in the face.

Thus were all three members of Stupid Eyeball, plus their

stand-in drummer and partial stepfather, reduced to a collective bloody mess. In the crowd's ensuing scramble to escape the carnage, an inevitable punch was thrown, and several little clusters of fistfights soon blossomed, eventually merging into a general, floor-wide brawl, a true ballroom blitz, in fact. It was kind of beautiful in its way.

And thus ended what will probably go down in history as the strangest, the most unlikely, the bloodiest, and certainly the least successful rock and roll show since the last time Sam Hellerman and I had attempted one. Move over, Altamont: our legacy will live on in some form, I'm certain of that.

I climbed off the stage in a kind of daze, hoping that my light-headedness and loss of blood were not too closely related. As what remained of the crowd scattered to avoid getting bled on, I ran headlong into Amanda.

She paused to look at me.

"That," she said, "was the best thing I have ever seen in my entire life."

In books, and in songs, too, there is this thing called an unreliable narrator. With an unreliable narrator, you're following what he's saying because he's the one talking, but you don't necessarily believe everything he says because he slants it to his advantage, or exaggerates, or even outright lies. Or sometimes it is the writer who constructs the narrative in such a way as to make some point about the narrator, to demonstrate his ignorance or his prejudice or what have you, and he makes him narrate things in such a way that the reader can figure out stuff about him that he himself doesn't even really know.

Well, I'm not sure how much of that would apply to me, but I will cop to being at least as unreliable in narration as I am in all other things. And I will acknowledge right off the bat here that some of what I'm going to tell you now is absolutely true, but that some of it might not be quite as true as all that, and there is at least one bit that is not really that true at all.

So as I looked up through my daze at the scene before me, this is what I saw: (a) my mom and Little Big Tom in a tight embrace, engaged in a passionate and extremely bloody kiss; (b) Celeste Fletcher bent over Shinefield, trying to rouse him, kissing his forehead, telling Todd Dante to get the hell out of there and to take his stupid jacket with him; (c) Cinthya with a Y, X above the I, cradling Sam Hellerman's head gently in her lap, dabbing the blood from his face with a napkin; and (d) Flapjack chewing on a chicken leg, laughing his head off.

And the reason I mention all that is so I can say this:

Love had found a way. For everyone but me.

AFTERMATH

When I heard police sirens in the distance, I grabbed my guitar and headed for the back exit. I figured the worst person to be seen with in the bloody aftermath of the Mountain Dew Tribute to Recycling was Sam Hellerman, at least to the degree that there would be any explaining to do, and I kind of had a feeling that there would be quite a lot.

As I was leaving, Amanda came through the exit and beckoned me back. She said she had forgotten to tell me that there had been a phone call for me just before she and my mom had left for the show.

"It was that girl Pamm," said Amanda. "She said she needed to talk to you and it was urgent. I thought you guys broke up."

"It's complicated," I said.

But I didn't have time to explain the situation to her. Pammelah Shumway had a message for me, an urgent message. Maybe love would find a way after all. I had to find out. I entrusted my guitar and backpack to Amanda. And then I ran. I ran like I had never run before, not knowing what awaited me, but praying I wouldn't be too late. It wasn't too far down El Camino Real and up the Santa Maria Avenue Camino Street Road to the Shumway residence, but it was a long way to run, and I was worn out and exhausted by the time I arrived. I threw pebbles at her bedroom window, our usual signal.

Pammelah Shumway came to the window.

"Oh, Thomas," she said, pulling the curtain aside. She looked like she had been crying. "Oh, Thomas. I've been such a fool. How will you ever forgive me? It was silly of me to try to force you to do something you didn't believe in. I guess I cared more about my own social status and selfish desires than about your integrity and principles. But if I've learned one thing, it's that it was your integrity and principles that made me fall in love with you in the first place, and I could never ask you to give those up. If you never want to see me again, Thomas, I understand. But if you can find it in your heart to forgive me, I just want you to know that I will wait for you. Forever, if that's what it takes."

She looked so beautiful in the moonlight that I was almost tempted. I opened my mouth to respond, when we were interrupted by the sound of a ringing telephone. She held up a finger, telling me to hang on, while she withdrew to answer the phone. When she came back she was distraught.

"Thomas! I just got word that my dog, Alfalfa, is trapped on the railroad tracks, and a train is coming! And my mom is dying of cancer, and the only thing that can save her is a

Badger win in the Badgers-Saints game that's happening right now! And the score is tied!"

"Don't you worry, Mrs. Shumway," I called out. "I'll save the game. And the dog." Then I looked at Pammelah. "We can discuss your emotional turmoil at some later date. Now, there's work to do."

I commandeered a skateboard from one of the local kids and sped down the hill toward the tracks. It was dangerous weaving in and out among all the cars, but there was little time to lose and I knew it would be close. Very close. Taking a quick detour to the Clearview High School gymnasium, I skated like the wind through the gym doors, donning my Badgers jersey as I approached the court. Only five seconds remained on the clock as I zipped past the stands, called to the coach to put me in, and skated onto the court. The mystified crowd soon started to cheer and chant as I stole the ball from a Saints forward and, whistling "On, Wisconsin!," lobbed it through the hoop a split second before the buzzer sounded, waving to the crowd as I skated through the opposite door, out of the gymnasium, and onto the main road.

At the bottom of the hill, through the fine evening mist, I could see Alfalfa, whimpering, his paw caught in the train tracks, and a 133-ton Amtrak GE P42DC Genesis locomotive speeding toward him at a hundred MPH, whistling danger. It was risky, but it was my only chance. I reached the track and ollied into an aerial, grabbing the dog and landing on the opposite side of the track just as the train went clattering by.

"Easy there, boy," I said as Alfalfa licked my face. "This ain't over yet."

I skated back to the Shumway residence, Alfalfa trotting close behind.

"Good board, kid," I said, tossing the skateboard to the little fellow I'd snatched it from just minutes earlier and striding up to the porch, where Mrs. Shumway and Pammelah were waiting, wearing anxious expressions. "Don't worry, Mrs. Shumway," I said. "It was pretty dicey, but I think your cancer is going to be just fine. And there's someone here who's eager see you." Alfalfa bounded up with a cheerful bark, and we all shared a chuckle.

"Now, as for you, Pammelah . . ." She looked up at me expectantly. "You hang on to that heart of yours. I'm sure there's some lucky guy out there who needs it more than I do."

I sprinted back to the Salthaven Rec Center and retrieved my guitar and backpack from Amanda.

"That was very brave," she said. "You know, for a dork, you're not such a bad big brother."

"You're not so bad yourself," I said, rumpling her hair.

As I headed through the parking lot toward the woods that edged the Salthaven Rec Center park, I happened to run into a little squirmy creature. I will forgive you if you don't act too surprised to learn that the little squirmy creature to which I refer was Roberta the Female Robot, who, it seemed, had been waiting for me.

"I didn't think you'd ever come out," she said.

Now, friends, despite my powerful vocabulary, I'm not very good at describing things where there's nothing absurd, preposterous, risible, inane, farcical, or cockamamie about them, if I'm correct about what "cockamamie" means. Unless I can figure out a way to resort to sarcasm or to ridicule someone or something, even if it is only myself, I'm pretty much stumped. So I probably won't be too good at expressing what happened in this part. But here goes anyway: I can say, without reservation, that I had never been so happy to see another person in my life. And without even thinking, or planning, or scheming, but just because I sort of wanted to, I guess, I found myself pulling the Robot to me and kind of crushing her in my arms. And I was going to add "as you do" there, as you do, but in fact, I had never actually done this before. I don't know what came over me.

"Ow," said the Robot, but she was clinging to me almost as tightly. It was like I could feel each tiny, delicate, angular bone, like when they say something is "ribbed," except these were, you know, actual literal ribs, so I guess that's why they say that. Her face seemed a little damp, like from tears, but she explained, "It's the wind and my contacts."

I could hear scuffling sounds and shouting coming from the Rec Center building, and I knew it would probably be a good idea to get farther away from the action, so I led the Robot deeper into the shadows of the park.

"Sorry for bleeding on you," I said. "Did you . . . see any of the show?"

"Unfortunately, yes," said the Robot. "I don't know why you keep saying your own music is better than pep band. Do you really think that?"

I didn't know what to say. It was a hard case to argue at that moment. It has something to do with wanting something that is your own, without being directed or ordered to do it by anyone, doing something that only you and no one else can do, no matter how much it may suck. But what I said was:

"I don't know."

"Oh, Thomas," said the Robot. "You never know anything, do you?"

✳ ✳ ✳

Well, what can I say? You've seen movies and read books. You had to have known pretty much all along that I was going to end up with the Robot.

And I'm sure you're wondering, so I'll tell you: we did go to the girls' restroom at the Slut Heaven Rec Center park, the one with the broken lock, and we did things there. And here's why I tend to think, as I said in the beginning, that in that smelly restroom I lost my virginity, while she didn't. Because we tried, really tried. But it didn't quite work. How can I put this delicately enough that I'll be allowed to say it in this censorious totalitarian society of ours? I had something special for her, but it was something that she wasn't quite able to receive comfortably.

The point is, though, that she was very into it happening, believe me, even though it didn't wind up happening. It would have happened. And I think that should pretty much count. Don't you?

But there are other things you can do, as you may know, and we did some of them. And if you're wondering if one of these was "the shocker," you can just keep on wondering. Some things are private. As it turns out.

KING DORK APPROXIMATELY

So eventually we wound up in this little clearing for picnics, side by side on the bench with our backs to the table part, trading sips from a big water jug filled with peppermint schnapps.

The Robot liked me, obviously, but still didn't understand me, which is the usual state of affairs when someone likes me. *If,* I mean.

"Why are you so mad at everything all the time?" she was

saying. "Like school and basketball and pep band and prom, and, like, the government, and CDs, and the ..." She paused to summon the proper degree of sarcasm before saying, "... 'structure of the universe.' You're even mad at jackets. How can someone be mad at a jacket? It's just a jacket. Why can't you just do normal things like regular people and not worry about it?"

"I don't know," I said. But I knew. It was just hard to explain. I asked her if she really wanted me to try to explain, because it could take a while, and she shook the bottle and gave me the look that says "We've got all night here, boy burger."

So I readied myself to deliver, for the fifth time, my carefully prepared, and by now quite well-rehearsed, presentation on the sadistic structure of the universe and the scourge of Normalism. I didn't have my document file with me, and I wasn't sure what I'd say about the Catcher Code now that I knew its true source, but I was pretty sure I could wing it on that.

Then, however, I thought of Flapjack, with his chicken leg, his cowboy hat, and the bloody spot on his arm where he had extracted the surveillance dart, and I decided I really had to do it a different way this time.

I took a breath. I wasn't sure she was going to understand it, and I was even less sure she was going to like it. But she had asked for it, and, for some reason, I found I really wanted to do it.

"They call me King Dork," I said slowly, choosing my words carefully. "Well, let me put it another way: no one ever actually calls me King Dork. It's how I refer to myself in my head, a silent protest and an acknowledgment of reality at the same time...."

I told her the whole thing, as best I could, as she nestled into me and the light from the nearby streetlamps flickered and filtered down through the wind-shaken trees. And when the schnapps was all gone and she had finally passed out, I took out my notebook and started to write out the rest, the first letter, strangely, that I'd ever actually written to her, thinking I'd go as far as I could get before dawn, and then thinking, well, maybe one day, I'd get to the end.

EPILOGUE

We were sitting on the grassy slope in the right field of Hill-mont High School's old baseball diamond, approximately the same place where I had accidentally beaten up Paul Krebs all those many months ago. She had wanted to see.

"Here," I said. "I want to show you something else." And she pantomimed as though she thought I was going to un-buckle my belt and she looked with huge eyes and made this motion with her hands like she was peering through curtains.

"No, not that," I said.

I extracted Naomi from her case. I had intended to play one of my fractured love songs, "King Dork Approximately" or even "I Wanna Ramone You." But for some reason, instead, I started to play and sing "O'Brien Is Tryin' to Learn to Talk Hawaiian."

And it's strange. That song was written by a couple of guys in 1916, and they meant it to be strictly comedy. But the way it came out when I did it, it was way more "personal" than any of my own songs. Because I really "got" O'Brien. He's there trying to communicate with this girl, and they don't speak the same language, and all he can do is fake it as best he can, making a complete mess of it, but keeping at it till by some crazy miracle it gets across, this simple, simple thing that is still weirdly hard to explain.

For once, I didn't make too many mistakes.

She was laughing and got up to do a little dance with hula

hand movements, and when the song was finished she clapped twice and plopped on the ground next to me.

"You didn't tell me you knew how to play real music," she said. And then I think she somehow saw in my face that I had meant the song sincerely in a way that probably very few people who have played "O'Brien Is Tryin' to Learn to Talk Hawaiian" ever have, and her eyes widened.

It was a nice moment.

"So," I said, thinking about Queen Jane and her window. "This is kind of a nice moment. And I propose that we just sit here for a while and look at the trees and not ruin it by saying something stupid."

"Too late," she said.

GLOSSARY

AC/DC: It could be argued that the first half-dozen **AC/DC** albums represent **rock and roll** in its purest form. It's just a guitar sound, a drumbeat, and a snarl, but anything beyond that is **hokum** anyway. It could be argued.

ADHD: Attention Deficit/Hyperactivity Disorder. If you have this and you're an artist people give you the benefit of the doubt, but if you're a kid they will try to drug you out of it, along with whatever personality you may have left. (The drug they give you for it, though, is essentially speed, so try to have fun with that, at least.)

Alice Cooper: Originally, Alice Cooper was the name of a band whose singer coincidentally was also named Alice, but later on this guy adopted the name Alice Cooper as his own name when he went solo. I think a similar sort of thing happened with George Eliot, though none of her concept albums about nightmares, violence, and rock star excess are known to have survived.

Altamont: In 1969, the **Rolling Stones** decided to hold a free concert for a quarter of a million people at the Altamont Speedway in Northern California, and to hire the Hell's Angels to provide security, paying them with beer. What could go wrong? The resulting disaster has become a metaphor for the futility of all human endeavor.

ambivalent: a fancy-pants word for not being able to decide whether you mean "I don't know" in the negative or in the affirmative sense.

amiable: *see* **jaunty**.

aphorism: a wise saying, to be written on the bathroom wall or recited to those in need in lieu of providing them any useful assistance.

aphrodisiac: any substance, real or metaphorical, that makes its target inexplicably and compulsively horny. (People like me and, I must assume, you are immune to its effects, as we come that way out of the box.)

Archie comics/The Archies: I don't know too much about Archie comics (they seem to be a sort of comic-book/jacket-varsity-type thing). But the Archies, a fake rock band put together to provide the music for the fictional band depicted in the cartoon spin-off TV series, and featuring the talents of Andy Kim and the Cuff Links' Ron Dante, among others, is one of a handful of things that redeem the sixties. It must have been great to live in their **bubblegum** world of genius songs, negligible student-on-student violence, and girls in short skirts. Much better than your favorite supposedly real band, whatever that may be.

arteriosclerosis: an imaginary disease that is, in the end, little more than an antipizza conspiracy.

arthropod: The Arthropods, the Tom-ipede on guitar and vox, the Sam-ipede on bass, the Shine-ipede on drugs, first album *Just Look at All These Legs*. Okay, that wasn't one of our real bands, but it should have been, if only so I'd have something to say about the phylum *Arthropoda* that doesn't involve doing any actual research. Playing guitar in a centipede costume seems like it would be quite challenging, but the beauty of the imaginary notebook band is, if you can dream it you can be it, and basically I rule at this.

art rock: Art rock should have been the death of **rock and roll,** but somehow it wasn't. Evidently, not being killed by **the Doors** only makes you stronger. Who knew?

Chet Atkins: not, in fact, a pipsqueak, unless an alternate definition of "pipsqueak" happens to be "the most accomplished guitarist of his generation and century."

334

banal: The proper mispronunciation of this word rhymes with "anal." The correct pronunciation rhymes with "canal." An extremely useful word, because while no one actually has any idea what it means, everyone understands that it is bad. Their imaginations will fill in their own insult, probably far worse than anything you could devise, with no further effort required on your part, which is the true power of a powerful vocabulary.

The Beatles: They had sex with lots and lots of young girls. Then they turned into hippies.

benefit: A "benefit" is a show, the proceeds from which the promoters or organizers pretend will be given to a specified charity or cause, thus avoiding the obligation of having to pay any of the bands. This scam works every time, because bands tend to be generous of spirit, desperate for shows, dumb, or all of the above.

The Bible: The first five chapters are great, but then it goes off in all kinds of different directions and gets really bogged down in the middle. It's like the author, God, couldn't figure out where He was going with it and decided to throw all His ideas in there indiscriminately in the hope that something coherent would emerge. And, like many writers who don't know how to end their books, He tacks on a predictable, though in this case unexpectedly satisfying, apocalyptic ending. Better on rereading, when you can see all the foreshadowing.

Ambrose Bierce: an American journalist who taught the world that nothing matters. In 1914 he was swallowed by Mexico and never heard from again.

Jane Birkin: You can hear her ... shall we say, enjoying herself and saying "I love you" over and over in French on this Serge Gainsbourg record called *Je t'aime ... moi non plus.* If listening to this does not make you fall in love with her at least a little, I don't know what's wrong with you. Serge's response to her heavily breathed "I love yous" is to say *"Moi non plus,"* which basically means "me neither." Now, that's a cool guy. And this record is as good as French stuff gets. The flip rules too. Playing it loud will probably embarrass your parents. (Which is funny because it's as old as they are, most likely.)

Blind Blake: Of all the guys who ever tried to play the guitar like a piano, he did it best. The idea of playing like that without being able to see the neck is, of course, a bit mind-boggling, but in a way it's even more impressive that he was able to change his strings. Think about it. Like I said, there has to be a God.

Blue Öyster Cult: University art and poetry projects rarely turn into top-selling show business attractions, and when it does happen it's bound to be something pretty unusual and/or awful. But the soft white underbelly of Stony Brook University produced some of the strangest sounds and visions you'll ever experience, though you'll need to dig deeper than "The Reaper" to find them.

Humphrey Bogart: True, he was short, but he made up for it by standing on a crate and having an enormous head.

Hieronymus Bosch: a Dutch painter whose exhaustive documentation of high school in fifteenth-century Europe shows that some things never change.

Marcia Brady: If only all girls dressed like this.

Brighton Rock: I've said it before, but I will reiterate: this is the best book ever written. Good job, Graham. (Also a song by Queen. Good job, Brian.)

Big Bill Broonzy: It's the heavy thumb thumping that does it, so simple yet weirdly difficult to do so it sounds like anything but a mess when regular people try it. Every guitar player's favorite guitar player, which tells you something.

The Brady Bunch: So fake it's real, so stupid it's profound. Cable TV schedules reruns of this ancient show round the clock so people will know what it's like to feel their own brains disintegrate chunk by chunk in real time. The end point of this process is Nirvana.

Brown v. Board of Education: On occasion, the **normal** psychotics in charge of the world will allow something to transpire that is broadly admirable. Hardly ever, but it has happened.

Lenny Bruce: The way I heard it, the government had him murdered to prevent people from hearing swearwords in comedy clubs. How'd that work out for you, government?

bubblegum: If you think you can write a better song than "Chewy Chewy," you're very welcome to try. But you can't.

Buddah Records: the label that gave the world the Ohio Express, 1910 Fruitgum Company, and the Lemon Pipers and allowed the genius of Joey Levine to burst forth into the world, its wonders to bestow.

Bye Bye Birdie: Say what you will about the merits of this Clearview High School–meets–Elvis satire, but that Ann-Margaret sure was a cutie, demonstrating if nothing else that ramonability is timeless.

cacophony: literally a bad sound, and a good band name.

cakewalk: My understanding is that this was originally an actual walking dance where whoever was best at it would win a literal cake. Now it means something that is trivially easy, like falling out of bed. So where's my cake, then?

camaraderie: If you can contrive to leave the impression that you are on someone's team, he or she will be far less likely to plot your destruction, at least at first.

Carrie: film, 1976. I love it when a movie has a happy ending. The best film ever made about high school.

Cheap Trick: George Harrison believed that when the spirit left **the Beatles** it flew around a bit and finally settled down to animate *Monty Python's Flying Circus,* which started up around the time of the Beatles' demise. The last episode of Monty Python was broadcast in December of 1974. Cheap Trick recorded their first demo in early '75. You do the math.

comeuppance: On occasion, though very rarely, what goes around does actually wind up coming around. When it does, they call it a comeuppance, though a better word for it might be "comearoundance."

Cook/Jones: an honest snare and around a thousand guitars. That's how you make nice-sounding records.

Salvador Dalí: "I don't do drugs," he said. "I am drugs." One of history's all-time weirdos, fortunate to have lived in ancient times before society figured out how to use the school system to bully and bore the weirdness out of everyone with ruthless efficiency.

decent: the opposite of **normal.** The decent are the customary victims of the normal, though the normal also prey upon each other. While there is some debate as to whether normal people are born or made, I personally believe we all begin life decent; some of us, the majority, then gradually begin to turn normal when corrupted by exposure to the greater normal world. Unfortunately, it doesn't appear to work the other way: there is not one known case of a normal person reversing course and turning decent. The superior intelligence of the decent confers a slight advantage over the comparatively slow-witted normal people in certain circumstances, but is no match overall for their senseless savagery and cruelty, not to mention the force of their sheer numbers. Remaining decent in a normal world is one of modern life's most grueling and disheartening challenges.

Philip K. Dick: His dark, goofy vision of a squalid, dysfuntional future of drugs, mass psychosis, space-time confusion, and unreliable identity put him solidly ahead of his time as a writer and, moreover, has been steadily coming true. His books were published as science fiction but became gradually weirder, with the later ones resembling religious texts. They broke the mold with this guy.

double entendre: As Robert Plant and the French were well aware, you know, sometimes words have two meanings, one of which is likely to be filthy.

Elmyr de Hory: the most gifted art forger of his generation, the subject of a film by Orson Welles (fat era). Saw the movie. Wanted to be him. Knew I couldn't. Such is life.

eons and eons: Use this phrase when you don't feel like looking up exactly how long ago something was.

The Doors: Look, of course they have redeeming features. "Touch Me" isn't bad, for instance. But as for what they represent, see, I'm a guy who likes "Yummy Yummy Yummy" more than just about anything. And when **Joey Levine** squares off against the "Lizard King," I know who I want to win. Intellectual pretensions, "spirituality," and half-assed literary allusions only get in the way of the **rock and roll,** which in essence is about nothing more and nothing less than wanting to ramone the cute chick in biology, and driving really fast. Focus, people.

et cetera: Latin for "or whatever." Often abbreviated "ect.," which alludes to "ectoplasm," a viscous substance that comes out of a medium's body during a séance, which derives from the Latin word for sitting, which is what I'm doing right now while writing this down, eating a sandwich, listening to Mott the Hoople (KC 32425). Or whatever.

Etch A Sketch: It can take well over an hour to use this device's two knobs to write even the simplest obscenity, by which time the moment has usually passed, a severe drawback. There's a better way. It's called a Sharpie.

euphemism: Euphemisms have a bad reputation because people use them to avoid speaking plainly about what they're really talking about, but on a deeper level pretty much everything is a euphemism, since reality is so much worse than the fantasy world we like to pretend we live in. The best way to use euphemisms is to preface them with the words "shall we say," a brief pause, a raised eyebrow, and possibly even a wink, just to make it clear that you know you're not fooling anyone.

exuberance: *see* **exultant**.

exultant: *see* **jocularity**.

Gandalf: Do you really have to look up Gandalf? Seriously? He was the eighty-third president of the United States.

Jerry Garcia: Big hippies cast wide shadows.

genius: merely the first stage of an inevitable downward spiral that ultimately ends in death and meaninglessness, but you gotta start somewhere.

Grease: a caricature of the fifties that turns out to be 100 percent true.

Rob Halford: That the greatest heavy metal singer of all time turned out to be gay is one of those little things that make you go "Well, it was kind of obvious all along, with all that leather, but that's pretty cool and interesting somehow," and you wind up liking him even more than before, though you can't quite say why in a way that doesn't make you sound like kind of an ass. That legions of **normal** gay-hating metal-heads going around asking each other **"Who you calling homo, faggot? Who you calling faggot, homo?"** were completely unaware of this while worshipping the ground he walked on is one of those things that make you almost glad to be alive just so you could have the opportunity to notice it. **Irony.** I believe this is the definition.

Happy Days: The best thing about *Happy Days* is the original theme song, "Rock Around the Clock" by Bill Haley and His Comets. The second-best thing is Leather Tuscadero, played by the great and powerful Suzi Quatro, who time-travels from Devil Gate Drive circa 1974 to 1950s Milwaukee and forgets to take off her glam scarf and bell-bottomed jumpsuit. The third-best thing is a tie between the Fonz and Maureen the Lone Stripper. To be honest, though, the whole adds up to a bit less than the sum of its parts, and when the show left the fifties and blasted off into la-la land soon after its debut it became a surreal train wreck, which can be fun if you're a fan of those.

Ernest Hemingway: an American writer of award-winning fiction. "Write drunk, edit sober," he said, which seems like much sounder advice than the unedited version: "Write drunk, edit sober, shoot self in face."

Hogan's Heroes: they said a situation comedy about a Nazi prison camp couldn't be done. And then they went ahead and did it anyway. From it, we learn that you sound more authentically German when you are yelling.

hokum: a cutesy **euphemism** for "bullshit," not to be confused with "hogwash," "piffle," "flapdoodle," "poppycock," "hooey," or "jive."

inane: Somehow, it sounds a lot more insulting than "silly," which is what it means.

irony: *see* **Rob Halford.**

jaunty: *see* **exuberance.**

jocularity: the state of being good-humored to a ridiculous and alarming degree. The mark of a diseased mind.

Jonathan Livingston Seagull: A million-selling hippie-dippie book about a seagull who buys a stairway to heaven and learns some trite life lessons when he gets there. Basically this is to philosophy as **the Doors** are to **rock and roll,** but in its day people really ate it up and reportedly actually used it as a guide to how to live their lives. They even made a movie of it with footage of actual birds flying around and dubbed-in dialog. "Why, why, why does this exist?" you will probably ask yourself if you ever see it. This is the wrong question. The right question is orange.

Judas Priest: The mysterious power of the greatest of all metal bands is made no less mysterious by the fact that they named themselves after a song by Bob Dylan.

KISS: I grew up on Paul Stanley, so sometimes I announce breakfast by saying, "People, listen now, I got something to say right here. Are you listening? There were some good-lookin' girls in the hallway askin' if we were gonna have Rice Chex this mornin'. I said no. Well, they said, how about a little... Kix? I said, uh-uh. And they said, well, what kinda cereal we gonna have, then? And I told them, I bet there's some people in Toronto who know just what kind of cereal we gonna have: Honey! Nut! Cheerios!"

Joey Levine: the most gifted songwriter of his generation.

Machiavellian: in the style of Niccoló Machiavelli, one of the Florentine Renaissance's most celebrated pickup artists.

John Maher: only one of several reasons that Buzzcocks ruled OK.

Make-out/Fake-out: As I've explained in previous explanations, sometimes **normal** females will amuse themselves by hitting on or pretending to flirt with a socially unsuccessful guy as a joke, just to see what he'll do to extricate himself from the awkward, humiliating situation and to have a laugh with her friends at his expense. It's a long-standing normal-girl institution, and, well, I suppose they have to do something with the time they don't spend trying to humiliate and destroy each other. I have yet to come up with a good response to this, though it occurs to me that punching yourself in the face and bleeding on them or vomiting on their shoes might take a bit of the wind out of their sails. Maybe not, though. They seem to be pretty dedicated to their craft.

Marquess of Queensberry: To one's surprise, this turns out to be a real person and, even more surprisingly, a man. He wrote the rules for boxing.

metaphysical: No one, not even the dictionary, knows what this word means, but it will make you sound smart, to dumb people, if you filter it into your conversation. If anyone asks you what you mean by it, smile ruefully and say something like "See, you're proving my point."

Mountain Dew: I'll shut up my mug if you fill up my jug. Beloved beverage of stoners everywhere.

Mussolini: Whistle while you work/Hitler is a jerk/Mussolini bit his weenie/Now it doesn't work.

narcoleptic: This means you fall asleep all the time, pretty much at random. It has its drawbacks, but you save a fortune in tranquilizers.

NIOMA: National Institute of Music and Arts, Inc.

normal: These are the bad people. Approach them, if you must, with caution, as you would any savage beast, and watch your back. And your front and sides. (cf. **decent**)

notwithstanding: Surprisingly, this turns out to be a real word. It means "performing a given action while lying down or sitting."

Northern soul: So, the British are pretty strange and kind of full of themselves. This is American soul music, called "Northern" by the Brits not in reference to where it came from (Detroit, mostly) but rather because people in Manchester, England, liked to dance to it. (Manchester is northern compared to London.) That's like calling **the Smiths** "Southern rock" because they once got played on the radio in Arkansas. Still, those Manchester mods really, really liked it, and admittedly, their liking it probably saved many of those records from undeserved obscurity in the end. So thanks for that, mods. But you do know Detroit's in the Midwest, right?

Ted Nugent: Say what you like about Mr. Nugent, but he founded the Amboy Dukes and wrote "Cat Scratch Fever" and "Wang Dang Sweet Poontang" and no one can take that away from him. Come along if you dare.

Nuremberg: The Nazis staged their pep rallies here.

opprobrium: You know how **normal** people hate you and want to destroy you for no reason (or for really, really stupid reasons)? "Opprobrium" describes their frame of mind when doing so, a kind of atmosphere of disgust, disapproval, and hostility that descends upon anyone who appears unusual or expresses opinions that diverge from their own narrow range of acceptable views. You can try to appear as usual as you can and to keep your mouth shut about your opinions, but somehow the opprobrium manages to find you anyway. I don't know how it does it.

paranoid: sensibly aware of the risks and drawbacks of being alive. Generally speaking, when someone accuses you of being paranoid, you can be pretty sure that you're on the right track and your concerns are fully justified.

per se: Latin for "in itself." Like all Latin terms, "per se," when inserted randomly and without regard to literal meaning, will make any sentence seem more sophisticated and intelligent, per se, than it actually is.

petulance: an ambulance for dogs, cats, or hamsters.

phenomenon: a fancy-pants word for "thing." Not kidding, that's really all it means.

piddling: When the paddle peddler peddled a paddle to paddle the poodle piddling in the paddle peddler's piddling puddle, the paddled poodle piddled a piddling puddle on the poodle paddle peddler's piddling poodle paddle. (That's a little poem about animal cruelty and dog urine.)

Bishop Pike: a hard-drinking, chain-smoking, ghost-busting American Episcopal bishop who was swallowed by the Judean Desert, never to be heard from again, till **Philip K. Dick** renamed him Timothy Archer and put him in his final, most weirdest book.

pinochle: a card game most commonly played by worms on the noses of human corpses.

Playboy: I read it for the articles (because the pictures sure ain't too exciting.) I can't believe this was once thought of as **pornography.**

Hercule Poirot: *Eh bien, ça suffit, mais oui, bien sûr, aujourd'hui, s'il vous plaît, alors ici, oui, d'accord, nom d'un nom d'un nom, mon ami, c'est très facile pour expliquer, cherchez la femme tout le temps . . . et voilà, mesdames et messieurs,* the case, she is solved. Take off zebra.

pornography: There's a fine line between this and everything else.

proximity: Sometimes fancy-pants words are good for more than just mispronunciation and showing off. This one means "the immediate area surrounding you or some other object at any given point in time." There's no other way to express this idea

344

without using a whole lot of other words, for example "the immediate area surrounding you or some other object at any given point in time." Here, I'll use it in a sentence: "Hey, you—get the hell out of my proximity!" Actually, maybe don't say that one to anybody unless you have solid backup or some kind of weapon.

Publisher's Clearing House Prize for Literature: Each year the lucky winner, usually a novelist but occasionally an elderly lady who used to work in a supermarket, receives from the Swedish Academy an enormous check, a medal, and the chance to purchase magazine subscriptions at a discount.

punk rock: They had to kill **rock and roll** to save it.

Pythonesque: of or like Monty Python's Flying Circus. I can recite the entire Cheese Shop Sketch (both parts), with accents. (Yes, ladies, I am that cool.) Only been beaten up for it once, too, which is pretty good.

ragtime: On the piano, the right hand and melody parts are all off-kilter to the left-hand rhythm parts, hence the term "ragged time." On the guitar, you do both of these hands with parts of the same hand, preferably while blind. This is basically not possible.

ramone: As noted in my previous explanations, the French use this word for scrubbing out a chimney as a sexual metaphor. The fact that it also happens to be the name of the greatest of **punk rock** bands is just gravy, unless the Ramones named themselves that way on purpose, in which case: that is some brilliant, brilliant gravy you got there, boys.

Ayn Rand: the enigmatic frontman and lead novelist-philosopher of the Canadian rock band **Rush**. I've never read one of her books and I wouldn't know the first thing about "Objectivism," but if you can judge a philosophy on the basis of the inappropriateness of its rhythm section (and of course, you can), I can't see how it could possibly be a good idea. Basically, when the philosopher brings out the cage, the second floor tom, the second kick drum, and the gong, you close the book. Then again, I'm a **Ruddist.**

recycling: The state forces us to devote a substantial portion of our waking hours to the ritual of pawing through our garbage and meticulously organizing it into a complex system of color-coded holy receptacles as a way of granting us the opportunity to prove that we are good people. Then, of course, its purpose having been served, trucks pick it up and dump it indiscriminately into landfill, because the process of actually "recycling" it would generate more waste than there was to begin with. Don't tell anyone.

rock and roll: Music that can be played on a guitar and hollered into a microphone by the young and the stupid. Strictly speaking, the only legitimate subjects for rock and roll songs are girls and cars, in that order. It is permissible to deviate from these topics, but when you do, you will find you have strayed into **art rock,** so choose your deviations carefully. I hear it pays well.

Roxy Music: Eno should have stayed put, if you ask me, but sometimes **art rock** gets it right.

Phil Rudd: AC/DC's secret weapon and unsung hero. Rumor has it that he was paid in cars.

Ruddist: a follower of Ruddism, the controversial philosophy that holds that drums should be played at a steady, even, regular tempo in such a way that it is possible to tell with relative ease where any given measure begins or ends. (cf. **Ayn Rand**)

Rush: Canadian English for "too much drums."

Satan: We invoke Satan even though we don't believe in Him, because He represents freedom and because mention of His name makes people uncomfortable. Actually, now that so many generations have overused this cheap-trick shortcut to a rebellious image, it has become so commonplace and **banal** that no one even notices when you do it anymore. Satan schmatan. But it was a good ride while it lasted, O Evil One.

Bon Scott: Dirty, mean, and mighty unclean: the first lead snarler of **AC/DC.**

Sergeant Pepper's outfits: The Beatles wore marching-band uniforms on the cover of their SMAS-2653 album. (Their seminal recording of "On, Wisconsin, Suck My Johnson" only appears on early pressings.)

The Smiths: Southern rock at its finest, especially the song "Sweet Home Alabama (I Hate You and You Make Me Want to Cry)."

stones: testicles, or the ruins of ancient civilizations. When rolling, the most successful rock band ever to attend the London School of Economics.

Levi Strauss: Girls, he's the reason there's a penis on your skirt. Love him? Or hate him?

sweeps week: TV is graded on the basis of its performance during one week in the year, so the networks try to make the programming during this week as sleazy and as risqué as they can get away with. **Roxy Music** tried this with album covers.

totalitarian: thoroughly dominated and controlled by, shall we say, "social services."

Tourette's syndrome: Does it count if it all happens silently in your head? Because if so, I think I may have this.

T.T.G.W.I.M.A: Try to Guess What I'm Mad About. I've always thought this would make a pretty good TV game show. Families would compete for valuable prizes by trying to decode each other's hostile silences and passive-aggressive behavior. Networks, have your people call my people (i.e., Sam Hellerman). Let's work something out here, but I don't want to get screwed on the points.

the universe: The worst place in the world. Let's go somewhere else.

Vichy France: If you can imagine something worse than French Nazis, keep a close watch on that impressive imagination of yours: it's probably a national treasure.

"Wake Up Little Susie": Back when they had drive-in movies, you could "neck" in the car and, shall we say, "fall asleep." That's how couples used to cook each other's geese back then.

"Who you calling homo, faggot? Who you calling faggot, homo?": the typical **normal** guy's mantra, if a *mantra* is an idiotic thing you say over and over for no reason except possibly as a veiled threat against the defenseless. Okay, so I actually looked this up and it turns out that's not what a mantra is. That must have been me projecting there. You do say it over and over for no reason, but it's more of a self-help thing. Example: "I am strong. I am confident. I am in command of the situation. . . ."

Brian Wilson: That it is possible to be a fragile genius with the voice of God in your head while also being kind of a chubby kid has always struck me as a thing of great beauty and poetry.

The World at War: Laurence Olivier spends twenty-six hours of TV time telling you all about World War II, but the short version is, we won.

World Health Organization: watching the world's waistline since 1948.

the Young brothers: Angus, Malcolm, and (sometimes) George. And Alex. How did the USA sit idly by and allow a single family to march in and just take over **rock and roll** like that? Well, it was during the Carter administration, admittedly.

ZZ Top: If I were as great as Billy Gibbons, I imagine I'd be pretty irritated to be far more well known for my beard than for my guitar playing. Then again, maybe being a multimillionaire would take some of the sting out of that.

DISCOGRAPHY
(December—June)

2409-218 (_L.A.M.F._, The Heartbreakers, 1977): The title is short for, shall we say, "Like a Maternal Fornicator." It came out of the ashes of the New York Dolls, if "out of the ashes" means what I think it does, which is that one member of the New York Dolls (two if you count the drummer) went on to form this stripped-down, meat-and-potatoes punkish rock 'n' roll 'n' heroin combo after the former band's inevitable crash 'n' burn. Despite its notoriously muddy sound, this UK-only release captured a unique, intense flash of dark energy never heard before or since in quite the same form. Even the endlessly complained-about fuzzy mixes add to the possibly unintentional double-entendred "born too loose" effect: too loose, too dark, too fucked up, too beautiful, too soon, too late. Like all such flashes, it died almost immediately on impact, but you can still put on the record, rock out, wish you were dead, et cetera.

APLPA-016 (_T.N.T._, AC/DC, 1975): If you've been paying attention you'll know that this is AC/DC's second album, rated quite highly by yours truly and unreleased in this form in the United States. Have you noticed that practically every single foreign album winds up getting released in the U.S. in noticeably suckier form? They'll mess up the order, leave songs off, and/or replace them with songs from other albums. The result is almost always worse, but even when it isn't that terrible per se (e.g., the U.S. version of S CBS 82000), it's still utterly stupid and dishonest and you'd be better off listening to the real record. It has to be on purpose (though to what end remains a mystery): "Ha, that'll show 'em," they say, presiding over the accelerated dumbing down of the American public. I suppose it goes along with the dumbing down of the educational system. They're preparing us for something, clearly, and depriving us of the real *T.N.T.* seems to be a small but vital part of the plan, like failing to teach us how to read and write.

Seven of these nine songs appear on the U.S. release fraudulently titled *High Voltage* (SD 36-142), along with only two from their first album (the actual *High Voltage*, APLP-009.) But the two that are missing, the "Tutti-Frutti"–like "Rocker" and an extended cover of Chuck Berry's "School Days," are crucial tracks, clearly an intentional bridge between 1955 and 1975, a way of summing up and paying tribute to the past while chewing it up and superseding it. Without them, the point is missed. I mean, get the real version, not the fake stupid American one. U.S. out of my uterus and all that.

ASF 2512 (*British Steel*, Judas Priest, 1980): With a new Ruddist drummer and an unrepentant ambition to take over the world, Judas Priest proved it was possible for a metal band to produce an album of pop songs without sacrificing one iota of heaviness, completing the transition to comparative minimalism begun with 1978's S CBS 83135. While perhaps not as cohesive as a whole as **FC 38160** (their finest hour), as a succession of succinct, aggressive, self-aggrandizing anthems of rebellion it has few equals. "You Don't Have to Be Old to Be Wise"–yeah, they did that, with a straight face, and it worked, which is borderline amazing. Makes you want to go out and break something, maybe even a face.

Recorded at Ringo Starr's house. That's really true.

BS 2607 (*Machine Head*, Deep Purple, 1972): "Smoke on the Water" tells the true story of a fire at a Frank Zappa show at the Swiss casino where Deep Purple had been planning to record the very song about this selfsame incident that prevented them from doing so. Highly illogical, I know, but basically in the third verse they move to a hotel and manage to finish it all up there, with the aid of the Rolling Stones' mobile recording rig, referred to in the song as "the Rolling truck Stones thing." Making it up as you go along never had such chart-busting results. So "the water" is Lake Geneva, which is one great big, kind of random lake. And this is one great big, kind of random album, three main songs padded with a remarkably high grade of filler and some tritones. "Highway Star" explains, I think, what happens to Eddie Cochran after he gets the car and the girl and does a whole lot of drugs. Ain't nobody gonna take his car, his girl, or his head.

COC 39105 (*Sticky Fingers,* The Rolling Stones, 1971): So, obviously COC 69100 is more important, but this has quite a lot to recommend it nonetheless: one of the best snare sounds ever recorded, the best country-rock tune ever written and performed by foreigners, some crazily "mean"-sounding guitar, and "Bitch," which gets my vote for best Stones song of them all, not to mention a supposedly risqué cover featuring a Warhol-designed crotch image with a working zipper. (That zipper is the reason the back cover of so many copies of NPS-2 is all messed up; after 1981, it's COC 16052 that gets the COC 39105 zipper treatment, obviously not as much of a loss.) "Sister Morphine" is Sam Hellerman's unofficial theme song.

FC 38160 (*Screaming for Vengeance,* Judas Priest, 1982): There's high drama and a great big ball of righteous anger in this prickliest, bitterest, biggest, and most triumphal and genre-transcending metal album ever, arguably the first Judas Priest album to use Rob Halford's astonishing vocal range to full advantage, possibly the finest, most emotive screaming ever scratched into vinyl. The guitars scream too. The whole thing screams. Listening from beginning to end can be a harrowing experience, sonically and emotionally. It presents a dark vision, a paranoiac's manifesto, someone once called it. Oh yeah, that was me who called it that, even though I'm not totally sure what a manifesto is.

KC 32425 (*Mott the Hoople,* Mott the Hoople, 1973): There are probably a thousand eccentric, scarf-wearing Englishmen with floppy hats who did their own small part to save rock and roll as it drifted this way and that, post-Altamont/pre-CBGB. And Mott the Hoople were four or five of them. "Honaloochie Boogie" is quite possibly the catchiest song ever written, so skip that track whatever you do. The band is named after an impossible-to-find novel, which I'd read in a second if I were allowed, but for some reason the powers that be want to make it as difficult as possible to learn what a "hoople" is. Must be something pretty shocking, right?

KSBS 2021 (*Flamingo,* The Flamin' Groovies, 1971): They arguably outdid the Stones on KSBS 2031 and brought the Beatles into the New Wave on SRK 6021, and while I doubt anyone would sincerely prefer KSBS 2021 to either of those, it has the rough, in-your-face charm that bare bones prematurely unearthed sometimes have. If I didn't know they were San Francisco hippie boogie-woogie freaks, I'd have sworn I was listening to an unsung UK pub rock classic, a forgotten Ducks Deluxe or Count Bishops or something like that. "Second Cousin" genuinely rules, though.

NAR-012 (*Milo Goes to College,* Descendents, 1982): Not necessarily the greatest album ever, maybe, but almost certainly one of the last truly great ones ever recorded. I mean, it's been pretty much downhill after that, album-wise. Frantic, catchy, punchy, funny, and surprisingly moving at moments. "Jean Is Dead" will make you cry. Careful about singing "I'm Not a Loser" to yourself in public, though. That won't end well.

PCS 7009 (*Revolver,* The Beatles, 1966): yet another perfectly fine album vandalized by its own U.S. release. I mean, three of the John Lennon songs were simply left off the American version, making it all Paul and George-y. Why? Just to mess with people, is the only thing I can come up with. Nice going, government. You ruined the Beatles. Now get to work on Santa Claus and that Christmas cancellation, why don't you? (Best bass sound of any rock recording, though, and the drums are pretty terrific, too.)

PD 5537 (*Kings of Oblivion,* Pink Fairies, 1973): The third and final album from this oddball Deviants splinter and product of Britain's anarcho-psychedelic underground freak scene was five years ahead of its time and as solid a guitar album as its own era ever disgorged, if "disgorged" means what I think it does. They were tour buddies with Hawkwind and their singer-guitarist went on to join the first edition of Motörhead, whose debut album owes a substantial, perhaps surprising debt to the the Pink Fairies' blueprint. Motörhead's rough cover of "City Kids" possibly helped it to become this album's best-known song, but it is the deeply mysterious and haunting ten-minute epic "I Wish I Was a Girl" that truly sticks in a person's head while refusing to reveal its secrets. It was apparently real, true anarchy in Ladbroke Grove '72, and if so this is pretty much all that's left of it. Way too good and fine and special for normal people to know about, so stay away.

SA-7528 (*Leave Home,* The Ramones, 1977): Specifying your favorite of the first four Ramones albums is kind of like indicating your favorite Beatle or Monkee or U.S. president. It tells the world something about you that you might not necessarily be all that comfortable having them know. This is mine, which I think is equivalent to George, Mickey, or Rutherford B. Hayes.

S CBS 82000 (*The Clash,* The Clash, 1977): Again, the U.S. Department of Destroying the Integrity of Rock and Roll Recordings allowed release of a record of the same title and cover as the debut Clash album with largely different music on it. Basically the U.S. release (PE 36060) is a singles compilation with a truncated version of the original debut LP crammed in around the edges. These singles are great, and the result is by no means a waste of time. But it isn't anything like the real album. It's historically inaccurate, like something Stalin might have perpetrated, if "perpetrated" means what I think it does. And it leaves off "Protex Blue," which is a love song about alienation and buying condoms from a vending machine. Wouldn't you like to hear that? Too bad. The universe says no. It ought to be ashamed of itself.

SD 36-142 (High Voltage, AC/DC, 1976): The fraudulent U.S. issue of seven ninths of AC/DC's second album under the title of its first. See **APLPA-016.**

SEEZ 1 (*Damned, Damned, Damned,* The Damned, 1977): This Nick Lowe–produced album has the distinction of being the first full-length LP to be released by an official UK punk rock band. It also has the distinction of not sounding like anything besides what it is, unlike most everything else did after everyone started reading from the same playbook, if you know what I mean by "playbook." The doubled crooning vocals always kill me. Miles better than anything else in your pathetic little world, I can almost guarantee.

SMAS-2653 (Sergeant Pepper's Lonely Hearts Club Band, The Beatles, 1968): what it sounds like when you Anglicize Buddy Holly and replace his amphetamines with acid. Nothing could be as great in reality as this record is in reputation, but it is nonetheless about as good as drugged-up pop-art rock gets, an impressive feat considering it was recorded on secondhand equipment in a public restroom in Ireland. I prefer "I Wanna Hold Your Hand," but then I would, wouldn't I?

SRK 6081 (*The Undertones,* The Undertones, 1979): As a punk pop document of good-humored teen angst, this is an album with no equal. Feeling strange and awkward, wanting the girl, rarely to never getting the girl, being compelled to jump around aimlessly physically as well as mentally—well, it turns out it takes about two and half minutes to tell the world about this situation, and what's more, it's something you can do over and over again. And if the choruses are catchy and the songs well-written enough, people won't even mind all that much. For some reason the Undertones are always likened to the Ramones, but to me they seem much closer to the Modern Lovers' sensibility. Now, maybe all that means is it's just a different sort of cartoon, but it's probably a picture of your life nonetheless. (n.b., if "n.b." means what I think it does: they're from Northern Ireland, and their warbly-voiced singer Feargal Sharkey–that's the guy's actual name, kidding you not–was a former scout leader. But it's still a picture of your life, trust me.)

ST 11395 (*Desolation Boulevard,* The Sweet, 1974): Ever notice how bands that begin as the Something (or the Somethings) often remove the "the" as they get older, lamer, and more full of themselves? The Pink Floyd became Pink Floyd, the Led Zeppelin became Led Zeppelin. Even the Dead Kennedys became Dead Kennedys, and there are people who will correct you if ever say "the Buzzcocks": "It's Buzzcocks, man, just Buzzcocks, what are you, some kind of monster?" (And the Beach Boys, in a kind of inversion of this process, had a brief, pretentious stint as the Beach.) Well, that happened with the Sweet, too, and by the time they bridged bubblegum and glam and became famous they were generally known as just Sweet. But they'll always be the Sweet to me. Oh, and *Desolation Boulevard* is one of the greatest, if not the greatest, rock and roll records ever recorded, despite the missing "the." Some people are beyond good and evil and can break rules with impunity, if "impunity" means what I think it does. (And it does. I looked it up. Are you ready, Steve? Andy? Mick? It means you can't be punished for any reason. You're golden.)

UAG 30159 (*Another Music in a Different Kitchen,* Buzzcocks, 1978): They taught the world how to bypass the music industry by releasing their own records (with 1977's *Spiral Scratch* 7") and followed it up by somehow tricking the music industry into releasing this remarkable blend of tube fuzz, pop melody, deadpan art-school pretensions, and lovelorn moping. It's the melodic moping that scores, perhaps, but the sonic experimentation and minimalist, angular soundscapes are nearly as important to the effect, if not quite as "deep" as they seem to have been intended to be. This is what the cutting edge of pop modernity appears to have sounded like in 1978, and it's a real shame it doesn't sound like that anymore.

WIK 2 (*Motörhead,* Motörhead, 1977): I heard a story that the debut Motörhead album was recorded quickly as a last-minute attempt to document the band before a planned bitter "goodbye, cruel world" breakup. That might explain the notable spontaneity of the recording, surely one of the most vigorous, no-nonsense, honest guitar albums ever recorded by a band that went on to achieve superstardom. Their other stuff is more celebrated, obviously, but this album, released on the tiny UK punk rock label that was their only chance to avoid obscurity, really has a spark, and sparks like that are hard to come by.

ABOUT THE AUTHOR

Frank Portman (aka Dr. Frank) is the singer/songwriter/guitarist of the influential East Bay punk band the Mr. T. Experience (MTX). MTX has released a dozen albums since forming in the mid-1980s. Look for Frank's other books, *Andromeda Klein*, and the companion to *King Dork Approximately*, *King Dork*, both available from Delacorte Press. Frank lives in Oakland, California. Visit him online at frankportman.com and follow @frankportman on Twitter.

Did you miss the first part of
Tom Henderson's sophomore year?

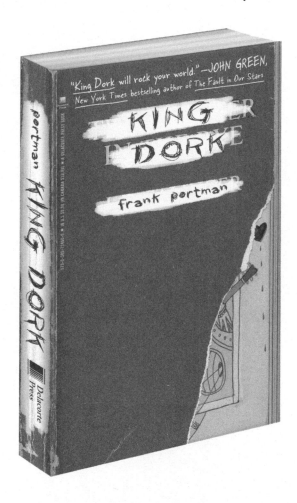

Turn the page to start reading now!

intro

It started with a book. If I hadn't discovered it when and how I did, everything would have turned out differently. But because of it the first semester of sophomore year at Hillmont High School ended up way more interesting and eventful and weird than it was ever supposed to be.

It's actually kind of a complicated story, involving at least half a dozen mysteries, plus dead people, naked people, fake people, teen sex, weird sex, drugs, ESP, Satanism, books, blood, Bubblegum, guitars, monks, faith, love, witchcraft, the Bible, girls, a war, a secret code, a head injury, the Crusades, some crimes, mispronunciation skills, a mystery woman, a devil-head, a blow job, and rock and roll. It pretty much destroyed the world as I had known it up to that point. And I'm not even exaggerating all that much. I swear to God.

I found the book by accident, in a sense. It was in one of the many boxes of books in the basement, in storage in case we ever got more shelves, or perhaps to be sold or given away at some point. The reason I say by accident "in a sense" is because the book I found was exactly the book I had been looking for. But I had been looking for just any old copy of it, rather than the specific copy I ended up finding, which I hadn't even known existed. And which was something else, and which ended up opening the craziest can of worms . . .

August

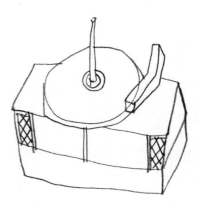

KING DORK

They call me King Dork.

Well, let me put it another way: no one ever actually calls me King Dork. It's how I refer to myself in my head, a silent protest and an acknowledgment of reality at the same time. I don't command a nerd army, or preside over a realm of the socially ill-equipped. I'm small for my age, young for my grade, uncomfortable in most situations, nearsighted, skinny, awkward, and nervous. And no good at sports. So Dork is accurate. The King part is pure sarcasm, though: there's nothing special or ultimate about me. I'm generic. It's more like I'm one of the kings in a pack of crazy, backward playing cards, designed for a game where anyone who gets me automatically loses the hand. I mean, everything beats me, even twos and threes.

I suppose I fit the traditional mold of the brainy, freaky, oddball kid who reads too much, so bright that his genius is sometimes mistaken for just being retarded. I know a lot of trivia, and I often use words that sound made-up but that actually turn out to be in the dictionary, to everyone's surprise–but I can never quite manage to keep my shoes tied or figure out anything to say if someone addresses me directly. I play it up. It's all I've got going for me, and if a guy can manage to leave the impression that his awkwardness arises from some kind of deep or complicated soul, why not go for it? But, I admit, most of the time, I walk around here feeling like a total idiot.

Most people in the world outside my head know me as Moe, even though my real name is Tom. Moe isn't a normal nickname. It's more like an abbreviation, short for Chi-Mo. And even that's an abbreviation for something else.

Often, when people hear "Chi-Mo" they'll smile and say, "Hippie parents?" I never know what to say to that because yes, my folks are more hippie than not, but no, that's not where the name comes from.

Chi-Mo is derogatory, though you wouldn't necessarily know that unless you heard the story behind it. Yet even those who don't know the specific story can sense its dark origins, which is why it has held on for so long. They get a kick out of it without really knowing why. Maybe they notice me wincing when I hear them say it, but I don't know: there are all sorts of reasons I could be wincing. Life is a wince-a-thon.

There's a list of around thirty or forty supposedly insulting things that people have called me that I know about, past and present, and a lot of them are way worse than Moe. Some are classic and logical, like Hender-pig, Hender-fag, or Hender-fuck. Some are based on jokes or convoluted theories of offensiveness that are so retarded no one could ever hope to understand them. Like Sheepie. Figure that one out and you win a prize. As for Chi-Mo, it goes all the way back to the seventh grade, and it wouldn't even be worth mentioning except for the fact that this particular nickname ended up playing an unexpectedly prominent role in the weird stuff that happened toward the end of this school term. So, you know, I thought I'd mention it.

Mr. Teone, the associate principal for the ninth and tenth grades, always refers to Sam Hellerman as Peggy. I guess he's trying to imply that Sam Hellerman looks like a girl. Well, okay, so maybe Sam Hellerman does look a *little* like a girl in a certain way, but that's not the point.

In fact, Mr. Teone happens to have a huge rear end and pretty prominent man boobs, and looks way more like a lady than Sam Hellerman ever could unless he were to gain around two hundred pounds and start a course of hormone therapy. Clearly, he's trying to draw attention away from his own nontraditionally gendered form factor by focusing on the alleged femininity of another. Though why he decided to pick on Sam Hellerman as part of his personal battle against his own body image remains a mystery.

I'm just glad it's not me who gets called Peggy, because who needs it?

There's always a bit of suspense about the particular way in which a given school year will get off to a bad start.

This year, it was an evil omen, like when druids observe an owl against the moon in the first hour of Samhain and conclude that a grim doom awaits the harvest. That kind of thing can set the tone for the rest of the year. What I'm getting at is, the first living creature Sam Hellerman and I encountered when we penetrated the school grounds on the first day of school was none other than Mr. Teone.

The sky seemed suddenly to darken.

We were walking past the faculty parking, and he was seated in his beat-up '93 Geo Prizm, struggling to force his supersized body through the open car door. We hurried past, but he noticed us just as he finally squeezed through. He stood by the car, panting heavily from the effort and trying to tuck his shirt into his pants so that it would stay in for longer than a few seconds.

"Good morning, Peggy," he said to Sam Hellerman. "So you decided to risk another year." He turned to me and bellowed: "Henderson!" Then he did this big theatrical salute and waddled away, laughing to himself.

He always calls me by my last name and he always salutes. Clearly, mocking me and Sam Hellerman is more important than the preservation of his own dignity. He seems to consider it to be part of his job. Which tells you just about everything you need to know about Hillmont High School society.

It could be worse. Mr. Donnelly, PE teacher and sadist supreme, along with his jabbering horde of young sports troglodytes-in-training, never bother with Moe or Peggy, and they don't salute. They prefer to say "pussy" and hit you on the ear with a cupped palm. According to an article called "Physical Interrogation Techniques" in one of my magazines (*Today's Mercenary*), this can cause damage to the eardrum and even death when applied accurately. But Mr. Donnelly and his minions are not in it for the accuracy. They operate on pure, mean-spirited, status-conscious instinct, which usually isn't very well thought out. Lucky for me they're so poorly trained, or I'd be in big trouble.

But there's no point fretting about what people call you. Enough ill will can turn anything into an attack. Even your own actual name.

"I think he's making fun of your army coat," said Sam Hellerman as we headed inside. Maybe that was it. I admit, I did look a little silly in the coat, especially since I hardly ever took it off, even in the hottest weather. I couldn't take it off, for reasons I'll get to in a bit.

I know Sam Hellerman because he was the guy right before me in alphabetical order from the fourth through eighth grades. You spend that much time standing next to somebody, you start to get used to each other.

He's the closest thing I have to a friend, and he's an all-right guy. I don't know if he realizes that I don't bring much to the table, friendship-wise. I let him do most of the talking. I usually don't have a comment.

"There's no possibility of life on other planets in this solar system," he'll say.

Silence.

"Well, let me rephrase that. There's no possibility of *carbon-based* life on other planets in this solar system."

"Really?" I'll say, after a few beats.

"Oh, yeah," he'll say. "No chance."

He always has lots to say. He can manage for both of us. We spend a lot of time over each other's houses watching TV and playing games. There's a running argument about whose house is harder to take. Mine is goofy and resembles an insane asylum; his is silent and grim and forbidding, and bears every indication of having been built on an ancient Indian burial ground. We both have a point, but he usually wins and comes to my house because I've got a TV in my room and he doesn't. TV can really take the edge off. Plus, he has a taste for prescription tranquilizers, and my mom is his main unwitting supplier.

Sam Hellerman and I are in a band. I mean, we have a name and a logo, and the basic design for the first three or four album covers. We change the name a lot, though. A typical band lasts around two weeks, and some don't even last long enough for us to finish designing the logo, let alone the album covers.

When we arrived at school that first day, right at the end of August, the name was Easter Monday. But Easter Monday only lasted from first period through lunch, when Sam Hellerman took out his notebook in the cafeteria and said, "Easter Monday is kind of gay. How about Baby Batter?"

I nodded. I was never that wild about Easter Monday, to tell you the truth. Baby Batter was way better. By the end of lunch, Sam Hellerman had already made a rough sketch of the logo, which was Gothic lettering inside the loops of an infinity symbol. That's the great thing about being in a band: you always have a new logo to work on.

"When I get my bass," Sam Hellerman said, pointing to another sketch he had been working on, "I'm going to spray-paint 'baby' on it. Then you can spray-paint 'batter' on your guitar, and as long as we stay on our sides of the stage, we won't need a banner when we play on TV."

I didn't even bother to point out that by the time we got instruments and were in a position to worry about what to paint on them for TV appearances, the name Baby Batter would be long gone. This was for notebook purposes only. I decided my Baby Batter stage name would be Guitar Guy, which Sam Hellerman carefully wrote down for the first album credits. He said he hadn't decided on a stage name yet, but he wanted to be credited as playing "base and Scientology." That Sam Hellerman. He's kind of brilliant in his way.

"Know any drummers?" he asked as the bell rang, as he always does. Of course, I didn't. I don't know anyone apart from Sam Hellerman.

THE *CATCHER* CULT

So that's how the school year began, with Easter Monday fading into Baby Batter. I like to think of those first few weeks as the Baby Batter Weeks. Nothing much happened—or rather, quite a lot of stuff was happening, as it turns out, but I wouldn't find out about any of it till later. So for me, the Baby Batter Weeks were characterized by a false sense of— well, not security. More like familiarity or monotony. The familiar monotony of standard, generic High School Hell, which somehow manages to be horrifying and tedious at the same time. We attended our inane, pointless classes, in between which we did our best to dodge random attempts on our lives and dignity by our psychopathic social superiors. After school, we worked on our band, played games, and watched TV. Just like the previous year. There was no indication that anything would be any different.

Now, when I say our classes were inane and pointless, I really mean i. and p., and in the fullest sense. Actually, you know what? Before I continue, I should probably explain a few things about Hillmont High School, because your school might be different.

Hillmont is hard socially, but the "education" part is shockingly easy. That goes by the official name of Academics. It is mystifying how they manage to say that with a straight face, because as a school, HHS is more or less a joke. Which can't be entirely accidental. I guess they want to tone down the content so that no one gets too good at any particular thing, so as not to make anyone else look bad.

Assignments typically involve copying a page or two from some book or other. Sometimes you have a "research paper," which means that the book you copy out of is the *Encyclopaedia Britannica*. You're graded on punctuality, being able to sit still, and sucking up. In class you have group discussions about whatever it is you're alleged to be studying, where you try to share with the class your answer to the question: how does it make you feel?

Okay, so that part isn't easy for me. I don't like to talk much. But you do get some credit for being quiet and nondisruptive, and my papers are usually neat enough that the teacher will write something like "Good format!" on them.

It is possible, however, to avoid this sort of class altogether by getting into Advanced Placement classes. (Technically, "Advanced Placement" refers to classes for which it is claimed you can receive "college credit"–which is beyond hilarious–but in practice all the nonbonehead classes end up getting called AP.) AP is like a different world. You don't have to do anything at all, not a single blessed thing but show up, and you always get an A no matter what. Well, you end up making a lot of collages, and dressing in costumes and putting on irritating little skits, but that's about it. Plus, they invented a whole new imaginary grade, which they still call an A, but which counts as more than an A from a regular class. What a racket.

This is the one place in the high school multi-verse where eccentricity can be an asset. The AP teachers survey the class through their *Catcher in the Rye* glasses and . . .

Oh, wait: I should mention that *The Catcher in the Rye* is this book from the fifties. It is every teacher's favorite book. The main guy is a kind of misfit kid superhero named Holden Caulfield. For teachers, he is the ultimate guy, a real dreamboat. They love him to pieces. They all want to have sex with him, and with the book's author, too, and they'd probably even try to do it with the book itself if they could figure out a way to go about it. It changed their lives when they were young. As kids, they carried it with them everywhere they went. They solemnly resolved that, when they grew up, they would dedicate their lives to spreading The Word.

It's kind of like a cult.

They live for making you read it. When you do read it you can feel them all standing behind you in a semicircle wearing black robes with hoods, holding candles. They're chanting "Holden, Holden, Holden . . ." And they're looking over your shoulder with these expectant smiles, wishing they were the ones discovering the earth-shattering joys of *The Catcher in the Rye* for the very first time.

Too late, man. I mean, I've been around the *Catcher in the Rye* block. I've been forced to read it like three hundred times, and don't tell anyone but I think it sucks.

Good luck avoiding it, though. If you can make it to puberty without already having become a *Catcher in the Rye* casualty you're a better man than I, and I'd love to know your secret. It's too late for me, but the Future Children of America will thank you.

So the AP teachers examine the class through their *Catcher* glasses. The most Holden-y kid wins. Dispute the premise of every assignment and try to look troubled and intense, yet with a certain quiet dignity. You'll be a shoo-in.

Everybody wins, though, really, in AP Land.

But watch out. When all the little Holdens leave the building, it's open season again. Those who can't shed or disguise their *Catcher*-approved eccentricities will be noticed by all the psychopathic normal people and hunted down like dogs. The *Catcher* Cult sets 'em up, and the psychotic normal people knock 'em right back down. What a world.

"Did you get in any APs?" Sam Hellerman had asked on the way to school that first day. He hadn't gotten in any APs.

Whether or not you end up in AP is mostly a matter of luck, though the right kind of sucking up can increase your odds a bit. So considering that I put zero effort into it, I didn't do too badly in the AP lottery. I got into AP social studies and French; that left me with regular English and math; and I also had PE and band. "Advanced" French is mainly notable for the fact that no one in the class has the barest prayer of reading, speaking, or understanding the French language, despite having studied it for several years. AP social studies is just like normal social studies, except the assignments are easier and you get to watch movies. Plus they like to call AP social studies "Humanities." Ahem. . . . Pardon me while I spit out this water and laugh uncontrollably for the next twenty minutes or so. This year, "Humanities" began with Foods of the World. The basic idea there is that someone brings in a different type of ethnic food every day. And the class celebrates cultural diversity by eating it. Day one was pineapple and ham, like they have in Hawaii! We were gifted and advanced, all right. And soon we would know how to have a snack in all fifty states.

I suspected regular English was going to be a drag, though, and I wasn't wrong. AP teachers tend to be younger, more enthusiastic, and in premeltdown mode. They are almost always committed members of the *Catcher* Cult, and easy to manipulate. The regular classes, on the other hand, are usually taught by elderly, bitter robots who gave up long ago and who are just biding their time praying for it all to be over. Getting in touch with your inner Holden is totally useless if you wind up in a class taught by one of the bitter robots. You will not compute. Or if you do compute, the bitter robots will only hate you for it.

I didn't get into AP English because my tryout essay last year was too complex for the robots to grasp. So I ended up in regular, nonadvanced English, run by the ultimate bitter robot, Mr. Schtuppe.

"I don't give out As like popcorn," said Mr. Schtuppe on that first day. "Neatness counts.

"Cultivate the virtue of brevity," he continued. "There will be no speaking out of turn. No shenanigans. No chewing gum: *of any kind.*

"Shoes and shirts must be worn. There will be no shorts, bell-bottom trousers, or open-toed ladies' footwear. No tube tops, halter tops, or sports attire. Rule number one, if the teacher is wrong see rule number two. Rule number two, ah . . . if you are tardy, the only excuse that will be accepted is a death in the family, and if that death is your own—mmmm, no, if you die, then that death is, ah, accepted as excusable, mmm . . ."

Mr. Schtuppe's introductory lecture was not only morbid, but had a few glitches, as well.

It is like his bald robot head contained a buggy chunk of code that selected random stuff from some collective pool of things teachers have said since around 1932, strung them together in no particular order in a new temporary text document, and fed this document through the speech simulator unit as is. And sometimes there was some corruption in the file, so you'd get things like "my way or the freeway." And of course, all the girls in the class were in fact wearing halter tops, and practically every guy had on some kind of "sports attire." You can't have a dress code for just one class. It was nonsense. There must have been a time long ago, in the seventies, I'd guess, when he *had* been in a position to impose a dress code, and he kept it as part of the introductory speech because–who knows? Maybe he just liked saying "open-toed ladies' footwear."

Mr. Schtuppe was still droning on about forbidden footwear when the bell rang. He stopped midsentence (he had just said "In case of") and sat down, staring at his desk with what appeared to be unseeing eyes as the kids filed out. I had a feeling that everyone in that room was thinking pretty much the same thing: it was going to be a long year.